## El Rancho De Las Estrellas, Sedona, Arizona

Lauren laughed in Americo Rios' face, defying him to deny her experience. Taunting him, she narrowed her eyes and poked him in the chest. "Listen to this, Americo, I was never just an empty cauldron waiting to be filled by you."

Unexpectedly, he saw a formidable woman who no longer needed him. He saw a free, wild spirit, with years of experience in her eyes, experience he had not shared. He saw a woman eager and ready to face the world on her own terms, willing and able to live her life without him. With anguish and loss in his heart, he detested the woman facing him. He detested her for standing in her own power and for denying him her neediness. And he was livid.

"You're a liar, Lauren. I was going to tell you how much I still love you, but I ought to kill you for sabotaging any chance we had with your wild, insane, secretive, thieving ways."

Screaming, Lauren twisted her body out of his grip. Insulted and angered by Americo's denial of her life, Lauren summoned fierce strength. She hated him, remembered all of the times she tried to tell him, wondered why he never asked and in a bold, but very appropriate gesture, held the red-handled broom like a bat and hit him over the head.

Americo couldn't help but smile, "Goddamn, a Witch and her broom are lethal weapons."

# Praises for Sunday Kristine Larson

"Fiction absorbs me. Good stories are just irresistible. *The Spinning Game* is such a story. It brings a whole new collection of people and events to the genre of fiction. Lauren and Americo will take you into a new world and on a remarkable journey. Their escapades are a journey into a vortex of reading exhilaration. The mystery and magic, the beauty of Sedona will capture your mind." *Maralyn Christoffersen, Scaly Mountain, NC.*

"The musical song of a windchime is one way to describe Sunday Kristine. Like a windchime, she is there in waiting until a burst from the universe plays her into motion and song. At the same time, she can be wild as the wind and daring in her discovery of the unknown. Her joy and laughter brings delight to those she touches with her mirth. A book by Sunday promises to be one of those intricate, can't-put-it-down, fantasy-journeys into the senses and the psyche." *Jacqueline Fogel, Salt Lake City, UT.*

"Racy, provocative, and possibly a real-to-life story - a must read." *Tom Bird, Sedona, AZ.*

"Sunday's tales are filled with a wonderful knowledge foreign to my small-town understanding, yet so very intriguing to my curious mind. A definite read for anyone who's been searching for their true inner self, heart, and mind." *Jamie Saloff, Saloff Web Designs, Erie, Pennsylvania.*

# The Spinning Game

A Sedona Story

Book One of the Sedona Witches Trilogy

## Sunday Kristine Larson

DJ & Mumm

Coming Soon from
Sunday Kristine Larson and
*The Sedona Witches' Trilogy:*

Filament and Witches' Knots:
The Journey From Sedona
*Coming 2003*

Brooms, Wombs, and Brains:
A Witch's Handbag
*Coming 2004*

DJ & Mumm
Copyright ©2002 by Sunday Kristine Larson

All Rights Reserved.
Cover: Graphics by Manjari
Layout: J. L. Saloff

ISBN: 0-9718661-0-4

# Dedication

**DJ, most of all, this is for You
and how life might have been.**

## Acknowledgements:

To Freda Cubera, my first teacher on the mystical path.
To Greta Bouchard and the magic she taught me.
To Annie, thank you for taking me to the garden and teaching me about stardust.
To Americo Yabar, a fabulous spinner of light.

This book is also dedicated to Love and Circumstances.

**To Brent Christensen,** My first crush and my first kiss. Once upon a time, in a land far away, there was a blue-eyed boy and a silly younger girl. Many years later, the girl, now a woman, came to a crossroads. She took the wrong road.

**To B.P.** Thank you for our time out of time, our interlude, and most of all for loving me as you did, unconditionally, openly, and thoroughly unashamedly. It was the secret and the gift, and with you it was the very, very best.

**To Bruce Sonen,** Thank you for the magical mystery tour.

**To Rick Lamont,** What a long strange trip it's been. I wouldn't have missed it for the world, and I thank you for being the best teacher and friend ever.

**To Daddy,** Can you see your little country bumpkin now? Daddy, you told me to reach for the stars, and I always have and I always will.

**To My Mother,** My outlaw blood has been a blessing and a gift beyond description.

**To My Wild Women Friends,** I love you all. Ramona Little, Chelsea Celine Little, Sunshine Kristine Little, Kelly Lamont, Phoebe Bergvall, Maralyn Christoffersen, Reta Lawler, Bobbie Pyron, Jan Scarbrough, Jacqueline Fogel, Sue Ring, Katrina Son, Jan Strickland, Pat Perry, Allison Rice, Susan Holiday Dunbar, Kathy Monahan, Marcia Fogel, and so many others. Keep spinning, Ladies!!!!!!

**To Rita**, the spinner of the Vortex, my psycho pomp and companion, I thank you for this story.

**To My Many Grandmothers,** all the way back to the dot.
**To Alberto Villoldo,** a healer extraordinaire. My life will never be the same.

I want to thank Tom Bird of Ambassador University for his guidance through this divine journey of self-exploration. Also, thank you Jamie Saloff, of Saloff Web Designs, the designer of my website, formatter of this book, and the most helpful person ever. Manjari, of Graphics by Manjari, you are brilliant, and you caught the magic. For your enthusiasm and support, my gratitude to Lane Badger of *Four Corners Magazine*.

Sunday Kristine Marquita Larson, the spinner of this tale, claims no authority on anything but her art, love, and circumstances. The belief systems, rituals, and ceremonies are a composite of her experience, however, time, culture, and location have been changed. The description of personality disorders is not intended to be diagnostic, and she does not encourage anybody to follow Lauren's decision. It was her choice, but it may not be a good one for you.

# The Spinning Game

A Sedona Story

Magic is nature unimpeded.
*The Magical Approach by Jane Roberts*

*He was the axis - She spun around him*
*He was the constant - She was the variable*
*He was the impetus - she was the response*
*He was the answer - She was the question*
*He was the particle - She was the wave*

*The Vortex created the map*
*They followed it to the end*
*It was their destiny*

## The Raven, The Bride and The Prize

A glorious, seductive scarecrow is an imperative to a gardener, especially if the gardener is a Witch. A scarecrow is even more critical if the garden happens to be shaped in a spiral. Every year, Lauren's Grandma Rita, The Witch of Sedona, created a scarecrow for her garden, even though there are not many crows in Sedona. Ravens are the black bird of choice for the Witches of El Rancho de las Estrellas, and the scarecrow is never designed to scare the ravens away. Rather...girls being girls, the intent is always the opposite. When a young Witch in training, Lauren helped Rita design and build the annual guardian and this year, finally, she created it by herself.

Lauren Auldney is wild, crazy, has a wicked little sense of humor, loves to shock people, and knows very well the power of a perfect disguise. In early May, Lauren set out to build a pregnant bride scarecrow and today she made a delightful, meaningful offering to her friend.

The pregnant bride was enchanting. Lauren found a used white wedding dress in a local thrift store, complete with veil, garter, and gloves. She stuffed the dress, making the bride appear seven months pregnant and then, hung her on a cross. Scouting around in the forest, Lauren found some slightly crooked branches for arms, but still, this wasn't good enough. It took her two days and thirty-seven minutes to figure out what to use for the fingers. "Ah hah," she said waking from a really good dream, "chicken bones will work." They did. Lauren secured the bones to the branches, but knowing details are everything; she decided her creation deserved a bit more consideration. She looked to the left and saw a dead Spanish Broom plant. The wild spikes were perfect for the hair, especially after being painted black, with enticing gold frosting. She then covered the unruly locks with a lacy, white, virginal veil. More, she still needed more, so under the veil Lauren strategically veiled a wee secret.

Veil, secret, and gloves in place, there was a finishing touch she couldn't resist. By nightfall, everybody on the rancho could see silky, shiny, red panties dangling from the bony fingers of the bride.

When the Goddess stroked dusky pink into the early evening sky, there appeared a very serious problem in foolish Lauren's plan. Somebody kept stealing the red, silky panties. It was a raven, and Lauren knew exactly which one it was, having often referred to him as the Magician. Through circumstances, Lauren happened to know this particular raven was wound a little tight, and usually stayed right on course. However, making the great escape, the raven flapped his black, shimmering wings, dropped the ball of skill, and taking a gamble on charm, looked back at the pantieless pregnant bride. Looking back, he lost sight of his destiny. Lauren giggled. "My dear friend, the Vortex of Sedona just gotcha, and you are about to take a spinning, wild ride." Sighing, she reached into her bureau drawer for another offering, and confessed, "As much as I love ya, darlin', there's no going back for you now."

☪★

# The Last Spin

*Tell me the landscape on which you live,*
*and I will tell you who you are.*
Jose Ortega Gasset

It is an old age, an eternal age. It is a time of spinning Grandmothers, wise brooms, shapely gourds, magic, eroticism, compost, seething cauldrons, spiral gardens, accumulated charms, witchy cats, wrap around porches, chiming bells, warm ovens, cracked cookies, and potbelly stoves. If you live in another age, or sadly, if your chariot has not yet shipwrecked on the shores of Complexity, Receptivity, Magic and Mystery, you will need this age defined. For those with enough courage to make the journey, very simply, the time mentioned was, and is, the age of the Wild Woman.

The place you will find the Wild Woman is a maze of red. Sedona is a seething, sensual, spinning, erotic, hot cauldron of pure, fierce, female energy nestled in the folded labyrinth of a red rock castle. The red-hot red cauldron of Sedona spins. It spins wildly in harmony with the Vortex. The Vortex is demanding, hot, and she wants you. If you harmonize with the Vortex, you will enter the spinning, gently, softly. If you decline, well...think of a twister.

Perhaps you have been on a journey alone and you want to return to something you don't remember, and yet you cannot forget. Standing alone on a snowy mountaintop, in the distance you will see the red rock land of the Vortex. You will feel a stirring within and become aware that the Vortex spins wildly from desire, a wish for the stars. While spinning, she will tell you that from her desire she births passion, love, and urge for her mate-the axis, the impetus and the cause. You will ask her, "If my love for another is born within the Vortex, will the excitement of perpetual motion and the sexual nature of the landscape bless our union with sensuality, magnetic attraction, and the wholeness of two?" She will answer, "Yes." Then she will counsel you, "You will know when love enters your body, and if you trust the Vortex, you will courageously surrender knowing you have no choice. The reward is waiting, wanting, desiring, and hoping. Your love may come at any moment, be aware, accept the circumstances, adjust your perspective, and you will not be denied this exquisite quality of love."

You will wonder, "How do I enter the land of wild love, passion, and desire?" If you have opened your eyes and have asked the question, perhaps you are the one who has been missing.

To enter the Queendom of the Wild Woman, one must first pass through a portal. Next you will pause, standing for a moment under an archway. What awaits you? Do you remember faintly, fleetingly, or maybe falsely? It will be dark and lonely with only the silhouette of an ancient castle to summon you into the distance. You will ask, "What lies between the distance and me? Is there a background behind the foreground? What have I failed to see? Did I stand on my head and spin in circles, while considering all other possibilities?" You will be afraid. Fear not, for a veil will now part, giving you an opportunity to consider the risk and benefit of your commitment. Once committed, there is no going back. This is not an illusion. You will have crossed into the land-of-no-return. Entering the land-of-no-return is a quest for power, and you will be transformed by your journey. Faint footprints will appear and if you wish, you may follow them along a rocky, wild sunflower lined pathway to El Rancho de las Estrellas, the rancho of the stars.

When the spinning vapors rise, you will be standing under the shadow of Cathedral Rock, the red rock temple of relationship. Perchance, walking along the path you will have discovered an ancient map or picked a sunflower. If so, you will ring your personal bell on the gate, take four steps onto the blood red painted porch, then wait to be summoned into the enchanted chamber. You needn't wait long. A silver haired crone awaits you and graciously, she will drop her golden spindle, then welcome you home from your odyssey. While you listen to her spin a yarn, she will magically and mysteriously weave your wild, pure, authentic love story.

## El Rancho de las Estrellas   Sedona, Arizona

El Rancho de las Estrellas awakens each morning under the watchful guardianship of Cathedral Rock. It is not a large ranch or even a working ranch. It is a ranch to retreat from the chaos of life. Wearing fur of gold, the small coyote scurries through the meadow. He reaches the meandering creek, sips the cold fresh snowmelt, looks to the left and spies a wandering wide-eyed doe. No, not now, he'll return later, in the darkness. From her perch on a dead branch of a sycamore tree, the horned owl watches, hoping the coyote disturbed some prey. In the moonlight, the javelina pigs trample the spiral garden and raid the compost pile. With whooshing wings, ravens stir the energy, making their playful presence known to all.

It is quiet on the rancho, but under the surface, passions reign. Passions fueled by the love of two central figures in the mysterious Cathedral Rock. There is a mystery the figures share, and only a few people know...the secret.

Scurrying quickly with short, sure steps along the meandering rutted lane, Lauren's long, lean, sun bronzed legs glistened in the moonlight. It was warm at 1:13 in the early morning, causing the person watching to wonder why she wore a heavy sweater with her running shorts. As they heard light footsteps, three coyotes stopped before running behind the shed, waiting for her to pass. She was nervous. The owl in the willow tree watched curiously. Lauren didn't want to be seen; yet was certain somebody watched her.

Silhouetted against the summer sky, the tall, gnarled junipers loomed black and mysteriously ominous with millions of needles forming web-like patterns against the horizon. The stars were brilliant, each dancing in harmony with the rotating spheres. She wore a purple bandana over her wavy, brown hair and carried a faded, threadbare, hand-woven satchel over her shoulder.

Hugging herself, Lauren shivered as she stopped on the red and gold adobe path leading to his door, wondering if the man who loathed her would read the invitation. The fragrance of lavender along the narrow path welcomed her, offering courage, causing her to remember. Fresh young apples silhouetted by moonlight beckoned her to stop, touch, and recall the night they planted the mother tree over twenty years ago.

Without taking a breath, Lauren slipped off her red flip-flop sandals, looked to the left and right, and quietly tip toed up the steps to Americo's door. Again she held the handmade envelope to her lips and sent a prayer that the invitation would be well received. She knew his habits and knew he stood in the doorway to welcome the dawn.

Far enough down the lane, she didn't hear the flick of his cigarette lighter, as the man watching Lauren sat alone in his apple orchard, unable to sleep without her. Shrouded by memories, Americo Rios didn't hear Lauren when she turned his direction and whispered, "Spin it, Rios."

Nobody knew what Lauren meant when she said, "Spin It." One day when three years old, she looked up from a messy plate of food and with a startled look on her face, held her little fingers to the sky and said, "Spin it." Often the words sounded like profanity, other times they sounded wise, but behind the words there was always the suggestion of a really great idea, tinged with the irreverent tone of a smarty panties.

The invitation was written in gold colored ink, only thirty had been sent and the message was provocative. The handmade paper, richly textured with organic material, reminded each recipient of Lauren's devotion to the Goddess and Earth processes.

> **On the eve of the Summer Solstice
> Internationally acclaimed
> Goldsmith & Doll Artist
> Priestess Lauren Cubera Auldney
> invites you to enter the Spinning.
> Surrender to your circumstances, and
> join her in the fairytale land
> of your deepest desires.
> Be aware of your perspectives, for
> they may be altered when the mist parts at the
> Langdon Gallery at 7:00 p.m.**

*Americo, I so miss our delicious conversations. Isn't it time to follow the circle, return to the beginning, and become once again what we were? I hope you and Alexandra will join me at the opening. We can toast our friendship with champagne. I promise it will be fun.
Love as always, Lauren*

Lauren Auldney is fey, funny, far out, and fantastically beautiful, in a way. She is also a nutty fruitcake. La Bruja is what Americo calls Lauren because she is a Witch. Lauren knows she has a few too many parts, but some of the most important parts are missing.

Like her Grandmother Rita, Lauren looks a bit witchy. Because of that, Lauren frightened her actress mother Sybille Ginot. She doesn't want to be recognized for her beauty anyway; after all, she is also very smart and very talented.

Some therapists have told Lauren she lives on the border.

Others have told her she lives outside of her body. She confuses everybody, especially those who think they know a great deal. Most of the time, she finds these persons to be very funny, because she knows how to navigate with ease in many worlds. Personally, Lauren credits her outlaw heritage for her outrageous escapades, claiming it's in her blood and she has no choice.

Lauren never fails to tell people part of her secret. Except the people she should tell. "Oh well," she says charmingly, "I'm just a little country bumpkin from a small town in Arizona, excuse me, what do I know?" Pretty soon she finds out everybody is a bumpkin. She knows with total certainty that everybody is from a small town, usually in their heads. Lauren knows very well that she is stark raving mad. She has to be. It's the only way she survives.

People who are somebody, liked the fact she looks like somebody and included her in their jet setting, high living world. Lauren learned to decorate herself and became a very pretty ornament. It was profitable. She decorated herself with the beautiful baubles and bangles she created. Then, thinking it a good business decision, she sold them off of her body at parties, on planes, and on yachts. For some reason, the men thought if they bought her jewels, their women would look like Lauren. The women thought if they wore the jewels, their men would think they were as enchanting as Lauren. "It's a strange world," Lauren realizes as she puts on her yellow straw hat to go to the beach. "But no stranger than the one in my head," she laughed as she danced. Her practical right side, she is really more left side, thought sensibly. "This is easy. I'll dress up pretty, go to parties, wear my jewels, and make a lot of money. Why have a store or a gallery? That would tie me down. Somebody might get to know the real me and I've absolutely got to spin. It's in my blood."

Dolls are her favorite companions because they keep secrets very well. Lauren collects dolls wherever she travels. She goes to many exotic places with secret lovers, and wonders why she forgets to mention things to people.

Now that she's older she makes dolls, imbuing them with her madness and magic. The dolls often wear the twenty-four carat gold baubles and bangles she creates in her studio. People pay a lot of money for her dolls of madness and her magic of gold. Sometimes the dolls find their way into the make believe worlds she creates for installation works of art. Lauren is good at make believe, it's part of her crazy spinning soul.

Nevertheless, she crinkles her lightly freckled nose, squints her deep-set, green eyes and gives people a silly grin. They think she's happy, especially when she blushes, giggles, and wears pink. Certain people have told her that she's very intelligent, successful, extremely talented, healthy, beautiful, and charming. What could she ever have to be sad about? Baring her straight white teeth, she scratches herself with a needle. "What a joke," she says to them under her breath. "If you only knew."

Words are ricocheting bullets, Lauren learned early in life. "If you shoot your mouth off and tell your secrets," she tells people, "the words you speak always come back. They shoot right through you, ripping your heart out." People say that trying to follow her words is like trying to follow a cat. Everybody knows you can't follow a cat.

Lauren is supposed to wear glasses to see in the distance, but she prefers the world to look a bit fuzzy. Sometimes she looks through a dark tunnel; it helps her focus. She has a hard time focusing because half of her is somewhere else, and she can't figure out where it is. But, she keeps searching and asking a lot of questions. When people tell her she should wear glasses more often because then she could see in the distance, she tells them, "Why should I, when I can already see everything that is between me and the distance? And believe me," she tells them with her eyes wide open, "we are not alone." When she does wear her glasses, they are always tinted pink. To her the world is prettier in pink.

She has double power, her teachers tell her, and a double edge. Wow.

The garden is her teacher, her university of life and she loves to get sweaty and dirty playing in it. Even though she has elegant carriage, aristocratic high cheekbones, and a heart shaped mouth, Lauren is an Earth child. All she ever wanted was a small cabin in the woods, but everybody thought she belonged uptown. "Oh well," she said as she danced on her spiral path wearing her favorite red shoes. "I can grow a garden anywhere, even if it's only in my mind. In my mind I can be the wild sunflower I was meant to be, instead of the hothouse cultivated rose the rest of the world wants me to be." Remember, Lauren is crazy and she is not at all certain that she wants to become stabilized. If she did, she fears the spinning top would topple over.

☪

The Vortex is contradictory and complete and like the still core within the spinning, Americo Rios is introspective by nature. Because he likes to bring everything in his life, including his thinking, to a high polish, he became a student of philosophy by education. He is a perfectionist and lives by a plan, a plan he refines daily. Americo is a hybrid, a cross between two cultural strains, with vigor and an enormous zest for living.

Americo learned discipline as he labored on the land. It was a discipline born of surrendering to the heat, the cold, and the winds without complaint. Sweating due to physical exertion cleansed his soul, and the quivering muscles of horses taught him of the passions that vibrate from a beings' body. Poker became his passion, and he found it difficult to separate the game he loved from the life he lived. Sometimes you win, and sometimes you lose. He rarely broke even. It wasn't his nature.

The practice of sorcery is a way of life for Americo. He starwalks to the highest rung on the ladder searching the galaxy to understand the woman he loves. He is well acquainted with the plant allies he acquired, and seeks their guidance as he follows Lauren on her spiral path.

As a young man he was popular with the girls because they loved his tall, lean frame, his rangy hips and swaggering walk. They loved his straight, black hair, his amber eyes, and the way he talked to them with his deep gravely voice when he made love to them. They liked his adventurous ways, and they liked that he made plans and stayed with them. Americo was deliberate and calculating in everything he did. He was willing to wait, to fulfill his gratification.

A person's walk reveals their nature and if you saw Americo Rios walk, you would know him. His long stride is confident and deliberate. He leads with his hips, revealing a sensual, earthy nature. His long legs swing from the hip, and his demeanor is composed and collected. Although he has a swagger to his walk, there are no ungraceful parts, for Americo knows what he is doing at all times. When he moves, he is elegant like a cat. His stride is fluid, and he can move invisibly when necessary. Americo's walk could be called sexy, masculine, effeminate, or tough, depending on who was looking at him. It wouldn't matter how he was described, because he would be remembered for his walk.

Now that he is a man, women love that he is a classy, sophisticated, successful, real cowboy who gambles for a living. The women find his qualities to be very appealing. He is a tough, hard man, but he can dance. He's a dangerous man, although he can't

remember why. His moods are dark and his frustrations intense.
Every day he fears for the woman he loves and his concerns spill
over into every part of his life. Searching for Lauren, he disappears without explanation to Mexico and the stars for weeks at a
time. Bar room brawls are not unfamiliar to him. He is selfish and
hard, and withholds his love while sharing his passion.

☪

## The Legend of Sedona

There is a legend of Sedona that has been told from the beginning. The legend was told before there was meaning woven into
the landscape. Invisible beings, water beings, Lemurian beings,
cosmic beings, and human beings have told the legend to all who
would listen and believe. The story changed, and part of it was forgotten, by some, but not by all. Often unnoticed, in many times, in
many ages, a woman returned to the red rock castle and she
remembered everything. She rarely told a soul, but the woman
even remembered where she dropped the hexagonal crystal the
last time she dwelled among the red rocks. One must be a perfect
listener and have a certain vision to remember the story.
Sometimes, as you listen and look, it helps to dance a little spinning dance.

Once upon a time, there was a tiny dot. The colorless dot
sparkled and pulsed as it radiated from its core. From the flutter
of vibrations an idea formed. Then, for a time the dot remained
motionless, drawing in and absorbing the intent of the Great
Spinner. A thought penetrated the dot, and the air began to rise,
creating an aura around the dot. When the crystal dot felt her
desire awaken and stir, she knew she was ready to create her
world. She knew her world would be red, and she knew that it
would spin. The dot was penetrated, began rotating, creating a
whirlpool of energy. As the energy spun faster, the Great Spinner
witnessed the forces of suction and retroaction, centripetal and
inertial powers. There was a moment of incurring and an out
swelling of release. The intimate relationship of opposing forces,
perception and conception, reconciled their differences. The axis,
the impetus of motion, stirred within the cone, stimulating near
translucent materials to spiral freely, joyously. The radius
increased, giving birth to the Vortex.

Spinning the red Earth into form, the Vortex whispered the legend to the land. The waters were stirring, and the air was whirling while the Vortex spun elements in her cauldron of gold. Fire burned furiously in the imagination of the Great Spinner. As if on a point, the Vortex danced on the tips of her toes, spreading her arms wide, spinning wildly, often changing directions. She laughed as she threw purple dots, indigo lines, red spirals, and yellow circles at the sky, charging the deep night with electric power.

The Vortex passionately tossed the dots, lines, spirals, and circles into the sky. Then, with her spinning fingers, she jealously drew them close to her center. Again, the Vortex spread her arms, pushed them away, saying with rapture, go play. She enfolded the dots, turned them inside out and gave them wings. The lines gained momentum, rotated and soared. The Vortex created enchanting spiraling curves, then repeated them in her bones, her heart, and in her womb. Admiring her beauty in a galactic star mirror, the Vortex molded her erotic red rock world to match the contours of her body.

Her consort stood still, waiting endlessly on the magnetic center point. She danced for him in the field of form, teasing him as she fractured, shattered, disappeared, and reappeared. Away and towards, reversals of perception confused her consort. Always waiting, he watched the visible and the invisible engage in an erotic mating dance. He knew, very soon, she would stop spinning and then gently rock him in her arms. But alas, he also knew the peace wouldn't last. The Vortex needed to spin faster, for she needed ecstasy to fuel the magic.

From her spinning womb, the Vortex birthed the first witnesses. From the red Earth element, the Vortex brought forth a woman and a man. She desired an audience to watch her magic. The Vortex thought the spinning delightful, and danced faster to the sounds of hands clapping. She imbued the first people with desire, passion, eros, and delight, and put little vortices in their red sandstone cells. To the woman she gave a spinning soul, a vortex in her womb. To the man, she gave a plan.

One of the witnesses looked to the sun, the other to the moon, in awe of what they saw. They spoke to each other, silently exchanging filaments, gazing at the past, trusting the future followed. They were given the task of weaving stories of the people into the red rock landscape. But, sigh, they didn't agree as to how it should be done.

"You create the warp," she told him, "then I'll weave the weft after I'm finished spinning."

"No," he said. "We should do everything together. I have a plan."

The first couple became contrary, fixed their perceptions, lost their awareness, doubted their circumstances, and forgot to surrender. That's when the problems began. And that was when the end of the legend was forgotten.

The Vortex sighed, smiled at the Great Spinner and said, "OK," as she giggled just a little. Thinking about what to do next, she took a bite of her frosted donut and made a pretty sunflower with lots of petals. "I'll put a little of this over here, a little of that over there, and right here I'll mix it all together. I'll hide the secret, the code, the key, the answer, the reason, and the magic in a tiny little bundle and put it in a cave. Someday, there will be a woman, maybe two or three or four..."

☪

The day begins early on a ranch, and the red Earth has seldom turned to greet the sun before the morning calls. Americo Saul Rios leaned his rangy frame against the half door jam of the freshly painted, barn red stable. He breathed deeply letting the hour of power fill his body with hope for a new day on El Rancho de las Estrellas. Americo unsnapped his gold and black plaid shirt and listened to the gentle whinnying of his twelve highly pedigreed brood mares waiting for the first feeding of the day. He could see the first intoxicating rays of the sun over the red rocks and smiled in appreciation for the quiet that enveloped his rancho, the rancho he worked on as a young man, inherited half from his father, and later acquired more from the Auldney family.

This holy hour, the morning hour of power, is the time Americo fills his body with filaments given freely from the sun. He smells the coffee brewing on the hotplate in his small office and knows the empty fireplace would, if needed, quickly heat the secluded corner where he does his pedigree work. It is his time, his time alone, to reflect on his life so far and to anticipate what lies ahead for him. He does this while making plans for his business, which is gambling, playing poker, the game of life.

With him as the central figure, the many threads of Americo Rios' life are integrally woven together into a single piece of tapestry. He cannot discover any disconnection between the practice of sorcery, the game of poker, his land, or his love for Lauren. He respects his Nagual, the man who guides him in the world of sorcery, and he loves the land he lives on. With astounding facility, Americo incorporates the lessons of sorcery into the game of poker, all the while loving Lauren. Yet, she is the single thread in the tapestry that keeps breaking. Americo had yet to decide what life holds for a man over fifty, a man with everything to give, and with no desire to share his life but with the woman who callously shattered his dreams by keeping her secrets.

Standing with his hands on his narrow hips, Americo sentimentally admired the small apple orchard in front of his house that had been planted over the past twenty-five years. Each tree reminded him of Lauren and how they had planted the trees together, one for each year she visited her home in Sedona. Americo knew each tree, the flavor of apple and the year it was planted. He also knew that the trees had been planted randomly, in a sort of circle, according to Lauren's design.

Many years ago, she told him that one day she wanted to stand with her man in the middle of the fairy circle of trees and feed him apples from the first tree they planted together. He called to mind the night so long ago when Lauren stood in front of him with moonlight illuminating her high cheekbones. She adamantly told him to pick only the apples he would eat or share, letting the remaining apples fall to the ground to feed the tree for the coming cold winter. Whispering, while swinging their arms together, she told him, "Americo, the tree doesn't care what happens to the fruit. She only cares that she bears fruit when it is her time. The tree will happily give birth to her young and then return her offspring to the Earth. That is the reason and the way, Americo." Lauren circled around him holding his hands in hers. "Every woman who has ever been born knows that."

The scene was pastoral. The mares in the paddock were softly whinnying to each other as the early morning sunrays bestowed their blessings on the luxuriant apple buds. In the foreground, luscious, velvety, purple Iris grew wild, contrasting with the backdrop of the sultry, red Earth. The copper panel on his front door was polished to perfection, except for one flaw that would not shine. The symbols engraved on the copper panel were meant for him alone, except for the small inscription made by Lauren the first year she returned to his bed.

The night before, lying restlessly in his bed, tossing and turning in torment, Americo agonized if he should open the envelope Lauren delivered to his door. He rationalized, staring at the moving patterns in the prayer carpets on his wall, "Mornings are a better time to receive bad news."

Americo Rios' hands are wrinkled and roughened, those of a rancher. His hands shook when he held a silver letter opener to the Sedona red envelope. His heart pounded, his breath quickened, and hope rose in his chest when the handwriting on the envelope reminded him of hundreds of letters kept in a carved mahogany box by his bed.

Sitting on the heirloom bentwood rocker on his porch, Americo stretched his legs and took a sip of his gritty cowboy coffee before reading the invitation for the third time. The warm morning sun kissed his body, easing tension, as he settled into memories of Lauren Auldney who had been his beloved mystery woman for most of his fifty-two years. He took his time, rolled a cigarette and grinned at her audacity. The invitation subtly seduced him, causing him to forget that he had felt nothing but contempt for Lauren in almost six months. Looking at the embedded desert flower, Americo noticed a raven feather next to her handwritten message and wondered if the invitation had been created especially for him.

He smiled, spread his legs, and leaned back in his rocker. "I'm surprised, Lauren. Are you stoking the fire, perhaps stirring the cauldron?" He rubbed the stubble on his face and wondered hopefully, knowing her subtle ways. "Or are you just being polite to your childhood buddy?" Americo blew a smoke ring in the direction of her cottage. "Whatever your reason, I'll be there, because believe me, Baby, I miss our delicious conversations also."

Sending his favorite chipped oversize coffee mug crashing to the deck, Americo's cat jumped in his lap begging for a morning treat. On the wings of another smoke ring, he wished her luck. "Lauren, love of my life, I'll see you at Rita's for dinner on Thursday and I'll be at your show on Friday. Good Luck, Princess, I'll always want the best for you. And by the way, Bruja, you still look incredibly beautiful in the moonlight."

☪

All across El Rancho de Las Estrellas, the gentle sweet sounds of bells collected by Rita Cubera Auldney could be heard chiming in the crisp morning breeze flowing along the creek. The bells suspended on the old rusty metal gate rang each morning, reminding Rita of her rich life on the rancho and her journeys around the world sharing her art, and searching for her past.

With her bare feet firmly planted on the blood red wrap around porch of her home, Rita greeted the morning sun. The old settlers farmhouse she and her husband Zachary Auldney moved two weeks before their wedding, was a home filled with the ambience of love and magic that Rita wove into their lives. Deep in each of their hearts, members of the Auldney-Rios clan knew that the cane Rita held in her left hand was a magic wand, rather than a staff used for the necessity of age.

Rita ruled, and Rita had two vanities. Her long, once black hair was the first, and the second was her bright red, painted toenails. The day was young, and Rita had yet to twist her waist length silver hair into a severe bun. Her long hair, soft and fluffy from a beer rinse, was either a halo or a veil, one simply could not tell.

As the filaments of light were bestowed upon her body she raised her elegant hand to the rising sun and whispered, "Gracias por la luz, El Sol." When the charms on her bracelet vibrated, she knew that once again he was there to help her make it through the day. Rita smiled mysteriously at the elderly Arizona gambler sitting straight backed in his rocker on the porch. "Good Morning, Zack," Rita whispered in a hushed tone. "Something is stirring. The Vortex is agitated. Can you feel it also, Darling? I thought so." Rita stroked the forehead of her indulgent husband. "Destiny is claiming its right to alter the circumstances."

☪

Zack Auldney, legendary gambler of the southwest, brought his young wife Rita Cubera to El Rancho de las Estrellas in 1922, looking for a place to retreat from the harsh realities of life. His eyes had seen too much in the dark smoky pool halls, whorehouses, saloons, and back rooms where he made his fortune, at the misfortune of others. For the rest of his life, he wanted to wake each morning bathed in the crystal clear light of Sedona with his bride in his arms.

Rita's eyes had seen too much, as she searched the cosmos trying to reconnect the knots of her past. Finally captured by the continuous thread of destiny, she arrived in Sedona and found she could see, so she quit looking.

With his own hands, the tall lean gambler, Zack Auldney, built a small log cabin on the rancho, that Rita, in celebration, named the Casino. Gamblers from the southwestern states came to match their wits and skills against the legend. Most of them failed, but hope springs eternal for those willing to risk it all.

☪

Using her hands, a shovel, hoe, pitchfork, and the spiraling forces of nature, the elegant world traveler Rita Auldney, created a spiral garden. When she wasn't spinning yarn or weaving, she was in divine communication with the Vortex of Sedona. Yes, she knew about it even then. Surrendering to the spinning brought her to Sedona. Rita and Zack met the first day she arrived in paradise and married one month later. But then, she already knew from a vision that he would be patiently waiting for her in the red rock castle. They had made a promise to each other in the last life they lived together on the red rocks that they would meet again on a sunny, winter day and continue their journey through time together.

Rita became known as the Witch of Sedona. The local women loved her, the men feared her, but she carried the secret.

Life was good on the rancho, even when the rest of the world was buried in depression or thrown into the chaos of war. Life on the rancho was rich with peace, and quiet was the way of life. The willows and sycamores swayed with the soft breezes and when the cold, winter winds howled from the north; the metal jalousie windows were tightly closed. The old settlers ranch house grew like a sprawling pumpkin plant. Rita refused Zack's offer of a new home, telling him that since she didn't have a history, she preferred to build upon the past and the house where they lived was an entry in the diary of Sedona. As they needed more rooms, together they mapped spaces between the gnarled manzanita and graceful willow trees, making space for new hopes and dreams. The home was vital and alive, breathing the healthy clean air of Sedona into their lives. The many wall-sized windows brought the exquisite scenery of the outdoors into their interior world.

While keeping warm by the potbelly stove, evenings found them breathing as one in their small living room, basking in their ongoing reunion. The cozy room was also Rita's studio where she spun the magic of the Vortex into their lives. In the corner there was a spinning wheel and loom. Behind the spinning wheel, stacked floor to ceiling, were skeins of yarn dyed the colors of the

great outdoors. The tile floors were dotted with geometric patterned Navajo rugs and a copper washtub stood by the fireplace,
filled with chopped wood that Zack had delivered each autumn.
Rita would spin the evenings away, the Vortex energy in, and
weave the story of their lives into mystical portraits. She spun the
yarn from strands of wool sheared from the lambs she lovingly
tended in the pen behind the shed. The yarn was dyed with natural colors from the soil and plants Rita found and collected on her
rancho. Mesmerized by the hypnotic whir of the spinning wheel,
Zack wrote in his journal, a habit he learned from his father, the
outlaw Jackson Auldney.

Jackson Auldney was a Texan outlaw on the run. With Olivia,
his gentile, aristocratic, Virginia born wife, he fled to Mexico when
charged with murdering a sheriff in the old west territory of
Arizona. The Saul Rios family owned the hacienda near seaside
fishing village of Guaymas, where Jackson sought refuge for his
family.

A Mexican bandito, Saul Rios collaborated with Pancho Villa
throughout the Mexican revolution and was charged with procur-
ing arms for the cause from wealthy men in the United States. He
did so by providing refuge at his hacienda for men who were wanted in the United States for crimes they did, or did not, commit.
They paid for his cooperation with arms, and he paid for the arms
with hospitality.

Zachary Auldney was born at the hacienda and spent the first
ten years of his life in the haven that offered protection to his
father. Olivia was buried in the Rios' family cemetery two years
before Jackson and Zack returned to the United States. A bond of
enduring friendship united the Auldney and Rios families and as
the generations passed, friendship became clanship.

For many years, the Rios hacienda was the refuge where
Zack took his wife and Jake, their only child, during the cold
month of January. At the hacienda, his son and Tomas, the grandson of Saul, became best friends.

On a dark moonless night a fierce fire swept uncontrollably
through the adobe hacienda, claiming the lives of Jackson
Auldney and Tomas Rios' parents, leaving him an orphan at age
ten. At that time Tomas became the second son of Rita and Zack,
living for the rest of his life on El Rancho de las Estrellas. In every
way he was Jake's brother and Zack and Rita's son. At the age of
twenty-four, after graduating from Arizona State University with
a masters teaching degree in history, he married Connie Allen of
Payson, Arizona. They had an only child, and they gave him the

name, Americo Saul Rios.

Jake Auldney, Jackson Auldney II, the only biological son of Rita and Zachary Auldney, was born at home, delivered by a midwife, at the stroke of midnight, exactly eight and one-half months from the day they were married. In every way he was a perfect combination of his parents. Jake was artistic and sensitive like his mother, and in his physical appearance he resembled Zack, with dark, copper-toned hair, blue eyes, and a tall, muscular, broad shouldered physique.

Jake discovered his destiny at age two, learning to record his experiences from his father. The evening hours on the rancho were often spent on the porch with Jake pretending to write, while his father made daily entries in his journal.

Jake grew up on El Rancho de las Estrellas protected from dark forces by the magical world created by the love of his parents. His nature was open, loving, and unsuspecting. He became prey. His innocence was his worst enemy and when he lost his innocence, he quit believing. Jake graduated from UCLA with honors, and before turning thirty earned an academy award for a screenplay called "The Arizona Gambler" based on his father's journals. It was the story of a gambler who learned skills needed for the gaming tables from a Navajo shaman. Trapped, Jake married a French starlet named Sybille Ginot on a day that started his decline into a life of self-destruction.

In a world filled with magic created by his parents, Jake learned how to write, but he didn't remember that you had to catch the magic. Next to writing the stories of his ancestors, he loved horses. When Jake quit believing, he quit writing; and when he quit writing, he entered into the fantasy world of race horses.

Trey Auldney, Jackson Auldney III, the first child of Jake and Sybille, reflected the bright sunbeams in the sky the day of his birth. His nickname, chosen by Zack, was a derivative of the Spanish word tres, meaning three. Sybille fell in love with her rambunctious little boy, staying with her husband only to keep her son. She had made a bargain at the time of her marriage to leave any children born to them with Jake should the marriage end.

Four years later, at 6:49 am, on a cold late January winter morning, three weeks late, Sybille reluctantly gave birth to a daughter, a daughter whom she could not love. She resented that her daughter bore no resemblance to her and more often than not left Lauren in the care of her Grandmother. Like Rita's, Lauren's all seeing, green eyes frightened Sybille because her deceptions could no longer be hidden. Lauren was born on a dark day, when the days were short. The light didn't shine on Lauren until spring, and by springtime she had fallen in love with the dark.

Eight years later, following a flagrant, passionate affair with Jason Baker, a local real estate developer, Sybille was asked to leave the family home. The bitterness preceding the divorce was staged openly, leaving the children to care for themselves as their parents indulged in the drama of their passions. When Sybille left the family to return to France and resume her acting career, she left Sedona without telling either of her children goodbye.

Home for Jake and the children was a southwest style, glass and adobe brick house, complete with household help, a swimming pool, and stabled horses. Jake made the rules, and they were non-negotiable rules. Jake was certain the rules would protect his children from the malevolent forces in the universe. Jake knew the forces, and he was certain the forces stalked them. He didn't want them to become prey, he wanted them to live the dreams he had lost.

☾★

A particular light radiates from a dying person; the surrounding light reaches to those who call from beyond the veil. The empty spaces yearn to be filled with awareness of the crossing. It is a pulsing, gentle light, unlike the bright light that surrounds a child. This light protects the person as they come to terms with their journey. Their senses are heightened, and they enter a time of reflection on what might have been. The lessons learned in this life become clear, and the dying person begins to understand the questions they should have asked, and the reasons and the patterns that seemed unfair or ambiguous at the time. Observing the light surrounding her beloved son, Rita watched him walking slowly towards her house and knew that he was dying.

Weather permitting Rita served morning coffee on the porch from the heavily embellished sterling silver service she brought to Sedona from Spain. Morning coffee with his parents was a tradition that Jake never dishonored as long as he lived on El Rancho de las Estrellas. Jake leaned back, rested his head on the chaise and took a deep breath before confiding to his mother. "Another beautiful day in paradise, Mom," Jake said as she poured a cup of hot coffee into the porcelain cup. "I'm beat, and I don't know how much longer I can keep it a secret, because I can feel it coming.

When I wake in the night, I feel death around me." Jake spoke quietly as he closed his eyes. "I have to admit, it feels seductive as hell."

Rita waited, understanding his feelings, knowing that soon she would also leave and return to her husband. "I don't think your time is here." Rita spoke tenderly before sipping her creamy coffee, "I watched you walk towards me and the light surrounding you tells me that you still have work to do." Rita picked a wilted leaf from the scarlet begonia growing vigorously in the clay pot by her chair. "Don't worry, my precious son, I birthed you into this world and my job is to help you leave." Rita stood as she spoke, absent-mindedly resting her cane against the house. "I'll know when it's time for you to go."

"I'm starting to wonder what my life has been about," Jake said as he lit a cigarette. "You and Dad gave me every privilege, and advantage a man could have. You loved me and took care of everything for me." Laughing with happy memories of his youth, Jake reminded Rita of her indulgence. "You allowed me to grow up wild and free here on the rancho, without a worry in the world. I had the best of everything, even my best friend, Tomas, became my brother." Amused by their antics, Jake pointed at the feisty blue jays darting for peanuts. "What more could I have asked for? Yet, Mom," he paused, "somehow I think I took a wrong road, maybe many wrong roads."

Rita felt a trembling in her womb remembering the passionate night her son was conceived. "You were our love child, our golden child. I knew the path you would take the moment you were born to us in this house. We love you with all of the love we share, and we love each other so very much."

Jake relaxed as gratitude to his parents filled his heart. Remembering that he thought all marriages were like his parents, he chuckled at his own naiveté. "That's why I've always worried about my own children, I didn't want them to fall prey like I did. I pushed them in directions I thought were best for them, but I guess they fooled me," Jake laughed wryly. "They found their own paths in spite of their old man. I thought with Lauren's high IQ, she would become a professor, and I thought with Trey's love of the rancho, he would take over the horses."

"Just like you found your path in spite of me," Rita laughed with him at the irony of life. "That's why we have parents. They provide the background for us to move away from." Rita traced the spiral pattern of her garden with her finger. "Thank the Goddess for the background of Mother Earth, because she accepts all of our pain if we offer it to her."

Jake chuckled as he coughed hoarsely. "I sure as hell learned that, didn't I, Mom? I'm proud of my kids, because they both share the love of the land and the rancho with us. Lauren's homecoming has been a real gift to her tired, old Daddy." Jake stood awkwardly to leave, running his finger through his thinning gray hair. "But I sure as hell wish it had worked out for her and Americo."

Taking his arm, Rita walked with Jake. "The story isn't over yet. Time, it just takes time. Remember," Rita stopped in mid-stride, "Lauren has proven that she doesn't need anybody to take care of her." Rita arched her finger, pointing at the apple tree that Lauren named Eve when she was a little girl. "Do you have the photograph Tomas took the day Lauren was on the swing that Zack hung from the apple tree?" Brushing her hair from her face Rita reminded Jake of the day. "It was following a rainstorm, the air was soft and moist, the light was muted by clouds, and Americo was pushing the swing. Lauren kicked her legs, trying to fly as high as the ravens. They were laughing, and she was looking over her shoulder, smiling at him while her long hair flew around her face. I'll never forget the moment, and neither should you."

The bells on the gate chimed as they stood by the dying apple tree, with the old swing still hanging by one ragged line of rope. "I don't have the photograph," Jake said pensively looking into the distance. "Maybe Tomas hung it on his picture wall." Jake leaned with his elbows on the gate. "Is she going to be happy now? She seems so vulnerable at times."

"Yes," Rita said resting her hand on his shoulder, "Our precious Lauren is going to be fine. You wouldn't understand it, these are things only a woman can know about another woman."

Jake laughed, realizing he would never understand the language Rita and Lauren spoke to one another.

"This is the last part of the journey, and you know we'll be together again, right here on our rancho someday, don't you?"

"I finally believe it; I just want to do it better next time."

"We will, Jake, we will."

☾★

Two bright lights met, fell in love at a young age, and made plans for a future, sensibly carrying out their plans. Trey, Arizona handsome like his father and a committed environmental studies professor, found in Sunnie Masterson the security he had never known. Sunnie, accustomed to brightening the life of her widowed father, embraced Trey and offered him the tenderness he so craved. The perfect couple, with perfect careers, a perfect daughter, and a perfect home they built by working together, Sunnie and Trey seemed to have it all.

The local people often commented that one of the brightest lights in Sedona was Sunnie Masterson Auldney. Popular all of her life, Sunnie was the girl in school the other girls gossiped with, not about. When she became the first girl in her class to sleep with her boyfriend, she was forever the Ann Landers, fashion advisor, and confidant of all the girls.

A football star in his undergraduate years and a guitar player in a band, Trey, three years older, never dated another girl. And when he entered graduate school at Stanford, he asked Sunnie to leave Northern Arizona University, continue her education in California and marry him. Life had been exceptionally fulfilling to Sunnie and Trey, and although Sunnie couldn't remember having an unhappy day in her life, she recently wondered why she now included her maiden name when referring to herself.

Working at her desk, Sunnie's face brightened when her incorrigible husband carried a table on his head to the front of the schoolroom. A luncheon meeting with parents of her students was planned and often, the questions posed were challenging, coming from parents making an effort to raise their children consciously. The colorfully painted interior of the building reflected Sunnie's devotion to providing sensory stimulation for the students, while also allowing them to participate in the maintenance, decoration and care of their school.

The parents of students at Sunnie's charter elementary school "Kids First" adored the vivacious teacher who took time to hold weekly meetings to inform the parents in lay language of the importance of raising their children with awareness. Asked by a parent about the ramifications of imposing a parent's hopes and dreams on a child, Sunnie started to speak. Long ago, Sunnie studied the writings of Alice Miller and along with her husband, referred to the writings often in the rearing of their daughter.

Trey settled in at the back of the room, proudly listening to his wife as she spoke with authority on the subject most dear to her.

"A child can crack," she told them firmly. "A sensitive child of two narcissistic parents can crack completely at a very early age.

A child weighed down with the burden of high expectations and loved only when she meets rigid standards and conditions imposed on her by confused unfulfilled parents, can crack beyond repair."

Although a small woman, Sunnie was a formidable presence. Pulling a chair from behind her desk, she met the gaze of parents she knew imposed expectations on their children. "Narcissistic parents will either be grandiose or depressed, because both are manifestations of the same condition. This confuses the child, because she doesn't understand the needs of the parents. A child caught between two dueling narcissistic parents learns the art of keeping a secret, because she knows plenty of them." Sunnie gestured, holding her hands over her heart. "Once she is their pawn, the prize, she holds her secrets even closer, because it's safer to stash her feelings in a bag and hold onto them. She becomes hypersensitive and over vigilant, because she hears too much, sees too much and knows too much, too soon."

"Hell, she's describing Lauren," Trey pondered.

"Soon the child becomes invisible," Sunnie paused, "because she hides the true nature of her soul in order to survive." Sitting on her desk, Sunnie revealed to the parents the behavior of the troubled child. "The decisions and actions that fall within the expectations of the parents are perceived to be the right ones. The child will construct her actions methodically, calculating every move she makes in order to show them what they want to see, even if it means killing her authentic nature." Sunnie paced in front of the group, presenting the most tragic element. "The child soon figures out that death, as in slicing off aspects of oneself a little at a time, isn't so bad. Soon, not even the narcissistic parents see the child because she, the real child, has for all intents and purposes disappeared, is dead, especially to their eyes." Crossing her arms, Sunnie counseled them, "It's safer to be invisible, safer but more frustrating." Waving her hand as if wielding a heavy sword, she warned them. "The cracked child is an executioner of the self, and she uses the sword with expertise, because she has been practicing all of her life."

Trey smiled in contentment. "No wonder our daughter is so damned wonderful, Sun. She has you for a mother."

Smiling back at Trey, Sunnie became more emphatic. "The cracked child adopts any persona that works for her, because she learns to show people what they want to see." Speaking rapidly, listing on her fingers the consequences, Sunnie counseled the parents. "If they want beauty, they get beauty, and if they want brilliance, she shines. If they want sanity and stability, she acts sane and stands very straight. If they want success, she succeeds and she wears all of the hats very well. If it serves her to act flighty and sound less intelligent than she is, in order to be in agreement, she does so, because it is expected. But, the other parts, the honest parts, rage and seek sensation. She wants to feel, to be, but while doing so, she spins, usually out of control."

"The manifestations of this syndrome can continue into adulthood," Sunnie said sadly. "The cracked child feels unworthy of someone who loves her unconditionally. She hasn't risen to any expectations to earn the love, so the love must be unworthy. Love, she knows without any doubt, has to be earned through achievement and recognition; it is the prize handed out for capitulation, agreement, and compliance. How could one respect the love of someone who gives it without any reason, as if love was ever reasonable?"

No longer appearing small, Sunnie commanded the room. "She finds a familiarity in the presence of those who make her feel invisible," Sunnie emphasized, "because they help her punish herself for being a murderer, a murderer of the self."

Trey started to clap; not realizing his wife had more to say.

Sunnie shook her head, flattered by his enthusiasm. "I encourage each of you to read the books written by Alice Miller. She explains the syndrome better than I ever could. But, and I can't say this strongly enough," Sunnie said reaching for the hand of the mother on the front row, "treat your child with respect and then you will never have to teach them to be respectful. Love them for who they are, not what they do, or what they become. Allow a daisy to be a daisy and a weed to be a weed. They are all beautiful, and nothing is as beautiful as an authentic self."

"Please," Sunnie pleaded with the parents, "don't rob your children of the vitality that they were born with by trying to make them fulfill your expectations and failed dreams." With tears softly gathering on her lower lids, Sunnie implored, "Protect the fragile, perfect soul in your care and let her grow towards the light according to her natural inclination." Sunnie closed her talk with a sincere plea to the parents searching their souls and motivations. "Don't disturb the natural ecology of the self in your precious child."

After making another offering to the scarecrow, Lauren wandered barefoot around the spiral path of her Grandmother's garden and swore as she sat on the ground to pull the cactus thorn out of her foot. "Oops, another thorn, damn that hurts. It's times like these I wish I dare let my fingernails grow." Propping her elbows on bent knees, she paused and wondered when her hands became those of a mature woman. "My hands must have aged during my sleep, because, I'm pretty certain when I went to bed I still had young looking hands."

Looking at the chipped red polish on her chewed nails, she rubbed her fingers, not recognizing her own slightly wrinkled and veined hands. Sighing, she resigned herself that her hands were beginning to look like her Grandmother's. "I think I like what I'm seeing, because I've earned these wrinkles and scars and after all, they don't look too old yet; they just look slightly used. My hands are without a doubt my best tools, and I couldn't have survived without making my art, working in the garden, touching, or cooking. Be prepared old hands," she laughed as she kissed her fingers one by one, "you've still got a lot of work to do."

The worship of the Goddess is a way of life for the women on El Rancho de las Estrellas. However, this way of life is not taught by memorizing a book of rituals or through a hierarchy of priestesses. Rita teaches the way of the woman as it was taught in the beginning, and Rita's lineage started with the woman who rose from the first dots of life that landed on the red Earth hundreds of millennia ago.

She teaches her heirs over the belly of a hot oven and the cauldron of transformation, the compost pile. She teaches it with a broom in her hand, a needle in her fingers, a dropped golden spindle, and by inserting her hands in the soil of her spiral garden. Rita's life is lived in ritual, never separating her practices from her daily life. Rita is a homebody Witch, and she digresses her heirs to first awareness knowing every good Witch has to make the entire journey on her own in order to fulfill destiny and to appease the fates. Rita believes that daisies should be daisies, apples trees should bear apples, and wild weeds should tumble with the wind. She insists that her women honor the Great Goddess, because she knows each carries her in their bodies and souls.

Rita knows that life spirals. She understands the nature of the Vortex and knows that life spirals outward and enfolds back into itself, thus insuring new manifestations of destiny.

Rita knows the secret. She also knows the power of observa-

tion. She knows the power of the mundane, because she honors
every act she performs as being sacred, holy, and perhaps the last
of her life. She teaches her heirs the power of the womb, sex,
desire, art, bells, chimes, cats, baking bread, spinning yarn,
brooms, flowers, long baths, window as transparencies, porches as
portals, and watching the cauldron of the fireplace transform
material into spirit.

Rita believes in eternal soulmates and natural inclinations.
She tells her heirs of the power of love, the elements, directions,
and the spirits. She believes in signs, not symbols and she knows
the difference. Rita wants the women to see, rather than look, and
to hear more than listen. Quietly she guides them into the mystery of endarkenment, telling them they must spend time learning
to love the dark, or the light won't mean very much when it shines
on them.

Spinning the fates of her loved ones, she teaches them the
pleasure of adoring their bodies, walking and touching. Never
denying the essential polarities of male and female aspects, she
also adamantly teaches her granddaughters the necessity of both
wild and domesticated energy. Always whispering quietly so the
men won't misunderstand, she tells them the wild is best and to
help themselves to an extra portion whenever they wish. When
Rita teaches the ecstasy of the wild, she does not mean reckless,
self-destructive, or meaningless defiance. While the wild is not
meaninglessly defiant, neither is it compliant to culture, rules
made by others, or constructions. Authentic, is the word Rita uses
to describe the wild, a state of natural inclination woven into an
environment. Authentic growth is adaptive, just as a tree branch
will wind its way towards the light, or a root will attach itself to a
rock. Authentic truth is not without relationship, but it is wild, it
is natural, unimpeded, and it is silent.

Rita guides her heirs carefully, teaching them the magic of
women's work. The tasks are mundane, repetitive, often relentless
and boring, until her heirs understand Rita's portal to the mystery.

Livvy had been given a set of tasks and the compost pile
needed turning. Livvy knew that Rita had surrendered the care of
her spiral garden to Lauren, passing the wand in a continuous
line that enfolded unto itself, as the seasons enfolded back to the
beginning. Rita is a strict taskmistress, knowing that repetitive
acts are the chariot to the mystery. There are no days off and no
excuses because Rita knows the freedom of timely work well done.

☪

Once again the raven ran away from the pregnant bride, proudly carrying red bikini panties from Earth to the curious, peeking stars. Livvy sat on the ground, inching closer to Lauren, touching her hand, wanting to create a bridge to her Aunty. Lauren hugged Livvy, thinking how similar they were in their habits, both of them loving the early morning hours.

Lauren squinted her eyes, scrutinizing Livvy's face. It took some time, but Lauren just had to count the freckles on Livvy's nose. "I win," Lauren proclaimed, tweaking Livvy's nose.

"Win what?"

"Tee hee, I have two and half more freckles than you do, so there." Lauren wiggled and grinned.

"What are you doing, Aunty Lauren? Why are you staring at your hands?"

Lauren looked out the corner of her eye, knowing Livvy had a backpack full of questions, and once started, she was in for a long morning of why's. Before Livvy could again mouth why, Lauren shushed her with a finger to her lips. Petitioning the wisdom of the spinning body, Lauren invoked the Vortex. Today, Lauren wanted to receive information from the belly of the Mother, so therefore, she traced the spiral with the cone to the Earth and the point to her chest. Had she wanted to transmit or send information to Earth, she would have traced the spiral in reverse. Very often the stars were good sources of wisdom for Lauren, as well.

"I was thinking how glad I am to have my hands. I was thinking about my chubby baby hands, the hands I had as a girl, and now I'm looking at all grown up hands. I've never noticed the changes before."

"Mom and Dad always said that when you weren't talking with your hands or chewing your fingernails, you were wringing your hands like a worried little old lady."

Lauren turned and stuck her tongue at Trey and Sunnie's house. "Little old lady, huh. Aren't your parents too funny? I wrung my hands so I could feel them." Lauren laughed, standing and brushing red dust off her shorts.

"Why did you stay away from Sedona for so long? It would have been so cool if you had been here all the time I was a little girl."

Lauren patted Livvy's cheek, wondering how long the conversation would last. "When I was very young, before I knew better and in order to survive, I made some bad agreements. They confused me, and I had to find the answers to my questions for myself. I kept a secret and when I started wandering, I couldn't stop. I wandered up and down the spiral path, sometimes coming close to home, but then the Vortex would change directions and so would I."

Lauren tried to decide how to tell Livvy, and not tell Livvy, about her life. "I made a few bad bargains, and vowed to do everything in life on my own. I struggled to hold on to that part of myself that was the real me when I was born. I knew what it was, and I could be that person when I was away, so I kept searching for a way to bring it home with me. I'd lose sight of it sometimes depending on the circumstances, but I always knew I wouldn't be truly alive until I could keep it with me all of the time."

Livvy wrinkled her brow in confusion, while Lauren recalled feeling trapped. "When I visited Sedona, I felt like I was trapped behind a transparency or a window looking at myself. I could see myself and hear myself, but I couldn't touch myself. I'd say things I didn't mean and act in ways that I didn't recognize, just to please people. Right now I'm struggling, but everyday I feel stronger and more in touch with the part of me that wouldn't die." Lauren placed her hand on her belly. "I know it's inside of me and whoever it is talks to me often."

"Will you tell me your secret?"

"Soon. I'm still coming to terms with everything it cost and it hurts too much to talk about it. When the light was too bright, I closed a lot of doors behind me."

"What did you do besides your art work while you were wandering?"

Lauren pondered while she watered the tomato plants. Sprinkling the water gently on the foot high green vines, she realized how much the hopeful young plant was like her younger self. "I tried to grow. I wanted to flower like a beautiful sunflower and be myself. Like a wild seed, the winds blew me far away from my home, but sometimes I found a good patch of soil to hide in for a while." Lauren laughed. "Like somebody told me one time, soil is a good place to grow from, if you don't believe me ask a plant." Using her hands to describe her experiences, Lauren used an analogy she discovered in a dream. "Many times when I felt myself growing towards the light someone would pick the delicate new flower, stomp on it, or cover it back up with more soil. Then I'd have to start all over again." Covering her eyes, pretending to be afraid,

Lauren exaggerated the overly bright light. "Many times I pulled my own flower back into the soil, because the light was so bright it scared me. Sometimes people took too good care of the flower because they didn't want it to die, so they kept it over sheltered. Other times people wished it was a different kind of flower, maybe a rose, rather than a sunflower. It happened again and again, but I never gave up. There were brief moments when I could see the light, but then I'd take another journey into the unknown interior of myself and Mother Earth." Lauren pointed to a small, yellow flower with a little ladybug creeping to the tip of the leaf. "I'm still waiting to blossom, but don't worry, I can feel the stirring of the Vortex, and you know what that means."

"Yes, Grandma Rita taught me."

"I guess what I'm saying is for many years I left everything behind and tried to find my way as I wandered in the compost pile of my mind."

"Sometimes you sound like Grandma. She always says things in ways that make you think you understand, but later you wonder if she told you more."

"So you inherited my old job. If you can imagine this, I felt like I was trapped in the middle of the compost pile. I was deep inside a little cave covered with rich brown powdery stardust. Everyday, somebody put leftovers on top of me, making it harder to see the light." Plunging the stirring stick into the center of the compost, Lauren rolled her eyes in mock despair. "I found out pretty fast, that the heat is in the center and all I had to do was put that hot stuff to work, and transform the crap into gold." Still stirring the compost, Lauren recalled Rita's wise words. "It's a matter of perspective, the way you perceive the circumstances you're given. At times I didn't know if I was upside down or right side up, and then one day it occurred to me that it simply didn't matter. The world looked pretty much the same from both perspectives. I just had to learn to move from the inside to the outside, from the upside to the downside, whenever I chose. It's so easy, once you get the feeling."

"What kind of feeling is it?"

"Livvy, you've spent a lot of time with Rita, so I know you know what I'm talking about. It's a feeling you have deep in your womb and that's where all good Witches do their best thinking. Now, put your hands in the compost and tell me what you feel."

Livvy squealed when she stuck her hand in the fermenting mixture. "Oh I do, Aunty Lauren."

"Tell me what you see, tell me in pictures so I can understand."

As she had been taught, Livvy lowered her lashes, unfocused her vision, and concentrated on the compost pile. "I see a big snake making a circle. I see a snake eating it's own tail. The snake is taking it's own life and making a new life from it. That's what happens in the compost, isn't it?"

"You've got it, my darling niece. That's the way for us and everything in the cosmos." Picking up a handful of fine red soil from the garden, Lauren sprinkled it over Livvy's head and then did a twirl on her tiptoes. "You are truly, truly, one of us."

Giving Livvy a kiss on the cheek Lauren had a great idea. "Let's go over to the Casino and have tea and creampuffs. Everywhere I traveled, the first things I looked for were the marketplaces, the bazaars, and a really good bakery."

Livvy looked at the snakeskin, hummingbird skeleton, eagle claw, owl feathers, mother-of-pearl crescent moon, gold coyote fur, cats' whiskers, and magic wand spread on the floor.

"What are all of these things?"

Lauren quickly picked up the picture of Americo and the lock of his hair. "I've been carrying a lot of things in the satchel Grandma made for me, and I've decided that it's time to lighten my load and make room for something new."

"Why do you have cats' whiskers? You don't have a cat."

Lauren tickled Livvy's nose with a whisker. "Americo and Rita saved their cat's whiskers for me. Whiskers are feelers and when you're wandering you need help finding your way."

"Why do you carry an eagle claw?"

"So I have a tool to help me hook power when I feel it moving. Sometimes it moves so fast you need a tool to help you snag it."

Livvy held a delicate hummingbird skeleton in her hand. "Why do you have a skeleton in your satchel?"

"Bones and stones hold all of the information."

"You love the crescent moon, why?"

Lauren softly touched the shimmering mother-of-pearl. "Oh, I do love the crescent moon. I think it's because for so long I was mostly hidden."

"This snake skin is really neat. It's so fragile."

"What we shed is fragile, but the new skin underneath is also pretty fragile until it's had some time to get used to the light."

"Where did you find the coyote fur?"

"On a walk over to Cathedral Rock. I found it clinging to a cats claw shrub, and it reminded me that the coyote is always watching and waiting for an opportunity."

"Look at all of your feathers. Can I have some?"

"Sure, take all you want, everybody needs to remember to fly."

Lauren laughed while serving tea in delicate, mismatched, porcelain cups and saucers. "Are you finished with your questions? You're just full of them today."

"Will you let me look at your bracelet?"

"Only on my arm, Honey. I've worn it since I was seventeen years old and very rarely has it been off my wrist."

"Where did you get it?"

"Somebody very special gave it to me a long time ago, and it's a secret only two people know."

Livvy imagined a dark, tall lover presenting the gift to Lauren. "I hope somebody gives me a bracelet like that someday."

"I do too, Livvy, I do too. It's the second best gift anybody could ever give you."

Although Lauren loved to spend time with her niece, when Livvy left the Casino, Lauren reached for her bell of silence. When clearing her world of unwelcome chaos, always, Lauren rang the bell on her charm bracelet. However, an imaginative and very essential design, beckoned the quiet. With the bell inverted and the chime suspended by chain, in the absence of contact, there was silence.

☪

Possibly, if not busy spinning another story in the Bell Rock area, the Vortex could have been blamed for the cloud of red dust. However, the whir of a speeding sports car convertible, and a clock on the dash obviously running as fast as the car, were quite enough to disturb the tranquil equilibrium on El Rancho de Las Estrellas. The steaks were marinated, the salad ingredients tossed and Americo paced, while Trey, annoyed at Lauren's tardiness, watched from the picture window.

Lauren's afternoon had been spent in town flirting with a cute, quite a bit younger cowboy, so she drove fast and worried hard. "I'm late and Grandma detests it when people are late. Damn, I hope Americo and Trey haven't started the steaks yet. Shit, why do I get myself in these situations?" The sports car stopped, the dust settled and the coals were perfect, just as Lauren had planned.

Taking refuge by her father, Lauren kissed Jake on the cheek, touching his thinning hair. Each lost in their thoughts; they stood together, not saying a word. A fleeting shadow marked Lauren's expression when Americo looked at her with unabashed love in his eyes. Jake saw the shadow, "Lauren, don't worry, you're a smart cookie, and you'll be fine."

Silently, Lauren answered, "Daddy, you never noticed, but your smart cookie turned into a cracked cookie, a very long time ago."

Fortunately or unfortunately, every young girl first sees herself through her father's eyes. Some fathers see their daughters as a princess and others see disappointment. Jake adored Lauren, seeing himself in his daughter. She was his princess, and he admired the many qualities of intelligence, wit, beauty, and talent she possessed believing they were a direct reflection of his own qualities. However, because Jake knew Lauren was exceptional in many ways, he thought it his job to push her to extreme levels of performance, never tolerating the average in any way. Jake could not tolerate imperfection of any kind, and therefore, the messages were mixed. On one hand, Lauren heard words of praise and adoration and on the other hand, she heard words of criticism and disappointment.

Believing he had comforted Lauren, deserved or not, Jake experienced a private moment of self-exoneration. "My silent wonder. She was so very quiet, always absorbing everything in her environment and processing it with her brilliant mind. She watched us play out our dramas in front of her eyes, analyzing everything until she resolved the mystery for herself. She's so accomplished and so independent, I must have done something right."

☪

Over dinner Lauren entertained her family with outrageous stories and funny commentaries on local politics, and Americo, much like the raven, waited to the side, watching for an opportunity. Thinking himself unnoticed by the others, he flew over, under, and around Lauren, searching for clues, wishing for time gone by and missing her terribly.

Americo extended his champagne flute, winked boldly and offered a toast. Never taking his eyes from the bracelet on her arm, he reminded Lauren of her place in the family. "To Lauren, our Princess. Lauren, I've always admired the beautiful gold charm bracelet you wear." Only Lauren and Americo knew that he had given her the bracelet thirty years ago. He stood with his hand on his fiancées' shoulder. "I'm bringing Alexandra to your show, and I hope she'll find something that pleases her. Good luck at your opening, I sincerely mean it, my friend."

Lauren blushed like a girl, and toasted him in return, sending another invitation, silently. "You need a haircut, Americo, and I know I'm the only one you've let cut your hair for twenty-five years. You look so tired. Darling, are you having the same problem I am?"

Americo's hair cast a shadow on the white embroidered table-cloth as he answered her with his eyes. "I am tired; you have no idea what leaving you has done to me. I can't sleep, food disgusts me, and I don't give a damn about having sex."

The conversation continued, the humming in the background remained, and time moved in a spiral as a ball of energy united and time spun backwards. Wild random energy can be organized, patterned, and channeled in many forms. Some people use patterns that are memorized, and others use random patterns, depending on their whims. Words are channels for energy, as are all images and works of art. Form channels energy, making it visible. Often, energy organizes itself into balls, such as thoughts, ideas, and feelings. However energy is organized, it can be blocked, cut, diverted, absorbed, or returned. In whatever form wild random energy is channeled, when a connection exists, there is magic. The energy spiraling between Lauren and Americo was not cut, blocked, or diverted.

Americo sat down when he felt the spiral connection between them coil and contract. Surprised, yet not in the least surprised, he felt Lauren's bare foot touch his boot. The touch wasn't intentional, but neither was it withdrawn. Like a yin and a yang meeting after months of separation, Lauren and Americo each sighed. Not a person at the dining room table heard the sigh, but one person caught the look on Americo's face.

Lauren Auldney is a brat, an irascible brat, and when her foot touched Americo's boot, she did not move it in shame. No, Lauren leaned towards him and with her face cupped in her hands, looked him in the eye and said, "Spin it." Everybody at the table, except Rita, thought she meant the real estate problem he was currently trying to resolve.

Casually, Americo reached under the table, and in a boldly

erotic gesture he touched her toes, weaving his fingers between them. Sending him a response, Lauren touched her fingers to her cheek, wiggling them as if bored.

Words were sent by the look in his eyes. "I can't forget you, no matter how hard I try."

Lauren reached for a roll, allowing her fingers to linger on the wicker basket. "Meet me halfway, Americo."

"I hate you."

"I love you."

"I love you."

"I know. Do you?"

Americo licked his lips and smiled, then answered somebody's question. "Yes."

With deliberation, Lauren cut a bite from her steak, held it to her lips, and said with her glance, "Do you remember?"

Americo responded, taking a drink of his champagne, "Do you?"

As the other sighed, each nodded their head in consent, surrendering themselves to their circumstances.

☪

Fifteen years ago Alexandra Kingston moved to Sedona from Beverly Hills. She arrived in Sedona well equipped with a large divorce settlement, a five-year old son who guaranteed her years of generous child support, a palatial home, and ammunition for more money from her former husband if needed. Her striking good looks, complete with flaming red hair and fair skin, armed her with the ammunition to become the most sought after date in Sedona. For five years she was seen on the arm of the wealthiest, most eligible men in town, most of them much older than herself. The arm she wanted belonged to Americo Rios, and for years she set her sights waiting for the time her charms would prove irresistible. She knew his reputation of being cold and ruthless to the women he dated, but Alex knew without any doubt that she could tame this local renegade, the most intriguing man in town.

☪

Feeling not even a tad sorry for shamelessly seducing Americo with her gestures, Lauren gave Alexandra a look of commiseration, hoping to divert her attention. Staring blatantly at Americo, Lauren spoke sweetly to Alex. "Your fiancé is a very generous man, and I hope one of my creations will please you."

Alexandra smiled insincerely at Lauren, knowing there were several reasons Americo would never buy a piece of Lauren's jewelry for her. She thought it too bold, too imaginative, too erotic, too avant-garde, too arty, and besides, Lauren rarely used faceted stones, Alex's favorites. However, the real reason was that Americo had never kept it a secret how he felt about Lauren.

The once lovely, glowing grin became tinged, carnivorous, fanged, and a little foolish. With her teeth bared, Alexandra stared at Lauren, wondering why the family hadn't noticed Lauren was obviously demented.

Half present and half with the devil in her satchel, Lauren listened to Americo go on about problems with Garry Baker over an easement the developer wanted to buy. Looking at the perfectly applied eyeliner, blush, lipstick, mascara, and base, Lauren pondered, "Why does Alexandra wear so much makeup? She doesn't need it."

Alex relaxed, sat a little straighter in the straight-backed chair and again smiled when she glimpsed the diamond on her finger. After all, Lauren was Americo's old friend, a crazy old friend, and feeling quite confident; Alex knew without question she had a fifty-eight faceted edge.

The clan gabbed idly, asking questions of each other and enjoying the familial bonding. Thinking he might want to take Lydia to Americo's hacienda for a week, Jake asked Americo about his ancestral home in northern Mexico. "Are you still having your housekeeper put flowers in the cemetery at Casa de Lorinda?"

Lauren gasped, wondering if anybody would ever figure out why Americo had renamed the hacienda Casa de Lorinda. Everybody had just assumed Americo named it for a woman in Mexico. Nobody ever met the woman; they just assumed. Americo glanced at Lauren before answering. His glance caused Lauren to spill champagne on her t-shirt.

Appalled that Lauren could be so indelicate, Alex sharpened her edge. "She doesn't have much to offer a man, after all, she's so unstable and flighty, and most men would never notice her looks. What on Earth is wrong with that woman? She's holding Rita's black cat on her lap while she eats dinner. I don't believe it! I think she's got red dirt under one of her chewed fingernails, how crass.

She would look ever so much better with a little makeup."

Alex knew she looked drop dead gorgeous in her very lovely Missoni knit pantsuit, and she should have looked gorgeous that night. She had spent the afternoon being clipped, polished, trimmed, rubbed, rolfed, oiled, conditioned, coiffed, read, made up, and pampered at a local day spa. She invested the time and money, hoping to impress upon Americo the contrast between her very composed self and the maniacal looking woman whom he still pined for like a college boy.

Almost startling calm in her demeanor, Alex felt very pleased with the results of her own years of therapy, hundreds of workshops, and personal psychic. "Maybe if Lauren went into therapy, she could lose that schizophrenic edge and the wild look in her eyes. She's with her family, getting all the attention, yet she seems so disturbed. What a sick, odd, freaky woman."

Alex crossed her legs and lovingly touched Americo's hand, feeling pleased with the strength of her place in his life. "What on Earth did Americo ever see in her? Hmm, I wonder if she ever slept in his house?"

Like a disintegrating shroud, the calm, poised exterior collapsed and Alexandra glared with contempt when Lauren stood. Teetering a little from the champagne and grinning mischievously, Lauren thanked everybody for the fun and good wishes.

Lauren smiled sweetly at Alex, hoping to put her mind at unrest. "By the way, Alex, the answer to your question is yes, many, many times."

Shocking her parents, Livvy giggled out loud. Never shocked by anything Lauren said or did, Rita discreetly covered her proud smile.

☪

By the light of the evening star, four luscious women dropped their robes and stepped nude into the cauldron of Lauren's hot tub. The small atmospheric fire in the red clay fireplace glowed soft, golden, and red. Making a final whoosh with their wings, the ravens passed into the night, leaving only the pattern of their wings silhouetted against the slow moving clouds. Lauren lit thirteen red candles in the outdoor candelabra and waved a stick of incense over each woman as she stepped into the bubbling scented water.

Ninety-nine-year old Rita slipped off her sandals and dangled her skinny, veined, crone legs in the tub, smiling proudly at the beautiful women who were part of her family. Gold glitter sparkled on her red toenails, glitter, that Lauren, feeling risqué, applied earlier in the week. Alexandra stood to the side, refusing to join the other women for a bawdy gossip session under the light of the moon. An overly friendly bat swooped low, found the sight of nude women delightful and swooped again, causing Lauren to lose her balance. She lost her balance and floundered to the bottom of the tub. Coming up for air the third time, she accepted a facet of her destiny. "Oh well, somebody has to be the Fool, the clown, or hang upside down. Seems like it's always me." Naughtily, Lauren flicked some water on Alexandra's sandaled feet. "Alex, you should join us for some fun. You haven't lived until you've howled at the moon with us."

Alex glimpsed at the naked women and then glanced at the men having drinks on the porch. "I didn't bring my bathing suit."

Lauren didn't see the problem. "Oh, Alex, if you're going to be a part of this family, you'll have to get used to some things. The men in this family are used to seeing our boobs and fannies all over the place." Lauren laughed tauntingly. "God, Americo and Trey have had to look at my bare butt since the day I was born."

Alex winced noticeably at the reminder that Americo and Lauren had shared more than a short romance together, but quickly played a flashy royal card. "No thanks, Lauren, I'll just go sit with my fiancé on the porch."

Lauren could trump that comment with a flick of her wrist. "Fine, but before you go, will you hand me the champagne from the ice bucket? Gorgeous, you're almost as sweet as you are pretty. Just think, when you marry Americo, we'll be almost like sisters."

Livvy laughed shyly. "Let's talk about sex. That's what we talk about at school when girls get together."

"Oh, no way," Lauren protested. "It's been so long since I've had sex, I couldn't stand to talk about it. The Vortex pulled me home and I guess her exchange was taking sex away. Yikes, all I do is fantasize about a long sexy night with a good man. We could drink champagne, feed each other luscious food, and then please each other's body in every way. Oh I hate it. I miss the candlelight, the massages, the flirting, and most of all doing it," she said pouting. "I miss having a man in my life and making love all night. Oh star light star bright, bring me a handsome, sexy cowboy tonight," Lauren giggled.

Feeling frisky, with a tarty grin on her face, Lauren made a toast, tantalizing the women by batting her lashes. "I think we should all toast Grandma, after all she raised us in an erotic cauldron of sexual energy and creativity. Grandma, you're living proof that we're all sexual beings from the day we're born until the day we die, and that there's not any part of our lives that's worth living if it's not motivated by eroticism."

Rita blushed slightly, feeling very proud that Lauren had learned her lessons perfectly.

Lauren turned to Livvy and smirked. "I hope you remember that when you do your homework, little niece."

Always the good mother, Sunnie told Livvy to study what her professors suggested and save the school of eroticism for her Aunt Lauren.

Although shocked by the openness of the conversation, Alex wished she could share with the women, and silently she did. "You're not the only one who's not getting any sex, Lauren. I don't know if it's because Americo isn't interested, or that he can't make love to me, but it's been months."

Lauren paused, then returned an affirmative nod, to a question felt, but not heard.

The amber liquid rested heavily in a crystal cocktail glass filled with three fingers of scotch. Americo and Trey winked at each other, thinking how much they would miss the sight of Jake with a glass of scotch and cigarette in his hand. Moths fluttered around the lantern light, darting at the screen door. A gentle awareness came to Americo, much like the soft flutter of the wings. "Lauren, there's never been anybody but you, do you know there never will be?"

Jake relaxed and stretched his legs, feeling proud of the two younger men in his company. "I sure as hell wish your father was here, Americo. You have no idea how robbed I've felt since he and your mother were killed in that goddamned car wreck. Tomas and I were like brothers as well as best friends and I've never found a friend to take his place." Jake paused when Americo nodded to Alexandra. "I have to tell you, son, I was extremely disappointed when you and Lauren broke up."

Americo sounded defeated and tired. "Jake, if it was a matter of love, I'd always be with Lauren, but I guess she's too complicated for me...or any man."

Jake absorbed Americo's words, listening as a writer would listen. He heard the pauses, the nuances, the emphasis on certain words, and he heard the underlying pain in Americo's voice.

"Americo, it's too damn bad you never found out who stole the gun Dad gave you, it was a hell of a piece, and it should have stayed in the family."

Americo remained silent, not wanting to share his fears for Lauren's safety with Jake and Trey. For eighteen months Americo had been tormented by the theft of a family heirloom gun from his car. Believing Lauren intended to harm herself Americo had relentlessly called, written letters and pleaded with her to admit that she had stolen the gun. Always, Lauren denied knowing anything about the theft, and yet Americo still woke in the nights wondering if someday Lauren would turn the gun on herself.

Jake interrupted. "Why doesn't Alexandra get in the tub with the other women? She looks lonely."

"Hell, I don't know." Americo laughed as he took a sip of his bourbon. "You have to admit that's a pretty formidable group of women, so maybe she's a little inhibited by how uninhibited they are."

☪

Already a little tipsy from the champagne, and feeling very mature with the older women, Livvy wanted to turn the conversation into an all night dorm room gabfest.

"Aunty Lauren, tell us about the first time you had sex."

Lauren splashed water on Livvy's face. "You're as nosy as your mother, and I will not tell you about my first time." Lauren wiggled her fanny, wanting to tantalize the others. "I'll only tell you this much about one of the first times. I was a dance major at the time, my body looked incredible, and a very cool, offbeat, long-haired architecture student asked why I kept my tiger body covered with a schoolgirl plaid skirt. We were all over each other on the dance floor, and then we did it with me sitting on the hood of his Porsche in a parking lot at U. of A."

"Oh my God, you didn't."

Rita chuckled at her irascible granddaughter and noticed Lauren scratching long, angry, red bruises on her thighs.

"Honey, stop scratching yourself, your legs are going to look terrible with the bruises you're leaving on them."

"Oops, Grandma, old habits die hard. Good thing my finger-nails are short, or I would do some damage."

Livvy loved Lauren stories. "What do you believe in, Aunty Lauren?"

"Do you really want to hear my list?" Lauren laughed knowing her list was long.

"You asked for it," Lauren said crinkling her nose mischievously. "I believe in the pattern of the Vortex and surrendering your filaments to the magic it holds. I believe in destiny, and I believe in the stories woven into the landscape. I believe in the beauty of the garden, cheeseburgers, hot sex, the power of desire, having great night vision, making art, and talking to my dolls. I believe in the magic of Earth processes, spaces between objects, experience, and the wisdom of your Grandmother. I also believe in living life to the fullest with passion and gusto, even if people do think you're crazy."

Fluttering her hands in the air with the grace of a maestro conductor, she continued, "I also believe in living by your own rules and in being aware." Lowering her voice to shock Alex, she whispered, "Most of all I believe in the unseen and the unknown. I don't believe in having habits, and I suppose that's why I identify with the deer. I believe in not taking yourself seriously, letting circumstances teach you, living spontaneously, catching power when it moves, and in adjusting your perceptions. I believe spirit resides in everything and most of all, women rule. Women rule because they carry the stories both in their wombs and on their backs, and what I wouldn't give right now to be on my back, if you know what I mean."

Sunnie winked at Americo when she saw his amused grin. "Lauren, you're the wildest person I've ever known."

Americo had his own opinion. "Lauren, you are the earthiest, most erotic, and magical woman I've ever known. So I suppose," he pondered rubbing his chin, "that makes you utterly deliciously female. I know better than anybody where your energy spins and believe me; you reflect this landscape inside and out. After all, you spun around me, like the Vortex spins around her axis."

Lauren laughed at her own hilarity. "We've laughed, now we cry. Tears are magic; they open doors and part the veils. I've never been with a group of women when we didn't end up crying. We'll all sleep so well tonight. I remember a time in my life when I didn't cry for over five years, so now I want to cry all of the time to make up for it."

"Aunty Lauren, have you ever really been in love? I mean really, really, deep down, totally in love."

"Yes, Honey, twice, but the first was the most special. It was so wonderful, beautiful and painful, but I wouldn't have missed it for the world."

"Now let's have a final toast to Grandma and my show tomorrow night. We'll knock them dead won't we, Grandma?"

"Honey, this show is your show. My weavings are just the background for your gifts to the world."

"Grandma," Lauren said standing to hug Rita, "you've always been the background for my foreground." With tears in her eyes she held her Grandmother with wet arms.

"That's just as it should be, Lauren. The past is always the background for the foreground. More importantly the Earth is the background for everything we do. Humans move in the foreground, and far too often forget the background that supports them. Life is like a painting, my dear girls, the background is the support and the ground, while the foreground is the active present, and we need both to keep the painting from floating off the canvas. Let the background of your lives support you, anchor your life to the four corners of Mother Earth, and live life in the foreground, the eternal present. I'm going to love watching you tomorrow night, Sweetheart, but now its time for this Grandma to go to bed."

☪

The fifty-five-year old log cabin, known as the Casino, had been transformed once again. In its life, the Casino had been where Zack Auldney held his high stakes poker games, a playhouse for the children, and is now a guesthouse where Lauren lives.

Colored patterned weavings, collected from her travels, decorate the walls and because Lauren loves candlelight, she placed tens of tens of candles of all shapes, sizes, and colors around the small living room sized building. Small, carved stone sculptures are displayed haphazardly, rarely seen in the same corner twice. Like life, Lauren believes art needs to move, breathe, and be free.

Soulful gray stone metates lean against the wall, the surfaces worn from hundreds of hours of grinding corn or grains, bringing to mind the repetitive motions of women all over the world. Lauren has always known that to be a woman and to do a woman's work, is a gift. The repetitive motion of spinning, sweeping, stirring, sewing, grinding, weeding, or chopping is a chariot into the mystery and that is why wise women smile as they work. Work isn't drudgery for a woman in touch with the Goddess, it's magic.

The womb shaped metate, and phallic like mano, embody the duality of male and female energies, forever reminding Lauren that one without the other is an incomplete process.

Two large Navajo rugs provide warmth on the saltillo tile floor, and the windows are covered with bamboo stick blinds overlaid with bright scarves, colored parejos, and flea market macramé hangings. The old brass bed is covered with an antique, delicately hand-stitched quilt that once belonged to America's mother.

Lauren dwells with the dolls she collected during her childhood and although she never played with them, they are her midnight companions and keepers of her secrets.

Lauren collects brooms. The small porch is lined with the broom sentries protecting her from ghosts that often follow. One never enters Lauren's space without awareness of lavender, vanilla, sweet grass, or Nag Champas incense. Fresh flowers, most often daisies or sunflowers, are placed throughout the single room in lovely leaded crystal vases. Before leaving the Casino Lauren cleanses it with sage and red carnations, knowing that the building is a living being, and welcomes time alone to renew the energy contained within.

Dancing from the porch overhang are spiral shaped chimes made by Lauren. Early in the mornings when a small gust of wind blows through the valley, the dancing spirals remind her of the Vortex and the pattern that informs her life. Lauren scatters gourds, her favorite ornamental plant, trailing them out the door and down the steps. Unable to sleep and alone on the steps in the nighttime hours, Lauren talks to the gourds, finding meaning in the shadowed contours of their bodies.

A small pine bench in a bright corner is her studio. At her bench, with her gifted hands, she channels the light into gold works of art. And with her designs, she celebrates the first constant in her life, that of being a woman, in love with being a woman.

☪

The Vortex stalled. A slight tilt to the right was corrected and Lauren claimed the peaceful afternoon for herself. She needed time, time alone to align her intent for the opening of her first show in Sedona. Early summers are filled with hope, offering one an opportunity to release pain and grow hopefully towards the sun, once again. Lauren had reason to smile, for once again the compost of her experience hinted at a new beginning. It was time to blossom fully and become a woman alone, alone but content with her art, her garden, her Grandmother, and the last third of her life.

Like ladies-in-waiting, the many brooms on the Casino porch offered choices. While on her odyssey, Lauren became very familiar with the land of choice, having crash-landed on the unforgiving, cliff ridden shoreline many times. Not always making the best decisions, Lauren sincerely wanted the broom she used to sweep the steps and the interior of her world to be exceptional. But...does a used broom clean more efficiently, due to experience? Or...perhaps, as the old Crones say, a new broom sweeps clean. The choice would have been easier if she didn't hear the sound of his footsteps or the emotion in his voice. Even the weathered brass doorknob, providing access to her chamber, taunted her with a choice she made many years ago. The raven, the relentless raven, stopped to caw, "Bruja, it's me, say something." He cawed over and over again, forcing Lauren to make a choice. The new broom bowed with the honor, promising they would learn together how to sweep up the dust and debris of a life and return it to a proper disorder.

One must always take time to acknowledge the messenger. Lauren sat down on the rickety old steps and smiled at the bodacious, old Venus gourd. "I think I'm going to be OK. It still kills me when I see him, and I'd give half of the rest of my life for one more night with him." Lauren and Venus each grinned mischievously at Lauren's sexy thoughts of what she would like to do to his body for a night. "He's been my Prince, my mate, my Magician and now, I find myself missing him most as a friend."

Fortunately for Lauren, Rita's words accompany her eternally. Rita had enjoyed many tasty times with Venus over the years and now that Lauren was old enough to be privy to the conversation, although taking a nap before the big night, Rita joined the lascivious women on the porch. Often when women gather, the nature of the deep exchange is what men call sewing circle talk. However on this afternoon, rather than talking about boys, the merits of a good broom were praised. Before Rita and Venus ventured far into the charming attributes of a broom, Lauren asked a most important question, deferring to the age and tad more experience of the older women. "Is a broom a phallic symbol? If so, why is it a symbol for Witches?"

Rita and Venus were aghast. "Well, of course not, how could

you say that?" Lauren shrugged, having just asked an innocent question. However, Rita didn't want her to linger too long on that assumption. "Lauren, doesn't the lovely slightly matted, V-shaped fiber remind you of something?"

Lauren pondered a little longer, catching a wink from Venus. "Well, Grandma, it certainly does." With not a moment to waste, Lauren abruptly grabbed the broom, but alas the moment of no return had long passed. "Well, let me tell you, this little hotty is having sex right in front of our eyes." Oh the audacity of a young red handled broom, with a lovely little V. Venus came to the rescue. After all, they all needed an immediate meaningful distraction in order to refrain from blatant voyeurism, regardless of the delicious temptation.

Like a strict disciplinarian and without hesitation, Lauren took the broom inside. Not letting the broom even consider reclining, Lauren authoritatively stood her in the corner by the fireplace. "Don't you know the bread needs to bake a little longer? You don't have any experience or any judgment, and Goddess knows what will happen to you now. How you could behave like this the afternoon before my opening, after I hand-painted that staff you're so fond of? Don't you know I'll worry about you all night long? Now you stay put, and don't you dare move until you ask me first."

Venus interrupted again. "Lauren, please tell us the purpose of the broom. Tell us just as your Grandmother taught you when you were a little girl and she needed her beautiful porch swept." Lauren became serious, the sweet memory returned and once again she was a young untouched broom, doing as her Grandmother bid.

The day in her memory was fresh, new, and alive. The unforeseen wind had cleared all unseen particles from the air, and even the birds that migrated over El Rancho de las Estrellas on Sunday were still visible. This was Friday. Lauren recalled the wise old broom in her hand. The broom, present at Rita's wedding, had been a part of the family for over seventy years. The beloved broom had swept many arguments, disagreements, tears, and fears from the covered portal of Rita's home.

Lauren sighed and spoke longingly. "Sweeping isn't about sweeping the little bit of nature that finds her way into our interior lives back to the source. As we sweep, with every repeated motion of the broom, we are also moving blocked energy from our body, mind, or soul. Sweeping is about motion, and everything needs to move. Sweeping gets into the corners where ghosts lie in wait for us and sends them to the great beyond. Sweeping gets under the bed, the chair, and the table, reminding us of things we may not have seen or have forgotten. Every Witch knows that a broom is for more than riding to the moon on the dark night, and sweeping helps us find the cat whiskers our earthly guides leave to guide us when lost. And so we sweep."

Alone again, Lauren closed the blinds and lit the candles. The circle was now cast, and red silk thread separated Lauren's world from all else. Recreating her life of experience from the core, Lauren placed a rag doll in the center of a geometric patterned woven cloth. It was a mother doll, embracing a child. An iridescent crystal ball caught the light, she sighed, and the shadows lingered. She kissed a small mother-of-pearl button, held it in her hand, still unable to relinquish the past. Finally, from a faded pink silk cloth she removed a small silver disc encircled by a serpent of shiny red enamel. Years ago, Lauren engraved the disc and embellished the directions with colored stones. The Vortex spiraled in the center and with a pass of her hand it halted, marking the moment warning Lauren that like the Wheel of Fortune, fate may stop on any color. Lauren offered a solitary sunflower to the circle and from a small vial she dripped sacred water into her miniature, silver cauldron. The water, tears shed from a heart broken open by love, sanctified the space, making it holy. One by one, the treasures of her past were revealed to the future and completing the circle of her circumstances, Lauren made one more offering. To mark a deep transition in her life, she placed a porous seashell, stained dark blood red, in honor of the last blood to flow from her womb.

The steaming cauldron of her bath beckoned with the scent of chamomile from her garden, and resting her head on a pillow filled with lavender, Lauren rubbed honey over her body. "I'm almost ready for show time." Even donning the fluffy, pink terry cloth robe could not contain her pre-opening jitters. "This is my biggest show ever, because this is the first in my hometown, and I'm the crazy girl they all thought would end up in trouble." Having acquired a bit of perspective along the journey, Lauren surrendered to her circumstances and finally, the awareness of all possibility peeked from under the Navajo rug. "Oh well, my life has been a little tragic and a little magic, but so far I haven't been in much trouble, not that I haven't deserved to be at times. Sedona, let magic reign, because tonight the real Lauren is going to shine."

Lauren didn't have a plan, but she certainly had intent and

looking hot was the horse her intent would ride into the night. Her style was subtle, yet packed with intrigue, and she knew very well the power of quiet luxury. Luxury, wrapped in small packages of pink, speaks more eloquently than an overbearing blast of purple, frilly, shiny stuff. Pink glitter powder, strategically placed on smooth shoulders and a hint of cleavage, is promising, touchable, and one must be rather close to appreciate the design. To reveal mysterious eyes, had it occurred to them, ladies of the night would have perhaps preferred dangling gold earrings set with peridot cabochons, rather than belladonna. Lauren's pupils, resting in a gentle pool of Caribbean Sea green, were deep, dark, a compelling whirlpool, promising unspoken delight.

The moonstones, although not precious to a gem dealer, were precious for what they signed. Three iridescent white moonstones set in a triangle against the soft, hand-polished background of a wide, gold bracelet, signed rites of passage in Lauren's life. "One for my maidenhood, one for what could have been my motherhood, and one for my cronehood. I think the best is yet to come." Lauren touched the third stone, whispering hopefully, "At least I hope so, because some of the other parts..."

☾★

The Vortex hummed gently, vibrating the frequency, birthing rich, potent, balmy air to the red rock paradise. The Earth sighed, surrendering to the inevitable. Once again she turned her back to the Sun, eager to dance alone in the night, offering her abandon to more distant stars. The hour of power was nigh. The daylight, always brilliant, muted in the near dusk, marking the separation, softening the details, adding mystery to the landscape. Lauren drove into the evening, the back lighting of the setting sun drawing awareness to those among us we cannot see in the day. Random clouds passed overhead, dropping purple memories on coppery shadows of the day, the vivid companions of the night. Her world, the night of her Sedona debut, was precisely the vision Lauren conjured.

At the same moment Lauren conjured, there was somebody conjuring Lauren, and just as a particularly bright last ray of the sun broke through the fleeting clouds, she caught her peeking.

"You, Rosy, I don't believe it, I haven't seen you since 30,313 BCE! The last time I saw you, I waved, but you were jumping on a little raft, leaving before the last wave washed us all to the sea. Did you make it? Was it a good ride?" The ride hadn't been good, in fact, she hadn't even left town.

"Honey, I'm so sorry to hear that, but don't you love living here? I do. Are you going to come to my opening? Believe me, I need my best friends to be there and you know why." Rosy knew very well why, after all, she had been watching Lauren's escapades for more than a few years.

Stone, our fundament, is impregnated with meaning. Meaning and the spirits of all those who once walked on the land are facets of the numinous, intrinsic, transcendent material. Stone resists time. It is perennial, cohesive, sacred and our terrestrial. Red rock, receptive, absorbent, red sandstone, holds the stories of those once here. The red rock also holds captive those who could not make the ultimate journey from her shores. Trapped, unable to move on, Rosy warned Lauren. "My friend, do you recall when your name was Copper Penny?"

Enthusiastically, Lauren shook her head yes. After all, she did start the first Jerome copper boom about a million years ago and to this day, drops a penny every time she parks her car, offering an unknown person good luck. One day, while wandering along a green river seeking sun seeds for flowers, Lauren tripped on a rather sizeable copper pellet. The connection was instant. Having the foresight to look into the future, she saw an incredibly convenient, sensible and pretty means of exchange. It was also very cool that the metal, being the connecting metal, helped her connect with her son up river hunting for his mother, who had once again ventured into another frequency, and sometimes took years to find her way home. She held it in her fingers and said, "Oha, kopa penie." Thus you have the name, the boom, and the bust. Rosy had always, for millennia, resented Lauren's keen eye and deft fingers.

"Penny, let me warn you, what you are now seeing may not be real. Held within this sandstone body of mine are multiples of meanings, many referents and your wild spinning soul has forgotten many, many things. Your lover has picked up his cards, started a new game with another and now that he's all grown up; he doesn't play poker for pennies anymore. Yet, you wait, hoping one day he'll forgive you and return."

Feeling haughty and looking exceptionally hot, Lauren defended her actions. "I'm not waiting for his forgiveness. I didn't ask him to forgive me because I made the best decision I could, and it was my right to do so. Gosh, Rosy, considering the time and circumstances, what would you have done besides stand there, silently disintegrating into a new form?"

"So I'm a little sandy, a lot dusty, and I've dropped a few slivers, at least I'm not keeping secrets. And, I might add, my form is rather devastating." Rosy added, "We'll see what your form looks like after the wreckage of revelation."

Lauren agreed about the form. A woman with red dust in her bones will always love the red rocks. "Hmmm. Well, I agree, now that I'm a little older, my satchel has been feeling a bit too heavy."

Being younger than Lauren by seventy-two million years Rosy had always felt superior.

Oh my, the arrogance of youth. "I didn't like your comment about my silently disintegrating. Perhaps you haven't been listening, but just wait till you shed your baggage."

Oh dear, the arrogance of a baby crone, the shiny copper only a touch tarnished. "Sure, Rosy, like I haven't already. Believe me, the crust on this little loaf of bread has already been eaten."

Maneuvering through the maze of local two lane highways, Lauren landed on stop in the shopping center parking lot overlooking the city. So characteristic of a high-energy womb like Sedona, the atmosphere was festive, tourists milling, shopping, and stopping for an early dinner. Waving to two flirtatious businessmen walking into a restaurant, Lauren spied a sleek, purring, black cat. Swearing softly, she nodded at Alexandra parking her new Jaguar.

Hope springs eternal. "I wonder why Americo isn't with her tonight."

Lauren pondered as Americo's car appeared. A vision of him making love to Alexandra then appeared. "I might just have to consider casting a spell so he can't have sex with the over dressed, over manicured, red headed bitch."

The scene in the gallery was one of intrigue, rich beauty and marvel. Opening her arms in delight, Lauren peered through the mist, still in awe of the display she created earlier in the day. Lauren whispered as she further parted the smoky mist veil. "Oh, how gorgeous, the mist machine gives the illusion of entering a fairyland." The fairytale mood was staged at the entrance. Smoky mist enshrouded a sunflower covered archway, offering illusion, dazzle, and charm, and once under the archway the guests entered a circle of thirteen vignettes, each designed to correspond with a passage of Lauren's life.

Weavings created by Rita were the backdrop, casting shadows of the past on to the yet untouched future. The textured gold pieces absorbed the diffused light, reflecting the mystery, the magic, and the emotion embedded in each work of art. Slowly walking from one vignette to another, she fussed like an enchanted girl with the dolls serving as props for her sumptuous, expensive, erotic, avant-garde, twenty-four carat creations.

Lauren stood alone by an abstract doll made from Peruvian clay. The eyes were amber, the hair was black and the sex of the doll was ambiguous, on purpose. The doll held her gaze, reached for her hand, and Lauren became emotional as she polished fingerprints from the cabochon ruby recessed deep in an incised triangle. Only Lauren knew the story told by the doll, and only Lauren knew it was yet unfinished.

Hundreds of sunflowers had been delivered an hour before and were placed perfectly according to her instructions. An extravagant bouquet remained anonymous, Lauren not having time to read the card. The gallery owner, letting Lauren know it was show time, offered her a toast as he walked towards the door, welcoming the first guests.

Lauren glowed as she circulated among her guests, radiating as brilliantly as the exquisite gold bracelet she wore. When Lauren stopped to visit with an intriguing customer, the woman noticed the bracelet emphasized the delicacy of Lauren's slender arm, giving her the illusion of being enslaved. The impeccably dressed, very refined woman graciously introduced herself as Graciela Ybarra. Complimenting Lauren profusely, Graciela said she had admired her work in a Paris gallery years ago.

"You looked so familiar to me when you walked into the gallery, Graciela, but I didn't connect it to Paris. I thought maybe I met you in Mexico where I spent time at a former lover's hacienda." Lauren laughed uncomfortably at the exchange. "You have a double, Graciela, but then, don't we all?" Lauren quivered when Graciela continued to stare into her eyes, yet determinedly took control of the moment. "Would you like me to personally show you some of my jewelry? Are you visiting in Sedona or do you live here?" Graciela explained that she was the wife of a Mexican government high official and had rented a home in Sedona for several months while her husband was out of the country on business. An hour passed quickly as Lauren personally selected a bracelet and two pairs of earrings for Graciela. The women exchanged phone numbers, promising to have lunch soon to become better acquainted.

To herself, Graciela Ybarra laughed viciously as she smiled at another guest making a purchase. "Americo, this is too easy.

You're with another woman, but I see the threads of your love wrapped around your Lauren. Thirty years ago, I told you I wouldn't let you go, the first night I looked into your amber eyes and made love to you. Si, you think we're friends. I know you don't love me, but I told you then, it's not your love I want. I saved every centavo of the money you paid me." Graciela gloated as she ran her fingers through her long, shiny black hair and admired the gold bracelet on her arm. "Tonight, I'll follow my plan. I know what I'm going to put in the locket of my new bauble. Your little princess overlooked what she knows she knows." Jealousy raged through Graciela when she saw Americo staring at Lauren. "Oh, how I remember watching the two of you at the hacienda when she secretly stayed with you. You watched over her as if she were royalty. You pampered her with everything she wanted, while I watched. Lauren wanted cream puffs for breakfast; somebody had to go buy them. Lauren wanted fresh eggs; somebody had to cook them. You kissed her fingers one by one and touched her cheek tenderly. For her, you put fresh flowers in your bedroom every day and every night you watched while she cooked your dinner for you. You made everybody taste the ugly, heavy tortillas she cooked on the outdoor stove. You brushed her hair, and sighed while she massaged your feet. You saddled her horse and took her to the sea. You introduced her to your friends and fed her shrimp and oysters with your fingers. I heard you both cry in ecstasy when you made love in the night. You served champagne to her on the veranda under the honeysuckle vines, and walked with her through the cemetery where your ancestors are buried. You kept special soft, silky sheets and blankets for her. You didn't allow anybody in your room but your Lauren. When I did your laundry and cleaned your house, Lauren took the broom from my hand, and said, 'Marquita go to town, have fun, it is very important that I care for Americo's house and clothes when I'm with him.'"

Lauren paused remembering a starry night fifteen years ago, when she and Americo were walking on the beach near Guaymas. She saw him bend to pick up a shell and blow the sand off before handing it to her. "I still use that shell for a soap dish, I wonder what made me think of that? I'll never forget the look of love on his face as he knelt in front of me, put his arms around my thighs and rested his head on my belly while I stroked his hair. He whispered to me, 'I love you, Lauren, I wish you wouldn't leave me tomorrow. I need you, Princess, I'm so lonely without you.'"

Guiding Alexandra towards the bar Americo paused as a vision of Lauren on her horse at the hacienda raced in front of his eyes. He felt her touch on his face when he raised the foot straps on the saddle. He saw the sunlight highlighting her hair and heard her giggle as the horse reared, wanting to run into the open spaces. Americo stopped to put drops in his irritated eyes. "What made me think of that?"

As minor duchesses will do, Alexandra Kingston swept into the gallery and graciously graced the masses with her presence. Her long, red hair was stunning and she shook her head often to give admirers the benefit of her exquisite mane. Her lovely hair was artfully styled in an effort to disguise a perky button nose that she always considered too small. She boldly scrutinized the other women, and then felt satisfied her attire was the most stylish in the gallery. Clinging to Americo's arm, she caught sight of Lauren holding court across the room and laughed when she saw the black, silk shift she wore. Alex fumed as she scanned Lauren's bare legs and hand painted ballerina slippers. "That woman has the worst taste I've ever seen. If she's the princess of Sedona, I really did choose a backwater place to live. When I think of the places she's lived and the people she knows, and how she gets away with doing nothing with herself, it just rasps me. She must think she's a goddess, the way she commands the attention of every man in the room."

Lauren waved sweetly to Alex and Americo, motioning them towards the display.

The slinky, patterned silk dress Alex wore clung to her voluptuous body, revealing her Scarlett O'Hara waist and generous breasts. She looked down, hoping her high heeled sandals compensated for legs she knew were slightly too short, denying her the possibility of ever appearing elegant. When she raised her head she caught Lauren's eye and knew without question by the little smirk, that she had read her mind. Alexandra felt a cold rush of panic when she saw the fleeting emotional exchange between Lauren and Americo, and in a huff she walked to the bar, glad that Lauren had enough taste to serve good champagne.

Rita stood at the sunflower covered helm, the billowing mist parted and regally the family matriarch entered the gallery on the arm of her son. The gold inlayed collar necklace Lauren made fifteen years ago adorned the neckline of a long red evening dress she had chosen for the affair. Gliding across the room Rita patted the silver bun that secured her long hair, stopping to visit with a woman about the hand-embroidered shawl she carried. Rita waved to Americo across the room and told the woman Lauren bought the shawl for her in the countryside of France, when she was a teenager visiting her mother.

The ninety-nine-year old woman took Lauren's hand, and the two women walked slowly, stopping in front of each display. Americo watched Lauren and her Grandmother sharing their stories and realized, as he silently intruded on their journey, he was indeed witnessing the wand of magic being passed to Rita's heir.

Jake Auldney stood tall, his six-foot frame imposing and his handsome face beaming with pride as it occurred to him that he had never before seen his daughter in her professional life. Jake shook his head as an old memory came back to him and closed his eyes, remembering the night of Lauren's high school graduation. Near tears welled in his eyes. "That was the first time I had a glimpse of the extraordinary woman she would become. I saw my little girl, my little rag picker, gliding down the staircase like a true princess wearing her pretty white dress. I saw her vitality and brilliance, and then she went away."

Lauren greeted Trey and Sunnie standing under the doorway surrounded by mist, their attention focused on one another. She deliberately guided the conversation to exclude Americo, who joined them, bringing Lauren a fresh glass of champagne. Alexandra glared from across the room, and Lauren waved, knowing friendliness was not what Alexandra wanted. For Alex's benefit, Lauren gave Americo a warm smile and a squeeze on the arm. The moment was too good to diminish. In a gesture of familiarity, Lauren allowed her fingers to linger on his back and then coyly dropping a lace hanky, she met Americo's hand when he bent to retrieve the white delicate.

Unable to quit watching her, Americo saw Lauren at the door having her palm read by a well-known local psychic. The longer they talked, the more he wondered what they were scheming. "What in the hell is she up to now? None of us are safe if she's conjuring something." Americo became perplexed when they both looked at him after reading the note resting on an elaborate arrangement of flowers.

Lauren, wrinkling her brow and pondering, held the small card to her heart. "These flowers have to be from Americo. Who else would say they've always loved me?"

Americo's fiancée demanded to talk to him privately and hissed as she possessively clutched his arm. "I'm leaving, Americo. You're embarrassing me by the way you keep watching Lauren." Her desperate eyes darted around the room suspiciously. "It's as though you're mesmerized by her. Why don't you understand she's nothing but trouble? I've heard the gossip, and it isn't very favorable."

Alex gulped the rest of her champagne, leaving an orange lipstick stain on the glass. "When you make love to me, don't you think I notice that you're rather mechanical and unemotional, in spite of your expertise? That is of course," she added sarcastically, "when you're able to have sex." Hoping to remind him of a commitment, she held her diamond for him to see. "I thought when you gave me this, it was over between the two of you."

They weren't playing the spinning game, and it wasn't a cute little Witch brewing the words, therefore, Americo didn't have the patience. "Do what you've got to do. I've told you before, Alex, you keep the chains too goddamned tight. If you want to be with me, you know damn well there are things I still have to work out, and whatever problem I have with Lauren is none of your business." He guided her towards the door, giving her no chance to change her mind. "You call it, lady."

Sunnie might have been looking adoringly at her husband, but she never missed the action. "I wonder what that was all about."

Trey smiled back at his tiny wife, fluffing her black and gray, wildly curly hair. "Hell, who knows, Darlin', but I'm not about to get caught up in Americo's love problems, even if he is my best friend."

Jake and Lydia watched Sunnie and Trey from across the room. "Jake, they're as much in love as the day they married. Trey's so rugged and masculine with his suntanned face, broad shoulders, and squint-lined eyes. Darling, he's almost as handsome as his father."

Trey didn't notice when Alex left the gallery, but after a few drinks, he did notice Sunnie. "Sun, I want to get a room and keep you for myself all night."

Sunnie stood on tiptoes to kiss him on the cheek, leaving the yes imprint of her luscious lips behind. "Where has the time gone, Trey? I feel like I've been trapped in a Dali painting. Thirty years have disappeared, and I can barely remember a thing."

The show was a rotating, spinning, spiraling, twisted success. There was a Princess and a Prince, separated by a moat that only the fearless dare cross. A regal dowager Queen, considering abdication in favor of the Princess. The King knew he was dying, yet rose to the occasion to accompany his lovely Lady to the ball. The brother Prince rediscovered his commoner wife, once again seeing the sunshine. The otherwise occupied rooms in the Castle were filled with a traveling merchant, a disgruntled duchess, and an evil sorceress. Not to mention a shadowy presence who could perhaps save the day.

Later in the evening, the festivity of the show traveled to a local restaurant and nightclub. The seductive rhythm of Salsa music was loud; the vibrations were stimulating and when Americo walked into the club, he had one thing on his mind. The guy has style, and his rugged appeal was not lost on four women tourists seated at a corner table. His ponytail was sleek, and the man looked cool wearing a white short-sleeved shirt, foot-molding calfskin boots, and chocolate-brown linen slacks. The tension in his body reminded them of a jaguar ready to pounce, and each one wished he would look in their direction. What a waste, a tall, handsome man, alone. He wasn't, but he seemed composed as he walked with purpose to a small table near the dance floor. Americo ordered a drink from the waiter, fixed his eyes on one woman and the woman he was fixin' to talk to was presently undulating her body to the sensuous beat of Latin music.

The bourbon was mellow, his thoughts were sweet, but the sight of Lauren dancing with his adversary Garry Baker, was bitter. He swore to himself, feeling a familiar dark pit in his stomach, then stepped outside to have a cigarette. Casually leaning against the wall of the building, he decided to tell Lauren he wanted to reconcile. Oh, he remembered and in spite of their estrangement, he couldn't help it, Lauren Auldney tickled him like he had never been tickled. "She's a delight to hold in your arms and damn her, she's a bewitching woman. Lauren is a hell of a show off, but I've never known a woman who danced with such wild abandon."

The music slowed, Lauren surrendered and a vision of Americo appeared. In her vision Americo tapped Garry on the shoulder. "I'm cutting in," Americo told Garry with authority. Through the fabric of his shirt, Lauren could feel his skin quivering, evidence of emotion yet unspoken. She blinked her eyes and smelled the scent of cinnamon cologne, the blend she brought to him from France. Home at last, Lauren leaned her head against his chest and surrendered to the security of his arms, remembering how perfectly they danced together. The vision ended, leaving her disappointed, bitter, and lonely. "Americo, it's only been six months and deep down I'm still missing you so much."

Americo saw the serenity in her expression, believing the reason was Garry.

Garry had an idea and Lauren responded. "Sure, it's fine if you want to come out to the Casino. I've got some champagne, and maybe we can figure out a way to be friends after all."

Laughing over their old feud, Garry and Lauren left the nightclub, infuriating Americo.

Old habits. "Damn her, what is she up to now? This is just like Lauren. She's going too far just because she's on a high. She'll crash tomorrow and hate herself." Americo yelled from the entrance of the restaurant. "Hey, Garry, let me talk to you."

The size had to go somewhere and with Garry Baker, it went to his mouth. "Rios, what are you, some kind of watchdog? Lauren invited me out to her place and unless there's something I don't know about," he paused waiting for a response, "what she does isn't your business. Hell, Rios, she's old enough to choose her own dates."

"Man, you don't understand," Americo protested. "Lauren's been through a lot lately. You shouldn't try to start something with her when you don't know anything about..."

"What's the matter, Rios, isn't our dear Alexandra enough for you?"

Americo wanted to focus. "Just leave Lauren alone, I mean it."

"Bullshit, Rios, what are you going to do about it?"

Americo ignored the question and Garry landed against his red Lexus SUV.

Lauren always had two cents worth of copper pennies to add. "You jerk, Americo, it's not like you could do anything the last time you tried."

"Lauren, shut the hell up and go home."

Lauren laughed at Americo, and seeing a man flattened against his car alters a mood. Feeling threatened, Lauren tarnished a penny with a little partial lie. "Don't even try to come to the Casino, Garry, I've got a gun and I know how to use it."

The lie opened a door and slowly, Americo turned towards Lauren and silently accused her. "Is there anything you haven't lied to me about?"

Garry taunted her as she threw her satchel and pink scarf on the passenger seat. "You're still a goddamned tease, Lauren Auldney, and you'll be sorry for this someday." Watching Americo drive away, Garry smirked, "So Rios is having a few problems. Interesting."

☪

The Vortex, adjusting direction and speed, had a problem keeping the landscape from dematerializing into frequency. Lauren gripped the steering wheel, looking for balance, something real to touch. Not knowing if red Earth touched the wheels of her car, she drove slowly onto the lane leading to El Rancho de las Estrellas, wanting nothing more than to disappear under the soft blanket on her bed, leaving the madness behind in another day. The car stopped, she didn't know how and Lauren could not move. "I don't know if I'm going to survive this or not. I feel like I'm disappearing again, watching everything from outside of my body. I miss him so much. Maybe if I send him a message, he'll come over." Her tears veiled the shadows of a juniper, but when her fingers touched the window, she knew he received.

Lauren clung to the rickety banister, looking at her feet, taking one step at a time towards the door. She stopped on the third step, shivering, certain somebody watched her. She looked on the porch, and nobody was there. She looked in the closet and under the bed, listened for footsteps, yet heard nothing but the silence of her own loneliness.

Ambiance, the setting was critical. Six pink taper candles, lavender incense, crystal champagne flutes, and a ready fire. Lauren heard his unmistakable footsteps, fluffed her hair, freshened her lipstick and placed the pink silk scarf on the stand. Lauren called when she heard his familiar tap on the door. "Come in, Americo, I hoped you might come over. Do you want some champagne?"

Americo didn't believe the ambiance was for him, and the gun was still on his mind. "Well, I seriously doubt the champagne is for me, but you can drop your perfect manners and listen, because I want to ask you about something before your company gets here." Sarcastically he looked at the candles, noticed the incense, and forgot the reason for his visit. "Christ, Lauren, are your panties still as hot as they always were? Is there anybody you won't bed?"

"Hell yes, they're hot," she hissed. "My panties are red-hot, red-hot, you jerk. It's been a long time for me, but I don't suppose you would understand that, since you're enga..." A silent truce prevailed, one point for him and two red ones for her. In the silence, their filaments reached towards one another. Lauren pled with him, looking down and making circles on the table with her finger. "If you're going to be rude, just leave. I can't take much more tonight, but thanks for the flowers, Darling, they're beautiful and I've still got the card."

Americo was more than a little pissed by now. "I didn't send flowers. That would hardly be appropriate since I'm engaged." Americo turned his back wondering who in the hell did send the flowers.

The air had just gone out of Lauren's balloon. "Oh." In a small voice, Lauren consoled herself. "It's good to know somebody will always love me."

"Princess, you could have had my love and everything else if you hadn't lied." Americo picked up the champagne flute wanting to crush it with his bare hands. "I still love you, but why did you have to change?"

"God, you're so sick, Americo. You're still in love with a mixed up seventeen-year old girl who hadn't had a chance to live. As long as our relationship was an extended honeymoon, you could pretend I hadn't grown up and gone through a lot of hell. I always knew it wasn't me that you loved, because the person you loved was some idealized fantasy you created for yourself. That was as unfair as what I did; don't you understand that? You made me invisible by denying my life and killing parts of me just like everybody else did."

"That's bullshit, Lauren. You lied to me every time you made love with me. But damn it, I'm so confused about how I feel, I don't know if I want to rip your clothes off and make love to you, or beat the hell out of you for all of your lies."

Lauren hissed. "Spin it, Rios. Spin it, and leave."

Americo lost it completely. "You bitch, you came home tired and worn out. You only came home to me because you thought you were losing your charms, and nobody else would want you." Americo knew he had gone too far. "I'm sorry, Baby, I didn't mean..."

Lauren narrowed her eyes and poked him in the chest. "Listen to this, Americo, I was never just an empty cauldron waiting to be filled by you." Lauren looked at herself from outside of her body. "Oh bullshit," she brought herself back to attention, "I'm not escaping anymore. If I'm angry or hurt, I'm going to show it. I'll never hide outside of my body out of fear again. This is real, and this is very personal, so get the hell back in your body, and face this man like a grownup woman."

Lauren shivered as she started towards him. "Don't you ever say you're going to beat me, Americo, I'll kill you if you lay one hand on me. Just the sounds of the words make me crazy. I don't care what you think or feel anymore, I've loved, I've lived, I'm me, and I'm free, free of you and all of the bullshit. And in case you haven't noticed, I don't dance in the dark anymore; I do everything where everybody can see me. Do you hear me? Now get the hell out of my house, you asshole."

"Hey, back off." Americo grabbed her arms, shaking her. "I said I felt like it."

Lauren laughed in his face, defying him to stay, and defying him to deny her experience.

Unexpectedly, Americo saw a formidable woman who no longer needed him. He saw a free, wild spirit, with years of experience in her eyes, experience he had not shared. He saw a woman eager and ready to face the world on her own terms, willing and able to live her life without him. With anguish and loss in his heart, he hated the woman he saw standing in her power, for denying him her neediness. And he was livid. "You're a lying little bitch, Lauren. I was going to tell you how much I still love you, but I ought to kill you for sabotaging any chance we had with your fucking crazy ways."

Screaming, Lauren twisted her body out of his grip, at the same time noticing a cool breeze blowing through the Casino. "You'd better get your hands off me, big tough Americo."

Insulted and angered by Americo's denial of her life, Lauren summoned fierce strength. She hated him, remembered all of the times she tried to tell him, wondered why he never asked, and in a very bold, but appropriate gesture, held the broom like a bat and hit him in the head. "Take that, you bully. You're always hitting somebody, aren't you?"

Americo couldn't help but smile, "Goddamn, a Witch and her broom are lethal weapons." Leaning his head on the mantle, he stopped the stars from spinning.

Lauren heard it first, but Americo felt the blast. The piercing sound of a bullet screamed through the Casino, and he fell to the floor. Lifting his head, Americo tried to see Lauren, afraid that she had shot herself. As if caught in the center of a hurricane, Lauren stood, staring at the open door, trembling in the cool breeze, hearing footsteps on the porch. Everything was in motion, spinning around her: the broom, her dolls, the champagne flute, the lace hanky, and the candles. Only Americo remained motionless on the floor. Again she heard footsteps. Running to the open door, Lauren tripped, tore her dress, skinned her knees, and gasped when she touched the dropped gun with her hand. Another shot blistered through the Casino. Lauren screamed when she felt the reverberations of the gun and remained frozen in place.

Lauren cried, and her legs shaking, she was unable to stand. She crawled to him. "Oh no, Americo's dead." Lauren whispered as she shook him. "I love you, Americo. God, who did this to him?" Tears ran down her cheeks as she kissed his forehead. "I can't remember what happened. Nothing makes sense."

She spoke calmly. "Hello, this is Lauren Auldney, and I'm calling from the guesthouse on El Rancho de las Estrellas. Americo Rios has been shot, and I think he might be dead." Her voice was flat, emotionless. "Please hurry, I don't know what to do."

Reeling from the contamination of a gun in her hand, Lauren stood over Americo. Like a cruel joke, the red handled broom stood by his body, the colorful zigzag patterns wiggling provocatively. Sticky blood ran slowly, making a forbidding red pool, staining the Navajo rug. Kneeling, she put her fingers over the wound, and felt his body quiver from her touch. Hesitantly, Lauren put her finger in the blood, tasted it, tasted life, tasted herself, and tasted him. "Americo, it's me. Talk to me. I love you. Who would want to kill you?"

Lauren rubbed her hand over his cold forehead. "This is the where we made love for the first time, Americo, please don't leave me, don't die. I'm going to try to help you, Jugador. Try to absorb the energy I'm channeling into your body." There was nothing she would not do to save this man's life. Lauren cast a circle around Americo and sprinkled him with sacred tears. She raised her left hand to the sky, connecting to the stars. Praying, she placed her right hand on his back, feeling the current of energy move through her body, into his body. With her eyes closed, she found the place in her body where she felt her love for him and connected, sending her love. When she felt the vitality rise in his back, she knew that he had received the love and responded. His lips moved, and she leaned closer. The ambulance stopped, and she heard him say, "Don't leave me, Lauren."

The police read her rights. Lauren stared blankly, not recognizing one of the officers she had known all her life. Confused, Lauren tried to see through the black tunnels surrounding her vision. She screamed as the paramedics wheeled Americo out of the room, begging them to let her ride in the ambulance. Crying, trying to move her arms, becoming frustrated by the handcuffs on her wrist, she begged the officers. "He asked me not to leave him. Please, Americo, tell them."

The last thing she heard was a weak, gravely voice. "That bitch Lauren tried to kill me. Don't let her out of your sight, or she'll runaway. She's a Witch, and you better watch everything she does, because she's crafty as hell."

☪

Dawn arrived early, overly anxious for the longest day, the shortest night, and time to play before dusk put the lid on the cookie jar. Dusk, dawn, it didn't matter, for at 5:07, tired and confused, Lauren Auldney was booked for attempted murder in the county jail. Oh, her hands had been dirty before, after all Lauren was a gardener and an artist, but when she saw the black smudges on her fingerprints, she squinted, feeling disgusted and confused. Lauren looked at her hands wondering if they were attached to her body. "Are those marks my fingerprints? They don't look like mine. You took my garnet ring," she accused the clerk.

The clerk had already heard Lauren Auldney stories from his mother and to him she was just another crazy from the New Age capital of the world. But, according to the stories, this crazy had been crazy, for a long, long time, even before there was a new age.

Lauren saw the pious look. "What did you do with my charm bracelet? I've worn that bracelet for thirty years, and it protects me."

The clerk was a punk, already having a bad hair day. "You're on your own now, lady."

Once happy free deer in a cold holding cell, feel trapped. A thin, gray blanket offers little solace to cold, bare shoulders and feeling fenced in, Lauren paced. "I didn't do it; I know I didn't. Why would he accuse me, after he asked me to stay? Americo, are you alive?"

Trapped behind fear, shock and silence, to Lauren the ugly metal bars seemed benign, penetrable and no longer formidable. Reduced to instinct, natural inclinations, and familiar patterns, Lauren started to spin. Lauren spun back in time, her future too uncertain to contemplate. Spinning further and further, she climbed the spiral to a warm, sparkling world, where the soft light shimmered, and patterns of yellow, blue, and red danced in the background, fluttering in and out of her field of vision. The spiral rotated faster, and twisting and turning, Lauren looked back on her jewel-encrusted path. Fearlessly, she climbed higher and higher, far away from the horror of her world. A constant, her lifeline and her destiny, tugged at her navel. The thread of gold contracted, pulling her to him.

The surgeons looked at each other as the lines and beeps on the monitor stopped. A young, dark-haired resident spoke to the aging head surgeon. "He's gone."

"Move over, kid, this man is going to live if it's the last thing I do. I knew his parents, and I'm not letting him go."

The gray haired surgeon worked furiously on Americo, and the monitor responded. "I don't understand this, the wound is closed, the bleeding has stopped and the bullet did very little damage. I think we better get him down for an MRI, I'm afraid there was a brain injury caused by the broom."

Soft words called to him. "Wake up, Americo, you look like Sleeping Man."

The thread of gold caught a beam of starlight and radiated. Americo breathed slowly and consistently, then summoned his strength and reached for the gold. The Vortex spun around an axis, a jeweled ladder, and beckoned him to climb. The coil twisted, turned, stretched, and almost broke. He screamed. "Stop, Lauren, the thread will break if you don't come back." She turned to him, fluttering her fingers, seductively motioning him to follow.

Secrets close many doors. Rusted locks and iron hasps resist entry, but a moment of light transforms fear into love and love into power, and with a pass of her left hand, Lauren opened the first of many doors once closed. Waiting for Americo to cross under the threshold, she took his hand and kissed his fingers. He kissed her hair, whispering, "Bruja, it's me, say something."

"I can feel you kissing me."

"I love you, Lauren, my Beloved Woman."

"We're still connected, Jugador. We were born connected, weren't we?"

"Many times, Baby. I was waiting for you when you were born carrying the wands of light in your chubby, little hands? Don't you remember handing one of the wands to me? I remember the red, knitted booties Rita put on your feet and I'll never forget how you smiled when you kicked your legs in the air. Lauren, do you remember us?"

"Help me. Maybe there are many things we've forgotten."

"Our place is on the red rocks, and we've always walked together in our paradise. Circumstances will always bring us home. I wouldn't have found my way to you if the fire at the hacienda hadn't made my father an orphan. Circumstances always return us to our soul family. Tragedies are not tragedies, Lauren, they are facilitators of destiny."

"Ghosts followed me to Earth this time, Darling. Why?"

"So you would learn the lessons you came here to learn. I think you got tired of me leaving you behind in many of our other lives." Americo laughed sorrowfully.

"Why did you leave me?"

"War, capture, death, adventure, hunting, many reasons, but I always loved you. There were happier lives, Lauren, at times we had it all."

"Do you want to go back, Americo? I can leave with you, I know how to die, I've always thought about dying."

"We have to go back; our work isn't finished. This is the next task and if we don't do it right, there will be more. We have to help each other because promises were made, and we can't afford to break anymore of them."

"I know, but we won't remember this."

"Our bodies will and when the time is right our minds will also. Princess, let's go back to Cathedral Rock and remember." The gold thread coiled tightly as together they traveled through the cosmos, laughing and smiling, the lovely Vortex pulling their filaments to her center. Americo held Lauren's hands, keeping her close to him. Clasping hands they sat on the red rock mesa where so many magical moments had been shared. Like two children telling secrets, they sat close to one another. They huddled together, feeling secure and safe, knowing everything they said was true.

"You go first this time, Americo. I wish you had gone first before."

"I know. Mistakes were made, and we can't go back. Why, Lauren? I still don't understand why."

"Because I love you, and I was afraid. I didn't want to ruin your life with my craziness, and you never asked the right question."

For twenty-five years Americo sent Lauren a ticket in November to return to his home for four days. She arrived at his door on the eve of the winter solstice, tired and limp from days of travel, looking sophisticated and beautiful in jewels, cashmere sweaters, floppy brimmed hats, sunglasses, and dark red leather boots. Falling into the arms of a desperate, lonely man, each year Lauren smiled shyly, crinkled her nose like a naughty girl and surrendered to his embrace. "Please wake me up, Jugador, I've feel like I've been in a long deep sleep without you."

They spent four days in seclusion, with Ignacio Verona as the guardian of their door. At her insistence, their time was private, a secret. During the days and nights, reconnecting the thread of gold, together they made enough magic to make it through the long months without each other. The only woman Americo allowed in his home was Lauren. A private man, protective of his space, he slept with other women where they lived or not at all.

"I still have the key you gave me when we were standing on the porch. Do you want it?"

"Keep the key, Lauren. Use it when you need me."

The moment of reunion often felt like a dream, Lauren appearing as an apparition, causing him to question her corporality. Needing assurance that the ethereal being in his arms was the women he loved, Americo held Lauren close and then carried her to a waiting bath. He undressed her slowly and then lowered her body into the lavender scented water before propping a soft pillow under her head. Surrounded by vases of sunflowers, bite-by-bite, he fed her cold shrimp, luscious, ripe, red strawberries, and sweet, gooey fudge. Bite-by-bite, she savored the delights, knowing that wherever she lived she needed sunflowers to remind her of his amber eyes. Sharing champagne from a single flute, he asked why she wouldn't allow him to provide more luxuries. "You never had to live as simply as you did."

"Yes, I did. I once made a list, and the first thing I vowed was to do it on my own."

Every year Americo lifted her wrist and looked sadly at the charms added to her bracelet by others. "The others are only decoration, Americo, the chain on my wrist is yours." He clasped the newest charm on the chain, once again making her his alone.

"I loved crawling into your bed, Americo. You held me while I looked at the small rugs, the magic carpets I gave you, hanging on the wall."

"When you weren't with me, I lost myself in the intricate designs trying to sleep without you." Their love story was written in the illuminated pages of the carpets. "We've made a lot of meaning," he paused, "in so few days over so much time."

"You always put a rug by the bed so my feet wouldn't touch the cold floor." Smiling at him with love, she reminded him of why.

"It helped having a rug under my feet that nobody jerked out from under me without notice."

Every year Lauren brought Americo a new gold concho for his belt. Every year she told him she would tell him the story, but alas the story changed, and she could no longer find the beginning or remember the end. "Each small circle tells part of the story of our lives together, and someday, if we have the chance... I loved the special red slippers you bought for me in 1979."

"You always had a list of rules for our time together, and you said the rules couldn't be changed."

"I was well known for my lists, Americo. They were the only way I kept my sanity."

"I remember your words, our time together is private, our secret. That's the only way I can be with you right now."

"I always reminded you that I didn't deserve your love and that someday you would know it. I pleaded that you not to ask for more than I could give you."

"You always insisted that I keep the blinds closed."

"Yes, inside of your mostly empty house was interior time. Time to peel back the onion and discover the deeper, hidden you, me, us."

Curled up on the cushions, Lauren always squinted and asked Americo to light the candles. "Talk to me, Americo, talk to me about your sorcery, and I'll tell you about my magic. Talk to me about ideas, not people. Tell me about your poker games and I'll tell you about my art. No please don't ask me those questions, you know I can't stay."

Like a young ballerina, she danced to his music. Each year she told him she was closer to her truth and that her truth was their truth. Yet, she did not offer hope. She always told him not to wait, that she might never find her peace. Lauren meant what she said, but she didn't say it loudly enough for him to hear.

"Do you remember watching me brush my hair fifty times, while you fluffed my pillows and warmed my side of the bed?"

"Yes, and then you would kiss me fifty times for loving you so much."

"My days with you were the happiest of my life. It was the only time I felt at home."

"I dropped my defenses when you were with me. You know I've always lived alone, and it was the only time I allowed another person to do for me. I watched in awe as you cared for my home, my meals, and my possessions. I reposed while you did for me, and I gave you full access to the spaces in my home, my heart, and my mind that I didn't permit anybody else. It was your way of making a home for me, and I knew it without question. When you left, I wondered how I ever made it through life without you."

"I forgot to spin during the time I spent with you. I forgot to spin, because I was safe from the world inside of your small, olive-green, board and batten home."

"I know. You surrendered to your love for me. You cooked our meals with the expertise of a master chef and served them on the small table in front of the fireplace, with a vase of sunflowers set on the corner."

"I told you I wanted to do everything for you."

"I remember. You trimmed my hair and shaved my face while I watched you in the mirror. You would inevitably nick my skin with the razor, lick the blood from my face, and say ahhh. Every year you sewed missing buttons on my white shirts. Some years you ironed thirteen shirts and other years only two. I never could figure out why." He laughed, adoring the magic of her complexity.

"It just depended on my mood and how I decided to make the magic."

"I always had a plan."

"I never did, I just spun whichever way the wind blew and from wherever I was standing. I guess that's why I had a hard time figuring out who I really am. I had lists, but not plans."

"I can still feel you massaging me with oils as you straddled my body, took me inside of you and rocked your body to the rhythm of the ocean within you. Ahhh, Lauren," he smiled as he pulled her closer, "you're the best. It's no wonder I love you more than anything in the world."

"The wonder is our story, Americo."

"We've chosen our battleground. You won't remember this, and neither will I, but I love you. Remember the gold thread and don't forget to check our personal telegraph."

"Will we survive the battle?"

"I don't know, but let's try, so we don't have to be apart next time. Deal?"

"Deal. If we do survive it, I'll put a candle in the window."

"Good, then you can take me back to the beginning."

The gold thread uncoiled, releasing them to destiny. The figures in the belly of Cathedral Rock turned for a moment, faced each other and smiled as they remembered part of the story.

☪

Americo struggled and tried to open his eyes when he felt soft hands stroking his damp forehead. He focused on the outline of a woman and whispered, "Baby, I'm back."

He recoiled and abruptly pushed away the hands of his fiancée. Deliberately, he lost consciousness, twenty-four hours passed, tests were taken and nobody understood why he avoided the world they perceived. He needed time to forget, time to forget what he couldn't remember.

Lauren cried as she sat in the cell alone and afraid. An open sore on her arm bled as she scratched and dug, searching for what she could not feel. "I must have drifted off to sleep," she decided as she heard the matron bringing her food. "I can't eat, just take it away. Where is Lydia? I need to get out of here. Please, will you call my father's house and ask when Lydia Fogel will be here?" she pled with the tough-looking desert woman. Lauren then saw Lydia walking towards her cell with a very grim look on her face. "I better toughen up because I think I'm in a lot of trouble."

☪

The debris filled public parking lot seemed an inappropriate setting for a Knight. His wild, galloping horse was at the airport, his lance was in his briefcase and his heart was on his sleeve. Yet, this Knight had saved this damsel's life once before and at any cost, Wyatt Kirkman would rescue her again. A tough southern man, Wyatt controlled a real estate empire with resorts in several southern states, yet wondering how Lauren would respond to seeing him after almost twenty years, at this moment his heart beat like that of an insecure schoolboy. The world of gambling is a small world, and when Wyatt heard Lauren had shot Americo Rios, he knew the woman he still loved needed him to right her circumstances.

The Lauren Wyatt remembered could not possibly face years in prison. Wyatt smiled thinking of Lauren, suntanned, standing on the beach counting the waves, wearing a pink, skimpy bikini bottom with a white, short sweater. He could still see her red, floppy-brimmed hat and remembered how she ran to meet him when he brought her favorite breakfast of cream puffs and fresh strawberries to the beach. "She taught this overly busy man how to have fun for the first time in his life." Wyatt smiled thinking of her eyes squinting over the top of her sunglasses that rested low on her nose. "Those years were the happiest of my life. Damn her sassy little fanny, she's a spoiler."

Giggling and crying, Lauren stood at the door as Wyatt rose slowly to greet her. "Wyatt, I never thought I'd see you again, much less be in jail if I did."

Holding her at arms length, Wyatt tried to hide his shock when he saw her haunted eyes.

Lauren laced her fingers through his steel gray hair and the years apart were forgotten.

Wyatt held her face in his hands. "What in hell have they done to her? Lauren needs to be wild and free, like a sunflower."

"Precious, I've missed you so much. What happened? Did he hurt you?"

"No, Americo wouldn't hurt me, I really wasn't afraid."

"Are you sure? I always thought he was overly intense."

Wyatt promised her the world that he could deliver. "If you don't want Lydia Fogel to defend you, I'll arrange for somebody else."

"Wyatt, Lydia is the only person in the world I would trust with this." Lauren cried as she held on to him for dear life. "They're going to take my passport, so even if I wanted to run away, I couldn't."

"Don't worry, Precious, if you need a passport, I'll arrange it for you. I've already thought about how to help you, and there's no damned way you're going to jail. Why did you make all of those scratches on your arms?"

"I couldn't help it, I felt numb and I'm confused. It helps me think, to focus. I don't know, Wyatt," she told him as she started to cry. "I've stopped at times, sometimes for a long time, then something comes over me and it feels so good."

"Witchy, was Americo the young man you told me about? Was he the one...?"

Lauren had long lived in the belly of the Ouroburos. "Yes, but how do you know him?"

"We met many years ago in Atlantic City at a poker tournament, but when I mentioned that I knew you, he abruptly ended the conversation. Do you have any money?" Wyatt asked protectively.

"You know me, I make a lot of money and I spend a lot of money. I have a little, but I've never been ambitious enough to earn all that I could have."

"Don't worry about a thing, Scarlet, my love, I'll fix it for you."

"Will you come to court and take me home to Grandma?"

"Of course I'll be here, Precious. Have you been happy living on your rancho again?"

"I've always wondered if I have a right to be happy, after everything that happened."

"Lauren, don't say that. What was it you always told me?"

Lauren rested her head on his chest and giggled. "Spin it."

The "click, click" of Lydia's high heels echoed ominously in the halls of the historic courthouse in Prescott, Arizona as the world of crime and punishment came to life for the day. There was a soft humming of voices, whispering about the most sensational case to be heard in some time in the peaceful northern Arizona community.

One month out of law school, Lydia Fogel came into Jake Auldney's lonely life like a fresh breeze from the low desert. They met at a dinner party, and within five minutes they were holding hands under the table. Only twelve years older than Lauren, Lydia had given a baby up for adoption and embraced Jake's children as her own. She could have been described as a too good woman, but she was not. She was strong, made a mistake and paid for it, loved a man fiercely and although she would not marry him, she committed her life to Jake. Lydia limited her practice and made the drive from Tucson to Sedona weekly, often staying a month at a time in the home of the man she loved. More than thirty years later, she was now defending the daughter of her beloved Jake, the woman she considered her daughter, the woman whose secret she had kept for twenty-five years.

Lydia walked confidently through the courthouse, looking striking in a white summer suit and heels, with her long gray and blonde streaked hair hanging to her shoulders. The public prosecutor stepped out from his office and nodded indifferently, wishing the defense attorney were a man, instead of a fifty-nine-year old woman, whose reputation for toughness and strategy preceded her.

In the stark impersonal cold conference room, Lauren paced. She paced, remembering thirty years of loving him, wanting him, being lonely without him, trying to forget him, trying to love others and trying to find her way home. She remembered their annual vacations to remote places, the days and nights at his hacienda, the letters, the desperate middle of the night phone calls, the weekly delivery of sunflowers, wanting to kill herself, wandering, never feeling at home, cutting herself with needles and tweezers, sucking the blood, trying to feel something, anything. Lauren relived keeping the secret, the drugs, the men, the women, and the pain of never feeling safe. Feeling the agony of always waiting for something that never came, her empty arms, the sound of a cry and the loss of her soul, racked her body. She stared at the coyote cloud in the sky and cried, remembering that he never asked for an apology, just her return.

Lydia sat across the conference table from Lauren, concerned by her client's ghostly pale face framed by brown hair.

Chewing her fingernails bloody, Lauren heard Lydia's voice droning in the background.

"Why, why, Lauren?" Lydia said in shock. "You've picked sores all over your arms."

Lauren spoke, her voice monotone, displaying no affect, no regret, and no embarrassment. "Just imagine how much fun I could have had if they gave me have a needle or tweezers, my preferred tools of destruction."

"Lauren, do you understand what this hearing is about? I've told you before, but I don't think you were listening."

"Oh I was listening; I was just listening with my other mind."

"The judge will read the charges and we'll answer with our plea of not guilty. He'll set a trial date and if it's not soon enough I'll protest. I may ask that the trial be moved out of this area due to all of the local gossip about you. Your entire past will be brought before the jury. The prosecutor will dig up anything that you have ever done, and I'm sure Americo will tell him anything he knows. Lauren, this is a class six felony and you could go to jail for a year. This is very serious, and I wish I could get more cooperation from you."

"Great, now everybody will get to know that I'm a thief, a liar, and a murderer. What happened to me, to us, to everything we waited so long to have? I hoped we would be married before the year ended, what a joke."

Listening to Lydia shuffle through her papers, Lauren laid her head on the scratched table. Through the shadows Lauren tried to imagine another prisoner sitting in the same room feeling the same frustration, trying to leave a mark that said that their life had also disintegrated.

Gently stroking Lauren's hair, Lydia told her to grieve for her losses and then release them.

"Believe me, I'm grieving even if I'm not crying all the time. The only thing that ever changes is the reason I need to grieve. When I'm not feeling pain or guilt, I'm numb, after all, don't I go from one crises to another, just trying to feel something?"

Lydia asked for Lauren's cooperation. "You could always use insanity as a defense," Lauren giggled. "I'm sure many people would corroborate it for you. I'll be glad to show my scars."

"Personality disorders aren't a good defense, and you aren't guilty, so drop the subject."

"Which personality disorder are you talking about, Lydia? The one where I live on the border, the one I need a mirror in front of me all of the time to know I'm alive, or the one where I take little trips and watch my life like it's a movie. Or maybe the one where I'm numb, or the one where I self-destruct all the time would be the most convincing? Why don't you just tell the bastards I've got a primitive mind, and I see the world from a different part of my brain? I've got animal instincts and I'll kill when I'm hungry or sick. Take your pick of my so called disorders, because I've got them all."

"Lauren, settle down."

"I'm fucked, Lydia, and you know it."

☾★

Having been released from the hospital that morning, Americo Rios, despite the protest of his doctors, sat in the courtroom.

Lauren stared at him defiantly, forcing him to see the freckles on her nose, contrasted against the ashen of her skin. She smiled slyly, readying for war.

"I haven't seen her so thin and wan in twenty-five years. Christ, she's picked herself bloody again."

Although his olive skin had paled, his lean body looked elegant in a white dress shirt, complete with gold cufflinks set with tiger-eye gemstones. His custom-made cowboy boots caught the eye of several envious men sitting in the gallery.

"Lauren Cubera Auldney, you have been charged with the attempted murder of Americo Saul Rios, of Sedona, Arizona. How do you plead?"

Lauren hesitated, took a deep breath, squared her shoulders and slowly removed her glasses. Surprising Lydia, Lauren turned from the judge to face Americo.

"I don't remember shooting him, but I do remember trying to kill him for years."

☪

Determinedly, with tears running down her face, Lauren carried the most precious of her belongings to her Grandmother's home. Stopping to stare at the dark, sticky stain on the Navajo rug, she bent to touch it with her finger and still damp, she laid her cheek on Americo's blood, feeling his hatred pulsate into her body. Shaking violently, with bloodstains on her cheek, Lauren stood in front of her workbench, trying to decide which tool to use. She held the sharp engraver, focused her eyes and slowly, as the ecstasy filled her body, cut a wound in her own hand. Holding her hand over the bloodstain, she felt relief as she watched her own blood fall, blending into his, becoming one. Over and over again, she heard his haunting voice echoing throughout the small building, "Don't leave me, Lauren."

When Lauren entered the living room, Rita stood and offered her a glass of sherry.

"My life is over, Grandma. How can you prove something that seems like a dream?" Lauren sat on the floor, brushing Rita's black and white masked cat, rolling the hair up in a small ball.

"Lauren, we've been given a gift. You will be under my roof for the rest of my life, and I told you earlier that I have a task for you. You may find it difficult on many levels, but it's something I've saved for you. Now, move over by my feet and listen carefully."

☪

The task was genius, brilliant, and contained a practical facet. Being a little older, now that she was a little younger, Rita needed some help around the house. Feeling childlike and adored by her Grandmother, Lauren scurried like a child to the scarred and chipped claw foot tub, eager to talk to her dolls. *"I don't think you've heard all of this story, so listen very, very carefully, because I need for you to help me understand."*

Annie, a child size rag doll listened attentively. *"Annie, you were my first doll, so do you remember when Grandma gave me the pink silk slip that I wore under my baby dress?"*

Annie remembered, because until that day, she held the dress in her hand.

*"Grandma instructed me to think of the things in my life that had caused me the most pain and make a tear in the silk as a sign of each one. Then she gave me a spool of fine thread the color of gold and a little gold needle to sew with. I didn't understand what she meant until a night when I was sitting under the Andean skies, looking for my special star."*

Massaging her body with a loofah, Lauren blew on a cluster of bubbles, sending them scattering into the air. Annie caught three. *"One by one, I recalled the moments when I closed the doors and left myself behind. I cut the holes with my Swiss army knife and some of them were jagged, one looked like a triangle, others looked like strike lightening. Some were large, and one was very small. Each one had it's own identity and as the pain came back to me, I started to sew the tears in the silk with the gold thread."*

Lauren dunked her head to rinse the shampoo from her hair, blowing bubbles with her lips, feeling young and refreshed. *"I sewed all night long by the light of a candle, crying and laughing all by myself in a small adobe hut. The thread made beautiful scars on the cloth, leaving it stronger than it had ever been before. On some of the scars, I put little patches that looked like doors, leaving them open to let in the light. The gold lines were different sizes and shapes, and don't you think the designs I embroidered on the patches are exquisite? When I finished closing the wounds, I felt whole again."* Wrapping herself in a fluffy, pink towel, Lauren looked in the mirror. The face looking back at her looked older, wiser, and wild, and Lauren continued to address the ladies-in-waiting listening rapturously to her tale. *"Do you remember the first night I told you about him? It seems the story has a very sad ending and I think I better go find my gold needle and thread, because this wound is going to need many stitches."*

☪

Rita sat on her porch impatiently tapping her bare foot on the deck. Checking her gold watch, she smiled when she saw

Americo's black Land Rover speeding towards her house. He
walked sheepishly through the gate, and Rita saw him flinch as he
sat on the steps in front of her rocker. Rita put her hand gently on
his shoulder, knowing that his pain was not merely physical.
"Americo, Lauren's sleeping in my home and this is where she will
be living until her future is decided, and perhaps she'll be here the
rest of her life. You know better than anybody else that my granddaughter has been building paths to nowhere in my garden and in
her life for many years. It is now time for her to finish them and
find her way home. That will be part of her task and who knows
where the paths will lead once they join."

Americo lit a cigarette and took a gulp of his coffee.

"I know you don't want to see her, so I'll speak very quietly.
You need to go away for a time, for you and for Lauren. I've given
Lauren a task and I'm doing the same for you. You must trust me,
Americo, at this time in my life I see the path of destiny clearly
and you must do as I bid."

Americo nodded his head in agreement to her mandate
"Grandma Rita, as always I'll do whatever you tell me, but I'm
still stunned that Lauren tried to kill me. We've both been hurt,
but the worst part is that the hurt kept happening again and
again."

"Parting can be sweet," Rita consoled him, "if it's occasional
and it can be painful if it's forever, but when it keeps happening
again and again, it can be devastating." Rita asked him to pour
half-cup of coffee, with one dollop of honey.

"When I dropped her off at the airport a year and a half ago,
she must have had the gun she stole from my car. When I discovered it was missing, I was afraid she was going to use it to kill herself and it made me sick thinking she would do it with my gun."
Americo recalled the numerous phone calls he made to Lauren,
always getting the same answer. Adamantly, Lauren denied knowing anything about the missing gun.

"I don't think she stole the gun, but time will reveal everything. Tell me how you're feeling, and I don't mean your gunshot
wound. Paint pictures with your words, Americo, so I can see for
myself what stirs within you."

Americo closed his eyes as pictures of his internal struggle
appeared to him. He cleared his throat and shifted his position on
the steps so he could look at Rita as he spoke. "My body feels like
the Vortex is coiled in my gut like a well-organized tornado. My
mood is like the sun, when it sends flares to the universe. I feel
like my state of mind is coming from a black hole that could turn

back on itself at any moment. There's an empty space to the left of me that could only be filled by Lauren. I don't remember when it started, but for years, I've had a pervasive pain in the left side of my gut. It's a pain combined with anticipation and fear of loss at the same time. It's related to Lauren, and you know why."

"I do know why," Rita said quietly. "It was destiny. First love, last love, or great love, all have a shadow side if something is hidden."

Americo rested his arms on his legs and as he described his feelings, he became aware of how long and deeply he had been tormented by worry about Lauren. "Destiny or not, even before it was identified, the feeling that lurked due to the loss of Lauren's loyalty had a very dark shadow. It's a dark shadow that hides behind my every thought and feeling, and it waits to jump out and say, fooled you, you dumb bastard; you should have recognized me a long time ago."

"I understand, my beloved grandson."

"What do you want me to do?"

"I want you to go to your orchard and pray. As you look at your trees, I want you to take inventory of your life. Then I want you to go to your hacienda and spend time with don Estaban, your Nagual. I want you to tell him to take you back to the beginning."

"Believe me, I remember the beginning."

"No, you don't, but don Estaban will know what I mean. Say those words to him and tell him I sent the message."

Americo nodded and scowled, knowing don Estaban had warned him that he would fail Lauren. Closing his eyes, he also heard Rita's words, asking him to be kind. The gift he had been given had been rejected and more than anything Americo Rios detested failing. The bullet wound in his back reminded him that he had broken a vow and in a moment of indulgence, had lost it all.

Rita could see the hurt in his eyes, the hurt of perceived rejection. "I can help Lauren because she's a woman, and I understand what she needs. Americo, you need the help of a man and I know how deeply you love and trust him. Be honest with yourself and him and be very cautious of the messengers who come to you. Listen very carefully to everything and know that words have but one true meaning, but others may say one thing while meaning another. Listen with your heart. I love you, Americo, so please trust me. This tragedy is a gift, and we must follow the markers on the path to the end. Trust the Vortex and I'll call you home again when the time is right."

Americo stood, knowing he had been dismissed. "I love you, Rita. Take good care of Lauren. You know I would do anything to go back thirty years and start over. I wanted to go after her when she left me, but she put up a shield and I was always afraid if I tried to penetrate it, she would never come back." Americo walked away quickly without looking back, knowing if he did, he would walk through Rita's front door directly to Lauren's small room.

Lauren stood at the window of her bedroom. She felt his turmoil and indecision, and cried as she touched the pane of glass with her finger. "Keep walking, Americo. I remember standing here when you walked away twenty-five years ago, when I had to go home to my husband. We both cried, you kept turning around to look at me and finally I pulled the drape closed because I couldn't stand it anymore. It isn't time, we have a battle to fight and whether you know it or not, it's our only hope. We each have to learn to forgive, not just forget. Convince yourself you hate me, see me as your enemy and then maybe one day..."

"You're right, Lauren," Americo answered her with his thoughts. "I'm in a very dark, ugly mood. My mood is darker than the raven's feathers I love and darker than the darkest forest you have ever wandered in. You don't know this side of me, but I'm afraid you will when we face each other in the courtroom. I'm afraid of what might happen, but I love you." He looked over his shoulder in time to see her blow out the candle in the window and turn away.

☪

Does evil lurk among us, ever pushing us closer to a ledge that has always compelled us? Who would do this to Lauren? Why would they want to further hurt her? Saturated by the putrid odor of burning hair, the corner of a hand-painted, pink silk scarf succumbed forlornly to the spell. A hand reached out and lit the last of many candles in the small room. A lock of Lauren's hair, placed on a shimmering seashell, covered a bullet hole in the scarf.

Like untamed electricity, energy sparkled around the room as a figure moved about, making precise hand gestures and articulating words, understandable only to the speaker. Pinned to the mantle was a photograph of Lauren working in her Grandmother's spiral garden. As the energy danced around the room, a small piece of the photograph was torn from the corner and held over a candle, quickly disappearing.

"This is the end for you," the person in the room thought as the candles flickered. "I've waited many years to destroy you, after everything you've done to me. I just didn't know how easy it would be. I never knew you would make such a fatal mistake. Ah ha, I always wondered if you would crack wide open one day." A ball of energy moved quickly in a spiral, resting on the altar. "You're a natural; your skills came so easily to you. Many of us have to spend years learning what you were born knowing, yet you've used everybody around you and played your little game." A strong wind, carrying gray shadows moved through the window. "Oh, lovely Lauren, you're a liar and a killer. My magic is stronger than yours because I had to learn it the hard way. I know where your energy leaks, and you think it's where you carry your power."

Stopping to scoop some ashes from a small fire, the figure sprinkled them on the pink scarf. "You always thought somebody would come to your rescue, but not this time, Princess. Enjoy your last game, because it could be over anytime. I can turn the gift you have inside out, and I can make it your worst enemy. You have a double edge. I can see it. You carry the power of two, but I have you trapped, and you have nowhere to hide. These gifts can be used against you. You can't fool me; I see more than you think I do. You came to take something that belongs to me and I'll stop you. You thought you came back to Sedona full of power, but do you feel yourself disappearing? Do you feel yourself disintegrating? Do you smell your hair burning? If you're the Witch you think you are, you should."

☪

Clouds were rolling softly across the sky covering the millions of stars vibrating in the sky above Sedona. The coyotes were content having already captured their prey. The owls were silent, watching. The breeze had ceased, and the branches on the trees were barely quivering. Not even the faint hum of a distant car interrupted the silence of the night. Using cat like vision, the figure hurried across the red rock landscape, moving with sure steps, shielded by an energy screen, hoping to remain unseen.

"It's me," the voice said breaking the silence.

"I know. I've been waiting."

"It's happening," she whispered as he pulled her mouth to his lips.

"I know, I've been watching."

"It's imperative that we keep the energy flowing."

"You're good," he said as he greedily pulled her body under his.

"I'm the best," she answered as she wrapped her legs around his waist.

"It's been a long strange trip, hasn't it?"

"It isn't over."

☪

When you live on a spinning orb, you can walk in circles and always end up back where you started. However, if you follow a series of dots called a line towards the stars, you will end up in a negatively curved land that looks like a two-sided saddle. Following the straight line, you will never end up back where you started, but in the land of negatively curved, you simply will never return. It is from the land of the two-sided saddle that the Great Spinner and Great Weaver perform their magic, and since it's a two-sided saddle, they each have a good seat, with a great view. They can see everything, but you cannot see them, even on a clear day in Sedona.

The old girls, affectionately known to each other as Spinny and Weavy, have been dropping spindles and looming on looms, creating all of creation together since a time before time. Like good friends often do, they help each other when a project is particularly difficult. They had a problem, and the problem was Lauren and Americo.

A weaver can't start the weaving until enough strands are dyed and spun into threads. Over the years, the Great Weaver wove the warp, but until recently she had to wait for more yarn to begin the weft.

Not long ago the Great Spinner stopped spinning, sighed, handed two baskets of spun yarn to the Great Weaver and said, "Go for it, girlfriend, I've finished my part for now and it's time for you to weave their story into the red rock landscape."

At first glance, the yarn looked perfect. The red, pink, and green yarn in the girl basket was mysteriously female. The amber, blue, and black yarn in the boy basket was rich with intense, raw energy. The Great Weaver had already experienced a few problems, but nothing compared to what happened yesterday.

Yesterday, The Great Weaver called the Great Spinner on the magic carpet of her side of the saddle. Tipping the saddle upside down, the Great Spinner looked at the weaving of Lauren and Americo. The Great Weaver was totally wefted and quickly becoming warped. "Spinny, why did you put all of the knots in the yarn? Don't you realize that now I can never make a perfect weaving?"

The Great Spinner answered like a spinner. "Weavy, it's rather difficult to spin when the directions keep changing. I kept losing my concentration and the threads kept breaking, so I stopped from time to time and tied little knots. But now I see what you mean, the threads do seem to be unraveling a bit, so maybe this weaving won't hold together."

To be a good weaver you have to be a good listener and as she picked through the threads of many colors, The Great Weaver had an idea. Hopefully adding a few translucent threads of light to the already damaged weaving, Weavy decided she was ready to hear the story. "Spinny, sit down on my side of the saddle for a while, my friend, and tell me how you spun the yarn. Maybe if I hear the story of how the yarn was spun, it will help me weave the weaving."

Eager for more texture and added interest, the landscape of red sandstone called Sedona listened with rapture. The already erotic landscape's heart beat faster, her mind twirled, and the red became redder as the two friends recapitulated the current life in the long story of Lauren and Americo that began before there was a time or story.

# IN THE BEGINNING OF THE SPINNING

*"Home is where we start from..."*
*T.S. Eliot*

## The Spinning Game

Adventures are born on lazy, cool Saturday afternoons, especially when the adventure walks hand in hand with a secret. Children know this, and young Lauren caught the wave of magic better than most. Yesterday, Lauren Auldney had an idea; she was full of them. Her head was always spinning with new ideas and at that time she made everybody listen to them, especially her older buddy, Americo Rios. He was kind, patient, easily amused, and thought she was very cute for a little kid. She had freckles on her nose and one dark dot above her upper lip that danced up and down when she smiled. Always a bit bossy, Lauren intruded into his room with pigtails in her hair and roses on her cheeks. "Hey, Americo, put down your cards and turn off your music for a while. Follow me to Cathedral Rock because I've discovered something and I've just got to show it to you." Lauren pleaded to Americo, wringing her hands together like a little old lady. "But you can't tell anybody else. Promise me, promise."

Americo grinned indulgently. "I don't have a lot to do today except hang out with my cat and fool around with the cards."

As if her hands were wet, Lauren shook her fingers, waving her hands with excitement as she stood in front of him almost jumping up and down.

"What kind of brew has the little Witch mixed up today? You're a real pain some times, Lauren, but you know I can never say no to anything you ask." Long ago, Americo discovered the intrigue of Lauren as she changed expertly and swiftly between her many personalities. That was why he tolerated and enjoyed this magical child, although he was a teenager, loaded with cool and on the edge of manhood. So in contrast with his own intense, deliberate personality, he loved the thrill of her extremes.

Americo took her hand having noticed her wet lashes. "Princess, why the tears?" Gently brushing a tear from her lashes, he said quietly, "Lauren, tell me what's wrong."

Lauren stammered, blushing with embarrassment. "Oh, it's nothing Americo, it's just Mmmama and Dddaddy. It's no bbbig deal." Instantly Lauren changed moods and patronizingly tilting her head, she sighed impatiently, "Jugador, I wouldn't bet the ranch on any of those hands."

Lauren scampered up the hillside like a little goat; her long coltish legs made strong and limber by years of ballet training. Reaching from one toehold to another, scratching her legs and arms on the shrubbery, she showed Americo the fastest path to the mesa. Stopping for a sip of water, she laughed because he had worn his cowboy boots that were slippery on the bottoms. Pointing out the exact, precise place they had to stand, she explained the rules to him as if reading from a list. Gesturing, with her hands fluttering like butterfly wings, Lauren told him how they were going to play the game, wiggling her fingers in the air trying to catch the words that flew out of her mind. Her mind spun so fast if she didn't catch them with her fingers, the breeze would carry her bossy, sassy words away. Lauren now had a captive audience and spoke to him like a master to a child. "You stand on the point and turn from where you're standing. When you're ready, you hold my hands really tight and spin me around. The idea is for both of us to get really, really dizzy."

Blushing when he ruffled her hair like a puppy, Lauren looked in his eyes and saw the gentle understanding he always shared. "It's sort of like when you ski, or ride a horse, or spin yarn, or dig in the garden under the hot sun, or climb trees, or run really fast. You just forget who you are." Stomping her foot, thinking he wasn't listening she pressed him for an answer. "Do you know what I mean?" Whispering and pretending somebody could hear, she told him a secret. "It's almost like dying, because you forget who you are." With the sincerity of an open child, she confided with a quaking voice. "I know how it feels to die because I die in my sleep all of the time, at least once a week." His eyes narrowed with concern for her. "So I really know what it feels like, and I like the way I feel when it happens."

Becoming a little nervous about how out of control she seemed, Americo wondered how terrible things really were for her at home.

In the next second she seemed like a typical little brat sister trying to get her way. "Anyway," she spoke loudly making sure he was listening carefully, "once we get really dizzy, let's stand back to back like the people in the center of the formation." Pressing her shoulder against his arm, Lauren looked up at Americo. "But let's touch, OK? Then, let's turn around really fast and face each other and see what we see then. You have to squint your eyes a little to shade some of the light." By dropping her eyelids, Lauren showed him her best example, thinking she looked pretty cute. Hoping he appreciated her smart and inventive ways, Lauren bragged, "I figured out yesterday if you let too much light in at the wrong time, you see things too clearly. If you don't do it right everything looks just like it looked before. You have to close your eyes just enough to change the way you see things, got it?"

Americo laughed as Lauren stuck her tongue out at him. "Let me see you open them just enough." Checking his eyes by waving her hands in front of them, Lauren was satisfied that her pupil had caught on to her game. Holding onto his hand really tight Lauren gave the final instructions. "I get dizzy really fast, so you squeeze my hand when you feel yourself losing control. Don't forget, back to back first." Cupping her chin with her hands she made a promise. "We can't forget the rules, Americo, because that's the way we'll always play the game, forever and ever."

On the warm red rocks, under the blue Sedona sky, they spun, they saw, and they were in awe. Americo didn't mind one bit spinning in place as Lauren twirled and spun around him. Lauren just loved spinning and stayed as dizzy as she could, for as long as she could. Together, Lauren and Americo discovered that the world moves, nothing is really as it seems to be, and what you see depends on which direction you look. They knew nobody would ever believe them so it became their secret game. When they opened their eyes, they realized that once you surrender, everything changes, and stuff really, really moves, if you're really, really dizzy.

☪

In the harsh, forbidding, desert landscape of Sonora, Mexico, an alliance born between an outlaw on the run and a fearless bandito was the beginning of the family weaving. The decades long bond between the two clans continued as Jake and Tomas Rios raised their families together on El Rancho de las Estrellas. Jake and Tomas were closer than brothers, for they were also best friends. Jake was flamboyant, worldly, and magnetic. In contrast, Tomas was sensitive, reserved, and radiated love and protection to his students and family. Their respect and affection for each other was fierce, each one ready to protect the other at all cost.

Together as boys, Trey and Americo became best friends as they crawled on Rita's floor, listening to Zack tell stories of the old west and the life of a gambler. Rita tossed balls of colored yarn and laughed with delight when they scurried across the tile floor, retrieving them like puppies. Americo's hair was black as the night, foretelling the depth of his soul and the darkness of his moods. Trey's copper colored hair glistened like electric sparks in the sunlight and like his smile, brought joy to each member of the family.

Clutching bright multicolored, shimmering lights in her hands, Lauren waited in the womb an extra nineteen days, letting the vortex in her body entrain with the Vortex of the land. Greeting Lauren, as Lauren greeted the world, was the figure of a tall black haired man with a feather in his hair standing to the side of delivery table. Because Lauren wasn't entirely certain she wanted to come to Earth, she felt relief following her long reluctant birth knowing he was there to guard her.

Two enchanted four-year olds, Trey and Americo, stood by her crib. They watched with awe as Lauren reached with her chubby arms for the star she had so recently departed. They knew she was special, because when they looked into her swirling eyes, they knew that she could see. Rita also whispered in their ears how lucky they were that their princess had found her way back to the red Earth after being away for so very long.

The two boys eagerly included young Lauren in their escapades, fascinated that she was born knowing how to capture the magic. They knew magic existed, but they didn't know where it came from. Lauren was born hypersensitive, precious, and precocious, and soon became their teacher and guide. Side-by-side, Trey and Americo fiercely guarded her from the lingering ghosts that followed her to Earth.

The children grew up sharing the horses, the pool, the Casino, and their grandparents. Basking in the shelter of Cathedral Rock, they shared their experiences, their secrets, their hopes, and dreams. The connection between them was profound, spanning time and space, and offered solace when the red dust blew in their faces and the baking sun scorched their backs.

The Vortex blessed them, claimed them as her own, and marked their destiny as they emerged from their mother's bodies. The landscape was imprinted on the children's bodies, souls, and minds as they explored the Sedona Valley on foot, bicycles, and horseback. The pattern that informed the land was imprinted on their souls. Two of them stayed home, living their lives in an axis straight line. It was destined. However, one of them had to spin to keep the Vortex alive.

They laughed when Zack called them his red rock babies, but they never disagreed. They knew deep down, if they could have looked inside of themselves, they would have seen the same landscape that they viewed with their eyes every day.

In a family related by clan or blood, there are moments that are forever captured in the memories of those who stand as witness. At such moments threads of connection coil, bringing people closer together as the sun shines softly, the breezes flow freely, and a moment of silence falls, opening a window into the future.

Tomas Rios stood on the porch holding his camera. As the official photographer for the family he made scrapbooks and movies, documenting the passing of time as the children grew up on the rancho. Jake put his arm over Tomas' shoulder, pointing to the three children in the yard. "You'll want this picture for your wall." Ignoring Sybille, who wanted to leave the family gathering early, Jake laughed watching Americo lift Lauren onto her pony. "Tomas, what do you think the future holds for our children, the grandson of a bandito and the granddaughter of an outlaw?" Tomas smiled wryly, wondering if Jake recognized the same look in Lauren's eyes that he did. As Americo checked the stirrups and bridle on Lauren's pony, Jake turned to Tomas, "Your son is quite the little man. I think he wants a sister the way he hovers over Lauren." Tomas picked up his Minolta camera and through the lens of the future, told Jake that Americo already had his soul sister and that she trusted him completely.

Filaments of light danced as seven-year old Americo led three-year old Lauren around the yard on her pony. They looked at each other and laughed with joy as a delicate gold thread connected their souls. As the family watched, the shimmering, twisting thread spiraled to the highest ring of the Vortex, stretching but never breaking.

Lauren was born curious; everything she saw, heard, and touched held endless fascination for her. She learned to listen. She listened quietly, enthusiastically, seeing pictures of the stories on a little movie reel in front of her eyes. She asked many questions and took time to listen to the answers. She felt what the others felt, and sometimes it scared her. "When I listen," she soon figured out, "I learn more than when I'm talking."

Proud of his daughter, Jake told his friends that Lauren was his silent wonder. "Still water runs deep," he told them.

Lauren absorbed the stories and the feelings of everybody in her life. It wasn't very long before Lauren couldn't talk. She couldn't even scream. Soon, the people around her didn't notice, for they enjoyed having a captive audience. One day, while counting the ants in a pile under the sycamore tree, a question came to Lauren. "I wonder if I look like a big ear? Everybody wants to talk to me, but nobody wants to listen to me, and sometimes I feel invisible."

☪

Rita and Zack's covered front porch was the gathering place for everybody on the rancho. The day began with coffee on the porch where the family counted the blessings Rita called in from the Vortex. Dinners at Rita's were mandatory, and she often summoned the family to her gracious table. Following cocktails on the porch, Rita called them to the table with a sterling silver bell. An artist lover in Spain presented her with the exquisite handcrafted bell when she posed nude as a model for his painting. The extraordinary painting that once hung in a Paris gallery, now hung above the bed she shared with her husband.

Serving sumptuous meals from elegant dishes, she showered those in her family with her love. Rita loved daisies and sunflowers and passed the affection for the happy faced flowers onto her granddaughter. Flowers were everywhere. Rita believed that flowers were gifts from the fairies, and the fairies bestowed their graces generously in Rita's yard and home. Many people in Sedona said that Rita sprung from the ground like an exotic plant transported from distant shores they had only heard about in stories. Zack said she looked like the luscious, sensuous purple iris that dot the red rock valley in early spring.

On the blistering hot summer day of July 4, during the family barbeque, young Lauren sat transfixed. Her twirling green eyes were busily searching through her grandfather's Spanish dictionary as her fingers turned the pages as fast as they could. Sitting pigeon toed on a step, pointing to a word on one of the worn pages, Lauren bestowed names on herself and Americo. "See here, a gambler. In Spanish you say it jugador, like who's there. Americo, you know how an owl sounds, whooo, whooo. Look, a Witch. Let's see, you say it 'bruja,' like 'ha, ha.' OK, from now on, forever, you are Jugador and I am Bruja. Is it a pact? Now say it for me so I know you've got it."

☪★

The skies are blue, and the sun shines in the small town of the red rocks three hundred and three days a year. It was an exquisite day, the sky was brilliant Sedona blue and wispy, feathered clouds winged across the horizon. Sparkling in the clear air, little filaments of light twisted and turned before landing on the red Earth. The red sandstone formations twinkled brightly when the light kissed the embedded crystal flakes good morning. The crisp, cool morning vibrated with anticipation children feel setting out for an adventure. It was another beautiful day in paradise, and that was the day Lauren, age eight, cracked.

Twelve-year old Americo ate his syrupy waffle and fried egg breakfast with gusto, then being tall for his age, he bent and kissed his short for her age, adoring mother goodbye. The morning sun lit his path as Americo rode his Appaloosa horse down the winding, willow tree lined lane towards the Auldney home. Eager and ready to spend a day exploring the red rock countryside, he stopped in front of the house waiting for his little buddy Lauren to go riding. Suddenly, he heard the screaming. While waiting for his friend, Americo tied Gambler to a twisted trunk of an old Manzanita tree and sat nervously tapping the toe of his cowboy boot on the pool deck. About to leave, Americo stood from the redwood chair and saw Lauren running down the steps, with her messy long braids flopping on her shoulders, to the sounds of her mother yelling at her in the background.

Sybille Ginot screamed at her skinny-legged daughter running away from her. "You little brat, you better get the hell back in here or I'll really give you something to cry about."

Lauren ran from her mother, skipping two steps at a time towards the deck, with her nose running, tears falling down her cheeks, and a look of horror in her eyes.

Standing at the doorway Jake shouted at his wife, "You no good tramp. You whoring Ginot bitch." Jake Auldney, tyrannical, tired, and suffering a hangover, caught sight of Americo on the deck. Embarrassed he slammed the door, thinking, "Goddamn, shit." Jake knew Americo would tell his parents about the problems in the Auldney home.

Startled, Lauren jumped at the sound of the slamming door, knowing she was now at the mercy of her mother.

A platinum blonde former movie actress, Sybille Ginot ran after Lauren, wrapping her powder blue silk robe tighter around her legendary body. Jerking her daughter's arm viciously, Sybille pulled Lauren close so she could look into Lauren's tearful green eyes. But, not close enough that Americo didn't hear the threats. Sybille tightened her lips, glaring at Lauren. "If you ever say one word to anybody about what you saw, Lauren Auldney, I'll leave you here to take care of your father. I'll take your brother with me and leave this red rock hell hole forever." Sybille rolled her big brown eyes as if the thought of the town of Sedona made her sick. "You think you're a princess, because you're the precious little daughter of the important cowboy, Jake Auldney. What's so wonderful, about being the princess of a small town in Arizona, a town full of red necks, cowboys, and hicks?"

Lauren cowered, thinking her mother would slap her face.

Sybille ranted, "Lauren, tuck in your shirt. I can see your panties, and you don't look like a little lady. Do I have to do everything for you?"

Lauren stood defiantly as Sybille hissed sounding like an evil witch. "Listen to this, Lauren. Just in case you decide to open your big mouth, and tell anybody what you saw yesterday, I'm going to tell everybody that you're a liar. Then nobody will believe a word that comes out of your mouth, not now, not ever. I'll tell them how you make up wild stories just to cause trouble for me because you're a daddy's girl, and you think your brother is my favorite."

All color drained from Lauren's face as her mind started to spin and spin.

Leaving Lauren frozen in place squinting at the sun that seemed too bright, Sybille stomped up three steps from the pool deck. Stopping, she felt Americo's stunned gaze. Turning with a vengeance, Sybille stormed down the steps and looking him in the eye, shook her finger in his face. "Don't you stare at me, Americo Rios, you have no business eavesdropping on my conversation with Lauren." Sybille challenged him. "I'm sure you've heard plenty of yelling in your home too, so drop the shocked look on your face and take Lauren for a horseback ride. I want her out of my sight for a while."

Furious that Americo didn't respond, Sybille attacked him again. "I've got some unfinished business with her father, and it's none of Lauren's business. I don't want the little sneak listening to matters that don't involve her. If she'd mind her own business, she wouldn't see things she shouldn't." Sybille threatened Americo, who was dumbfounded, having never heard such language in his parent's home. "Keep your mouth shut, Americo, or I'll cause some problems for you, too."

As if walking in her sleep, Lauren held her arms close to her side, carefully placing one foot in front of the other. Wiping her tears with the sleeve of her purple sweatshirt, she sat on the edge of a chaise staring into space. She didn't see her furry, brown dog offering consolation, the water ripples on the pool, a murder of ravens circling overhead, or the roadrunner scurrying across the lawn. Lauren did see the flashing dance of light and shadow, but that was all she saw as the bright Sedona sun illuminated her pasty, white face.

Feeling big brotherly concern, Americo self-consciously put his arm over her shoulder.

The little girl's knees shook violently, her feet bounced on the flagstone deck, and her teeth chattered so loudly Americo worried they might break. Becoming frightened, he saw her lips were as white as chalk against the light olive of her skin. Americo tried to console Lauren and not knowing what to say, he enticed her with their horseback ride. "Hey, Lauren, don't let your mom get to you. They say things sometimes they don't really mean. Come on,

Princess, I'll help you brush your horse and get her bridled up, then we'll go for a long ride together, OK?"

Americo's eyebrows turned into caterpillars, his mouth looked like a cavern, his amber eyes looked like gold pinwheels and when Lauren tried to speak, words couldn't find the path from the abyss of her mind. When Lauren stammered, the small, dark freckle above her lip danced to the cadence. "Aaaaaammmmerico, I ddddon't think I can move. I'm so ccccccold and my head feels so heavy I ccccan hardly hold it up straight." Her lightly freckled face wore no expression as she tried to speak. "My mmmother always says things like tttthhhat to me." Cold sweat poured from Lauren's face and neck.

The day Lauren was born, four-year-old Americo assumed the role of her guardian. He stood, holding her clammy hand and offered her his Levi jacket. "Lauren, let me put my jacket over your shoulders, then you'll feel better." Wishing somebody would help him, Americo asked hopefully, "Where's Trey, did he hear the fight?" Americo waited for an answer that never came. Lauren's appearance changed, her once green eyes became staring ice blue, making him wonder if she were blind.

Not recognizing Americo, Lauren wondered the name of the nice boy with gentle amber eyes. Americo stood helplessly watching as warmth flooded Lauren's body. Shaking ferociously, she held her head, willing the ache to leave. Trying not to faint, Lauren saw the world spin uncontrollably.

Believing himself a cowboy rescuing a damsel in distress, awkwardly Americo tried to lift Lauren into his arms.

With a vacant look in her eyes, Lauren asked Americo to help her to her Grandmother's house. Her legs wouldn't move, her mind wouldn't still and as she pleaded for his help, suddenly Lauren started to cry. "It feels like the time Trey jjjjjjerked a rug out from under me when I wasn't looking, and I'm afraid I'll fall if I try to walk. I want the black bbbbblobs of shadows dancing around in front of my eyes to go away. I fffeel lllike I'm cccaught in a wwwwhirlwind or somethhhing."

Without warning Lauren giggled wildly. "What are you doing, Americo? Did I pass out again? Sometimes I even try to make myself pass out, it feels like you're dying if you do it right. The other day I was lying under the big willow tree after Daddy and Mom had a big fight, and you'll never believe it, but when I came back it was almost dark." Lauren spoke to him in a little voice. "I have an awful headache. Will you come with me over to Grandma's so she can give me an aspirin? Maybe she'll have some cookies for us, then we can go for our ride."

Later in the afternoon, Americo stood in his mother's kitchen with his elbows on the counter, twisting the heel of his boot on the floor. He wondered, remembering Sybille's threat, if he should tell his mother about Lauren.

Safe in her Grandmother's home, Lauren huddled up in her bed and trying desperately not to worry, she pulled the pink, quilted comforter over her head and pretended to be asleep.

Squinting at the sliver of light under the covers, Lauren tried to stop the black shadows that spun in front of her eyes. Placing her hand over her mouth as if to stifle a word, she made a silent promise to anybody else listening to never again cause trouble. Still shivering, Lauren hugged herself. Donning her fate like a cloak of doom, she wondered why her mother had kissed a man who wasn't her daddy, or Santa Claus. As Lauren dreamed, she shot out of her body into space, dying, feeling free as she looked back at her body, saying goodbye.

Listening to the radio in his room, Americo stared at the cracked plaster ceiling, wondering why his mother hovered over him by offering him second portions of dessert. Haunted by the vision of a little ragamuffin looking at him with big eyes that didn't recognize him, Americo changed the radio station and made a promise to his tabby cat that he would guard Lauren forever.

☾★

The dream came fast and left fast. Crying in her sleep, Rita woke Zack and as he held her she told him the dream. "It was a cloudy day, Zack, and I saw Lauren outside in the yard, standing quietly, looking at the old Sycamore tree. I know something terrible happened to her today because I saw a mirror in front of her that was fractured into a thousand shards. Her eyes were opaque, and when she walked away from me I knew she didn't recognize me."

Zack held Rita, listening to her weeping softly as he offered solace and protection. "Now, now, Darlin', we'll take care of her. Wasn't Americo a good little man today?"

☾★

The oatmeal, garnished with a dollop of raspberry jam, fresh yogurt, and three almonds, remained uneaten. Hypnotically stirring with the special silver teaspoon her Grandmother handed her, Lauren looked helplessly at Rita, unable to swallow.

Jake called his mother's house ordering Lauren home. Accompanied by Rita, Lauren stood in the foyer staring at the suitcases stacked in the entry. As she stared, the suitcases seemed to float on the heavily waxed saltillo tile, reminding Lauren of still pond water crawling with brown and gold slimy algae.

Composed and costumed in a champagne gold traveling suit, holding a mink stole over her arm, Sybille glared accusingly at Lauren and Rita. Hung over and disheveled, with a hoarse voice and blood shot eyes, Jake stormed out of his study and informed them that he and Sybille were divorcing. "Lauren, your mother is returning to France. You and your brother will be staying in Sedona with me."

Afraid of stammering if she spoke, Lauren remained silent with a world of black shadows spinning crazily in front of her eyes. Quietly Lauren climbed the staircase to her brother's room, determined not to make a sound and never to cause problems again.

☪

At the poker table in the Casino, Zack looked at the serious amber-eyed boy sitting opposite him, and challenged Americo to make a decision on the cards he held close to his chest. Americo took his time and waited while making a plan. Zack smiled a slow easy smile, a smile as slow and charming as an Arizona drawl. He knew he faced his heir and his most worthy opponent. A real gambler, like a real artist, knows another when they look into their eyes.

"A gambler is a sorcerer, a sorcerer who stalks his prey," Zack Auldney told the enraptured fourteen-year old Americo Rios as they sat at the poker table in the Casino. "A sorcerer stalks his prey by assuming many roles. When you play poker, Americo, always take the first card as the map of what comes next. Don't raise me now, wait for the sign," the old gambler said cautiously. "Watch your fellow gamblers, but don't follow their ups and downs. If you watch them carefully you will see them cracking at their seams. Stalking your opponents with the proper attitude and means, makes you able to benefit from any game. Be impeccable in everything you do. The game doesn't end at the table, and I can't emphasize this enough." The crusty old gambler told his apprentice, "Don't take yourself too seriously, Americo. Have an abundance of patience, and be ready to improvise on a moments notice. Games can change quickly and you as a warrior must be ready. You are in combat, they are your enemies, take no prisoners, yet be willing to change directions anytime. Every card may be your last card, every game your last game, be willing to wait and then act quickly, decisively, and efficiently."

"Good job, Americo, some day I'll give you my coyote and raven bolo tie," Zack told his heir with a reserved smile. "It'll bring you good luck, and you can forget all of the above if luck is flowing through you, however, I prefer to call it power. You must watch for power, and when you feel it make certain you grab it so fast it makes the other's heads spin, because if you miss it, it won't return. Don't forget your natural enemies, as well as those you haven't met. They're out there." Zack admired the natural reserve and preparedness of the young man holding all of the cards. "When it's all said and done, Americo, the one thing you must remember, is that none of it mattered anyway."

In the mid of a dark November night, under the guardianship of Cathedral Rock, the past, present, and future were again entwined into the eternal braid of destiny. Gracefully capturing the inevitable, the nimble fingers of the Great Weaver randomly wove delicate gold strands of light into the long silvery locks of the Witch of Sedona.

Standing in the middle of her spiral garden, Rita Auldney, a woman without a known past, and an indefinitely long future, lifted her hand to the stars and elegantly traced the pattern of the Vortex with her finger. As the spiral garden gathered energy and began to spin, Rita initiated her granddaughter in a ceremony gifted to her by the first woman of the Vortex. Barefoot, with toenails painted blood red, Rita dipped her fingers in a solution of tears and red soil, and then marked fourteen-year old Lauren with the pattern of the Vortex on her head, heart, and womb.

As Lauren's soul surrendered to the Vortex, the aristocratic high cheekbones of Rita's timeless beauty were reflected back in the mirror of her granddaughters face. Shades of moonlight resting on Lauren's heart-shaped mouth glistened as she parted her lips, sighing in awe of the translucent vibrating rainbow colors of the Vortex. With her sea-green eyes sparkling, Lauren surrendered to her destiny, ecstatically swirling her wavy hair with wild abandon to the pulsing rhythm of the spheres.

"Granddaughter, at the time of your birth on El Rancho de las Estrellas, the spinning in your mind, body, and soul was entrained to the Vortex. You are now a woman of the Vortex and with that honor you must live a life of surrender, awareness, respect for your circumstances, and the knowledge that your perspectives will change as the Vortex spins."

Grounded on Mother Earth, with her feet covered with red powdery soil, Lauren lifted her young eyes to the sky, instantly recognizing her star of origin. Feeling the deep stirring of menarche, Lauren shivered under her Grandmother's watch. Drawing wisdom from the oracle beneath her feet and stained by the red spiral mark of the Vortex, Lauren answered her own question with awe. "Oh, Grandma, now I know how I'll know. When I feel a stirring in my body, I'll know that I'm connected to the Vortex and I'll follow the path she predestined for me."

"Lauren, you have no choice but to surrender, regardless of your circumstances. You will live a spinning, wild life full of magic, misery, and mystery; such is the nature of the Vortex. But, my little Witch in training, one day, it may be soon or it may be at the end of your life, you will stand with the man you love in the still hollow center of the Vortex and at that time you will know that it has all been worth it."

Lauren held her hand on her womb, feeling the stirring of the cauldron. Her world spinning madly, Lauren breathlessly made a promise. "I'll never forget what you've taught me, Grandma, no matter where I go or what I do."

Rita smiled knowingly. "Yes, you will forget, but when the time comes that you need to remember, you will."

☪★

Everywhere in the world on the night of the full moon, if you look in windows and see candlelight and sweet cookies, you will know that women are meeting to share the mystery. Even if you could listen, you wouldn't understand unless you had accepted the path of the Goddess. In spite of the protests of their men, Rita guided the women of Sedona on their paths to the riches of spirit. Thirteen nights a year, on the night of the full moon, the women gathered in Rita's living room to have their lives renewed.

Serving peppermint tea and sugar cookies on a silver tray, gangly fourteen-year old Lauren smiled sweetly at each of the women and carefully poured tea from a flowered porcelain pot into the delicate cups. Feeling very grown up by being included in the women's mystery group, Lauren wore her best black and white wool plaid pleated skirt with a red cashmere sweater and white blouse. She tied a white ribbon in her long hair and put small gold coyote earrings in her ears.

As Lauren served the cookies she felt the stare of Lucille Baker, the grandmother of the boy Lauren made cry by winning an arm wrestling match at summer camp. More than anything, she hoped the gossipy old lady wouldn't confront her, knowing occasionally when challenged she stammered her words. As soon as the thought crossed her mind, she heard Mrs. Baker telling one of the other women about the incident. Lauren cringed when Mrs. Baker said that Lauren was wild and for the safety of everybody in town, her Grandmother should keep an eye on her. Lucille whispered behind her hand that Lauren was uncontrollable, even though she had the best grades in her class. Lauren stared at the older woman feeling a rush of naughtiness. Defiantly she held the woman's gaze until Mrs. Baker uncomfortably lowered her face, looking into her porcelain teacup. Lauren smirked, confidant that she had won the contest, fully planning to send Mrs. Baker reminding looks throughout the rest of the evening.

Barefoot as usual, Rita sat regally on her carved rosewood chair. Her bright red toenails peeked from under her long, black skirt as she called the gathering to order. Rita looked elegant with her salt and pepper hair in a bun and a touch of lipstick on her lips. Her kaleidoscope eyes were sharp and intense warning all that she suffered no fools, who didn't know they were fools. On her wrist she wore the gold charm bracelet her husband gave her on their wedding day, making bell-like sounds as she moved her arm in the air, enhancing her vivid descriptions. Rita spoke with a far-away look in her eyes as she channeled the words. "Ladies, as I've told you so many times before, the spiral caught my energy threads and spun me to Sedona so that I could meet my husband, Zack. I had a vivid, delicious dream of the red rock castle that had been my home several times before." Rita reaffirmed the mystery of her knowledge, making the women wonder about her past. "Many of you have curious minds and have asked me about the nature of the spiraling body and although I'm not a scientist, I do know how the Vortex spins. The ancients have understood this for thousands of years, in fact, they understood the laws of nature long before Einstein and the other physicists discovered the principals of energy. I've known some of the finest mystics in the world, and I'll share what they've told me." Stopping to take a small bite of cookie and a sip of tea, Rita suggested that the women might want to take notes. Not caring if they did or did not, she continued speaking in her hypnotic voice that sounded like a spinning wheel to Lauren.

Lauren stared at the ceiling, comfortably curled up on the floor with her head on an embroidered pillow. Feeling cozy warm by the fireplace, Lauren didn't care that her long legs peeked above her red knee-lengths or that her red Sunday panties peeked below her skirt.

Rita spoke mysteriously as the women enjoyed the magic she brought to their lives. "In the beginning there was a dot." Rita meant the beginning, long before the creation of humans, plants and animals. "As a matter of fact, there was an extended line of dots. We can interpret the line of dots as the axis, because like I told Lauren when I taught her how to draw, any line is just a series of dots. Each dot increases the many possibilities within the spiral, and you must keep that in mind as we travel the Vortex."

Lauren fidgeted with her knee socks, repeatedly pulling them up and down.

Rita taught the women with concrete examples, knowing that esoteric concepts are often difficult to grasp. After asking Lauren to put more wood in the stove, Rita then told the women to close their eyes and use their imaginations. "Connected to the first dot is a collection of threads. Try to think of each thread as a person or an event." Taking a skein of yarn out of the Anasazi woven basket by her bare feet, Rita clipped off a foot long thread with her small gold scissors. Pulling apart the many strands of wool that had been spun into a single thread, she held them up for the women to see. "As you can see by the nature of the threads, each person, or event, is made up of many strands. Each strand is an aspect of the person, or a possibility, and they are infinite," she said with a flourish of her hand in the air. "However, to keep a person or event coherent, the strands are spun into intensive energy threads. You might also think of the strands as folds that describe the multitude of facets of each person, or perhaps they indicate aspects of their destiny," she said arching her brow provocatively. "The threads are attached to the first dot, and as the axis starts to turn, the threads begin moving in a circular pattern. If you close your eyes and imagine the axis turning faster, you will see that the threads will form a perfect cone and at that point you have the spiraling pattern."

As the spiral in the weaving above the fireplace started to spin, Lauren dropped her lashes, causing the sharp details to soften and float. Carefully following the path of the vortex woven into Rita's Sedona red and sky blue weaving, Lauren drifted into reverie, stopping at each turn to gaze in the other direction.

"The spiraling pattern can compress, release, widen, tighten, reach as far as the stars, or reduce to a small circle, depending on the mood of the Vortex. Think of a hurricane, or how cake batter looks when stirred. When you imagine the infinite possibilities, think of gravity, levity, radiation, and magnetism. However, there is one more thing I want to touch on briefly," Rita continued in her spinning voice. "At the point of the vortex there is an abyss, or a gap. On the other side of this abyss there is the equal and opposite counterpart of the spiral, and in the abyss there is everything and nothing. Some possibilities fall into the abyss, others are ongoing in their opposition as we speak."

Not having missed the remarks Lucille made about Lauren, Rita wanted to bring the gossiping woman to attention. "Think of it this way, Lucille, the decision you made to marry your husband instead of the man you loved is ongoing in this life, but on the other side of the gap is the life you didn't choose. Or, perhaps the possibility fell into the abyss and never happened." Rita continued speaking in a drum-like cadence. "The gap, or abyss, is the instant of decision. It is the instant before your mate enters your body, it is the second prior to conception when the spirit says yes or no, it is the place where the holy dove of power lands and gives you the chance to accept it or reject it. It is the place of all possibility and no possibility."

Rita calmly sipped her tea, looking out the corner of her eye at Lauren, giving the women time to absorb the profundity of her words. "The spiral is the Great Spinner of all things. While she spins, she provides our stories to the Great Weaver, who then weaves our stories into the landscape. The body of our beautiful red rock landscape was created by spiraling the threads of our stories together and forever weaving them into her red rock body."

Rita spoke firmly to the women, not wanting them to over romanticize the Vortex. "The spiral is never sentimental. Although it loves you and has captured your energy filaments, it will demand that you surrender, or you will wish you were dead. It is never static, however, it does vary the intensity and direction that it spins. It creates circumstances, ruthlessly eliminates boundaries, and alters perceptions, whether you are aware or not."

The women in the circle didn't realize that Lauren was being initiated as Rita's heir. At times during the gathering, Rita spoke only to Lauren. "Lauren, I have given you the four key words and I hope you are listening to me. They are surrender, perception, awareness, and circumstances, and if you remember these terms you will understand the Vortex. Remember also, the spiral does not transform or transfigure, but if you are in harmony, the spinning motion refines everything to a fully polished state, although the journey may be painful."

Offering words of hope regarding the magic of the Vortex, Rita told them of the reward if one lives in harmony with the phenomenal pattern of their environment. "If you are not in harmony with the Vortex, it will disassemble you and that is the painful, but necessary aspect of it's magic, for once disassembled, you have the opportunity to recreate yourself in a more harmonious order. The spiral soars, grounds, attracts, and releases. Yet, within the center of the spiral, my dear friends, there is a still hollow center. If you surrender you may, if you are very lucky, find yourself there one day. The story of your life will read more beautifully after you surrender to the Vortex, become totally aware, realize that your perceptions will be altered, and accept your circumstances that are infinitely wiser than you are. Then and only then are you in harmony with the spiraling body we live within."

Rita walked her guests to the door, offering each of them a small gift before telling them that she needed to send Lauren to bed. Later, Rita whispered to the young woman drifting off to dreamland. Holding Lauren's hand, Rita counseled, knowing the words were entering her awareness. "Surrender to the Vortex, my dear, and your life will be less painful. The warp of your story is being created and later we will weave in the weft as you have your life's experiences. We will both see the footprints of your journey in the spiral garden. Experience and awareness are everything, and whatever happens to you, you must always trust circumstances. Circumstances are a gift from the Goddess, and she is so very wise. Sleep well, my precious girl, have beautiful dreams of open doorways and hands that reach out for you, and know that I understand."

☪

Under the scorching full noon sun floating in the clear blue Sedona sky, Lauren received a gift from the stars. The gift came to Lauren as the creek flowed by, while the ravens circled overhead, and a star exploded in the distant sky. Surrounded by the swirling Vortex energy, yet feeling safe and protected in the still hollow center, Lauren knew she had touched the mystery of her Grandmother. Lauren and her enigmatic Grandmother were frying their brains and licking sweat from their lips while working in the enchanted spiral garden. As if the blast from the star had landed on her head, Lauren got the message. "I've got it figured out, Grandma Rita, and now you don't have to think about where you were born or who you are, because I already know." Lauren stood with her hands on her hips, with a voice filled with mischief and wisdom. "You can't fool me anymore, I know you came from the Pleiades, and you're one of the sisters who came here to teach me the magic."

☪

The spinning of the Vortex hummed in Lauren's left ear as she took notes for her class with her right hand. She turned pages of "One Hundred Years of Solitude" by Gabriel Garcia Marquez with her left hand and listened to the voice of her teacher, Tomas Rios, lecturing on Arizona history. The high pitch whirring, round and round and up and down, organized her mind. When Mr. Rios suddenly called on her to answer the question he had already asked the class, she was ready, this time. "Lauren, how does history move itself forward? What is the driving force of humans within history?"

She answered him, without lifting her head, putting down her pencil, or stopping spinning with the Vortex. "History does not move forward in a straight line," she said in a dreamy voice, with a little bit of a sigh and a lot of indication of boredom, as she continued to read the words of Garcia Marquez. Rolling her eyes to the left, Lauren saw herself dangling by the threads of destiny, dancing her life's dance on the tips of her ballerina toes. "Humans don't have a thing to do with it. We're just the actors or puppets."

Lauren blinked, saw a vision of a snake eating its tail, and offered a plausible parallel. "History eats itself. History consumes the past, changes the style, alters the form, and moves in a circle, and I know this to be a fact because I can see it happening. History is driven to ingest the past by some unnamable impulse. I like to think of it as a ghost or a spirit. But never fear, Mr. Rios, whatever makes it happen, it will always spit it back out, prettier, uglier, here and there, more or less." Lauren ended her analysis of history at large in a few short sentences, giggling wildly and feeling very proud having surprised her teacher.

☪

Rita and Lauren carefully placed their bare feet in the soft soil, leaving their footprints for the Goddess to follow as they stood together holding hands, trying to keep their balance as the swirling motion captured their filaments. On a spring morning as they were setting the seeds to plant in the garden, Rita chatted with her granddaughter. "A gardener is a lot like God. He orders the chaos of creation in order to provide for all of us. However, a woman who is a gardener is like the Goddess. If she is in touch with her random soul, she will let her garden grow according to it's own will, providing only the seed, the water, and the compost."

Although sixteen, Lauren looked like a happy twelve-year old with red mud smeared on her face and a handful of seeds ready to toss in the air. Rita had just explained that a seed often remains dormant for years, waiting for perfect circumstances to open the container of experience.

A gardener with exceptional talents, Rita had her own way of entering into partnership with the soil. "The woman in touch with her wild nature knows the Goddess and understands her ways. She will let the garden find its own natural order and companions. The garden of a priestess is rarely set out in straight rows or planted in monoculture beds. We wouldn't find that very beautiful, would we, my dear?"

Rita winked slyly knowing Lauren felt the secret in her soul. As the Vortex aligned with the spiral garden, Rita tossed a handful of sunflower seeds in the air. "A woman will throw the seeds in the air, knowing that more than enough of them will germinate, and just as I did the first year I was married, a woman will capriciously plant a willow tree in the middle of a tomato patch, trusting that just enough light will filter through the graceful limbs."

Rita pointed to the desert willow dancing among the tomato vines. "You will find sunflowers and rose bushes in the middle of my potato patch, and the nasturtium and daisies we plant now will dance among the pole beans."

In delight, Rita spun with the Vortex under the early morning sunrays. "A woman will dig in the soil with her hands, forsaking the ease of the larger tool. A woman will let the soil in the garden rest, never violating it with a plow. She knows that all beneath the surface will rise in its own time. That's right, Lauren, dig with your hands and fingers. Doesn't the body of Mother Earth feel delicious?" Rita called Lauren closer with her finger. "A woman has a natural clock, and she doesn't need a Farmers' Almanac to tell her when the moon is full. We know the secrets, don't we, Lauren?"

☪

Peeking under the clouds, while weaving perpetual stories into the landscape, The Great Weaver watched the border town where, poised with promise, a geographical mating dance began, again. Safe, with her belly on the body of the mother, marking the land with winding meanders, the low desert energy crawled slowly, often looking back at what she left behind, towards her opposite, her destiny, her other, and her beloved. Ecstatic, filled with passion, new desire, and sparkling light, he from the northern alpine blew briskly down the ancient corridor towards the inevitable. In rapture born of recognition, there was the initiation of a tentative courtship, a creative interaction, a convergence of opposing forces, synergy, magic, the reconciliation of opposites, and...extreme consequences. A self-contained system, a love child, a Vortex, was born.

☪

The redtail hawk dipped and soared, his eyes fixing a bead on the small scruffy packrat seeking shelter. The bobcat shaped like a cloud tried to hide from the bear in the air as Lauren and Americo stood by the fence looking out over the grassy meadow. The creek sang a meandering tune when Americo put his arm over Lauren's shoulders, captured by how adorable she looked wearing a white puffy sleeved blouse, red shorts, and raggedy, old tennis shoes. Amused by her earnest expression, he wished she were a few years older.

Lauren leaned against Americo's damp, dirty, white t-shirt, holding onto a fence post with both hands. "He smells so good." She let herself soar with the hawk as the combination of sweat and cinnamon scent tickled her nose. "I think next to the smell of horses, I like the smell of Americo's sweat more than anything in the world." Lauren added the tidbit to her list of personal markers.

Americo's body and soul felt satisfied after a hard days work in the hot Arizona sun. "Hey, Lauren, isn't the rancho the greatest place on Earth? What do you say we get married someday and live on the rancho the rest of our lives? We'll have ten kids and love each other madly for the next seventy years. What do you think, Princess?"

Lauren smiled back at her best friend. "And you think I'm crazy, Americo. You better just go off to college, get your law degree and I'll see you here at Christmas every single year for the rest of our lives. I'll check out the girl who says yes to having ten kids with you."

Lauren giggled as she visualized him with a chubby blonde housewife. With a faraway look in her eyes Lauren said with certainty. "I'm never going to get married. I'm going to travel the world, and someday, I'll have a handsome lover who won't tease me so much."

☪

Seated in his office chair, Jake put on his reading glasses and yelled as he signed her report card with a firm J. Auldney II. Standing up in order to look down, he ranted, "Lauren, an A- in geometry, I'm mortified. The finest minds in the world understand algebra, geometry, and chemistry, and I expect the same from you. Don't ask to go anywhere but school for the next thirty days, and then I'll think about whether you get to leave the rancho, mind you, I said I'd think about it."

Defiantly Lauren had glared back at her father, never averting her gaze.

Jake growled, looking at her pleated mini skirt. "Go up to your room and memorize the Lincoln-Douglas debate and when

you're finished with that I'll think of something else for you to do."
Lauren bent over to pick up her purse and once again, Jake commented on short skirts. "Lauren, I don't want to see you in a skirt that short again. I expect you to look like a lady, not a bimbo. You're unique, you're not like the other girls and I won't have you looking like them. Why do I get the feeling you're not listening to a word I'm saying?"

Acting somewhat repentant, Lauren asked for special circumstances. "I'll try harder, Daddy, but I've already tttttold Sunnie, Trey, and Americo I'd go hhhiking tomorrow."

Jake yelled at her, detesting any imperfection. "Goddamn it, Lauren, stop ssstuttering." Seeing her tears, Jake relented. "Yes, you can go hiking with your brother and friends tomorrow, but no telephone, no television, and no dances. I only want the best for you, after all, you're Jake Auldney's daughter, and you're expected to be the best at whatever you do. You know how I feel about losers, and you're not one of them." Jake continued in a conspiratorial tone. "Lauren, don't ever be a good loser, be a winner, a big winner." Pointing towards his Oscar, he bragged, "It's the only way to fly."

Taking off his glasses, Jake leaned back in his chair and admired his daughter, not realizing he had hurt her feelings. He looked at her ethereal, deep expression, the brilliant light in her eyes, and liked what he saw. He saw his own potential reflected in her face. "Baby, before you go, pour your Daddy another drink. Pour three fingers of scotch, just like I taught you. You're a beautiful girl, you're special and I'm damn proud of you. You're all Auldney, and you have to live up to your legacy because you don't have a drop of your mother's blood in you." Jake believed he had just been a very encouraging father.

☪

Hiking fifty feet ahead of the others, with a floppy brimmed, pink hat over her long curls, Lauren spotted the ancient water carved cave first. Running as fast as she could over the red stony path, she tripped once, skinned her knee and didn't care. Lauren stood at the entrance staring, and then held the small perfectly preserved agave thread basket to her heart. "I found it, I really found it," she whispered. "It was here all along, just like in my dreams."

Sunnie stood back, holding hands with Trey.

"Can you believe it, Sunnie? It was here all the time."

Carefully, Lauren tipped the basket to inspect the bottom. "I wonder if it still holds water." Aware of the looks the others exchanged, she stuck her tongue out between her perfect teeth. Lauren giggled, tantalizing Americo with her teasing gestures, holding the Sinagua basket she unearthed in the cave. "You want it don't you, Americo? You really want it." Lauren held his stare, squinting her eyes and crinkling her nose. "What do you have to trade with, Jugador?"

After wrapping the small, fragile basket in a purple bandana, Lauren demurely asked Americo to lift her pack on her back. Giving him her most mischievous smug look, like I've got something you want, she took off hiking ahead of the others. They stood dumbfounded, not believing that she had known exactly where to look for the basket.

Americo looked at Lauren, felt something curiously familiar, then looked at the cave stained with white, yellow, and purple water lines, guarded by erosion formed sentries.

☪

Red dust flew as Americo Rios pulled his jeep onto the willow-lined lane on his way home from Northern Arizona University. The Grateful Dead music on his radio pounded the silence, he had aced his midterm in philosophy 301 and he had a date with Annie Lafferty, the prettiest cheerleader at NAU Friday night.

Lost in her thoughts, Lauren crossed the lane on her way to Rita's house to compost the garden. She walked in a trance, not hearing Americo's jeep, not hearing the chimes hanging from the branches, and not seeing Brown Dog running to greet her.

Americo waved at Lauren. Realizing she hadn't seen him, he stopped his jeep, backed up, and gave her his usual whistle, calling her back from her walking reverie.

Life was good. Americo tapped his fingers to the beat of the song and watched the long-legged, graceful girl walk towards him. "Man, is that really Lauren? I swear she didn't look like that last week when we played poker."

Lauren smiled, her sensual mouth revealing her natural warmth, and suddenly, Americo wasn't as excited about his date with Annie.

Lauren emerged from her trance and arched her brow, wanting to remind him she had cleaned up last time they played poker. "Hey, Jugador, did they teach you anything in school about playing poker?"

Americo answered awkwardly, not feeling big brotherly towards her any longer. "Nah, got an A on my midterm, but now that I think about it, I don't know what I learned this week."

"What were you thinking about, Princess? You didn't hear my jeep or see me wave at you."

"Oh, nothing much. I was just worrying about something silly."

"You worry too much. Why?"

"I can't help it," she said in a small, shy voice. "I figured out when I was a little girl if I worry about things ahead of time, then they don't come true. So I try to think of anything bad that could happen, so it doesn't."

Concerned about Lauren worrying about things that probably wouldn't happen, Americo pretended to look at Brown Dog jumping up on the door of his jeep. Not wanting Lauren to leave, Americo thought of something to fill airtime. "Do you want me to give you a ride over to Rita's?"

Jabbing him on the shoulder, she gave him a naughty smile, wondering why he seemed so nervous. "That's silly, I'm only thirty-six steps from Grandma's door."

☪

Every good Witch knows that magic begins in the dark, warm, moist center of the compost pile. The transformation of the old into the new is the secret that all wise women hold most dear. Endarkenment is as powerful as enlightenment, and the women laugh when they listen to the fathers rapture on about the light.

"Watch me," Rita told Lauren as they stood by the compost bin. Rita added oatmeal, banana peel, morning toast, and hair from her brush. "Everything I put in this compost pile is a remainder of the past. In this magical cauldron it will be transformed into fertilizer for everything we'll grow in the next garden. The same thing happens with your life's experiences and circumstances. The transformation of the old is the best food for the new. Lauren, just imagine that the hair from my brush will probably be a beautiful sunflower next year, and the year after that it may become a tomato that you'll eat from our garden. Isn't it wonderful to know that we can live many lives in one?"

Lauren stared as if hypnotized by her Grandmother's rhythmic voice.

"It's the involution of the old that feeds the evolution of the new. It's so simple, just like most of the important lessons in life are. However, there is a recipe because only experience can provide ground for the new, so watch carefully. At first your experiences will be differentiated, but after the magic, they will be transformed into wisdom. Wisdom is not fragmented like knowledge; it is whole and singular." Rita held her arms in a circle, capturing several rays of sun. As the rays concentrated on the ground, the cicadas began their symphony, with crickets joining in. Entranced by the gift from the Goddess, Rita waited for the performance to end. "Think of the enclosure as a round of love. It is the container for the magic and love is always the finest enclosure."

Wondering when it was going to fall down, Lauren looked at the rickety chicken wire and board enclosure. Following Rita's instructions, she held her breath, then pitch forked dried manure into the compost.

Rita gave Lauren a sly wink, before reminding her of the secret. "First we add the leftovers, then we add some red soil for the color because everything must be beautiful, and you already know that's the most important part of the secret. Now, add some of the old compost to the new because it requires the old and the new to make magic."

Following the recipe to the letter, Lauren added manure and old compost.

"Now, we'll add a little bit of water. Let's sprinkle it with our fingers, because the drops of water are fairy tears and because tears bring blessings, we want them to fall very gently on the mixture."

Lauren listened with a sensation of anticipation growing, as Rita pointed at the stirring stick. "I want you to stir the mixture once a week," Rita told her emphatically. "We have to let the heat build in the center, because that's where the magic begins." Rita spoke with mischief in her voice, "Once you mix some of the new, some of the old, some of the eternal, and a few fairy tears, the process begins. In a few months you will have gold, my dear granddaughter, gold that is really stardust from the heavens. Isn't that just like life?"

Americo woke with a start, kicked his books on the floor and before the light from the lamp lit the room, he knew he was in love with Lauren. Staring at the early light filtering through the window, he said it out loud, "I love Lauren." He didn't know when it happened, but he had fallen in love with an irascible, enchanting, tomboy ragamuffin.

Americo knew the rules and Lauren had not been allowed to date yet, but he thought considering the circumstances; her father would make an exception. Puzzled and unable to recall when his feelings had changed from brotherly protectiveness to love for a woman, Americo envisioned her, knowing he had just observed the first budding of her womanhood. "Man, she's going to be some kind of fox in a few years."

Making a plan was Americo's specialty, and on his way down Oak Creek Canyon from school he decided what he wanted to say to Jake. "I'm probably walking into a lion's den, Jake's so damned strict with her, and he's got a hell of a temper." Americo spotted Jake's tan colored Scout parked in front of the horse barn. "Oh hell, here goes, might as well give it my best shot."

Americo opened the door of the stable and walked confidently through the door, hoping Jake was in one of his rare good moods. Seeing that Jake was grooming his most promising colt, Americo picked up an old horse brush and started grooming the mane. After several minutes of friendly horse talk, Americo sat on a stack of hay bales, nervously chewing on the toothpick in his mouth. He looked Jake in the eye as he spoke. "Jake, don't lose your temper, but I really want to ask Lauren to go out with me. I'll respect any curfews or restrictions you decide on, and you know I'll take good care of her."

Silence prevailed.

Jake started to yell, holding a pitchfork in his hand "Jesus Christ, who in the hell do you think you are, Americo? I'm not about to let her get hooked up with some local yokel like you, and let you ruin her life. She's going to leave this place and make her mark on the world. I don't want you or anybody else talking her into settling down here. Stay the hell away from my daughter, Rios, or I'll run your ass off this rancho. I haven't allowed her to date anybody and you're too damned old for her. I mean what I'm saying, Americo. Keep dating that pretty blonde cheerleader, there are plenty of girls like her out there and Lauren's not one of them."

Americo stood directly in front of Jake, hoping he could restrain himself from punching the older man in the face. Knowing how demanding Jake was, Americo told him what he thought of his comments. "Jake, Lauren doesn't know anything about this and I won't tell her, but let me tell you something. You're driving her crazy with your restrictions, expectations, and demands, and one day she's either going to crack up or leave this place forever." Americo turned away hoping tears of frustration wouldn't come to his eyes. "Can't you see how special she is? Don't you realize that she worries all of the time?"

Jake, somewhat taken back by Americo's candor, tried to calm the atmosphere in the stable. He took his Stetson off, rubbed his forehead, and spoke more civilly to the white-lipped, young man confronting him. "Of course I know how special she is, why do you think I try to keep her so safe? Remember she was advanced a grade so I can't let her do things the others are doing. Lauren doesn't have a damn thing to worry about, she's gifted and she'll be fine. Kid, don't worry about her, let me do that, because I expect big things from her."

Americo countered Jake with the fact of his life long friendship with Lauren.

Patting the dark bay two-year-old on the rump, he chuckled at Americo's sincerity. "Go ahead and be her friend, but get any notion of being her boyfriend out of your head. Now get the hell out of here, I've got to get this horse ready to ship to the trainer tomorrow in San Diego. This one's going to be the big one. You can mark my words on that, Americo."

With his lips drawn tight and two dots of pale white skin throbbing above his eyebrows, Americo stormed into his mother's kitchen refusing to eat the snack she had waiting. Stomping into his room, he threw his book bag on the bed. He held his head in his hands, feeling confused by Jake's tirade, because Americo had never before doubted his self worth.

On the mesa under Cathedral Rock, where he and Lauren played their Spinning Game, Americo swore that one day Jake Auldney would get his due. Retrieving a part of himself Jake had stolen from him, Americo made a vow. "One day, you mark my word on this, Jake, one day, I'll own the whole rancho." Lighting a cigarette and blowing a perfect smoke ring around the distant image of the ranch house, he made a promise to his future. "I don't know how I'll do it, but I will." Americo spoke to the image of the young beauty he adored, with absolute certainty that he was right. "Lauren, I'm so damned sure I love you and someday, I'll figure out what to do with that also. You just wait, Bruja, because, you'll be mine. It'll just take a little time to make a plan."

☾★

Wearing her first long party dress, with her first corsage on her shoulder, Spring Prom at the high school was a big night for Lauren. When Trey, Sunnie, Americo, and Annie pulled into the parking lot, the double dating foursome saw the crowd gathered around Garry Baker's car and knew there was trouble. Opening the car door Trey started to mumble. "Sisters are such a pain. We better go over and see what's going on, Americo. You girls stay here," he told Sunnie and Annie as he looked in the backseat.

"No way," Sunnie piped up putting her hot pink lipstick in her small evening bag, "Lauren's my best friend and I want to see what's going on." Looking like a fairy princess in her long, powder blue chiffon dress, with dyed to match high heels, Sunnie got out of the car. In a gossipy, confidential tone, Sunnie told Annie, "I can't stand Garry Baker. Did you know his father had an affair with Trey's mother?"

Annie kept her eyes on Americo, acting indifferent, letting Sunnie know she was bored going to a high school dance.

Sunnie prattled on, being quite certain she was discussing something important. "The way Garry teases her all of the time, I don't know why she said yes when he asked her on a date. There were a lot of other boys who wanted to ask her to the dance, in fact, every boy in school wants to date her. You just wouldn't believe how popular she could be." Sunnie sighed in exasperation, knowing that going to a dance without a date would be a fate worse than death.

The four of them, Trey and Americo walking ahead of the girls, who were making "click, click" sounds with their heels on the concrete parking lot, headed towards the action. As soon as they got close enough to hear Garry yelling at Lauren, Americo readied himself for a fight.

The first thing they heard was the complaining sound of Garry's voice. "Hell, Lauren, I thought you'd have hot pants like your mother, but you're nothing but a cold fish." As they got closer they could see the blood running down his face. They saw Lauren standing by his car, her face as white as Garry's shirt. Trey took over immediately. "What in the hell is going on here?"

Americo put his suit jacket around Lauren's shoulders and as he rolled up his shirtsleeves, Lauren, laughing through her tears, told him she had punched Garry in the nose.

Garry answered him defensively as he held his handkerchief to his nose. "Lauren and I were kissing, and all of a sudden she swung at me with her fist. That little bitch broke my nose."

Lauren screeched loud enough for all of the parents to hear. "That's bullshit, Garry, all I did was let you give me one little kiss and you felt my butt. I'm not even your girlfriend and when I told you to stop, you wouldn't, so I hit you and I wish I'd hit you harder." Lauren tried to go after him again. "This isn't the first time I've made you cry, weasel."

Americo pushed Garry against the brick wall while Annie screamed in the background. Pinning Garry with his left arm, Americo towered over the senior boy and demanded he apologize to Lauren immediately.

"Not on your life you mother fucking spic. I don't take orders from half-breeds like you, even if your Mexican dad is a school-teacher."

Annie screamed again. Americo threw Garry in his car, with a final warning. "Now get the hell away from here. We'll take Lauren home and don't be surprised if her Dad comes after you." Protectively Americo pulled Lauren away from the car.

Not knowing what to do, Trey motioned for Sunnie to help Lauren, who was sobbing and swearing at the same time. At the same time, he overheard Annie mumbling under her breath that once again Lauren had ruined their fun. "Annie, watch what you say. Long before you came along it was the four of us and nobody comes between us." Turning to Americo, Trey demanded, "Get your girlfriend back to the car before I say anything else to her."

With her curls askew, cheeks blazing red, eyes bloodshot from crying and with her hands rumpling her yellow dress, Lauren smiled shyly at Americo, feeling special that he would protect her. With a soft tissue from her evening bag, Sunnie wiped Lauren's tears.

Deliberate but not reasonable when it came to Lauren, when the dance ended, Americo put Lauren between himself and Annie in the back seat of Trey's car. The five rode back to the ranch in silence, the thirty-minute ride home seeming like an hour. Lauren gloated, Annie sulked, and Sunnie fretted that she wouldn't be alone with Trey later. Trey was pissed at the evening being ruined and Americo basked in the touch of Lauren's skin.

☪★

Queen of hearts, nine of swords, the Magician, the Heirophant, the Empress, oh my, so many, many possibilities when a young Witch in training asks the big questions of the Great Spinner and Weaver. The candles were lit, the incense wafted, and Lauren's eyes were half closed in trance as she shuffled the deck of cards gifted to her by her Grandmother. Lauren sat on her just big enough for one Navajo blanket, a magic carpet already vibrating, ready to carry her on a flight into the mystery.

Two weeks before graduation, Sunnie needed a future life reading and asked Lauren to consult the cards regarding her fight with Trey the night before. With the flowers of their souls poised to bloom, the Casino was the perfect setting for two young women to have a sleep over, talk all night, and speculate about their future. Accompanying Lauren on her magic carpet ride were her crystal ball, special feather, small silver cauldron, a hummingbird skeleton, her gold spindle, and a lock of Brown Dog's hair.

Draped in her pink afghan, Lauren whispered to Sunnie very confidentially that sometimes she felt a chill when spirit moved through her. Feeling the warm current of spirit enter the room, Lauren commenced the reading by jingling a small bell over Sunnie's head, further opening the channel of the future.

After the reading, with her lower lip in a pout, Sunnie looked petulant and very cute in her blue tights and baggy shirt. "I'm not surprised, Trey is so possessive and he wants to get married before I graduate from college, but I don't agree." Sunnie looked at herself in a small mirror. "He has all of his stuff, I mean, he plays football, plays guitar in the band and all he wants me to do is follow him around. We had a huge argument last night, that's why I'm so glad we decided to sleep over tonight."

Lauren contemplated her own problems. "I don't feel very sorry for you, at least you have a date for the dance and you don't have to go to France to see the movie star." Lauren rolled her eyes very dramatically. "I just hate the thought of leaving here for the summer again. All she does is criticize me for being a hick from Arizona and then introduce me to sons of her rich friends."

Listening to one of Lauren's favorites, Steppenwolf's "Magic Carpet Ride" on the tape player, Sunnie served the chips and dip she brought from home. Lauren poured wine she stole from Jake's cellar and rolled a joint from the pot she pinched from Lydia's stash. Something was hiding under Lauren's magic carpet. "Sunnie, if you don't mind, I'd like to practice part of my graduation speech tonight and have you tell me what you think."

Just as the performance began, the girls heard the growl of America's jeep when he revved the engine announcing their arrival. Before Lauren could stop Sunnie, reminding her that she was really mad at Trey, Sunnie ran outside, showering him with kisses. Exuding the energy of wet, muddy, and sweaty young lions, Trey and America, were high on life and invited or not, they eagerly joined the party, bragging to the girls about their day four wheeling near the San Francisco Peaks.

Thinking she looked rather adorable in her father's silk, striped pajamas and one of Trey's old baseball caps, Lauren ignored the guys when they called her a ragpicker. Testosterone talk can be very boring when you've just returned from a flight into the unknown that became known, so after passing the joint and pouring the wine, Lauren settled in for some much needed reverie. Some things can interrupt the best of reveries and a good looking pair of muscular, long legs on a very cool guy always brings you back to Earth. Looking at America's long tan legs it dawned on Lauren for the first time that he was handsome, and not just brotherly handsome.

Unaware of admiring green eyes fixed on his legs, eyes that were wondering if Jim Morrison's legs would look as good, America tucked his long hair back in a ponytail and put his baseball cap back on his head.

Sunnie, sounding a little giggly, snuggled up to Trey on the couch. "Stop, you guys, we've heard enough of how strong and wonderful you are. Lauren wants to practice her graduation speech, and the least you could do is listen since she doesn't even have a date for the dance. We all want to hear it, don't we?"

Delighted to be the center of attention, Lauren took the stage and hurried to the end of her speech. "My dear classmates, I know I'm supposed to leave you with elegant quotes from great minds, but..." As she giggled and wiggled, Lauren ended her speech, sounding more than a little stoned and high from the wine. "But I want to share a small problem I have with you. I have been provided with an incomplete education at this fine school in this fair burg, and I have a complaint. I'm leaving all of you to go out into the big world, and I'm still a virgin." She paused, "I consider that to be a major failure on your part."

Sunnie squealed. "You wouldn't say that, would you? Oh I just know you would if you were in the right mood, and your dad would just die."

Trey wondered what in the hell was wrong with her. "Christ, Lauren, grow up."

Lauren taunted him, performing a few perfect pirouettes on her bare toes. "But that's what I'm trying to do."

Always very sensible, Trey was annoyed with his sister, thinking she always caused him embarrassment. "Come on, Sunnie, let's go for a ride. I'll bring you back here in a while."

Looking at Americo with a secret grin; Lauren fished around in her satchel. Laying her many treasures on the floor in a circle, she found the woven basket still wrapped in the purple bandana.

Americo turned slowly, his blood shot, sunburned eyes resting on Lauren's proud face as he recalled all of the pottery shards, little stones, feathers, and bones she had given him. "Wow, Bruja, are you sure?"

"De nada, it's nothing. Maybe it even belonged to you in another life."

Americo shivered, reached to his left leg that suddenly ached.

Lauren felt warm, afraid, in a hurry.

The brief, timeless moment passed.

"Do you want to play a few rounds of poker before lover boy brings Sunnie back? If you don't have time, I'll just hang out and listen to music until she gets here."

Americo was reserved, but he quickly seized an opportunity that had green eyes, wore her dad's pajamas, and a silly grin. "Sure, your deck or mine?" They had long ago figured out how to play poker with a tarot deck as well.

Lauren answered emphatically, totally understanding the mystery of her deck. "Yours without question. My deck is resting from the reading I gave Sunnie."

Lauren sat cross-legged, staring into the cards as if willing her hand to be a winner.

Americo shuffled his special deck of cards, dealt the first hand and asked about her graduation dance. "Princess, you don't have a date for your graduation dance, why not?"

"Oh, it's no big deal. I think the guys are afraid of me after the Garry thing." Lauren pouted just a little. "I'll just go by myself and dance with all the other girls' dates."

Americo examined his hand. "Hell, I wouldn't mind going to another graduation dance. If your dad will let me, I'd like to take you." Americo could not yet read the thoughts hidden in Lauren's wild curls, backlit by the flickering fire.

Lauren sat on her knees with a very poker face, analyzing the excellent hand he dealt her. "Wow, right on, that's so cool, Jugador, but I have a couple of rules now as far as dates go. I drive my own car, I arrive late and leave early, so if you want to take me to the dance knowing that, I'll ask Daddy and tell you tomorrow." Lauren tried to assure him he would have a good time. "I'm having a pool party for a bunch of the kids after the dance." She then had one of her infamous funny thoughts that usually showed up as little pictures. She giggled hysterically, lying on her back kicking her long legs in the air. "Don't worry about what color of flowers you buy because I'll be wearing white like all good virgins."

Americo shook his head, grinning shyly at the goofy ever-changing girl, knowing if he said one more word he would tell her how much he loved her.

☪

Before the commencement Lauren retreated to the girl's restroom, hiding in the stall, trying to stop her legs from shaking. Against the pale of her skin, her apple-rosy cheeks perched above the startling whiteness of her lips. Her new pink flowered spaghetti strap sundress looked happy, the waves in her hair looked carefree, but Lauren was frightened. Wishing she could disappear, she dabbed her eyes with a tissue and held her head in her hands. "I have to give a perfect speech. I just can't make a single mistake. If I stutter just one little bit Daddy will be so embarrassed. I haven't done it for a long time, but I never know when it's going to happen. It feels like somebody is trying to take over my body, and then I can't find my own words."

When the second speaker concluded, Lauren heard the applause and knew that her name would be the next announced by the principal. Wondering whom he described, she listened as he introduced her to the audience, listing her awards and honors. Twirling her gold spindle, she stood behind the heavy drapes dreading the walk to the podium. Finally relaxing, she felt a wave of warmth and saw herself walking across the stage looking poised and confident. Lauren stared at the audience, watching the people start to quiver like waves in the ocean. She heard her voice, thought it sounded different, then looked at her family beaming with pride. Looking straight at her father, she wondered if her family realized she wasn't inside of the girl giving the valedictorian speech. When Trey and Americo nudged each other and gave her their special sign, she knew then she could continue.

Lauren smiled at the audience giving them her most charming expression. "I am now at the end of my speech. I know you are all thinking this is the best part, but...it will not be what you expect to hear."

Trey's mouth flew open. Sunnie looked at Jake. Lauren giggled and grinned when she saw Trey and Americo exchange horrified looks. Lauren paused, knowing what they were expecting to hear. "I know you're expecting me to quote a very famous or wise person that you have read about in your classes, and I'm supposed to remind you of their sage advice to guide you through the next years of your life, but I'm not going to do that." Lauren rested her elbows on the podium, continuing to tantalize the audience. "What I want to tell you is this. Go to the garden, get dirty and sweaty, and then put your hands in the soil. After your hands are good and dirty, plant seeds that will grow into beautiful plants. Water them with fairy tears, then think about what happens in the compost pile. There is magic in the garden," she said dropping her voice, "in fact, the garden is the best university you will ever attend. Play in nature, fly with the birds, hug trees, chase butterflies, and sit under a waterfall." Fluttering her fingers, she continued to advise her classmates. "Spin yarn, bake bread, grow flowers, carve wood, weld metal, do whatever you care to do, but make beauty with your hands. If you don't believe me, ask my Grandma Rita," she said seeing the relief on her brother and friends faces.

"I hope you all have really happy lives. When you come back to Sedona for visits, be sure to look in the local paper, because someday you'll see my name in the headlines. I'm going to try to do something really exciting with my life; I promise you. I hope the same for all of you."

☾★

Matching the eyes of the cat watching Americo, the gold and tiger eye cufflinks Rita and Zack gave Americo for his graduation rested on the oak dresser. Buttoning the mother-of-pearl buttons on his shirt, Americo looked at the new suit his mother pressed, hoping he hadn't spent too much money from his growing savings account on new clothes for the dance. Securing his now almost shoulder length hair in a ponytail, he exhaled a sigh of relief that he was finally going on his first date with Lauren. Almost ready, he snapped the cufflinks in place and called for his mother to help with his tie.

Ecstatically holding her arms in the air, Lauren twirled in front of the cheval mirror, watching her white eyelet, floor length dress swirl. She had watched enough movies to know how to make an entrance and imitating the actresses, Lauren practiced walking down the staircase several times when home alone. When Lydia called that Americo had arrived, Lauren held her breath, made herself wait a few more minutes counting the time on her new gold watch.

Heeding Sunnie's advice, she added a touch more green eye shadow to her eyelids and quite a bit more cotton candy colored lipstick to her lips. Lauren bent at the waist, shaking her hair so it would look wild and fluffy. "I look so pretty, Americo probably won't even recognize me when I make my entrance." One more time, she checked the clasp on the seed pearl necklace her Grandfather gave her for graduation.

Peeking over the banister of the circular staircase, Lauren giggled when she saw Americo grinding the heel of his left shoe on the tile floor while making nervous conversation with Jake and Lydia. Stopping at the top of the stairs so that all eyes would be on her, she began her descent, offering them a small shy smile as she walked slowly down the circular staircase.

Jake cleared his throat and stood in rapt attention as his princess daughter stepped gracefully towards them. Lydia beamed, wishing that Lauren were her own. Americo paled at the sight of the girl with her eyes locked on his.

Lauren stopped, her fingers resting on the wood banister. Still looking at Americo, questioning whether he would notice how pretty she looked, Lauren tilted her head to one side. She crinkled her nose, asking for his approval with her eyes. "Do you see the real me? Do you see everything that I am, Americo? I'm not just a mixed up girl, I'm growing up and I want you to be proud of me tonight."

Americo responded, speaking only with his eyes. Noticing her long neck, graceful shoulders and rosy cheeks, he answered her from the love in his heart. "For me, Lauren Auldney, there is only you. I see everything you are, and everything you will become. Princess, I promise you, someday you'll be mine."

Stopping at the bottom of the stairs in the large foyer, Lauren twirled for her audience like she practiced in the mirror. She smiled at Lydia, gave her father a kiss on the cheek, and curtsied in front of Americo, while he stood frozen in place. "Somebody, say something, please," she giggled, wondering if she had acted too silly.

Americo spoke first, his voice sounding squeaky and his hands shaking. "You look really pretty, Lauren. Let me pin the corsage on your dress."

Lydia became impatient after Americo pricked Lauren's chest with the pin. "Oh, Americo, I don't want any blood to stain Lauren's white dress. Let me help you do that," she said, fussing as she took over the pinning of the sunflower corsage.

Lauren blushed, loving everybody's attention. "Daddy, can you believe it? Americo remembered that sunflowers are my favorite flower. Isn't that just too cool?"

Jake cleared his throat, hoping to refrain from emotion as he looked at his lovely daughter who seemed so happy. "Yes, Honey, that is just way too cool." Jake then started to sound like a strict father. "Now, Americo, no drinking until you get back here for the party. Do I have your word? I checked the air in the tires on Rita's car this afternoon myself because I don't want any accidents."

From deep in the Sedona sky, millions and millions of sparkling suns swing daintily from fine gold threads, hanging close enough to the land that if you reach for them slightly, you can touch them with your fingertips. Seeing the stars in her eyes, Americo reached for Lauren's hand and with her fingers to his lips, he saw her face illuminated by moonlight.

"Trey, there's Daddy's Lincoln, oh Americo, hide that joint so they won't see it if they come to check on us." Like a little girl, Lauren took Americo's hand and held it with both of hers. "Oh, I don't want to get in trouble tonight; I'm having so much fun."

Trey rolled his eyes at his sister's overreaction, sensibly rolling down the windows and turning on the air conditioning to clear the air. Sunnie giggled, and instructed everybody to pretend they didn't see the parents. Feeling pleased with herself, she offered words of wisdom for the evening. "If we don't see them, they won't see us. Lauren, lean forward and I'll act like I'm telling you a secret. Americo, you look out the window, and Trey, you fiddle with the radio."

☪

Lauren and Americo paused under the archway. The archway divided realities, and Lauren sighed, wondering what marvel awaited her. Standing under the arch, Lauren felt a wave of change, a new frequency, and looked behind her wondering what she had left behind. She blinked, the veil lifted, her vision altered and the light became brighter in the new circumstance of her experience. The cloak of her youth had been replaced, her classmates looked different, her perception of herself had changed, and looking at Americo she became aware of feeling hope, love, and surrender. Magic awaited under the archway dividing the passage of girlhood to womanhood.

The faceted orb cast flickers of silver light over the yellow and pink crepe paper flowers in the music filled room. Americo and Lauren passed under the archway, smiling at each other as a translucent energy body surrounded them, joining them together in the plan. Lauren, with her arm linked with Americo's, gave smug smiles to the other girls, having told none of her friends the name of her date. She loved knowing they were probably jealous that she was with a college guy, the handsome Americo Rios.

The Auldney-Rios-Masterson group held a collective breath at the sight of the beautiful couple. Rita gasped seeing the bubble of pulsing gold light surrounding Americo and Lauren.

"Zack, look at them, Americo looks like an Aztec God with his queen. He seems to be presenting her to the world as his beloved woman."

Zack smiled a reserved, wry smile as he checked out Jake's expression. "Lauren is his beloved woman, haven't you realized that before? I've known it for years. Darlin', you're seeing first love and last love. They're just too young to know it yet."

The first dance began with Lauren in Americo's arms. He wanted her all to himself, alone on the dance floor, under the lights, with her head on his shoulder, her heart next to his. He touched the soft, white dress with his fingers and felt the satin ribbon in her hair on his cheek. He closed his eyes and imagined what it would be like to wake up and see her wavy hair spread like a fan over a pillow.

Closing her eyes, Lauren rested her cheek on his chest inhaling the scent of his cinnamon scented clothes. Enchanted by the softness of her fluffy hair touching his lips, Americo mouthed, "I love you, Lauren." The music stopped, and Americo bowed deeply in front of her. As Lauren blushed furiously, trying to cover an embarrassed smile with her hand, Americo made a silent vow. "Lauren, you are my princess, and I will bow to you everyday of my life."

A pink organza dress and baby white roses, it was the perfect dress, for the perfect girl on the arm of her boyfriend who was already flushed from kisses and beer. Like a delicate doll, Sunnie Masterson crossed under the archway on Trey's arm, her black, curly hair messy and her many freckles dancing over her cheeks.

Jake relaxed with his elbows propped on the bleacher, looking handsome in his linen suit and well-oiled cowboy boots. Enjoying watching his two attractive children on the dance floor, he smiled remembering his younger days at UCLA and how he had fallen deeply in love during his second semester. Jake couldn't help himself, he wanted to smile and enjoy the romance of the moment, but daddies will be daddies. Telling Sunnie's father he needed to cool the situation off a bit, Jake watched Trey nuzzling Sunnie's neck, and Americo's hand creeping ever lower on Lauren's back.

Stopping as he passed Lauren and Americo, he gave Americo a friendly pat on the shoulder. "Not so low, son," he whispered soft enough that Lauren couldn't hear.

Surprising Trey, since everybody knew not to cut in on the perfect couple, Jake tapped him on the shoulder, ruffling his hair like a little boy "Trey, there's a time and place for everything and people are watching the two of you. Go to the men's room and pour a glass of cold water over your head. I'll finish the dance with Sunnie."

Jake winked at Sunnie's father as he took the tiny young woman in his muscular arms. "Sunnie, don't hide your pretty face, nobody's angry with you. We were all young and in love once and Trey just got a little carried away." Jake walked the red-faced girl back to Trey waiting by his grandfather.

☪

Twirling gaily on her side of the two-sided saddle Spinny sighed, feeling romantic as the Great Weaver wove threads of pink love into the weft of the landscape. The Great Spinner, already partial to her offspring the Vortex of Sedona, knew that throughout the cosmos this night would live on in memory. All over the rancho, threads of destiny vibrated with anticipation, knowing that soon... There was a flutter, a desire, the time was now for the next thread to be captured and spun.

The spinner remained in trance, the sweet fragrance of a good cigar filled the room, an elderly man sipped his bourbon while pondering the expression on her face, and the sound of a whirring spinning wheel summoned the Vortex. The soft firelight cast shadows on the vivid skeins of yarn, as Rita remained deep in thought, unable to forget Lauren and Americo standing under the arch.

"I wonder what's on her mind tonight. She hasn't acted quite the same since I told her I've known that Americo has been in love with Lauren for years." Feeling especially proud of Americo, Zack considered Americo's demeanor on the dance floor. "I like that young man, he's going to be a hell of a poker player someday if he'll just keep practicing what I've taught him. He has a natural simplicity in everything he does, he fears nothing and relaxes and abandons himself to his feelings." Affectionately Zack looked at his wife, admiring the softness of her expression, reading the diary of their fifty years together on her now lined face. "He's chosen his battle and he's taking a stand. I can't blame him, because Lauren's as mysterious and enchanting as her Grandmother."

Rita stopped spinning, wondering if Zack needed a fresh drink "Why are you staring at me?" A light pink blush crept over her high cheekbones. "Zack, you're such a romantic, tell me, do you really believe Americo is in love with Lauren, or is it just brotherly love?"

Zack stood by the spinning wheel running his finger over her rosy cheek. A love, although old in years, had remained romantic and sensual. Zack touched his lips to the charm bracelet on Rita's wrist, the charm bracelet he first clasped on her wrist moments after they wed. Tens of gold charms for the bracelet had been accumulated over the decades, and decades later Zack remained eternally bewitched by Rita's ever-accumulating personal charms. "There's no doubt in my mind. The wheel is turning, and history is creating the next version of our story. He loves her completely, he knows it, and he'll wait for her. I didn't meet you until I was much older than he is, and I waited alone. He's known her all of her life, and he'll still have to wait alone. Lauren's not ready for him yet, but trust me, he'll wait."

With his arm over her shoulder Zack walked with Rita into the candle lit kitchen, recalling the first night she poured sherry from a decanter once in his mother's trousseau.

"I'm worried about Lauren." Sitting down at the old pine kitchen table Rita put her head in her hands, and wondered how many more times her elderly husband would sit across a table from her. "Lauren was so happy and having so much fun tonight, but she always disappears into sadness when she becomes so thrilled."

Zack leaned back in his chair, scrutinizing the look on Rita's face. He took a sip of his bourbon, and waited while Rita pondered Lauren's capricious ways. "She's so sensual and female, in spite of her tomboy ways. She has a natural tendency for passion, and she tends to lose herself in the moment whenever she discovers something that excites her senses. I've watched her work in the garden, pick apples, swing by her arms from the tree, and bake bread," Rita paused, "and she loses herself completely whenever there's a wave of magic in the air. Her capacity for joy is as profound as her capacity for sadness, and I wonder if she's ready to leave us." Rita finished with tears in her eyes.

Zack stood up from his chair knowing she needed the comfort of his arms. He blew out the candles, and kissed the top of her head as he tenderly removed the pin that held her long silver hair. "Rita, let's go to bed, I want to hold you."

☪

A fierce fire rages in the belly of a young man, especially a young man in love. The few lumps of hot coals in the belly of the large clay fireplace had dwindled, and ending the night alone was not part of Americo's plan. Dancing in his arms, Lauren had confirmed to Americo the depth of his love and before she left for Monaco, he wanted to ask her to come home and be his girlfriend. Americo had waited, waited long enough to make Lauren his own. With a cigarette dangling from his lips, he continued to pace, his white shirt open, his tie long discarded. His hair, still damp from a swim in the pool, hung loose against his neck and his right hand ached. Americo found three more pieces of wood and stoked the fire. "Damn her, the least she could have done was say goodnight." He remembered how yielding her body had been when they danced. "The look she gave me before we got in the car sure as hell said something." He saw a shooting star, then another, then again saw Lauren descend the stairs. Americo closed his eyes and smiled thinking of the radiance of Lauren's smile when she looked at him, her head tilted, a question in her eyes. "Damned, she's a looker and I know she sent me a message with that question on her face."

The wood popped several times as Americo heard Trey and Sunnie's footsteps on the deck. "Oh hell, they probably want to be alone." He heard Sunnie whispering and realized he should let his presence be known. "Hey, don't get carried away like you did on the dance floor; you're not alone."

"You still here," Trey asked as they sat down on the bench by the fire. "What happened? Did you pass out or something?"

"Americo, what's the matter? Why are you alone?" Sunnie noticed his mood. "Where's Lauren, did she go to bed?"

"Your goofy best friend has really done a number on my head, and I don't know where she is. She ignored me during the party, didn't say two words to me. Lauren spent all night goofing around in the pool, flirting with the boys and tormenting the girls as usual."

Trey opened three cans of Jake's imported beer. "What do you mean, she's done a number on your head? Christ, Americo, you haven't fallen for my wild sister have you?"

"Stop it." Sunnie knew she was about to hear something interesting. "I think that's rude. Lauren's really cool, she just hasn't figured out who she is yet." Blessed with a nose for a story, and endlessly curious, Sunnie wanted more. "You were really holding her close at the dance, she never dances that close with guys."

Americo held his head in his hands, leaning his elbows on his knees. "I must be pretty drunk, or I wouldn't tell you this, but I realized a couple of years ago I'm in love with Lauren."

Sunnie was shocked. "Americo, I thought you really liked Annie. She's wildly in love with you. If you knew you were in love with Lauren, why didn't you ever ask her on a date, instead of leading Annie on like that? That's not fair."

"Sun, I never led Annie on, I told her a long time ago I couldn't fall in love with her, but she doesn't want to believe it. I promise you; I haven't lied to her. I asked Jake two years ago if I could take Lauren out, and all he did was yell that he'd run my ass off the rancho if I tried to be her boyfriend, so I just put it on hold."

Looking out the corner of his eye, Trey lit a cigarette and blew a smoke ring around the moon. Startled, Sunnie grabbed Trey's hand when the haunting sound of a coyote yodel echoed across the rancho. Bats flew overhead as a cool breeze blew from the San Francisco Peaks, causing them all to move closer to the fire. Trey tried to find an excuse for the way Jake spoke to Americo "Jake's really protective of Lauren, you know that. She's got some problems, so it would probably be a good idea if you just forgot about her. She's a holy terror, but in a way she's pretty immature." Americo laughed.

In the game of poker, Lauren considered her protégé to have awesome potential. With the mind of a young woman, she also thought Americo had fine potential in the game of life. Under her tutelage, Americo had learned to play poker from his center, not his head, and only when he lapsed did she win. However, recently she won often, and she won big. Lauren had an excellent poker face, a photographic memory, and nimble fingers. In the game of poker Lauren held a big IOU from Americo and he vowed that one day the table would turn. "I really would like to win back some of the money I owe her; she thinks she's such a hot shot. Someday I'm going to be collecting a lot of money from her, just wait." Americo grabbed another beer for the walk home. "To hell with it, I'm going home to bed." Taking one more look at the dwindling coals, he slung his jacket over his shoulder and started down the path made dark purple by moonlight. "I can't believe I fell for that brat. You're one stupid ass, Rios."

Watching a coyote cross the path in front of him, he stopped, listening to the silence of the Sedona night. To break the silence, Americo kicked a red rock off of the path. "Man, when I hear Sunnie and Trey talk about their plans it makes me so damned jealous." Becoming more frustrated as he took long frustrated strides down the path, Americo looked at the silhouettes of the red rock formations surrounding the rancho and then stopped when he saw the candle in the window.

The Casino, tucked between the junipers, was where Lauren disappeared before the party ended. Under the stars, the bluish yellow aura of the junipers beckoned for the thread of destiny to connect. The owl hooted at the moon, the thread danced precariously close to him, and he knew he had to make a decision. Swallowing the last drop of his beer he spoke out loud. "Man, you are at one of the crossroads of life and you better take a minute to think. I know if I go in there I'm going to want to make love to her." Nag Champas incense wafted from the window and the voice of Jim Morrison singing "Touch Me Baby" wafted softly into the night. "Oh shit, just keep walking dude. You know what you want, don't try to kid yourself." Americo stood on the small stone entry to the Casino. The chime in the breeze caught his attention as he reached out, paused, almost put his hand on the brass knob of the old wood door, but stopped. "I better think about this."

Spinny sighed again, tipping over to wink at Weavy. "He has

too many plans; he's too cautious. I think we better do some fancy spinning here, maybe take it the other direction. He should have opened the door, you know."

C☪

Lauren took deep breaths, twirled her gold spindle, and tried to release the chaotic energy she absorbed at the party. "I'm so awful; I didn't even thank Americo for the sunflower corsage." Lauren giggled just a little, remembering the moment just before they got into the car to go home. "I almost kissed him tonight." Remembering him kissing her hand in the car, she wondered why she stopped herself. "It's probably a good thing I didn't, because he's got a real girlfriend, and I can tell she doesn't like me." Lauren giggled at how gaggy Annie usually acted. "She's always flipping her long blonde hair, watching every move Americo makes, and looking in a mirror to check her eye makeup, yuk. I didn't dare talk to him at the party, because I felt silly after almost kissing him." Feeling embarrassed, Lauren's cheeks turned pink.

The footsteps on the path interrupted her solace. Grabbing a tissue, hoping it wasn't her father; Lauren shushed Brown Dog with her finger. "Shhh, darn it, I didn't want anybody to know I was in the Casino."

Americo stood quietly, then turned the brass knob and opened the door with authority. The silhouette of her delicate profile in the candlelight caught his eye, and the husky sound of his voice caught her attention. Out the corner of her eyes she saw his silhouette in the doorway. She saw his long hair hanging around his face, his unbuttoned shirt, his jacket flung carelessly over his shoulder, and his hand resting against the doorjamb. She shivered when she heard him speak, in a voice that sounded unfamiliar, "Bruja, it's me. Say something."

C☪

Jake spoke quietly hoping Lydia hadn't fallen asleep. Stoned, Jake was worried about Lauren and felt suddenly insecure about his relationship with Lydia. "Lydia, Sweetheart, are you awake? I can't seem to fall asleep, that treat of yours was something else."

Lydia answered with a sleepy voice, wrapping her arms and legs around his large masculine body. "Jake, what is it?"

Jake spoke with uncharacteristic openness. "Lydia, you know I love you, don't you? I can't offer you everything a young woman like you should have, and sometimes and I worry that you'll leave me. I have a hard time trusting love, as you well know. You should be married, have children..." he let his voice trail off.

"I don't believe in marriage, I have you and that's enough."

"I hope so." He spoke softly, not knowing if she had fallen back to sleep. "I want so much for my children, but I worry, knowing how vulnerable they are, especially Lauren."

"Jake, why are you talking about this tonight? You should be proud of Lauren; she was so lovely tonight."

"My silent wonder, I hope life is good to her. She's always been so quiet, always watching. Still, I don't want her settling down; she's got so much to accomplish."

Lydia stared out the large window in Jake's bedroom when she heard Trey and Sunnie leave the house. Looking deep into night blue sky, knowing Jake was as mysterious to her as the night could ever be, she held his hand to her lips, hoping he would continue sharing. The dark, she knew, offered Jake a sanctuary.

"I can't coddle them, I can't over protect them the way Zack and Rita treated me. I didn't know people could be calculating, devious, and manipulative. I have to prepare my children, motivate them. I was too naïve and trusting."

"Jake, you know what I think, but that doesn't matter. You know I think you only make three mistakes in life, not writing enough, expecting too much from your children, and wasting your money on horses."

Jake patted her fanny. "Yeah, yeah, you sassy broad, I know what you think, but there are a few things in life even a brainy dame like you doesn't understand." Jake pulled her closer and spoke in a husky voice. "There's nothing like a good woman, the land, and hard sweaty work." He laughed knowing what a city girl she was. "I wonder why Sunnie looked at me when Lauren told her classmates to work in the garden and make art. She's a funny young woman, she acted like I would be surprised."

"Sunnie and Trey are going to get married, you know that, don't you?"

"Yeah, I do and I'm glad." Jake stood by the window looking out over his land, smoking a cigarette and waiting for Lydia to come back to bed with their drinks and a midnight snack. Standing together with her head on his shoulder they noticed smoke from the fireplace in the Casino. "Looks like Trey took Sunnie to the Casino for a little lovin' tonight. I was relieved when her father told me she's taking the pill. They're good kids, they're sensible, Lauren's the one I worry about."

"I'm sure as hell looking forward to our vacation this summer. Time alone together, away from here during the hot month of July. Are you sure you want to spend a month in the rugged interior of Alaska, flying around in bush planes, stalking wild game, and looking for native art with an old man?" Jake put his fingers in her long sandy blonde hair and started to kiss her. "Why don't you turn the music on again? I don't want Lauren to wake up and hear us."

☪

There are some moments that will live forever in the memories of those present. The Great Spinner had done her best spinning and returned Americo to his place within the plan. A crying girl, a comforting brown dog, a fireplace stacked with wood, moonlight, and room on the sofa for Americo.

When the flames in the fireplace rose Americo knelt before her and immediately noticed the tears in her eyes. Gently, he brushed the tears with his fingers and cupped her face, hoping for a smile. "What's the matter, did you have too much to drink tonight?"

She shook her head no, refusing to look at him.

"Did that jerk Garry hassle you?" Teasingly, Americo mussed her hair. "Goof ball, you're such a showoff sometimes." Americo lightly pinched Lauren's cheek. "You were the prettiest girl at the dance." Americo stood, noticing how fragile she looked wrapped in her afghan. "God, I want to hold her so much."

Lauren started to sob and her body shook, "I'm sssorry about tonight, Americo. I felt so pretty, and I had so much fun, but I feel like something changed and I'm confused."

Americo held her hands, trying to get Lauren to look at him, wondering if he dared... "Man, I'm going for it. No way is she leaving for France without knowing how I feel. To hell with what Jake says, I'm tired of waiting."

They both started to talk at the same time, then, looking at each other, started to laugh.

"You go first."

"OK, all I wanted to say was thanks for punching Garry for me. I really hate him, and I almost hit him again myself, but Jake was watching so I just walked away," Lauren giggled. "It's a good thing I've got you to look out for me like a big brother."

Americo did not feel brotherly and her response hurt his feelings. "Damn it, that pisses me off. I'm not her damned brother. Oh hell, I'll just show her the little treat I saved for us, that ought to cheer her up." Moonlight and marijuana, the combination for making madness in the middle of the night appeared. Grinning mischievously, Americo waved the joint in front of her eyes. They sat in silence, each of them stroking Brown Dog's velvety coat. He broke the silence. "Lauren, I had a few things I wanted to say to you tonight, but I want you to remember one thing, I am not your brother."

The yes or no moment arrived. Should he stay or should he go? With his back to Lauren, Americo noticed the raven feather and picked it up. "Lauren, I'm sorry I forgot to take the feather with me the other night. I'll put it in my felt hat and wear it until you come home in August. But just remember, when you come home I want to talk to you about some serious stuff."

In her dreamy gaze Lauren liked what she saw when she looked at the tall hunk standing with his elbow on the mantle, his unbuttoned shirt looking stark white in the moonlight, and his white teeth sparkling in a shy half grin. Giggling just a little, Lauren tried to guess what was on his mind, knowing full well what was on hers. "That is one cool dude standing over there." She smiled, thinking about giving him a kiss. The big moment comes in every girl's life, the moment they become aware of their mystery and the style they choose to first unveil their magic. Sassy and full of her womanly charms, Lauren paused for a second. "He smelled so sexy tonight and his arms felt so good around me, I could hardly believe it. I'll take the fates in my own hands and if he runs like hell, I'll send Brown Dog after him." She giggled loving her own funny thought, and the image of the feisty, brown dog chasing him down the lane.

Luxuriously stretching her arms, Lauren stood with her feet in a ballet fifth position and then bent over slowly. Lightly touching her fingers to her toes she shook her curly hair suggestively, giving Americo a wicked grin. In baggy jeans and pink sweater, she sashayed barefoot with a sway to her walk, keeping her eyes locked with his, not giving him a chance to misinterpret her intention. Pleased when she saw the stunned look on his face, she held her arms out, seductively wiggling her fingers. Lauren looked at his sparkling eyes and firm lips with naughtiness on her mind. "He's such a cool college guy, let's see how he handles this little surprise. I can tell he's going to be one hot guy someday. His mouth is starting to look like a man's mouth, and I wonder how his lips are going to feel touching mine."

Americo wondered if she realized how desirable she looked with passion in her eyes and the moonlight shining on her face. His body started to respond. "I better make up my mind fast, because once I kiss her there won't be any going back."

Lauren put her arms around his neck and pulled him close to her body. Letting her support him, he buried his face in her hair and pulled her closer with his arms. Running her fingers through his black hair while kissing him, she thought to herself, "Why not tonight? This would be the best graduation present I could give myself."

Slowly, deliberately, Lauren pushed his shirt off of his shoulders and with the raven feather started to tickle the skin on his chest. She saw his eyes close and watched his body shudder when she slowly ran the feather zigzag across his bare skin.

The second time she kissed him like a woman. Standing back to look at him, she held his gaze and following the flow of magic handed him the feather. "This started long before he walked in the door." Again she caught a glimpse of how powerful he looked standing in the doorway. "I wonder if he has any idea what he started at the dance." Feeling her power, realizing what he had been saying to her without words, Lauren dropped all inhibitions. Remembering her girlish fantasies about her first night with a lover, Lauren stood in front of the fire and slowly, expertly, pulled her pink sweater over her head, leaving only her lacy, blue chemise top. "I might as well give him the whole show. I'll take my time undressing so he can savor every second." She handed him her sweater, touching his hand lightly with her fingertips. Slowly, she let her torn at the knee jeans fall to the ground, stepping out of them with graceful ballerina steps. Red satin panties shimmered in the moonlight as she seductively pulled the blue chemise over her head. Wearing only a strand of seed pearls around her neck and a white ribbon in her hair, she reached out to him.

Americo stared boldly at her tall, shapely body that he had been imagining earlier. Flames from the fire danced with her as she swayed slowly to the music, running her hands over her body in abandon. "God, I am so in love with her." Americo ran the feather over every inch of her body. "She loves this; she's a natural."

Her arms reaching above her head in full ecstasy, her fingers fluttering with anticipation, Lauren arched her body like a serpent on the antique Navajo rug.

Intensely memorizing every line and curve of her body, Americo followed the tip of a florescent raven feather with his eyes. Americo whispered as he placed the raven feather on her belly and rubbed his hands over her rounded hips. "You are so damned beautiful, Lauren. Baby, I want to do something with you I've never done with anybody before." Americo gently parted her thighs with his hand. "I want to do it with you; I want to kiss you down below." Americo wondered if her silence meant receptivity, and watched as she held her breasts in her hand and moved sensually on the diamond-patterned rug.

Crying out, Lauren moved towards him in readiness. Americo kissed her lips to share the wonder of what he had tasted. Lauren held his face in her hands as they looked deeply into each other's eyes expectantly, promising and loving without words.

Lauren ceremoniously removed the rest of his clothes piece by piece, holding each piece to her cheek, smelling the scent of cinnamon and of his body. Holding his clothes to her heart she closed her eyes, committing the memory. Stopping once to look at him she leaned her head against his abdomen and with her arms around his thighs, she told him in a dreamy voice, "Promise me, do it for me. Promise you'll always wear a white shirt when you play poker, because if you do, I'll be with you."

Americo whispered. "Touch me."

She had a funny thought and giggled as she looked up at him. "I guess I won't be a virgin when I leave for France after all. Thanks, Jugador, you'll have saved me from a life of hell and I won't have to wear white like a little girl anymore either."

He answered, squeezing his eyes closed, holding her head against him. "Oh hell, anything for you." Lying on the floor he placed the raven feather between her breasts and spoke to her in a husky voice. "Be quiet, I've hoped for a long time that I'd be your first lover, but now that I think about it, it had to be this way." Through his kisses he told her with raw intensity in his voice, "This moment started a long time ago."

"Ouch," he heard her say as he moved inside of her.

"It's her first time," he remembered, stopping to look in her eyes for a sign. "Lauren, do you want me to stop?"

Lauren pointed to where the scratch had been made on her skin. "No, no, I love it, but the feather just scratched my belly." Americo stopped, put his lips near her navel, tasting her blood. A rush of power moved through his body and without thinking, shuddering, looking into her eyes, he took the feather and brushed it slowly over the cut, letting it absorb the blood.

Through time and space, from the stars to the core of the Earth, through the crystal tunnel, through the story filled layers of time, under the water that once floated on the land, he filled her, and she was fulfilled. Like interlocking parts, not knowing who was on top, or who was on the bottom, they forgot who they were, became one and one with everything. Together, they remembered, forgot, and absorbed. To remember the stories, the amber of his eyes searched the sea of green answering his desires. There was the sun, the moon, the sea, and the land. Was it Lauren and Americo making love? Or was it another man and another woman, in another time, on the same land? Who was making love to whom? What were their names? How long had they loved? Were they making love, or was love making them?

Spinning in the sensations of their lovemaking, she felt his tongue in her mouth, his hand on her breast, and she inhaled every breath he exhaled. His body moving in perfect rhythm with her own, she responded by lacing her fingers in his tangled hair and then rubbed her hands over his back and thighs. Deep in the wonder, Lauren started to remember. She moved towards him, wanting to feel whole, one. She felt an explosion deep inside her body and in the deep sky she saw two stars falling, spinning, colliding. When the brilliant stars became one, Lauren knew she had fainted.

"Princess, Bruja, Lauren, I love you."

☪

The candle retired, the moon moved across the sky and the darkness provided a container for honesty. Neither of them knew what this would mean and the quiet beckoned truth.

"I could hold her forever." Americo wished he could take her home to his single bed. Holding Lauren's relaxed body and feeling her head on his shoulder, he ran his fingers over the contours of her face. He memorized the lines, knowing she was leaving in three days. Rolling over, he stared at her profile and the dreamy expression on her face. "I need to remember how she looks right now, so when she's gone I won't forget."

Lauren floated in his arms with her head on the small rug. "I'm going to lay here until the magic ends because I don't want to break this spell we're in. His fingers feel so good on my face."

Touching his fingers laced in her messy hair, she felt a shiver run through her body. "I didn't know it was going to feel like this. I didn't know the explosion in my body would send me like that, I even saw stars colliding. If only this soft heavenly feeling would last forever. He said he loved me."

"Jugador, I'm in such a trance you wouldn't believe it and I soared so far in space I even saw shooting stars exploding into each other." She paused wanting to hear his voice. "Was it the same for you?"

Americo took his time answering, wondering what her question really was. "Lauren, you're going to be my Bruja forever." Americo turned Lauren's face so he could look into her eyes. "Baby, I've got to tell you something and I'm not just saying this, I flew and I'm higher than I've ever been before. Lauren, I lo..." He stopped when she put her finger on his lips.

"You don't have to say that just because we had sex together. You don't have to say you love me."

Americo stared at the beamed ceiling in frustration. "Lauren, just be quiet and listen," he pleaded with her. "I've been trying to tell you all night, and every time you interrupted me. I do love you, Lauren, I've been in love with you for two years, if not longer."

Tears started to form in his eyes. "What are we going to do with what just happened? Lauren, say something. Please don't go to Monaco, I want us to be like Sun and Trey, a real couple, making plans."

Lauren spoke in a small voice. "I'm so thirsty, will you get us a glass of water, please?" Americo held a teacup of water to her lips. "I hope this scratch leaves a scar; it can be a reminder of this night forever." Lauren held his fingers to the scratch on her belly. "Maybe you'll change your mind while I'm gone. I'm glad you were the first though, I mean it so much I have flutters in my stomach."

Troubled by his silence and feeling his hurt, she pulled him down and rolled on top of him, rubbing his cheek with her finger. "I guess it's up to me to try to make sense of this. I've always been afraid of missing something in life, but now I'm afraid of missing what I already have. Does this make any sense to you? I don't want you to miss anything either."

"Lauren, listen to me, because I'm not bullshitting you like some guys might." He paused, "Most of the stuff you just said were Jake's words, not yours and I know it. If we were a couple, you could still do anything you wanted because I'd make sure of it."

Americo sat up uncomfortably, wishing he didn't have to mention the subject. "Damn it, there's something else we have to talk about. I know you're not on the pill, but if anything happened, you know how I feel. I mean it, I love you and I'd give up anything for you. You didn't do this by yourself and in a way I hope you are pregnant, then we could be together. Just like I said before, we could stay on the rancho and have nine more kids."

Lauren giggled, and thinking he was very naïve, spoke with full confidence. "I'm not the least bit worried, girls can't get pregnant the first time, don't you know anything? I'm pretty sure I heard that from somebody."

America had something else on his mind. "You smell so good, why is it you don't wear perfume? I love it that you smell like you, not like some sickening flowery stuff."

Lauren giggled, put her head on his shoulder. "I prefer the smell of your sweat, horses and now that I know what it smells like, sex."

"Well that sure as hell broke the spell of the moment, you little nutcase." America tickled her under her arms. "At least you're not still a virgin."

Lauren gave him her sexiest naughty grin. "No I'm not, but now, my man, the least you can do is help me get dressed, because Jake would kick your ass if he knew all the sexy things you just did to my virgin body."

America whistled, calling Brown Dog back into the Casino.

"Oh don't blow out the candle yet, I want each of us to pick a Tarot card before we go home. After what we've just done, I think we ought to take a little peek at our future."

Like an excited little girl she emptied the contents of her new satchel on the floor, looked up at America, then shuffled the deck like a pro. "You go first, now close your eyes, and pick one. Don't peek or it won't work."

"I don't believe it; you got the Magician. How perfect, you're a gambler and I just know someday you'll be a famous poker player. Now, don't forget what I've taught you and don't forget to wear a white shirt, promise? I want you to keep this card so you'll never forget me. Now you shuffle for me."

Lauren looked solemnly at the fan of cards, waving her hand to pick up the vibrations. Seeing the card in her hand, she felt dejected and turned to America for assurance. "The Fool, wonderful, I really wanted the Queen of Cups. Oh well, it's either the best or the worst card in the deck, I wonder which it will be for me."

Counting the fence posts Lauren touched the feather with her finger. "This feather ought to be a good luck charm for you after tonight."

With her messy bedroom as a backdrop, Lauren stood nude in front of the cheval mirror rubbing her hands luxuriously over her body. She looked carefully, trying to discover a difference in the appearance between the girl who went to the dance in a long white virginal dress and the girl in the reflection in the mirror. Staring into the mirror, Lauren pretended she could see Americo's eyes looking back at her. "Personally, I think I can see a difference in my eyes." Half closing her eyes, she opened her lips as if ready to be kissed. "So this is what you look like after a guy makes love to you." Lauren proudly examined the small scratch on her belly. "I wonder if this is how my body felt to Americo when he touched me." In the mirror, Lauren saw the face of a very experienced woman. "One thing for sure, having sex sure gives you rosy cheeks."

In her pink baby doll pajamas, Lauren snuggled up under a goose down comforter. "I love having a guy make love to me. I'm so glad Americo was the first, I wonder if he really does love me. Wouldn't that just be too cool if I already have a boyfriend when I start college."

Lauren kissed Brown Dog goodnight, and to the thirteen ladies-in-waiting watching their princess she told them a beginning of a story.

*"Dolls, wait until you hear my stories tonight. This is a beginning of a new kind of story, a love story. I wonder how many chapters I'll have to tell you during my life. I hope they're all as good as this one. You absolutely won't believe what I just did. Now listen very, very carefully, because you have to hear every single word. Once upon a time, there was a girl everybody called Princess. Once upon a time, there was a really cool boy who said he loved her. The boy took the Princess to her special dance and gave her sunflowers and kisses. I wonder how the story..."*

The meandering lane was a gift, offering Lauren near circularity as she circled back and almost touched the sweeping curve of the past. The meandering lane narrowed, intensifying her recent experience, causing feelings that yet confused her. Walking alone, Lauren felt womanly, proud, receptive, giving, soft, vulnerable, provocative, and shy. At one near juncture, Lauren almost touched the untouched girl she had been just two days before. She looked back and feeling the tug of her future fluttering in her body, Lauren walked on, letting her quiet footsteps lead her to her destiny. Around the bend, she saw Americo sitting in his jeep and knew in a moment he would pick her up to go hiking. She checked her satchel to make sure the snack she packed was covered and then took a sip from her thermos. Holding the mother-of-pearl button she found when she tidied up the Casino, she wondered if she should give it back to him. Excitedly, Lauren rubbed her hand over the tightly woven, small Navajo rug. "I wonder what he'll say when I give him my special rug. I want him to have something to remember me by and besides, it was so cool the way he remembered sunflowers are my favorite." Almost wishing she left the blanket home, she heard his jeep rounding the bend.

Americo smiled when he opened the door and noticed the blanket in her arms. "Bruja, are you too grown up to sit on the rocks anymore? Bringing a blanket is something my mother might do."

Lauren's cheeks blushed. "Americo, it's not for me, it's for you. I just wanted to give you something before I left for Monaco. I really loved the sunflowers."

Americo squeezed Lauren's hand and winked. "Are you serious? Zack gave you this a long time ago. Isn't it too special to give away?"

Lauren wiggled in the seat, wishing he would take the present. "That's why I wanted to give it to you, because it is special." Lauren felt embarrassed. "Let's go hiking, the way you're looking at me makes me feel silly."

"Thanks tons, I'm going to hang it in my room where I can see it from my bed, and every time I look at it I'll think of how much I'm missing you." Americo gave her a kiss on the cheek. "Did you bring your cards?" Americo put the jeep in gear and took off. "Cool. Will you give me a reading while we're up there? I want to ask the cards if you're going to come back and be my girlfriend."

Silence descended over the dining room as Rita stood and put her hand on Lauren's shoulder. Smiling at Americo and Trey with a sparkle in her eye, Rita looked at the other members of her family with pride, sending each a message of love with her glance. Speaking somewhat cryptically, she left instructions. "I'm going to take my granddaughter for a walk, and I want one of you boys to pick us up at 6:30. Perhaps we'll be walking home by then, and you will find us somewhere on the loop road." Rita continued in a seductive voice. "We may be walking in another world, and perhaps we won't notice you, so give us your whistle and we'll know you're there. In the meantime, I want Trey and Americo to do the dishes and let Zack and Jake enjoy an afternoon on the porch together. Lydia has work to do and Sunnie can practice her spinning while Lauren and I walk. I have a gift for Lauren, and we'll find it along the way." Turning to Lauren, Rita brushed hair from her eyes and crumbs of chocolate cake from her chin. "Lauren, I want you to bring your satchel; you never know what we might find as we take our afternoon walk. Sometimes Mother Earth has many treasures to offer on our journey through our life."

The day was warm and bright and as they donned their hats, Rita chimed their departure by ringing her dinner bell. When they stood at the gate, Rita began telling Lauren what she considered an essential lesson for life. "Lauren, walking is a very special gift. You're starting a new part of your life, and you will have many exciting adventures. Some of your adventures will take you far from home, and sometimes, even though the Vortex will keep your energy threads attached to Sedona, you will be lonely. Walking is a gift of power and if you walk you will always find a way to see. When you feel homesick, Lauren, walk. Walk until you forget you are walking, walk until you are no longer separated from the Earth. The Mother should always be your reference point, wherever on Earth you are. You will never be lonely if you walk, because when you recognize the body of the Goddess, you are home."

Lauren skipped ahead a bit, holding her arms to the sun, catching rays in her hand. She grabbed three and offered them to Rita and as Rita carefully put them in her bag, she continued to speak. "When we are lonely and sad, we tend to talk to ourselves. We try to recall what it felt like when we were happy. We try to recall the world that we were familiar with, and we tend to do this all the time, but especially if we are troubled or confused. Let walking take away the conversation in your mind and allow yourself to just be. Usually it's better to forget who we are, because who we think we are, isn't us at all. Do you understand what I'm telling you?"

Stopping to chase a lizard chasing a bunny, Lauren didn't answer.

"When you walk you will become part of the story, the mystery, and when that happens it won't matter what troubles you, because you will know that none of it matters anyway. The only thing that matters is that we forget to remember."

Lauren protested. "But I like to think about home when I'm away."

Rita laughed softly, loving her granddaughter more than ever. "I'm not telling you to forget us, but I want you to have command of when you are remembering and when you are not. You must practice moving back and forth between the two natures of awareness. I don't expect you to remember all of this or to become adept right away."

A small fluffy pink cloud floated over, reminding Lauren that she had worn her pink Saturday panties on Sunday. Rita called her back to attention by taking her by the hand. "I've always taught you through experience, and you must learn from the things you do, even more than from the teachers in your life. Only experience can provide wisdom, and you, like myself, are guided by the wisdom we hold in our wombs. Our wombs are the containers for wisdom, not knowledge, and there is a difference. The vortex in our wombs is entrained to the Vortex we live in, not only in Sedona, but in the entire cosmos."

Lauren started walking backwards, talking excitedly. "Grandma, look back at Cathedral Rock and see the sun shining on it. The sun's highlighting the man and the woman standing in the center and the way it looks is so cool. They're always sheltered by the rocks so they probably love having the light on them."

Rita smiled. "Yes, it's very cool. Do you see now that you can never be lonely if you walk? You already have a gift of power."

Lauren put the little gem of power in her own satchel.

"When you walk, if you choose, you can see your past because it is always in front of you. Sometimes when you walk, seeing your past will be your intention. Our past is our diary and all of it is good, even if we don't realize it at the time. We can learn from it, but we shouldn't dwell on it because it can rarely be changed. Our future is behind us." Lauren turned to look at the future. "Now don't look over your shoulder, we can't see the future until it's in front of us as our past."

Lauren waved at a tourist driving slowly, gazing at Cathedral Rock.

"You will make many decisions in your life that you will question later. Don't question them because they are all the right decisions. Honor your path and trust your destiny no matter how difficult or joyous it is. There is a lesson in everything and that is the light. One second of light erases years of pain."

"I want my life to be happy, Grandma. I don't want to have a life full of fighting and problems."

"Your path will be what it is. Don't judge other people's destiny. They are learning their lessons, just as you will. We all have our battles, and usually, they are within ourselves. The important thing is to recognize the light when it shines on you."

Rita pointed to the east at a formation that reminded her of a resting warrior. "Lauren, I call him the Waiting Man. He's waiting for his woman, his lover, to wake him when she returns and I hope I live long enough to see the day it happens. His eyes are closed, but isn't he handsome with his noble nose and forehead? He's waiting, and he will wait forever until the times come for him to open his eyes, but while he waits his spirit climbs a ladder to the sky."

"But where is she?" Lauren felt sorry for Waiting Man.

"Lauren, don't feel sorry for Waiting Man. He made the choice to wait for his lover. He hasn't forgotten who he is waiting for, but because he looks at the sky all of the time he isn't seeing her as she changes."

Rita then added another little gem of wisdom for Lauren to put in her satchel. "I'll tell you something, if you promise never to forget. Men are always making plans and looking up either at the sky or to an authority figure, but a woman knows better. We know that if you look inside of something or within yourself, that's where you'll find true wisdom. Women's wisdom is seldom on the surface or in the sky, and we know this because we have a container of wisdom inside of our bodies."

Lauren pestered Rita about where Sleeping Man's mate might be hiding. Rita picked up a cracked red stone revealing the crystal inside and spoke slyly. "Now I'll show you where Waiting Man's lover is, but it will be our secret. I think it makes women more mysterious to have a tidbit that we keep to ourselves. There is always a time to tell the secret, but only we know when the time is right. Lauren, keep this stone with you and someday you'll understand why it is so important."

Lauren pleaded like a little girl, wringing her hands and standing on her toes. "Grandma, tell me now. Maybe I'll never figure it out."

"You will, my dear, you will. I know, because I already know your story."

"Oh, Grandma, you always say things like that." Lauren thought Rita might be teasing.

"You know that I've lived here many times before and so have you. This is our place, and we will return again and again, because we are in the same circle and we travel together. Maybe you'll be my grandmother next time, and I look forward to that experience. You will have a great deal to teach me, because your life is going to be so interesting and rich, and you will have learned so much."

Lauren looked askance at Rita, wondering if sometimes her Grandma told stories.

Rita swept her arm over the horizon, with awe in her voice. "Each time I've lived here I've learned different stories, stories that explain the creation of our beautiful paradise and stories that tell of the people and the land. Sometimes, people make the mistake of adopting the myths and stories of another time, rather than seeing the myth they live within. What I'm going to show you is part of the myth I learned while walking on the land in this life and this is the myth you need to remember."

"Do you really think we see the same people over and over again? I hope so because I'd just die if you, Grandpa, Americo, Trey, and Daddy weren't in my life."

Rita knew Lauren wasn't ready to hear the end of the story. "Absolutely, unless there is a reason that one soul chooses not to make a particular journey. Never fear, those in your circle will always be watching over you even if they leave early or decide to rest a bit longer."

They tiptoed across the rocky land carefully avoiding the cactus and scorpions. Rita held her hand to the sky connecting the filaments of the sun to the formation in the horizon. She touched her fingers to Lauren's chest, sending vibrations of love and reception into her body and closed her eyes seeing Lauren's story. "Look over there and tell me what you see."

"Oh that's easy, I see Thunder Mountain and Old Gray Back."

"Let me tell you the story this red Earth told me about Beloved Woman. Before I tell you the story I want you to promise me something, do you agree to that?"

Lauren nodded her head enthusiastically, sitting very close to Rita.

"The promise I want from you is this, wherever you go, and wherever you are walking, I want you to look for the eternal female in the landscape." Rita drew a sweeping spiral in the air with her left index finger. "Look for her breasts, her womb, and the holy gateways marking the entrance to her interior mystery. Look for caves and contained bodies of water. Remember that all streams are male and ultimately they all flow into the container of Mother Ocean. Look for caverns and crevices, for they will remind you of your own body. Never forget your womanhood, because it is your most precious gift."

Rita held Lauren's elbow. "If you stand right here, you'll see what I'm talking about. Remember the drawing lessons I've given you. If you walked down the street a ways, you would see something different. Perspective, remember perspective, everything in life depends on where you are standing." Tracing the outline of a formation, Rita called Lauren's attention to the imposing figure in the distance. "Many groups of people consider Sedona to be a sacred place, and they are each correct. Each group gives names to aspects of the landscape that speak to them. You've heard the stories from our Yavapai and Hopi friends that Sedona was the birthplace of their people. Some say Montezuma's Well was the place of origin, and others say that Sedona was the birth opening. We know of course, they did not call their sacred place Sedona, because Sedona is a new name and a beautiful name. Whatever the name is, the meaning is the same because it always refers to a woman. When you look around this beautiful land we live on, can you doubt that it resembles a woman?"

Lauren didn't exactly understand, but shook her head yes anyway, wanting to please her Grandmother. Rita wanted to emphasize the imprint of Lauren's environment on her life.

"Lauren, the landscape surrounding us is a holy temple to the female body."

Lauren imagined her body as the land, and wondered how the landscape could be a temple. "I don't think I get it, Grandma."

Rita continued spiraling deeper into the description. "The nature of the folded, creviced, labyrinth-like red formations we live within resembles the erotic qualities of a woman's body. Lauren, that means it is female, fierce, and it is sexual. The Vortex, the spiral, is a powerful female aspect and it is born from the body of our red rock paradise. The energies from the San Francisco Peaks flow down the crevice of Oak Creek Canyon and when they meet and mate with the energy from the low desert in the womb we call Sedona, the lovely Vortex is born from the reconciliation of opposing forces. The Vortex we live in is fierce, and you should never doubt that it exists. It exists in its entirety and in the vortices within the Vortex. Some people say the quality of energy in Sedona is masculine because it is so fierce." Rita chuckled slyly.

"Lauren, let me ask you, do you think there is anything fiercer than a woman? A woman fighting for her man, her child, or her soul, is the fiercest being on Earth. And like a woman, the Vortex refines and cleans her environment. The Vortex creates the world we live in and it continuously polishes, rearranges and makes everything more perfect. We are the same because each time we cook, sew, garden, make art, we are refining our world, making it more beautiful."

Lauren knew what she had been taught, but as she imitated Rita by drawing a spiral in the sky, she pondered that oftentimes it just felt like work. Rita read her mind and in amusement continued her story. "Some people call the formation we're looking at by other names, but she tells me that her name is Beloved Woman. The sun is her lover, and for him she is open and receptive and in her large pregnant belly she holds the secrets. To be receptive is to be a woman, and it is a gift from the Earth. Every woman holds the secrets in her womb because in each of us there is a vortex."

Lauren wondered if the feeling she had while making love came from the Vortex. Rita patted her hand, understanding her perplexed expression.

"Beloved Woman's headdress, a majestic eagle, watches each morning for her lover who rides with the sun. Adorning her toes is the head of a serpent, looking west, waiting for the darkness." Rita smiled with a secret. "During the day she absorbs the love of her man into her body. Look at her full breast reaching for his love. At the end of the day, when Beloved Woman turns from the sun, she wiggles her reptilian toes in happiness as she tells him goodbye. Without his watchful eye, each night she dances and reaches deep into Mother Earth with her serpent toes and soars to the heavens on the wings of her eagle. While she journeys into the night, the Vortex spins wildly in her belly processing life internally."

Lauren sat with her chin in her hands, mesmerized by the sound of Rita's words.

"As the Vortex spins the rays of love from her lover, she processes, refines, and cleans the energy of our valley for the coming day. The light of his love helps the Vortex spin stories of the mountains and the desert into beautiful threads for the Great Weaver. The rays are the impetus, the axis, and the cause." Rita now whispered, "And someday she'll dance in the light while her lover watches, rather than by herself in the dark."

Lauren squinted her eyes, trying to see the rays of the sun being absorbed into the belly of Beloved Woman. Shielding her eyes, she caught a glimpse and turned to Rita saying, "She really does, doesn't she?"

Rita smiled and patted Lauren on the head. "Look very carefully and you will see her wide-open eyes. Women are so curious they rarely shut their eyes for very long, because we are afraid we'll miss something. That's the way we collect and create the stories for the Great Weaver. We know there is magic in everything we do and that we have to catch power when it moves. Men spend energy like the sun, so they need to sleep more."

Rita laughed, trying to read Lauren's earnest expression. "Someday the sun will fail Beloved Woman because he will have given all of his energy and time, and she will cry because her Vortex will no longer spin. That's the way life is, and when it happens she will know to surrender to the inevitable. But, perhaps there will be a small seed of powerful energy that will burst into light, and once again her lover will return to her."

Lauren stuck her tongue out at Sleeping Man. Rita scowled and told her to be patient; sometimes it takes a man longer to wake up than a woman.

"Perhaps the elements will have eroded her into another form, or perhaps she will have disappeared into nothing. Perhaps, she will have become composted into a new creation, or perhaps she will nourish a new plant or animal. But always remember, a part of Beloved Woman will remain in whatever form she's in, just like the chocolate in our cake, regardless of the form, is still chocolate."

Lauren became antsy and stood to stretch.

"Beloved Woman talks to her lover everyday while he sends his love to her. Sit down, and I'll tell you what she says to him as she receives his love on her glorious body. These are words of love, and someday you will say the same thing to the man you love more than anything else in the world."

Lauren settled down, stretched her legs on the large flat red rock that resembled a table, and closed her eyes while Rita wove her story from threads the Great Spinner generously shared.

The red Earth whispers as she wakes from her long deep sleep. "Yes, I'm ready for you, My Dearest Man. Kiss me, My Love," she whispers softly as she pauses, arching her body towards his light. "I can feel my body turning towards you." She exhales with her lips half parted. "Yes, I turned away from your radiating light for a time as I traveled another circle of my spiral path. Yet, I feel the promise of your first warm kiss as I return to you, as I must, again and again." The most erotic landscape on

Earth sighs as the hour of power opens the window of mystery upon the surface of her red sandstone body. "I feel the promise of your kiss." She feels the first warm flutter of desire. "You make visible my ever spiraling story that I spin from the gift of your threads of light." The pulsing heat reaches her core. "Never fear, My Darling." Beloved Woman sends her thoughts as she opens to receive his love, "I will always return to you; I have no choice."

She pulls the ray of his love more deeply into her warm magnetic core. "You channel your light into my core, and there I hold it, waiting. I inhale your love as I turn away from you into the dark." Beloved Woman is breathless as her faithful man further awakens her with his insistent love. "I hold your love deeply within my body, quietly, for then it is mine alone, for an instant. When I return to you in the first light, I then exhale." She paused, feeling a quiver rush over the surface of her body. "I return the love from your light that I have stored deep within me on my ever-changing path." She smiled seductively, fully awakened by his power. Exhaling from deep within her body she sighs, again feeling his fingers touch her skin. "I know you give your rays to another when I turn away. Do not worry, My Love, we have no choice and that is not why I cry. Yet, my moon sends your love to me on the wings of her reflected glory." She pauses with stolen delight in her eyes. "Sometimes, I receive nothing and other times your full expression. My moon is your messenger, and I receive your love on the chariot of her unselfish magic."

The layered sandstone woman whispers with her arms reaching towards his body, "Do you understand what I am confiding in you?" She whispers to her man with dark spots in his amber eye. "I know you are always there for me, but I have no choice, I must turn and look the other direction at times. When I turn away from you, My Bright Light, all that grows beneath my surface is nourished from the absorbed warmth of your love." She stops, waiting for a sign from him. "Then I am able to make visible the life that grows within me." Earth speaks excitedly, pulling his firm lips to her own soft mouth, "I am always being revealed by the love of your constant rays."

Earth breathes as she opens herself fully to him, feeling her temperature rising. "My core is a magnet charged by my desire for your love. I entice your love that travels on rays of light with my own love that is concentrated in my core. The spinning begins when my love greets you at the point. The spot, oh yes, there, My Love. There the story begins." She waits patiently for the motion to resume. Her breasts heave towards him as he caresses her hips and thighs with the long fingers of his intense midday rays. Her once dreamy eyes, now fully opened, reveal their secrets to him one by one, taking time for him to transform them into light. "Yes, My Love, I will rise to witness your love, never doubt me. My body connects to your center with a thread of gold. It is a thread that cannot be broken as I follow my spiral path." She shows him with her hand on her belly.

"The tears of rain we create together cleanse my body as you hide behind the clouds. Never fear, the rains of our tears erode my body so more secrets of my soul are revealed to you each day. In that revelation, that which is washed away becomes a fertile bed for new growth from my body. We are forever young and forever old, My Sun. Our love is eternal." She begs the sun with a whisper, "Please erode away my surface with your intense love, then one day the secret of my core will be yours to know. The wind, My Demanding Lover, scatters particles from my body to the other side. Perhaps you are never without a part of me under the rays of your insistent love." She pauses to let him absorb that what she transmits back to him. "My Love, look at the rosy pink and indigo sky we share. The sky is the lovely scarf you use to cover my eyes as you make love to me with your light. Look again with your eye of gold at the owls, the coyotes, the raven, and the deer that play in the sky, keeping me company when I leave you. Don't worry, My Dearest, for I am never alone."

Stretching, she turned away. "Don't be jealous, My Love. Please, don't plead with me to stay, for I cannot yet do that." She felt his sense of loss, for without her, his light remained invisible.

"When I leave you, I prepare myself to return to you, to receive you, and absorb more of your love. I've never promised anything else to you." She sighed as she inhaled his love from afar. "Keep reaching for me, My Dearest Man. I must continue turning and circling, but never forget, I hold your precious rays within me." She feels the beginning of the spinning. "At times you are so intense, My Sun. You send flares from deep within your body, and I feel your restlessness. What causes the dark spots that releases the intensity of your soul?"

"Someday, My Bright Light of Love, you will know the deepest secret of my soul, for I will have found my own light. You see it, you feel it, you wonder about it and when it doesn't matter anymore, you will know." Beloved Woman speaks to him in a voice not quite loud enough for him to hear; but loud enough for him to know there was something he missed.

Lauren exhaled, opened her eyes, her tears falling freely on the red rock.

"One day, Lauren, this will all make sense to you. But never, ever forget what I've told you, because this is the place where magic begins."

Lauren was enraptured by the story of Beloved Woman. "Grandma, I love you and I'll never forget a word you said today."

"Yes, Lauren, you will forget."

The desk was mammoth, the leather chair rugged, and the dark wood paneling reminiscent of back rooms at exclusive clubs where men smoke Cuban cigars and drink expensive whiskey. The office mirrored the big man with an imposing stature who dominates any room he occupies. Twisted, ground out cigarettes filled his ashtray, hinting at the lurking depression. Jake was already missing Lauren, and his heart was breaking as the realization descended. "She's leaving me and not just for the summer. My little girl is almost grown up, and it will never be the same."

Jake heard Lauren scurrying down the stairs, taking two at a time, with Brown Dog nipping at her heels. He heard her say goodbye to Lydia in the foyer and met Lauren with an awkward hug when she walked into his office, wishing he could tell her how lonely he would be without her. Lauren cringed, knowing by the gruffness of his voice that once again, Jake was upset. Rolling her eyes to the ceiling, she half listened, being more excited about the ride to the airport than listening to her father ranting.

Jake sensed her agitation and resented her eagerness to leave. "I've made a list of books I want you to read this summer, because I want you to use your time wisely, and be ahead of the game when you start college this fall. You were accepted into the honors program, and I want you to be the best in the group. I was first in my class at UCLA, and I want the same from you."

Lauren felt the pressure building. "I will, I promise."

"Did you pack your nice dress? I want you to go back upstairs and do something with your hair, pull it off of your face. You look like a pauper in those torn jeans. Don't you want to wear something nice for traveling?"

"Daddy, all I do is sleep on the ppplane, you know I hate to fly. I'm comfortable like this. Come on, DDDaddy."

Jake spoke in an ornery voice. "One more thing, Trey said

Garry Baker told him you were kissing him before he got fresh with you at the spring dance. Don't be a tease, or sometime you'll get what you ask for and Trey and Americo won't be there to defend you. You have no idea how important this is, and you better not be lying to me. I'll defend you if you're honest, but if you're not, you'll be on your own. Make me proud of you and don't act like your mother."

"It was only one little kiss, Daddy, no big deal. It wasn't like I was leading him on. I dddidn't do anything wrong, honest. I won't let you down, I pppromise."

With only her backpack and satchel Lauren stormed out of the house, her green eyes flashing. She slammed the trunk closed, then for emphasis slammed it again, glaring at her father on the landing. "Fuck, Trey, why doesn't he just deal with his own problems instead of laying them on me, like I need him to tell me not to be like our so lovely mother. God I hate their relationship, sometimes I think I would rather have not been born than to be their daughter. When I'm around Daddy, I feel like I'm being suffocated."

Trey ignored Lauren, giving her good reason to elaborate.

Lauren loved to mimic Jake. "Lauren, comb your hair, don't act like your mother, did you take a pretty dress, here's a list of books to read, only buy really good stuff, are you going to wear those ratty levis on the plane. It's not like he's going to miss me."

Lauren giggled when she saw Americo's bemused expression. "Do you have any damned pot?" She folded her arms in a pout. "I've got to mellow out before I get on the plane. You guys know how I hate to fly." Lauren turned to the backseat looking at Trey accusingly. "I swear, he only likes me when I'm ppperfect. Why did you tell him I let Garry kiss me? He made it sound like I asked for what Garry tried to do." Lauren took two quick hits from the joint. "Thanks Jugador, I'll just take a couple of more hits, OK? I don't give a shit if Jake does see me, I'll just blow the smoke in his face if he says one more word to me." The others were silent as Americo waited for Lauren to stop ranting, wondering how the girl with moonlight on her face could have become such a holy terror.

When Americo held her hand, Lauren felt the looks from the backseat. "Haven't you ever seen friends hold hands before? God, you two are so horny, you think sex is all anybody thinks about. Give me a fucking break. Let's get this car moving, Americo, I wish we were going alone."

Trey snapped at Lauren. "Lauren, shut the hell up. Americo, let's just get this brat to the airport. Lauren, I swear, you're so damn crazy, you're going to kill somebody someday."

"Well, if I do, it might be you. If I knew how to fire a gun, I'd shoot you for telling Daddy what you did about me." Still agitated that Trey didn't have to visit their mother, Lauren decided enough was definitely not enough. Sunnie hadn't defended her, so Sunnie felt the brunt. "Sunnie, I loved those strappy high heels you wore to the dance the other night. What was it you called them, your...me shoes? Oh, I won't say it in front of Trey if you're going to blush like that. I'll just say it like this, can I borrow some of your, I'll say it this way, kiss me lipstick."

She caught the look on Americo's face, and her belly fluttered. "He really is hurt that I'm leaving. Wow, I probably shouldn't have seduced him." When she saw his pale drawn lips, Lauren was certain she made a mistake. "But after the way he was all over me on the dance floor, he kind of asked for it."

Sticking her tongue out at Trey, Lauren gave Americo a coy grin and sweetly whispered loudly enough for everybody to hear. "Americo, will you walk me to the plane by yourself? That way lover boy and Sunnie can stay in the car and do what they do best."

Lauren shrieked, clapped her hands and laughed until she cried as she looked at her torn jeans and lime green sweater. "Oh no, I forgot to bring my suitcase. Now all I've got to wear at the villa are my Levis and some cutoffs I stuffed in my backpack. Won't that please the lovely Sybille? I was so pissed at Jake; I forgot to go back in the house."

Lauren chattered flippantly when they walked across the hot pavement, giving Americo last minute poker lessons based on a dream. "Come on, Jugador, put this little country bumpkin on the plane." Lauren pulled her sweater over her head, revealing a skimpy t-shirt. "God it's hot down here in the low lands, hotter than hell."

Lauren nonchalantly opened the Butterfinger candy bar Americo bought at the newsstand. "Candy, cool." Facing him before the final boarding call, she teasingly put the candy bar to his lips. "Wanna bite? Just have a little one because I'm already really hungry."

Startled, Lauren stepped back when Americo raised his voice.

"Damn, Lauren, look at me, and get that candy bar out of my face." Americo put his hands on her cheeks. "Maybe I'll come and see you later in the summer if I make enough money. For some reason I'm afraid if I don't, there won't be any hope for us."

Mischief reigned, and Lauren grinned with a twinkle in her eye. "Do you have your knife on you? I'm going to cut a piece of hair and give it to you. Hair is the same as a person and if you keep it, you'll think I'm with you."

Knowing Trey would advise him not to, Americo handed his knife to Lauren.

"Aren't you a lucky guy? It will bring you good luck too, so don't you dare lose it, OK?"

Americo grinned as he folded the hair in a bandana. "Lauren, you are so damned goofy, why don't you just say you love me too?"

Lauren paused when she heard the question and as she put the sweater over her head tears rolled down her cheeks. "I'm sorry I was such a bitch on the way down here, I guess my period is about to start, or something girly like that. I think I might be getting cramps, like flying isn't bad enough. Tell Trey and Sunnie I said sorry, OK?"

Americo held Lauren and stroked her hair.

"I loved waking up holding your hand, Jugador, and I'll think about everything you said, I promise. Maybe you'll change your mind and decide you like the older girls better."

Lauren turned to walk away, and he answered, "No damn way, I'm waiting for you." A jolt stabbed Americo in the gut.

Lauren placed her hand on her belly. Returning the kiss she threw, he walked away humming the Dylan song, "Just Like a Woman," thinking it described her perfectly.

Lauren smiled at another passenger as she boarded the plane. "Americo doesn't know it yet, but he's got himself a girlfriend. I don't care what Daddy says, what can he do, kill me? Hmmm, Americo thinks he's pretty cool, so maybe I'll wait and tell him the good news in August. On second thought, I'll write Americo a letter right now, and tell him I love him too." Looking in her satchel for paper, Lauren began composing the letter in her mind.

> *Dear Americo,*
> *Guess what, you've got a girlfriend, me. I still have a hard time believing it, but, like you said, it had to be this way. Maybe it's destiny. I'll have to ask Grandma when I get home. After all, we do*

*know how to spin together, don't we? I hope we don't end up hating each other like a lot of couples do. I worry that maybe I'm too crazy for you and that I'll drive you nuts. We'll see. Maybe I'll write more about that another time. Sometimes I scare myself.*

*You better be good, cuz I love ya, and not just like a friend either. See, there wasn't any reason to worry and you should always believe there's hope for us. I really, really, really, really, really mean that, Americo. Please, Jugador, no matter what happens, don't ever, ever, ever, ever give up on us. I mean it so much it makes me shiver and I'm pretty sure I'm going to mean it forever.*

*Wait until I get home to tell anybody so we can tell Daddy together. If we're going to be a couple we should do stuff like that together, right? I don't know very much about being a couple, so you'll have to teach me, OK?*

*Save your money. I'll be home before you know it. Have a fun summer, but not too much fun, if you know what I mean. Will you ride my horse for me? She gets so lonesome when I'm not there. Play with Brown Dog, OK? Write to me tons. I get really homesick, and now I'll miss you more than ever.*

*Your girlfriend, Bruja*

Lauren smiled as she drifted off to sleep.

"I guess I better get the pill, cause I can't wait to do it again."

Standing on the balcony of the light creamy yellow stucco villa, one overlooked the bluest water and most sought after harbor on Earth. Decorated like a lovely bejeweled woman, the Mediterranean Sea stretched far into the horizon with luxury yachts anchored to the sea bottom, some swaying rhythmically on the lapping waves. Flowering shrubs were in bloom and could be seen from each picture window in the villa. The tile deck jutted over the hillside, suspended as if floating in space. Ornate objet d'art decorated the spacious rooms quartered off in intimate seat-

ing arrangements by plush heavily patterned rugs, and a perpetual fire burned in every fireplace, with slow moving fans luxuriously moving the scented air.

Inside of the villa, the woman was as beautifully manicured
as her gardens. Her bedroom, swathed in white mink was made
silent by a thick, luxurious carpet. Lazily, she wrapped a baby
blue silk kimono around her petite body, appreciating what so
many others have admired. And as she sat at her dressing table
she touched her hair, resenting that dark roots were again visible.
Sybille Ginot looked at her delicate features in the rose tinted mirror and sighed dramatically at nothing and everything. Her sigh
indicated the distress in her life, her daughter.

As Sybille gazed through the large picture window at the
yachts in the harbor, Lauren sunbathed on the deck. Angry that
her youthful dreams had been shattered, Sybille jealously scrutinized her daughter's long legs and graceful tall figure, knowing
she again read the letter she received in the morning mail.

Lauren slowly opened the envelope, wishing she could turn
back the clock a few short months. As she started to read the
words her heart started to break.

> *Dear Lauren,*
>
> *Hope you miss me as much as I miss you. It
> just isn't the same in Sedona without you. A king-
> dom isn't a kingdom without a princess. I've been
> counting the days till you get home. I love you and
> miss you tons. I'm still working hard and saving
> my money.*
>
> *I have a great idea for how we can celebrate
> my graduation from NAU next spring. After school
> is over, let's hit the road. We can take a trip togeth-
> er in my jeep, camping and hanging out. Maybe we
> could go drift around in Mexico and check out the
> old hacienda where our relatives lived. Just think
> Princess, the two of us, totally alone, on the road.*
>
> *I had the money saved to come and see you,
> but the day before I was going to buy my ticket, I
> fell off of your horse and broke my leg. Sorry. But
> in your next letter tell me what you think of my
> idea. I'll have plenty of money saved, and I can't
> wait to have you all to myself for a few months. The
> more I think about us being a couple, the happier it
> makes me. I wish it hadn't taken us so long to tell*

*each other how we feel. I love you even if you are*
*crazy, maybe it's because you're crazy, either way*
*you're mine. Don't worry about it; I'll always take*
*care of you.*
    *Write soon. A*

Tears fell, tears that she couldn't stop. She held the letter to
her chest and closed her eyes, wondering how she would get
through the next few days. With a prayer, Lauren spread the
Tarot cards on the deck, asking for help.

☪

Sybille Ginot, the daughter of the famed Parisian art histori-
an Phillipe Ginot, loved three men in her life. She adored her
father, who abhorred her chosen career, preferring that she follow
her sister Blanche into academia. In spite of her motivations, she
fell completely in love with Jake Auldney who married her only
because she was pregnant and never let her forget it. Trey, her
handsome young son, would not see her again after the divorce.
She loved three men, and the three men she loved had broken her
heart. Her daughter Lauren frustrated Sybille to frenzy. Hating
Lauren as she watched her out the window, she wondered how she
could ever have given birth to such an odd child.

At fifteen years of age, Lauren created her own Tarot spread
and as she looked at the ripples on the pool she shuffled the cards
with her question in mind. Hypnotized by the lapping sound of the
sea she hesitated before placing the cards on the clay brick deck.
Wondering if she really wanted to know the answer, she thought
back to the night in the Casino and how a few brief hours had
changed her life. The black bird flying overhead reminded her of
Americo saying he wished he were a raven so he could see everything, especially the cards of his opponent across the table.

Lauren gasped as she looked at the fan of cards, foretelling
her fate. "This couldn't be worse; there are swords everywhere. I'm
going to crack up completely, I can feel it happening and I'm going
to lose everything. Oh no, the nine of swords, I can't stand it."
Holding the letter from Americo on her heart, she cried. "It's
already started. I can feel the sword go right through my heart. It
was going to be so fun to have a grown up boyfriend and go to college with him. We could have ridden to school together, gone ski-

ing, and to dances, and parties. Now he says he wants to take me on a trip next summer. I'm losing everything even before I have it." Lauren held her head in agony, wanting to scream, yet could not. "Every time I call home, I think I'm going to tell Daddy, but he'll just say I trapped Americo like Sybille trapped him. He'll just yell that I've let him down, that I haven't made him proud of me."

Scattering the cards across the deck with her foot, Lauren damned herself. "God, why didn't I get the pill when Lydia offered to take me to the doctor? I just didn't know I'd be doing it with anybody, and I didn't think you could get pregnant the first time either. I don't want Americo to get blamed for this. It was my idea, but nobody will believe me because he's older." Lauren brushed the tears on her cheek away with a swipe of her hand and swore. "Damn it, why did I send that first letter to Americo? Now he knows I love him, and I'm going to have to tell him something else, I just don't know what. Should I tell him we're going to have a baby? Should I have an abortion? Should I run away?"

Lauren stood forlornly on the edge of the deck wringing her hands until they were numb. "I don't want him to quit school. He has so many plans for his future, and he's so smart and gets good grades. A road trip with a baby wouldn't be very much fun. He sees me as this wild, fun girl, but I wouldn't be like that anymore. He probably wouldn't even like me if I couldn't do fun stuff like dancing, riding, and hiking with him. But he's a good guy, I know he'd pretend and I couldn't stand that."

Lauren ran to her room as a wave of nausea flooded her body. Sitting on her bed, she put her head on her knees to keep from fainting. "God, I wish I could find some pot here, it's supposed to settle your stomach." The soft, yellow throw offered little comfort as images of flashing lights and dancing shadows distorted her vision. Lauren fell to the cool tile floor in the bathroom hoping she wouldn't get sick. With the cool tile against her cheek she remembered how safe she felt when Americo held her after they made love. She lifted herself from the floor and turned on the faucet thinking of her father's angry face. "Maybe I'll drown myself, then I won't have to face anybody."

"Both of my parents think I'm a slob, well, wait until they see this mess." Lauren raised her arms in the air looking at the small razor blade in her hand. "I think I'll find a commune to live in when I run away." Lauren smiled, drawing the razor lightly across her wrist, so the blood rose to the surface. "I can do this I've always known how to die, so if I kill myself, no big deal."

☪

Taped on the round ruffled mirror was a photograph of America wearing a cowboy hat and a sweat dampened t-shirt, grinning as he looked down at her from his horse. Haunting Lauren with his eyes, he stared relentlessly as she crossed the room, picked up the silver backed brush and slowly ran it through her hair. Staring back at him, with tears suspended on her lashes, Lauren recalled when he touched her face, her hair, her body, and her heart. Lauren lit a match, held the first of America's letters to the flame and then stopped, holding the flame to her fingers instead.

The brilliant lights from the harbor announced a night of festivity and celebration, not realizing the sadness within a young woman's heart. A light came on inside of Lauren, a light of possibility. "Maybe I should just get an abortion, that would solve the problem and nobody would ever have to know. I could hitchhike over to Nice and find the hippies because I'll bet some of them would help me. If I could only get my hands on some money." Lauren started to scheme. Standing in front of the mirror, Lauren imitated the foppish mannerisms of her mother's young lover, Didier Chesnel. Steam of disdain rose as she planned the encounter with Sybille. "Oh, she will look so beauuuutiful tonight. I think I'll go torment Sybille for a while, and I know it really pisses her off when I call him Smelly. But he is in the perfume business, or so he says. So why not call a rose a rose, that's what Daddy says." Lauren chuckled wickedly at her evil thoughts.

Without knocking, Lauren belligerently entered Sybille's white mink boudoir and with obvious contempt on her face she looked at the silk covered walls and gold leaf furnishings, raising her eyebrows with exaggeration. Setting the scene, she jumped vigorously on her mother's large round bed, stretched her legs and propped her chin on her hands. "Hey Sybille, putting on your pretty face for the yachty pawty? How can you stand all of that war paint? I've tried makeup a few times, and I think it feels slimy and gross, but don't worry, I think you'll look realllly pretty."

Sybille sighed with annoyance, having until that moment been proud of her efforts. "Lauren, for your information it wouldn't hurt you to wear some makeup or lighten your hair."

Lauren giggled quietly. "Who ever heard of going to beauty parlors when you're seventeen and pregnant?"

"No thanks, mother dear. I'm not you, and I never will be." Mocking Sybille, Lauren imitated her mother's preening gestures by turning to each side, pretending to check the lines on her face. "I prefer an honest face and I like my hair just fine, I just thought I'd come up here and ruin your night."

The expression on Lauren's face turned the key to Sybille's latent fury. "How dare you look at me with that expression? You're face is like an open book, and I want you to wipe that look off of your face now, or I'm going to slap it off."

Lauren heard her cue. Sybille had freaked and was now several shades redder that she had been a few moments ago. "All right, this is what I've been waiting for, the big opening. I just love it when she loses her cool, and I'm getting better at tipping her over the edge all of the time." Lauren shook with glee at the stage she cleverly set. Irritating Sybille further by drawling her words Arizona style, Lauren walked into the opening she created. "Wellll, you might as well hit me because you're the only one who does. Not that I planned to ruin your party or your life, but you're going to be a grandmother sometime in late January. Congrats, Sybille."

Stunned, Sybille slowly turned to Lauren. Seeing the smirky look on Lauren's face, she screamed. "You little tramp. Does your father know about this? Who is the father of your little bastard?" Sybille knew the answer to her question. "The father is Americo Rios, isn't it? He talked you into having sex with him, didn't he? Where did you sleep with him, in the stable or his car? I'll call your father right now, and he'll have Americo arrested. You're not even eighteen years old, and Jake will be so disappointed in you, he might even shoot Americo."

Lauren felt suddenly proud and stood with her hands on her hips, challenging Sybille to continue with her threats.

"How could you, a Mexican peon for the father. He looks pretty cocky to me, it's no wonder you fell for his line."

Listening to her mother insult Americo, Lauren's body shook savagely and with her cheeks blazing red she rested her hand on the bed for support. Fear for Americo rose in her chest and viciously she slapped Sybille's face. "Listen to me, movie star, he's the best friend I have and he's a hundred times better than your gigolo. He's brilliant and handsome, and his father owns as much of the rancho as we do. You are so shallow, it's no wonder I've always told people you were the perfect example for me." Lauren laughed in her mother's face and added for emphasis, "Don't get me wrong, I mean an example of exactly what I don't want to be." Grabbing

Sybille's arm, Lauren hissed and gritted her teeth. "Sybille, just think of the headlines when I tell the press how you made Daddy marry you and how the legendary Sybille Ginot is seen through the eyes of her pregnant teenage daughter."

Trying to placate Lauren, Sybille suggested that she could arrange for an abortion, telling Lauren that a young girl should be concerned about parties, pretty dresses, and rich young boyfriends.

Fury rose in Lauren's body, fury that shook her body uncontrollably. Towering over her petite mother, Lauren made the rules. "You're worried about the parties I'll miss and how I look, while you're suggesting I abort Americo's baby. Believe me, I will never get rid of this baby."

Rushing out of her mother's bedroom, Lauren found Didier climbing the wide carpeted staircase and glared at him through her tears. "You better watch out for me too, smelly, Smelly." Lauren liked the sound of the word more and more. Lauren yelled, holding the shocked debonair man's gaze. "I've been keeping my eye on you and when I need it, I've got a big mouth." Lauren pushed past him on the stairs almost knocking him over. "Your old movie star meal ticket is in her dressing room, and she looks fabu-uulous as usual."

Lauren stormed back to her bedroom, throwing herself on the bed near collapse. She held her hand on her chest trying to slow her heartbeat, wondering why she couldn't stop shaking. "She always does this to me." Lauren sat, her long hair hanging straggly around her face and her cheeks beet red, "She sucks the energy out of me until I think I've turned inside out." Carefully placing the contents of her satchel on the bed, Lauren sighed with relief when she found the little woven bag Rita made for her spindle. Trying to think sensibly as the pendulum rotated and the circle growing wider and wider, her body shuddered at the thought of an abortion. "This problem is too big for me to handle on my own and I don't know what in the hell to do. I didn't know the idea of an abortion would make me feel sick until I heard Sybille suggest it. That is definitely not an option and neither is calling Jake or Americo."

Sitting cross-legged on her bed watching the spindle rotate slower and closer, Lauren decided if she had money she would run away, keep her baby, live on the land in a commune, grow a garden and forget everything else in her life. Wondering what to name her baby, Lauren had an idea of how to accomplish her plan. Standing in the bathroom soaking her face with a cool white terry washcloth, she squinted at herself in the mirror trying to imagine a baby who looked like her and Americo.

Listening carefully with her ear to the door, she heard the car taking Sybille and Didier to the party and then set about carrying out her plan. Moving quietly, so not to disturb the live in maid, Lauren went to her mother's room. Counting on Sybille being distraught, she opened the closet door and found the jewels. Digging furiously to the bottom of her mother's jewelry chest she found a treasure she hadn't expected. There, buried as if in a tomb, beneath Sybille's many pieces of precious jewelry, wrapped in a piece of indigo velvet was the engagement ring her father had given her mother. Lauren clutched the five and a half carat, marquise-cut diamond ring to her chest knowing she had found the way to carry out her plan.

Lauren stared at the ceiling from her bed, sending an update to her dolls waiting in her room at home.

*"Dear Dolls,*

*"The princess is lost, and she probably won't be coming home for a long, long time. By the time she finds her way back, the boy who loved her will probably have three kids with another girl. Won't he be surprised when I introduce him to his son or daughter? Oh well, Grandma says that there aren't any wrong paths, so whatever happens will have to be OK. Maybe it's destiny. Maybe someday I'll forget what might have been, but you won't, will you?"*

☪

The end of the day on El Rancho de las Estrellas found the men on the porch leisurely having after dinner bourbons, smoking cigarettes and sharing the camaraderie of each other's company. Zack sat in his bentwood rocker listening to Jake talk about his month in Alaska with Lydia, bragging about the Inuit sculptures he collected and telling tales of adventures in bush planes flying over rough terrain. Watching a gray cat cloud stretch and float across the sky on a streak of red, orange, and pink, Americo and Trey sat on the steps playing with Brown Dog.

Jake sipped his drink, leaned back in his chair feeling relaxed from his month alone with Lydia, and wanted to catch up on some news. "What do you hear from your folks, Americo? Are they having a good time in Europe? I remember when Tomas and I took that trip together after our sophomore year at college. We had a hell of a good time, just the two of us catching trains and moving around whenever, wherever we felt like going."

Americo whistled for Brown Dog running after a chicken. "From the postcards it sounds like they're having a great time, I guess they'll be back the day before school starts."

Zack asked Trey about the masters program he was about to start at The University of California at Davis, telling him the only consolation was that Americo, Sunnie, and Lauren would still be at home attending NAU.

Jake agreed and offered Trey some advice. "I'm proud of you, son. You're really taking the bull by the horns. Get out there, get your education, come home, marry Sunnie and stay on the rancho, leave the gallivanting around to your sister."

Jake shook the ice in his glass, trying to interrupt Americo's musing. "They just don't it know yet, but Lauren and I will be together, and living on the rancho someday too." Americo sent a message to her with his thoughts. "Wow, I can feel you beside me, Princess, knowing you love me makes it seem like you're already here."

Half way around the world, the other half of a divided whole lay sleepless in her bed, remembering a night that seemed a hundred years ago when a young man first said, "I love you, Lauren."

Americo felt whole and he knew what he wanted. Lauren Auldney by his side for the rest of his life had become the driving force of his life plan.

☪

Silence dropped like a heavy, wet terry towel over the sun filled kitchen when Lauren found her mother and the maid talking over morning coffee. Sybille was particularly cheery, waving her manicured hand as if she could change the course of destiny with one elegant gesture. She told Lauren that she and her sister Blanche had talked for hours on the phone making a plan. Sybille claimed to understand Lauren's abhorrence at the thought of an abortion and told her that she would live in an apartment in Paris under her aunt's supervision and then give the baby up for adoption. Sybille had schemed and thought of every eventuality and explained to Lauren that if they told Jake she would be attending the university in Paris he would agree, especially if Lauren told him she wanted to spend more time with her mother.

Watching Lauren sulk and stir her tea with a cinnamon stick, Sybille again reminded Lauren of Jake's temper and how vindictive he would be towards Americo. Feigning simpatico, Sybille told Lauren that she knew Jake's hatred began when he learned of her pregnancy. Appealing to Lauren's efforts to please her father, Sybille countered and trumped every protest Lauren made, including the fact that Jake didn't care if Trey and Sunnie were having sex. Slyly and cleverly Sybille reminded Lauren that she was Jake's princess and he would care more about her than any other girl. As Sybille gaily pointed out the happy faces of flowers in her impeccable kitchen garden, Lauren saw a transparency of glass shedding tears she dared not cry. Making designs in the moisture beads on the paned window, Lauren pondered Sybille's scheme. "God, what happened to me in my sleep, where did my spunk go? For a while last night I felt kind of excited to think about my little baby and me being gypsies together."

Struck by the reality of living in an apartment, Lauren pleaded to hide in her room if she could stay at her mother's house. Her request rejected, and feeling disgusted by the conversation Sybille feigned, Lauren stuck her tongue out behind her mother's back.

Sybille reminisced, sounding like a swooning teenager. "Jake, sometimes I detest you, but other times I remember what a handsome young man you were." Lauren didn't know that Sybille had plotted her ultimate revenge by denying him the knowledge of his first grandchild.

Sybille touched her cheek and rolled her eyes looking at a daydream in the air. "Lauren, please quit chewing your nails and take off those glasses that make you look so bookish." Sybille laughed a silly laugh, making Lauren want to gag. "My, when I was your age I was already an actress and I was so popular with the men."

With her hair in messy braids Lauren slouched in her chair as thoughts of Americo tumbled through her mind like the red rocks of Sedona. She had been defeated, and she knew it. "It's probably the best thing. Americo doesn't deserve to have this problem, I started it and it was my fault for not being on the pill." Listening to her world crashing down around her, the white wrought iron table made red indentations on Lauren's face when she listened to one side of her mother's conversation. "My fate is sealed. I can't find the round house this time, so I'm cornered with nowhere to go."

Smiling with satisfaction, Sybille stood in the foyer with her

hand resting elegantly on the phone. "This is very good. The cowboy can't ride in and rescue his little princess, and he'll never
know he had a grandchild. But, oh yes, I will know and depriving
him will be the sweetest revenge ever."

Numb with shock, Lauren listened to Sybille pierce her heart
a thousand times as she outlined the next several months of
Lauren's life. When Sybille finished speaking, Lauren left the
kitchen walking as if someone had tied ropes around her arms.
With her tears staining the delicate, already water-marked paper
she wrote to him.

> *Dear Americo,*
>
> *I really am sorry to be writing you this letter,
> but things have changed. I wanted to tell you
> before you heard it from Daddy. I know I told you I
> love you, and I do, but I don't want you to wait for
> me because I don't know when I'll be coming home.*
>
> *I'm really sorry that you broke your leg when
> you fell off of my horse. I can just see you hobbling
> around on crutches. Don't fall down, Americo, I
> can only imagine how hard it would be for some-
> body to pick you up.*
>
> *Sybille wants to get to know me better so I'm
> going to go to a university here and then on a ski
> holiday with her at Christmas time. Like I said,
> things have changed, and she's trying really hard,
> so I guess I should too.*
>
> *I really do love you, and maybe we can talk
> about it when I get home next time, if you still want
> to. I'll send you my address in Paris so you can
> write to me, but I'll understand if you don't. I'll
> really miss you, and your plans for us did sound
> fun, but I guess I'm too young and flaky, just like I
> told you.*
>
> *Your Friend, Lauren*

Feeling poisoned, betrayed, jealous, and confused by Lauren's
decision, Jake needed to let off steam. Irritated that the letters he
picked up from the post office had been mailed a week before

Sybille and Lauren called, Jake needed an excuse to yell, and Trey and Americo had broken a rule. "Christ, they know better than to work on a car in the driveway. Goddamn it, they've probably spilled oil all over the bricks." The minute he stepped out of his car, Jake started yelling, waving his arms and hat. "Trey, what in the hell is wrong with you two? You know I don't like you working on your car in the driveway."

"Sorry, Dad. We haven't been changing the oil or anything. Mellow out."

Steaming at life that he didn't understand, Jake stood sorting the mail in his hand.

Americo raised his eyes from the engine when Jake told him he had a letter from Lauren.

White-lipped and furious, Jake gave them the news. "I heard from Sybille and Lauren last night, and your sister isn't coming home. She's decided to attend a university in Paris."

Barely able to hold the wrench in his hand, with his knees shaking, Americo kept his head down pretending to work on the engine.

"Why is she doing that? Sounds pretty weird to me."

"Christ, I don't know. Something about spreading her wings, the usual bullshit. Sybille said something about wanting a relationship with Lauren, woman to woman. Shit, beats the hell out of me, she's never been that motherly."

Americo viciously threw the wrench in his hand against the adobe retaining wall. "Jake, I told you this would happen; I told you two years ago." Stuffing his letter in his pocket, Americo put his baseball cap on and limped away on a cast.

"What in the hell is wrong with him?"

Trey calmly wiped his hands on his jeans and started putting the tools back in his car.

"Ah, I think he likes Lauren a little."

Jake found another window to yell through. "Oh for Christ's sake, I told him a long time ago I didn't think Lauren was the right girl for him. Isn't he still going out with that cheerleader?" Jake gestured towards the crumbled adobe, swearing louder than before. "Look at the hole he made with that wrench. You tell him I expect him to repair it and pretty damn quick too. You kids give me nothing but heartache. Think about it carefully before you have any children of your own."

☪

The woman the moon, brought the man in the moon, to talk to the little boy inside of Lauren. Lauren knew they were there, she heard them talking, but she didn't know what they said. All she knew was that when she woke up the next morning, her final decision had been made. Getting ready to assume the role of maturity, Lauren tucked her hair under a small felt hat. Turning to look at herself in the mirror, she believed the conservative black dress and nylons made her look at least thirty. "I have to look sort of rich or he'll never believe that I would have a ring like this. I'll wear these gloves and carry this little purse so I look like a society woman, and maybe when he finds out that I'm an American, it will make a difference."

Calm and deliberate would describe every move she made. Lauren moved like a girl walking in her sleep, knowing if she allowed her thoughts to wander, she could lose her courage and have to give up her plan. Her eyes were opaque, her cheeks were gaunt and her lips were pale. And although four months pregnant, she was startling thin. When shopping for her costume Lauren spotted a small, side-street jewelry store and today she paused at the entrance appearing poised as she looked around for the older man in the store yesterday.

Instantly spotting the hallmark of an international jewel thief in the making, the jeweler emerged from behind the safety glass, putting his wire rim glasses on to better see the young con artist at work.

Trying to give the illusion of maturity, Lauren felt more at ease when she saw his bent back, thin hair, and thick glasses. She smiled wanly at him hoping he would feel sorry for her. She then reached in her small bag for the ring she had stolen from her mother.

"Yes, that's right, my husband left me for his college sweetheart. He said he still loved her even after we were married. Oui, I speak French quite well. I studied languages in college. No, I am from the west coast of the United States, San Francisco, California. Yes, it is a beautiful city isn't it? No, my parents are dead and my brother is traveling in Asia right now. I plan to go home and get a job teaching school. I love children." Lauren reached for a white lace hankie in her small bag, with the suggestion of a tear in her eye. "My husband didn't want to have children with me because he didn't love me, and it broke my heart."

Almost kissing the elderly man, Lauren tenderly touched his hand with the charm of a woman much older than herself. "Will you really give me that much for it? Oui, cash would be better. I don't have a checking account here, so I'll take the cash to a bank and buy travelers checks, they're very safe, you know." Lauren believed she sounded very worldly.

Lauren smiled at him, carefully putting the $4000.00 worth of francs in her small bag.

"Monsieur, thank you very much. I feel better already."

The old jeweler watched Lauren as she left the small shop, staggering slightly as she wandered down the street. He walked to the entrance and as he saw her turn to the right, he thought to himself that the young woman who had been in his store would probably make headlines someday for committing a big crime. One more time, he held the exquisite diamond under his loupe, knowing he had just purchased stolen goods. Feeling pleased that he hadn't overpaid and knowing her story was a lie, the jeweler immediately removed the diamond from the setting, certain that he could sell it that afternoon for a quick substantial profit.

☪

The small apartment in Paris was dark, impersonal, and lonely, the perfect backdrop for Lauren, who sat uncomfortably on the firm couch with her new best friends, a needle, tweezers, and a razor blade. Alone in Paris, armed with money and a secret, with Americo's initials carved into her thighs, Lauren wrote convincing letters to her family, fully describing her apartment with friends, even including descriptions of the posters on her bedroom wall. Deception became easier, much like a game she played to entertain herself.

"Merry Christmas, Lauren." She laughed hysterically. "Doesn't every seventeen-year old girl spend Christmas alone, feeling fat and old?" Christmas presents from home, thoughtfully selected for a young college girl, had been opened and carelessly left on the table. Living in a state of unreality that was very real, Lauren spent more time opening a window into her now numb body, trying to understand why she no longer cared if she lived or died.

Heartbroken, Americo continued to write, offering every reason for Lauren to return to Sedona. A gold bracelet adorned with a raven charm arrived for Christmas, with the vow that he still considered her to be his girlfriend. Guilt ridden, she read the letters and with the bracelet dangling on her wrist, the fiber of her soul unraveled quickly to the deepest interior of her being. Unable to cry, Lauren continued to carve. "He's crazier than I am, and I think he's the fool not me. He told me that my magic is good because I'm honest, and I'm not."

Almost screaming with a ferocious headache, Lauren hurled her glasses across the room, believing she was going blind. "I feel like I'm in a black hole, and everything seems so fuzzy. I wonder if I'll ever feel young again. I feel so old and tired." Lauren ran her fingers through her sweaty damp hair. "I hope the hair I cut off at the airport brings you good luck, Americo, but it probably won't because I'm a terrible person." Believing she was dying, Lauren made a promise to Americo. "Someday when I tell you about this, you'll hate me and I won't blame you, but you'll just have to believe that I didn't want to ruin your life or have Daddy send you to jail."

☪

Snow fell, and the temperature dropped on the Northern Arizona University campus the first day of classes in January. Students were hurrying to classes, some of them visiting with their friends, catching up after Christmas break. There was an electric feeling in the dry air, static making hair stand on end. Faces were red from the frigid cold wind. The students were wearing colored parkas. Some were red, others green, yellow, orange, and blue, giving the campus a surreal flavor, hinting at spring, giving hope for flowers.

Americo Rios stopped two hundred feet from his jeep unable to walk further, feeling a stab in his belly. He stood frozen in place, losing track of time. He looked at his watch and seeing that he was already late for class, he lit a cigarette and dropped his book pack on the wet blacktop. "Something's wrong, somewhere. I know it." With his eyes cast down looking at the snow covered blacktop, Americo returned to his jeep. Feeling guilty for missing the first day of class, Americo turned on the engine and closed his eyes.

Not knowing why, Americo drove to the administration office and parked his jeep in a red zone, not caring if he got a ticket. He walked as if in trance to the window and handed the secretary an official withdrawal form. His voice sounding huskier than usual, he spoke abruptly to the woman behind the counter. "Yes, I want to drop out of school. No reason, I just have to."

C★

After being rushed by taxi to a landscape disguised private clinic on the outskirts of Paris, Lauren bared her teeth and laughed viciously as she threw the adoption papers in her aunt's face.

"Fooled you all, Aunty Blanche, there's no fucking way I'm giving this baby up for adoption."

Sweaty haired and with green eyes blazing, Lauren, bent over with contractions, vehemently told her aunt not to call Sybille under any circumstances. Sybille had failed to visit Lauren during the months she had been confined to an apartment and Lauren realized without any doubt that her mother was dead as far as she was concerned.

Through Demerol fogged eyes Lauren squinted at the kind faced doctor, trying to form a question with slurred speech and a dry mouth. For ten days Lauren had been in labor and being unable to dilate, the doctor was considering performing a cesarean. However, when he checked Lauren's vital signs for the fourth time in an hour, he was convinced cesarean was no longer an option. Lauren spoke slowly, saying the words carefully, trying to find meaning in the haze. "How long have I been here, Doctor?"

"That means I've been here almost two weeks. Why haven't I had my baby yet? I can't take any more pain. Am I going to die?"

"Young lady, yesterday you were in such a good mood, why are you so frightened today?"

"I don't remember yesterday, am I going to die? I feel like I am, it's like I can feel it around me. I really don't care if I do, so you can tell me, I won't freak out or anything."

The doctor stood at the foot of her bed, reviewing her chart and making notes of the many cuts and bruises on her body. "We are doing everything we can for you, young lady, whoever you are. Your body is very young and not well prepared for childbirth. We have given you all of the medication we can, and I hope you will not die, but perhaps we should call your husband or father just in case. Will you give me their names?"

Lauren surprised herself at the comment she made. "They're both dead and I'm on my own in the world, so don't bother trying to call anybody." Struggling to hang on to consciousness, Lauren closed her eyes, not wanting to look at the doctor. "I'm spinning around in a funnel, and I can't get out, I feel like I'm about to fall out of something, and I can't hang on." Lauren tried to sit up as the old doctor took her blood pressure. "I want more medication, and I want it now."

The doctor refused to give Lauren more Demerol telling her that her labor contractions had intensified and pain medication could stop them. Offering her a small sip of water, he noticed she seemed less coherent and more disoriented as her labor progressed.

Never screaming, Lauren fainted. The doctor reached quickly for his stethoscope, feeling her pulse diminishing in strength. "Please Doctor, I can't see anything but swirling black clouds. I thought you were supposed to see light when you die. God, this is killing me, isn't it? What's going on?" Lauren asked with a dull voice. "Will somebody say something?" Lauren yelled as she heard the doctors and nurses moving quickly around the dark delivery room. "You're going to do what to me? No fucking way are you going to cut me open down there."

The feeling of emergence a woman longs for, and never forgets, came too soon and sadly for Lauren. As the baby emerged from Lauren's body, she heard the nurses whispering quietly behind her. "I can hear a cry..." Urgently, the nurse called to the doctor telling him the baby needed help. The doctor yelled back, "So does this young woman."

Lauren lost consciousness and shot quickly into star filled space, losing all care, feeling no fear, surrendering to the silence. As she floated into space Lauren did not feel alone. She reached for somebody, barely touched their hand and then the hand slipped away. Already lonely for the hand that touched hers, Lauren kept turning from side-to-side, losing track of her companion. Slowly returning to her body, she felt the doctor shaking her and heard him pleading with her to stay. The doctor tenderly rubbed her cold cheek while a nurse covered her shaking body with a blanket. "I am so sorry, young woman, but your baby did not survive the trials of birth. Your body fought against the labor, and we almost lost both of you. We'll make arrangements for you to see your son before his body is taken away for cremation."

Her mind lost in unconsciousness, Lauren's body tumbled backwards. Blackness surrounding her, she rolled past everybody

in her life moving in the other direction and desperately she cried
out to them.

C★

Lauren struggled and as she focused on the gray clouds in
front of her eyes, she felt the nurse gently shaking her shoulder.
"Lauren, you must wake up. You cannot spend any more time
sleeping. You have been asleep for twenty-four hours."

"What happened in the delivery room? I heard a cry, and then
it stopped, and all I heard were voices whispering. I kept rolling
down a hill, and then..."

The nurse interrupted her, and as she wiped Lauren's face
with a cloth, she tried to console her. "You must cry for your son,
Lauren, don't ask so many questions. Don't hold your pain inside
of you or someday you will be sorry. Here let me put my arms
around you. Where is your mother? Please, young lady, cry."

Lauren clung to the bosom of the plump nurse. "I can't cry
anymore. I quit crying when I moved to Paris, and I may never cry
again." Lauren averted her eyes to the window. "I don't know if I
should see my baby. I didn't even get to tell my son that I loved
him even though I wondered all of the time what the baby would
look like."

With grief on her own face, the nurse wondered what was
going to happen to this girl with the haunted stare. "I'm going to
bring your baby to you. It's very important that you see your son
so that you will know without a doubt that he didn't live. He is
with the angels now, and he is happy."

With her breasts aching with desire to nurse her son, Lauren
held her baby boy, wanting to feel, not knowing what to say, and
tentatively, she touched her finger to his soft, black hair. "I wondered what a baby who was half Americo and half me would look
like. You have his hair, would you have had his voice, and his
walk? Would you have loved horses, the rancho and me, like your
Daddy does? Do you know that you were made from stardust and
light? I saw two stars falling through the night, they collided,
became one, and then there was you. Did you hear your Daddy say
he loved me? Were you there when he tasted me, when he stroked
my body with a feather, when he was first inside of me? Do you
know that deep down I always knew I loved your Daddy?" She
touched his cheek, feeling his soft, cool skin and wondered how he

would have sounded if he could cry. Lauren had so many questions that could never be answered. Almost willing her son back to life, she talked to him. "Can you hear me, can you see me, do you know that I'm your Mommy, do you know who your Daddy is? I'm so sorry, why couldn't you stay? We could have lived together and then later gone back to Sedona and told your Daddy. He would have loved you, even if he hated me." When she looked at the baby's hands she saw her own long fingers and with tears almost forming, she told her son, "I wish I could see your eyes; I wonder if you have my eyes or Americo's?"

Lauren turned to the nurse, "Would you let me cut some of his hair? I want some of his hair to keep with me; it's almost the same as having the person you know."

"Of course, let me help you. I'll find a small bag for you to put it in. Would you like for me to do it for you?"

"No."

"Do you want the ashes of your son?"

"Yes, I need to take him home."

Before handing the body of her son to the nurse, Lauren kissed him on the forehead and fingers. As the nurse walked out of the room carrying the swaddled baby, Lauren felt a deep part of herself rush from her body and follow her son. The part of her soul that left her followed her son on a gust of cool wind that formed in the deepest part of Lauren. Coldness filled her body, yet she couldn't shiver. The nurse touching Lauren's skin thought she felt less life in the frozen young woman than in her dead son. Lauren, feeling limp and alone, stared out the window at nothing but loneliness surrounded by a black tunnel. Wanting to hug her son, she hugged herself with arms of lead. The need to hold somebody was so great she bent over and moaned, clinching her fists. "If I call him TJ, after our father's names, at least I'll have a name to call him when I think of him."

When all was quiet Lauren sat in her bed and listened. Knowing most of the staff went home at night, she quietly wandered the halls looking for the medications. Spotting the glass front case, Lauren spied the bottle of 500 Demerol and quickly stole it from the pharmacy. Hiding it in her satchel, she found a way through her grief.

☪

Three days later, one day before her eighteenth birthday, Lauren counted her stash of money and pills and put her son's hair and ashes in her satchel. With nowhere else to go, Lauren returned to Monaco. As the plane descended over the Mediterranean city of Nice she knew she flew in the direction of her state of mind. Lauren accepted her fate as she watched festive passengers depart the plane. "It's not over yet. This story is only beginning. I'm on my own in the world, and I better get used to it because I wonder if I'll ever feel safe again." Trying to rise from her seat, Lauren also tried to see her future. "Why does everybody look so fucking happy? Why can't anybody see that I'm dying? I know a few things for certain, I can't go home yet, I've got to stop thinking about Americo, and I need help."

The driver of the taxi wound the car up the narrow street to her mother's hillside stucco villa. Lauren stood at the door, not wanting to face Sybille, but when she opened the door she heard her mother's lilting voice calling from the living room. "Lauren, darling, please join me, I've been waiting for you to arrive. Now that you're a woman, would you like to join me for a cocktail? Come, sit with me by the fire."

Lauren stood under the archway, stunned. "Lovely, I have a baby boy and he dies, so I'm invited to have a cocktail. Now, if she'd roll a joint for me, I might take her up on her offer." Shaking her head in dismay, Lauren felt invisible. "No thanks, I'm going to my room and sleep, I don't know why, but I feel a little tired."

Sybille challenged her with an offended expression on her face. "Are you sulking about something? Of all the ungrateful attitudes." Sybille exclaimed with aghast, "I make all of the arrangements and you treat me terribly."

Lauren continued to stare at Sybille in disbelief.

"You should be thankful for what happened, it was a blessing in disguise." Sybille raised her lovely bejeweled hand to the sky. "Now you can get on with your life like it never happened. Think of the parties, the dresses, and the boys you will love."

Seeing the look of astonishment on Lauren's face, Sybille decided to promptly put an end to Lauren's attitude. "You are really something, Lauren Auldney, acting like something terrible has happened to you. What on Earth could you have to be upset about? You're young, beautiful, talented, and intelligent, you have everything in the world, and you have absolutely nothing to cry about."

☪

Holding two Demerol on her tongue, Lauren again heightened her stupor. "Will this nightmare ever end? If I get out of this bed and see Sybille, I'm pretty certain I'll kill her." Lauren schemed in a moment of lucidity. "I've got to figure out what to do with my life. I've been in my room for two days without seeing anybody, I wonder if they know I'm lying in here dead. Maybe I'll light just one candle and read my birthday cards from home." By the light of the flickering candle Lauren opened a card from her father. "God, I'm so awful, would it really have been so awful to tell you about the baby? But, what if you did have Americo arrested? You used to brag on me so much, well you wouldn't be bragging now, because I've really let you down. My baby probably wouldn't have died if I had been happy and at home with Americo."

She held the next gift, staring as if she might see into it unopened. "I must be a masochist." Lauren saw the gold raven charm and wished she had thrown the package away.

> *Dearest Lauren,*
> *Happy Eighteenth Birthday, You're legal!*
> *Well, sort of legal.*
> *I found this charm in a store in Sedona, and it reminded me of our night together. I'll never forget it. I wear the feather in my hat all of the time, but I'm thinking of putting it away, because I don't want to lose it.*
> *I'm waiting to talk to you. I still don't understand. I dropped out of school because I feel like there's something wrong with you. I feel frozen in place, waiting and worrying. I still think we're connected, because I think I feel what you're feeling.*
> *I'll finish school this summer, and then I'm heading to Mexico, with or without you. I need to know more about that part of my history. I think there's something there for me, don't know what.*
> *I love you, Bruja, and nothing has changed for me. I still want you to be my woman someday. I know how young you are, so have some fun, and then come home to me.*
> *Love, A*

Her heart hardened, and Lauren decided he should be the first person to know her plans.

"I might as well let him get on with his life without me, a liar, a thief, and a murderer." Lauren found her pink, water-marked stationary in the bureau drawer, sat at her desk, set her chin and wrote the letter.

*Hi Americo,*

*Thanks tons for the bracelet and the charms. I wear them all of the time. I almost lost my bracelet the other night at a party when I was dancing. I tell everybody my best friend from home sent it to me and when I show my friends your picture they think you're really handsome.*

*I probably either had the flu or a hangover when you were worried about me. You better get your butt back in school. Don't wait for me because I've turned into a total flake as far as guys go, if you know what I mean. I'm way too young to get serious.*

*I've made a decision, and you are the first to know. By the time you get this letter, I'll be gone. I hate school, so I'm running away. Everybody does it, don't they? Watch for me flying over on my broom, I'll be the one with a black and white cat. I don't know where I'm going or when I'll be home, but when I see you again, I'll kick your ass in poker. Wait and see! I'll send you letters from wherever I am, probably just as I'm about to leave.*

*Do you still spin now that I'm gone? Now, I'm just spinning in circles, having fun. Do you still like the Grateful Dead? Be good but not too good, if you know what I mean. Are Sunnie and Trey still doing it all of the time? Have a puff for me, OK?*

*Your Friend, Lauren*

*P.S. Girls might not like it if you call them your woman. That's old fashioned, Americo. You know how we women's libbers are. Really, person-ally, I wouldn't mind it, but then I'm crazy and we both know it. Ha Ha.*

In the semi-darkness, Lauren stood in front of the mirror looking at the outline of her body. She held the candle in her hand moving it across her face, staring into the huge pupils of her eyes. Staring through the dark tunnel surrounding her vision, she saw a faint almost faded memory of the night Americo made love to her and told her she had suns shining in her eyes. "Well, that sun has died out. No wonder I feel so cold."

Standing in front of the mirror, Lauren examined the fullness of her breasts. Noticing the new roundness of her hips, she felt them with her hand remembering his cheek resting on her belly. "I don't look like a teenager anymore." As she felt the hollowness of her cheeks, she realized her appearance had changed. "I think I look more like Grandma now."

When Lauren looked at the picture of Americo on her mirror, she felt a stirring deep inside of herself. The feeling came from deep in her core and it had nothing to do with Americo. She thought of her Grandmother, Eve the apple tree, the Vortex, the red rocks, the story of Beloved Woman, the compost pile, the chocolate cake, the spiral garden, and her spindle pendulum.

"That's me, whatever I'm feeling is me, and I can't lose that because if I do, I really will want to die." Lauren didn't define it until three years later, but at that moment she knew the driving force in her life was not sex, but sexual creative energy.

Thinking of graduation night she asked herself, "If I could wave my magic wand and make it all go away, would I?" When she visualized him looking down at her while making love, she answered, "No." Lauren clasped the small gold feather to her bracelet and made a vow. "The day I take this bracelet off, I'll know I don't love him anymore." Lauren compared how she looked to the photograph on the mirror. "I looked so pretty the night of my graduation." Lauren said with finality to her reflection in the mirror, "That girl is dead."

Systematically, as if in a trance, Lauren went through her drawers, coldly throwing out anything that wouldn't fit in her backpack and satchel. Throwing down the purple sweatshirt of her brothers, she thought to herself, "If I'm going to live in this spinning nightmare, I don't want anything to slow me down. If I'm going to carry everything by myself, I might as well make it a light load." Stuffing the photographs in her satchel, she took a final look at Americo's face.

"Who has time to grieve? Hah, not me. I've got to get moving. I don't care what the doctor told me, if I kill myself or somebody else, so what? I've already murdered a little baby because I didn't take him home to his daddy." With her heart hardening and her mind clearing, Lauren recalled one of her father's favorite sayings. "I remember your words, Daddy, and I'm pretty sure I know what you meant. Those who travel alone, travel the fastest." Zombie like, sitting at her desk, with her back straight as an arrow, Lauren made a list. She made no unnecessary motions. Setting her chin defiantly, she allowed her future to unfold. First, she wrote letters to her family and her mother. Next, she planned her escape.

At the top of her list in bold letters she wrote: **Do It On Your Own**. Next on the list was get birth control pills, marked by a star. Try to have fun for a year or so, find some magic, and try to forget. Then go home to Sedona. When I get home this is what I need to do: Get a job, buy a car, find a boyfriend, act happy, and get my ass in school. And never forget, don't tell anybody anything, and don't take shit from anybody, ever again.

*"Dolls, I know you aren't here but I'm pretty sure you can still hear me. If I ever forget my list, will you remind me? I guess it wasn't a love story after all, but I'll be happy again someday. Make sure everything is OK at home. I miss you.*

*"Do you remember me telling you about the Princess? Well, the Princess is pretty sad right now and it looks like she's going to get lost for a while. The nurse told me I needed to cry, but Sybille tells me I don't have any reason to cry, because I'm lucky. Maybe she's right, because I can't. That's OK though, cuz don't fairy tales always have happy endings? Ha Ha."*

☪

# Life Really Starts to Spin

*All wandering is from the mother, to the mother,
in the mother - Nor Hall*

The sweet, poignant calm before the storm had long past. The unexpected early March storm was ominous and on the wings of black clouds raged tragedy and bad news. The winds were howling and the chimes were chiming as Rita listlessly closed the shutters and stoked the fire in the potbelly stove. Rita was agitated, something was stirring and pulling the last shutter closed; she knew her fears were for Lauren.

The revving motor of America's jeep startled Rita from her concerns. With their heavy footsteps creaking the wood plank porch, her grandsons raced to the door. Trey twirled Rita around, teasing his Grandmother for going barefoot while cold snow fell outside. Preoccupied by her fears, Rita fixed hot chocolate and sandwiches for their lunch, not wanting to dampen the spirits of the adventurous young excited by a precious late winter day on the slopes.

Life on a ranch has a flavor of its own. There is no separation between work and leisure, nor are there are set hours of a work-day. The laws of nature dictate the schedule on a ranch, along with the hours of daylight and emergencies in the dark hours of night. Everything depends on the livestock, the weather, and the whims of the people.

The home is the office, the gathering place, the retreat, and even a place to nurse sick newborns. As Rita paced, wringing her hands, she remembered the baby lamb in the laundry room need-ed feeding. Stirring and stirring, Rita stared at the rich mixture of formula heating in the copper pot, realizing that saving the baby lamb's life may mean the life or death of one of her own. After care-fully pouring the precisely warmed sustenance into a liter bottle, Rita gently lifted the head of the weak lamb and offered the large nipple to the soft lips of the infant. As she held the lamb's head on her lap, she stroked the fine wool with her hand and felt the life force strengthening as she channeled energy into it's weakened body. Rita prayed for the lamb and to the lamb. As she prayed, she made a promise that the life of the lamb would hold special mean-ing and would not be without profound purpose. Rita's tears fell, mixing with the small droplets of saliva resting on the baby's chin as she envisioned the story of Lauren's life, seeing images of a spinning spiral path marked by many doors, some open and some closed.

"If you live, precious lamb, I'll spin your strands of wool into threads for Lauren's life story weaving. Using rose-petals, I'll dye some of the strands pink. Other strands I'll dye light green with leaves from the willow tree, and petals from the iris will make a beautiful purple. I'll use silver thread for the moon and for the spi-ral and stars; I'll weave in threads of gold, real gold. The back-ground will be dyed from the red soil and for the sky..." She pon-dered, "For some reason you came to me now when I'm missing her so much."

Rita was alone on El Rancho de las Estrellas, and these moments were precious. Unlike other women, Rita did not lose her husband to hours on a job, so therefore, she did not have set hours each day for herself. Quietly and softly, as she made herself available for his needs and desires, she wove her spinning and weaving into the warp of Zack's life. Rita was never seen at work and yet, magically, her home held the ambiance of peace and tranquility. Fresh flowers brightened every room and light from candles flickered, casting mysterious shadows on the walls. The potbelly stove was ablaze in the winter, and the windows thrown ecstatically open in the spring. Zack's pipe and journal rested by his easy chair and the skeins of yarn behind her spinning wheel caused the wall to vibrate with color and promise. Rita's weavings adorned the walls, enhancing the tranquility with mysterious symbols and stories.

Everything in Rita's home glistened, yet nothing was polished. The floors were covered with woven rugs and a soft, white chenille spread, with a pastel orange afghan rested on the high poster bed. Lace hung over the windows in stark contrast to Zack's cowboy hats that hung on a wall in the living room. Zack's rugged boots lined the wall by the front door coat tree, protected by Rita's embroidered shawls draped sensuously from above. Polished copper pots hung on the wall of the kitchen and the coffee pot was always full. Most often there was a sweet delicacy baking in the oven waiting for a visitor to share the magic of Rita's kitchen. Usually, one could hear the whirring of Rita's oak spinning wheel in the living room and see the outdoor gardens through the picture windows. It was a portal to serenity, quiet, and enchantment. Whenever one entered the sanctuary, they were transported to realms rarely accessed.

Rita knew the secret. She had been born knowing the secret. Ritual is not something to be performed; it is something to be lived. One could pass Rita on the street, find her in her spiral garden, or see her staring into the fire with her drop spindle in her hand and you would never stop, point and say, there's a Witch. No, being a natural Witch, she knew about the nature of props and persona and she had little use for either one. Rita knew that props, rather than calling in the magic, dropped veils between herself and the mystery. To all who asked her about the secret, she would tell them, "The mystery is my story, nothing more and nothing less." There were no divisions in Rita's day. There was not a time set aside for prayer, meditation, cooking, sewing, spinning, weaving, making love, making bread, serving cocktails to her husband, or nursing a newborn in desperate need. Time was all time, no time, and any time. Everything she touched received the same degree of love and respect. For Rita, there were no clocks, no judgments or priorities, only surrender and love. Every action was entered in a frequency determined only by her personal intent. As Rita sat on the rag rug nursing the baby lamb, she had a vision of Lauren.

Wearing a knit hat on her head, a purple scarf around her neck, and a backpack on her back, Lauren sat on steps carved into a rugged hillside overlooking the sea. Lauren held the gold spindle Rita gave her, watching it rotate and stop. Rita heard Lauren's question.

In answer, the pendulum moved east to west as Lauren's lifeless eyes stared vacantly, not seeming to focus. Looking closer, Rita noticed a difference in Lauren's expression. There was a look of maturity, and she seemed more womanly, sad and yet serene, accepting, and uncontrolled. Rita had seen the expression before, and she knew there was only one experience that gave a woman access to the particular veil of wisdom cloaking Lauren. It was a cloak of honesty, vulnerability, and surrender, and she knew Lauren stood at a crossroads. Rita cried out. "Lauren, please go to the left, the west."

As if hearing her Grandmother's words, Lauren turned her head to the left. Still unfocused, she serenely smiled her acceptance, then put the spindle back around her neck, tucking it carefully under her shirt. Lauren stood on the hillside as little tears glistened, then retreated. Shouldering her pack, she turned to the right.

☪

Lauren held her own gaze ruthlessly and defying herself to sacrifice her plans, she looked in the mirror, knowing today she would make her escape. Speaking to her reflection in the mirror, she followed the path the spindle beckoned. With hard finality in her voice she closed another door. "They don't know the new me, because I don't have the right to have fun or be silly anymore. That girl is dead."

Systematically she layered a pair of shorts and skimpy top over her bikini. Next, she put on a pair of jeans and two t-shirts, one long sleeved and one short sleeved. A long flowered skirt covered her jeans, and she tied an Irish cable knit sweater around her shoulders. Birth control pills were in her satchel along with her letters and pictures from home. Her money and passport were in a money belt under her clothes. With a look on her face that said,

"Don't fuck with me, I'm crazy and I'll try anything," Lauren ran away.

Lauren had made a decision to live by choice not surrender. She had purchased a ticket to the United States and put most of her cash in a vault at the bank. Taking enough money to last a short time, she decided she would reconsider her choice in a few months. Looking in the mirror a last time she offered herself courage. "If I can just get through the next few days, I know I'll be able to do anything. Pain can't last forever and if I just put it away somewhere inside of me, pretty soon I'll forget." She had two keys to the vault; one hung on the chain around her neck and the other was under a sticky piece of duct tape inside her backpack. Her pack was old, nothing she wore was new or conspicuous, and with her sleeping bag strapped to her backpack she was prepared for anything. Lauren left the home of her mother with a gold charm bracelet on her wrist and a gold spindle hanging from a chain around her neck. Even when running away from herself there were some things she couldn't leave behind. After tossing a note to Sybille on her pillow, Lauren walked the streets of Monaco.

> *Sybille,*
> *Wish me luck. My son is dead, you're dead and*
> *if I'm lucky, soon I'll be dead too.*
> *Lauren*

Remembering Rita's advice, Lauren walked. As she walked she stopped thinking and became one with the streets, the people, and the sea. She disappeared. Hours passed as she sat in the Chapel of Mercy, alone and quiet. Lauren sent messages to her family from the Exotic Garden, walking among the cacti that reminded her of home. The mysterious limestone formations in the Observatory Cave transported her to a part of herself that was not attached to the world, as she knew it.

Rita knew she had to walk. The blustering storm couldn't deter her, for she needed solace for the coming news. More than anything, she feared for her husband and son. Rita did not use props, but she did use tools, tools to help her access the frequency she needed to enter. She also wore a bracelet, a gold charm bracelet that was her portable altar. Removing the bracelet from her arm, she held it next to her heart and then over a candle.

Bundling up against the elements, Rita wore a bright red wool scarf covering her silver hair and a woven cloak, seldom seen by others, covered her clothes. Resenting the winter boots between her feet and the Earth, she scooted hurriedly towards her special place among the red rock folds near her home. The wind was at her back, accelerating her speed. A small rabbit scurried back and forth across the trail as if guiding her home. She stopped, touched a charm on her bracelet, the doorway opened and Rita entered.

☾★

Zack, Tomas, and Jake, each lost in their own thoughts, drove home silently from the coffee shop. Jake held an opened letter from Lauren, while others, addressed to Americo and her grandparents, rested on the dash. Zack's Saturday morning tradition of sharing coffee and news with his sons had ended in heartbreak when Jake read the letter from Lauren aloud.

Still handsome at ninety, Zack held his cowboy hat and took Jake's elbow as they made their way up the old wood steps. Concerned about Americo, Tomas followed, knowing Lauren's news would further devastate his son who seemed already on a path of self-destruction. Surprised to find Rita away from the house and nothing baking in the oven, Zack asked Tomas to pour more coffee. Cold with fear, Jake stood by the window as though expecting to see Lauren walk through the gate.

Stopping to touch the velvety petals of purple pansies in old clay pots decorating the steps, Rita listened to chimes hanging from bare branches in the trees. The picket railing wore snow flake white hats, causing Rita to wonder whom the soldiers were guarding. As she tiptoed up the red painted steps, the door opened and her son met her, his body shaking, as he could no longer contain the tears she felt on her cheek. Needing the comfort of his wife, Zack pulled Rita to his lap before handing her the letter. Before opening the pink envelope Rita asked Sunnie to pour a glass of sherry.

The baby lamb needed feeding and again Rita offered the nipple to the baby. "Lauren, the threads that connect you to your home are stretched and thin, but you are still tied to us and to the Vortex. You will never be released, no matter how far away you go."

The questions in Trey and Americo's eyes contradicted the healthy red on their cheeks when they walked into Rita's home where the family gathered. The bad news vibrated across the room and Trey immediately noticed his father's tears. Tomas Rios motioned for Americo to sit by him on the couch and handed him the letter from Lauren.

Sunnie started to cry as she held Trey in her arms. "It's Lauren, she's run away."

Americo held the letter, and afraid to open it, he stared at the familiar handwriting. He paled and the high energy he felt after a day on the slopes drained from his body. Americo looked at each person hoping for connection and panic rose in his chest. His eyes were clouded with confusion and vulnerable, he looked at his mother as a young boy might, wishing she could comfort him, yet knowing she couldn't. Americo stuffed the letter from Lauren in his pocket, looked at his father for reassurance and then leaned back on the couch, staring at Jake. He gripped the coffee mug, holding on to it as a lifeline. The room darkened, he couldn't see the details, just outlines of the people and the potbelly stove. The room was full, yet seemed empty because there was something missing, and it was the girl he loved.

Americo felt a cold, empty space to his left side as he watched Trey and Sunnie offering each other comfort. It was a space waiting to be filled and until the last few moments he believed he was saving it for Lauren. It is a space one saves for a mate, the space for the vibrations that match your own and when empty, can become filled with the unwanted. The space one holds for a loved one that remains unoccupied becomes a place haunted with poignant longing, waiting, hoping, and expectation. Tomas broke the silence as he stood to take his wife and son home. Nobody said a word, but everybody knew a heart had been shattered, a young man had received a blow that he couldn't respond to and again, silence fell over the room.

☾★

Still high, Americo Rios groaned as he rolled over and looked at the long, blonde hair of the pretty cheerleader in his bed, remembering their acid trip the night before. He shook the girl's shoulder, feeling rude and disgusted. "Goddamn shit, I had sex with Annie last night pretending she was Lauren and that's a bull-shit thing to do."

Americo couldn't remember if he had won or lost during the poker game the night before. "How in the hell did a one night poker game turn into a three-day binge?" Panicked, he tossed dirty clothes and food boxes to the side and looked desperately around the room for his felt hat, worried that the raven feather might be missing. Running his tongue over his gritty teeth he sat on the edge of the bed holding his head in his hands. "Fuck, I'm really screwing up, I should have stayed in school this semester."

Americo growled abruptly, waking Annie. "Hey, wake up, we've got to get out of here. Get up and I'll take you back to your dorm. It's almost 9:00 and I've got to head home and get some fresh air, because I feel like shit." Americo's voice was hoarse, and he ran his fingers anxiously through his tangled black hair. "I'll shower first, and then I'll clean up the mess in this fucking room while you get yourself together." He looked at his white lips and stared at his swollen, red eyes in the mirror. Hating himself as he stood by the dirty sink, he swore to his reflection in the mirror. "You stupid, fucking bastard."

The steaming water streamed over Americo's tired body as he felt a wave of dizziness pass through him. "Christ, why is it, every time I think of Lauren, I feel like I'm spinning out?" Leaning his head against the tiles, with his hands on the back of his neck wait-ing for the sensation to pass, he wondered once again, "What in the hell is going on with her, I know damn well something's wrong. Where in the hell is she now?" Americo grabbed the thin gray washcloth and tried to scrub away the traces of the last three nights from his body, knowing he had to make a decision. Hating the feel of his dirty white shirt, Americo realized he was in descent. "I'm only twenty-three years old, and I shouldn't feel this hammered." Feeling a stabbing pain in his gut, he wondered if he should see a doctor.

Americo snapped at Annie when he walked out of the bath-room and saw her picking up wine bottles, pizza boxes and empty-ing ashtrays. "Annie, I told you I'd do that, it's my goddamn room. If you want to shower, hurry up, cause I'm leaving here in fifteen minutes. Damn it, don't cry, I told you if you wanted to go out with me again; you had to accept the fact that I love Lauren. I didn't kid you, now get dressed so we can go." Opening the torn drapes to see the San Francisco Peaks Americo squinted his hung over eyes as the bright light blazed into the room. "Christ, I can't stand it in here anymore."

Driving his white Jeep down the snow sprinkled switchbacks of Oak Creek Canyon, tapping his fingers on the steering wheel, Americo felt a stirring like springtime in his body. Catching sight of the red rock formations looming over the entrance to the Sedona Valley an idea came to him. "Yup, I just might do that, I'm sure as hell wasting my time here, but right now all I want to do is take a nap. I've got to stop this shit."

Leaning his head back on the seat, Americo sat in his jeep waiting for the music to finish and saw his mother looking angrily at him from the porch. Giving her a quick peck on the cheek, Americo tried to dodge her questions. "Sorry, Ma, the game just lasted a little longer than I thought it would." Seeing the look of concern on her face he gave her a hug. "I'll be OK sooner or later, I've just got a little thinking to do."

Still yawning, Americo rummaged through the drawer of his nightstand looking for Lauren's letters. "Yup, I know how I'm going to make my decision." The blood soaked raven feather in his fingers stared back at him when he tenderly ran it over the palm of his hand. Stuffing the letters in his Levi jacket pocket Americo left for Cathedral Rock to make his decision. He looked to his left, thinking how right it would have felt to have Lauren sitting next to him again. Cursing the fates, Americo pulled her letters from his pocket and then lit a cigarette. "Shit, it didn't have to be like this." Blowing a smoke ring in the air, he surrendered his fate to her letters by tossing them into the air. "You make the call, Baby."

The letters landed in front of him, and he laughed wryly, recalling Lauren when she made a decision. He pointed to the letters, accepting the sign. "Eeny, Meeny, Miney, Mo. Well, you always told me to follow the signs, so here I go, Princess." Feeling defeated he put the letters in his pocket, saying goodbye to no one in particular, "Goodbye Sedona, goodbye spinning game, I won't be seeing you for awhile."

Rummaging in the barn Americo found an old saddlebag he remembered Zack hanging on the wall years ago. The old saddlebag now cleaned, he took it back to his room and sitting on his bed Americo carefully laid out his most precious belongings. He found a green bandana in his drawer and wrapped the raven feather he used to make love to Lauren. He kissed a lock of her hair in a small silver box and stuffed it in his pocket. Americo put his lucky dollar bill in his wallet, hoping to use it for some liar's poker along the way. The Magician Tarot card fit perfectly in the side pocket, along with the deck of cards Zack gave him for his eighteenth birthday. Hurrying, he stuffed his journal and a few pens and pencils in the compartment and took his savings account passbook from his nightstand drawer. Americo wistfully checked his empty wallet. "I don't know how long $4,203.75 will last me. I don't know yet if I can make a living playing poker, so far I've done just OK."

He checked his stash of pot and thought ironically about his destination. "This ought to be enough to get me to the border." Looking under his bed for his camping gear he saw his fishing pole. With a half grin, he imagined himself fishing for his dinner. "Why not? If blow my money at the poker table, I'll feed myself by fishing."

The rusty gate chimed Americo's arrival and with a postcard from Lauren in her hand, Sunnie ran to greet him. They whispered together quietly, wondering why Lauren was in Crete. Twirling Sunnie around, Americo felt a wave of homesickness already enveloping him. Arm in arm they walked into the cozy warm ranch house kitchen where the family gathered for drinks. When Americo walked into the room with purpose, Jake and Americo's mother lifted their heads and looked at him expectantly. Taking a deep breath and sticking his hands in his pockets, he took the family by surprise when he looked directly at his mother and Jake. "I've made a decision, and I don't want to hear any crap about it because my jeep is packed, and I'm ready to leave. After I go to the bank in the morning, I'm leaving for Mexico and I don't have any idea how long I'll be gone. I'm just going to drift around for awhile."

Unaware, Americo bent a spoon in half. "Jake, I love Lauren, I really do and she's not coming home for a long time." Brushing his hair from his eyes and blinking to hold back the tears, he continued, "I've been in love with her for three years, if not longer, but I've got to get out of here and get my head on straight or I'm going to ruin my life. I can feel it happening and I'm scared. She wrote and told me she loved me too, Jake, it's not like it's just me."

Giving Rita a hug, he heard her whisper, "I understand completely what you're going through. Circumstances, Americo, you have to trust them. Lauren will be home to stay someday and so will you. When the time is right, I'll spin both of you back home. One day we'll see her footprints in my garden and know our Princess is back to stay."

The fragrance of dinner made Americo homesick and again, his heart started to break. "Grandma Rita, feed me, I've been living on cigarettes, booze, and cold pizza for three days."

The intense gaze of Lauren's grandfather interrupted Americo's time with Rita and when the crusty, old gambler motioned for Americo to join him in the living room, Americo was certain Zack would try to stop him. Looking down at the floor, twisting the toe of his boot, he said in a hushed tone, "I'll be fine; I've got to get over Lauren because she's really messed with my head."

Zack affectionately hugged Americo, recalling how quick and adept he was at the game. "You're a warrior, my boy, I know you will. Be prepared, like I've told you so many times. The game of love, like the game of poker, is the game of life and you are beginning the most important game you will ever play. I trust you'll remember what I've taught you. Stay as long as you need, gather your power and make a plan, a plan you can change on a second's notice."

Americo spent his last night on the rancho alone in the Casino. With twisting, entwining images, his cigarette smoke surrounded him as he spoke to Lauren. "Baby, I guess I better write you one more letter. I'll send it to your mother's house, hope you get it someday." Roughly Americo ripped a page out of his journal and wrote quickly, not wanting to stop his heart from breaking.

> *Dearest Lauren,*
>
> *I'm leaving tomorrow for Mexico. I'm following the signs. Write to me at my parents address, they'll know where I am.*
>
> *I can't spin without you. Keep having fun. Beware of strangers, not everybody will love you like I do. Who knows, Bruja, when we meet up again here at the rancho one day, maybe I'll still love you and maybe I won't. If we need to talk then, we will. Thanks for the memories.*
>
> *Zack gave me his bolo tie tonight. With all of my other lucky charms, including your hair and the feather, how can I lose? Wish me luck and I really do love ya. A*

The instant he gripped the steering wheel, almost anybody could have stopped Americo from leaving his home, and as he looked back, he almost hoped to see his mother or Rita waving for him to stay. He was alone with a pain in his gut, and tears in his eyes. Nobody heard him drive away to the sound of gravel, rocks, and the rough growl of his jeep. Resignedly he put his baseball cap on the seat, forwarded a Creedence Clearwater Revival tape, and looking back at the red rock formations, he gunned his jeep and turned west. With only Lauren's presence to listen, he lit a cigarette and said, "Do it for me, Lauren, someday put another candle in the window just like you did the night of your graduation."

Twelve hours later, tired and dirty, Americo Rios arrived at the old hacienda near Guaymas, Mexico, where their great grandfathers collaborated during the revolution. Sitting in the courtyard watching the scurrying chickens, the only residents of the broken down property, he said to himself. "Someday never comes, or so they say. You might as well go for the gusto, Rios, because you've got nothing left to lose." Forlornly opening a warm cerveza and lighting a cigarette, Americo sent a message to Lauren via the stars. "This is where it all began for you and me, Bruja." He offered a toast to their grandfathers and as he raised his beer bottle to the sky he said, "Here's to Saul Rios and Jackson Auldney, thanks for the beginning." As he looked at the starry sky, another message was sent to Lauren, "Without everything that happened here, we would never have met and I can't help but wonder, now that we're both so fucked up, where it will end."

Americo considered restoring the hacienda, hoping he might restore the love of life he had already lost. "Maybe I ought to put this old place back together while I'm trying to put my life back in order. Buena Suerte, good luck, my beautiful, young, goofy bruja, wherever you are," were the words he sent to Lauren.

☾★

A soft blue sky hovered and waited for the Goddess of Empathy to drop a veil over the harsh details of life, allowing the illusions to linger through the dark, lonely night. Near the hippie caves near Matala, on the west coast of Crete, the Earth turned slowly towards the seductive buzz where candles were burning low, dripping layers of colored wax over the porous boulders. The porous boulders were receptive and absorbed the fragrance of incense and pot as the young people in the commune stirred, waiting to gather for the full moon celebration. The soft goat milk cheese and sticky baklava were shared, and cheap wine was sipped from jewel colored bottles. Small handmade gifts from the farmers market were exchanged, and promises were made for the night. Spirits were high, the drugs were plenty and the rules were few. The moon of the Vernal Equinox made a promise, a promise to witness their dance of life. Life was being renewed, and hope burned deep in the hearts of the young and disillusioned. Among them was a young runaway who didn't believe in hope, her heart was broken and she was alone.

The sun had fallen over the horizon, and the stars were brilliant in the distant sky. The reflected light of the moon danced on the tips of waves lapping rhythmically on the shore. The air was chilly. The drummer beat his drum slowly. The drumbeat pulsed, calling the hippies to dance. They danced in a processional, a snaking, winding pattern around the bonfire. Within a spiral she made on the beach, Lauren mesmerized her companions, dancing on her toes, twirling like a ballerina. An axis, a small labrys she bought at the market stood in the center of the spiral, providing a focal point as Lauren spun. Lauren's feet danced gracefully on the hundreds of fresh flowers offered by the dancers, and she shook her tambourine in harmony with the chanting in the background. She danced with her arms wide open, wiggling her fingers, reaching for something nobody else could see. Her bare feet squished the wet sand and she shook her hands in the air with a rhythm that matched the waves lapping on the rocky shore. She danced ecstatically to the heartbeat sound of the drums as the hippies watched the fire flicker over her shapely body.

Lauren took a breath and then shuddered as she stood still in the center of the spiral. She gazed at the Earth and with her arms at her side harmonized her energy with the Vortex of Sedona. She surrendered to the vibrations of the Vortex, and the filaments of her energy body sparkled, pulsing with the light of the stars. Shuddering as she felt a wave of ecstasy, Lauren saw a vision of her Grandmother with her drop spindle, spinning the strands of her life into a thread of yarn. Lauren danced in circles, tossing her hair in complete abandon. The cells in her body danced when she matched her serpentine movements to those of the Milky Way. She held her face to the dark and opened her fingers wide to catch energy from the stars. Lauren bent at the waist to place her fingers on the sand, releasing star filaments to the Earth. She closed her eyes, sacrificing herself to the whole.

Lauren rocked her hips to the rhythm of the waves, matching her movements to the element. She circled her hips as if meeting a lover. She touched her fingers to her face, knowing the hands she felt were not hers. She ran her fingers through her long hair, slowly and passionately. She lifted her face with a small smile on her heart shaped lips, waiting for his kiss. She was remembering Americo.

Lauren saw his face smeared with streaks of red Sedona mud

as he sat in his jeep after a day of four wheeling. She saw his white dress shirt glowing in the moonlight. She saw the look of passion on his face when they made love. Feeling his lips and hands on her face, she squeezed her eyes and shook her head, wishing she could release the tears that throbbed insistently behind her eyes. The scent of cinnamon wafted through her senses as she felt her cheek resting on his chest when they danced. Lauren watched as he walked towards her, swaggering his hips, wearing his rust color cowboy hat. She saw him sitting confidently on his Appaloosa horse while carefully making his way down a difficult trail. She felt the vibrations from his sweaty body as they stood by the fence overlooking the rancho. Lauren saw him holding a door open as if waiting. She smiled sadly and looking into his eyes, she shut the door and danced.

Lauren twirled wildly in place making her yellow and pink flowered skirt fan open. "Grandma, you always told me to dance from the heart." Yellow flowers were tossed in the air. "Dancing is like making love or having a baby, because it renews our life. You said a woman must dance to attune the vortex in her womb to the cosmos, because everything is alive and everything dances. You told me that I could reach ecstasy if I released heavy energy through my feet and let it descend into the body of the greedy Mother. Only then can the light in my body be released and ascend to the stars." Lauren stomped the sand in perfect rhythm, forcing the sadness to descend from her feet. "When I dance, I'm free. When I stop, I go away."

☪

The chaos of the commune was unbearable to Lauren and even the patient lulling of the sea could not still the longing she felt for solitude. Sitting by herself, lost in memories, she longed for the harmonious setting of the country home on the large, nearby farm. The next day would be Lauren's last in the hippie cave commune, and she felt eager to spend time at the home of Beatricia Cholis, a woman she met in Iraklion the first day she arrived on the ferry. Lauren had found her first job and for a month she was going to work as a maid for the wife of the wealthy landowner.

Lauren giggled when she watched the beekeeper gathering honey from the hives. Asking if she could help, Lauren put long gloves on her hands and arms and said, "I can do that." Lauren said happily as she took the left over food from the kitchen to the compost pile behind the barn, "I can do that. My Grandma let me stir the compost pile at home every week. She told me about the magic that happens inside." Lauren mixed the ingredients together for a rich, gooey, chocolate cake. "I can do that, I used to help my Grandma in the kitchen all of the time. The oven is like a woman, Beatricia, it makes magic if you put the right ingredients together and stir it just enough." Lauren took the broom from Beatricia's hand. "I can do that. Grandma says it's very important to sweep your house everyday. She says it cleans the energy as well as the floors. I think it always feels better after the house is swept. Now we should go outside for a little while and give the house a chance clean itself of any bad energy. I've already put fresh flowers in every room, so they can work their magic while we sit on the porch. I can do that," Lauren told Beatricia, as she weeded the kitchen garden. "It's easy if the moon isn't full. My Grandma told me that the Earth releases when the moon moves to the other side."

Beatricia sat down by Lauren and kindly told her that she didn't have to try so hard to please everybody. Lauren was stunned. "I thought I did."

A day alone, shopping in the farmers market lifted Lauren's spirits. Beatricia watched Lauren walking home with a cloth tied around her shoulders like a peasant woman; Lauren not realizing her burden was already showing. Excitedly Lauren emptied the cloth to show Beatricia the gifts she bought at the market. "Look what I found, I found a charm like the labrys you have hanging above the front door. Will you clip it onto my bracelet for me?"

Enchanted by the young woman who shared so little of her feelings and experiences, Beatricia was happy when Lauren showed her another gift. Lauren unfolded a small wool rug and then tenderly picked some lint from the center symbol. "Look what else I found. This is for my boyfriend; no, I mean my best friend." Lauren pleaded with her eyes for Beatricia not to question her. "I'm going to send it to him when I leave here. There's a labrys woven into the design." Holding the cloth woven from gray, blue and gold threads, Lauren looked at Beatricia with questioning eyes. "I gave him a special small rug before I left home and this will be the second one for his collection. I'm going to buy a little rug for him wherever I go." Beatricia had never seen Lauren so animated and it was the first time Lauren had mentioned a boy.

The next day, Beatricia found Lauren sitting at the outdoor table, playing in mud and asked what she was doing. Not taking her eye from her project, she answered, Beatricia having never heard her speak so excitedly. "I'm making a doll for you and one for my Grandma. The Goddess comes from the land so what better material could I use? I can't wait to go home and make dolls from the red soil there. My Grandma would love a doll like that. I just know she would. I have lots of dolls at home, and I talk to them every night before I go to sleep. They know all of my secrets. See all of the little sticks and stones I found. I'm going to make them a part of the doll. Do you like it so far?"

The last evening Lauren worked on the farm, they sat on the veranda sipping lemon verbana tea and eating oatmeal cookies Lauren baked that afternoon. Beatricia told her how much she was going to miss her and told her that she was a fortunate young woman to have been raised by a wise Grandmother. When she inquired about her mother, Lauren was shocked at her own response. "My mother is dead; she died when I was eight years old." Crinkling her nose like a naughty child, Lauren tried to explain the Vortex to her friend. "We live in a Vortex, and she keeps us spinning around, so I guess that's why I'm so mixed up."

> *Dear Grandma and Grandpa,*
> *I'm leaving the island of Crete today, but I can't tell you where I'm going. I've already met some really cool people, especially the woman I worked for while I was here. Grandma, she reminded me of you, only she wasn't as pretty. I lived in a cave with some hippies for a while, but I didn't like it very much. There was too much confusion, and it didn't feel like home. I still haven't found what I'm looking for, but I have a feeling I will pretty soon. I'll let you know. Say Hi to everybody. I love you and I'm fine. Grandma, we have matching charms now. I hope you like yours. It's called a labrys and I'll tell you about it when I get home.*
> *Love, Lauren*

☪

Broken hearted and alone again, Lauren walked the streets of Monaco. Bearing the weight of her backpack she climbed the hillside and stood outside her mother's villa, wondering if she should confess her crime, take the punishment and return home to Sedona, having failed at her adventure. "I should feel like a school girl now, instead of tired, dirty, and alone. In a way I'm just killing time so I don't have to face Americo, but he wouldn't even care, cause he's probably got a new girlfriend."

To pass the days Lauren wandered the streets, looking in shop windows and admiring attractive tourists as they filled the afternoon shopping in elegant stores and sipping wine in the restaurants. She stopped as she looked in the window of a small gallery and saw the same black haired man she had watched for two days. The intense looking man working over his small work bench seemed deep in concentration, until he raised his eyes and held her gaze. "Who are you, my young sister with the stormy sea in your eyes?" Benito Yupanqui asked with his heart as he looked at the forlorn girl staring at him. "I want to know your story, the one you've lived in this life. I see many shadows in your eyes, far too many for one so young."

Lauren answered him with her eyes. "I want to tell you my story, because I think I've been waiting my whole life to look into your eyes. Who are you and where have you been?" Energy connected them as he motioned for her to join him in the gallery. Benito spoke to her in a low, melodic voice and scanned her energy body with his deep, slanted, dark eyes. "What is your story, my young friend? Why do you watch me instead of going to classes or visiting with your friends? Why are you alone on such a beautiful day?"

Shyly, Lauren sat down her backpack and looked at him. "Who are you? Why do you want to know my story?"

Benito chuckled as he continued polishing an exquisite earring. Speaking as a matter of fact, he told Lauren, "We meet people unexpectedly who are part of our family. I have often wondered when I would meet my sister again."

Lauren didn't know what to say to the stranger who didn't feel like a stranger.

He smiled at her with reserve. "Welcome home, hermana, it's been a long time."

Lauren spoke to him in broken Spanish. "When I looked at you through the window, I told myself I had been waiting my whole life to meet you."

Benito laughed wryly, acknowledging her age. "Well, that hasn't been very long. You are an old soul, but you are very young in years."

Lauren felt a void in her life being filled. "How do you know I'm an old soul?"

"I know everything about you from reading your energy body. I am from the Andes of Peru and that is how we greet people. I suppose you could say we are cautious because if we don't like what we see, we look the other way, and that is the end of the contact. I am Benito Yupanqui, and como se llame?"

"My name is Lauren Auldney. I ran away from my home, and a few months ago, I had a baby boy who died. I didn't tell my boyfriend and I'm afraid and alone." Lauren's cheeks blazed red as she turned away from him. "Why did I tell him? I haven't told anybody, not even Beatricia."

A lovely Spanish looking woman walked gracefully into the gallery and stopping his conversation with Lauren, Benito stood to greet her. Kissing the woman with undisguised passion, he introduced her to Lauren. "My woman, Feliciana Mora. Lici, I want you to meet my sister, Lauren. She has traveled for many hundreds of years to find me and it's time for us to take her home." Benito pointed to his goldsmith bench and winked at Lauren. "She wants to come to Cuzco and spend time with her brother learning his craft."

Lauren gasped. "What? I didn't say that."

"Yes, you did. You told me with your eyes."

"But my home is in Sedona, Arizona, in the United States."

Benito made the plan, offering Lauren no escape as he explained the nature of their relationship. "That is your pacarina, your birthplace, your special place. You are my sister of the soul, Lauren, not of the body. You must understand, for me there is no difference. It doesn't matter that we have different pacarinas, because there are many things that only a brother and his woman can teach you. Is there any reason you cannot leave with us next week?"

Not knowing why she agreed to go to Cuzco, Lauren shook her head, "No."

Feliciana took Lauren's hand, looking at her dirty fingernails and the scratches on her arms.

"Sister, do you have a place to sleep, or would you like to join us in the lovely apartment the owner of the gallery provided for us?"

Again, Lauren shook her head, "No."

"I thought so. You will come with us."

In the desert of northern Sonora, alone for the first time in his life, Americo Rios made a plan. When he left Sedona, he left behind what he believed to be the best of all worlds. As a young prince, he grew tall and strong on El Rancho de las Estrellas with adoring parents, his best friends, grandparents, and the rancho he loved. As the foster grandson of Zack and Rita, Americo already had a stake in the rancho. Although he was a prince, he was not a wealthy prince, and Americo made a plan to afford a larger stake when the time came.

Zack Auldney had seen the look in Americo's eyes, the look that only another gambler recognizes and had trained Americo to play poker like a magician. Americo reached deep into his heartbreak and found a sword to carry to the games. Discipline and hard work ordered Americo's life, and the bubble of love he had been raised in remained intact, providing Americo with confidence, a sense of purpose, and a strong intent. His love for Lauren was the driving force behind his efforts and his belief that she would return to him did not waiver. There were days he wanted to despise her and others that he desperately longed for her, but regardless, Lauren was perpetually on his mind.

Americo was alone, but not lonely in Mexico. He spoke the language and had a family heritage in the area that many long time residents still recalled. His circle of friends grew as did his reputation as an excellent a poker player, and Americo did not lack the companionship of women. He kept a space in his heart and on his left for Lauren, but the space to his right was often filled by one of the young women he met in the seaside city of Guaymas. Americo's plan was well defined. He made a commitment to stay at the hacienda for five years, each year restoring a different quarter of the dwelling and the surrounding landscape.

The rugged landscape surrounding Guaymas had become a mecca for the movie industry, and the town was alive with the infusion of people from Hollywood, the money they spent, and the jobs they offered the local population. It was time for Americo Rios to put his money to work, and he vowed to every year double his money at the poker tables where the high rollers held nightly games. His stake was at stake and Americo went to the tables armed with purpose, an inner core fired by love, his skills well honed, and a disarming inner strength for one so young.

Americo's workday started early, regardless of the time his night ended. Rising with the sun he cleaned up debris that had accumulated over the years in the yard. Working alone he planted bougainvillea vines on the adobe walls surrounding the courtyard and encircled an abandoned fountain with fruit trees. When not at a game, evenings found Americo writing in his journal, drinking alone, and staring at the stars wondering where in the world Lauren wandered. His body was tired, but the hard, solitary work honed his mind and refined the skill he took to the poker tables. In the six months he lived at the hacienda, the interior of the fire-damaged building had not been touched. In the hours he walked through the dilapidated rooms, he felt the ghosts of his ancestors and waited for a sign that they were ready for him to reclaim their home.

The small family cemetery where his grandparents' rest beside Lauren's grandmother and grandfather became a place of refuge for him as he opened himself to the stories only they could tell. Every week he ritually placed flowers in the enclosure, inviting the presence of people he never knew to share his life.

Americo's charm and skill did not always serve him well. He left the tables with too much money, refused to drink with his opponents, and maintained a private life far from the community and Hollywood industry. There were those who resented his confident reserve and believing his qualities were those of arrogance and aloofness, schemed against him. Although not unaccustomed to barroom brawls, Americo rarely provoked the fight. His fists were ready but only to defend, and when he left a Friday game a winner at 2:00 in the morning, Americo was accosted from behind and beaten brutally. Left unconscious on the street, Americo was rescued by a man he had yet to meet.

Regaining consciousness, Americo felt somebody wiping his brow with a soft damp cloth. His voice was hoarse when he asked, "Who are you?" Flinching from the pain, Americo tried to make a fist. His head pounded and his stomach lurched from the taste of blood in his mouth, and slowing inching through his mind were memories of the night before. Through the slats of his eyes he looked at the woman standing over him and squinting, Americo pleaded with her. "Where's the little silver box I had in my pocket?" Barely whispering, "I have to have that, please, look around for it. It's the most important thing I own."

She taunted him with her voice. "Why is it so important?"

Just before losing consciousness again, he answered, "It's all I have of..." Fighting his way out of the black tunnel, he remembered his winnings and trying to form words with his swollen lips, he asked her, "My money, where is my money?"

The woman answered in a soft lilting voice as she wiped the sweat dripping from his hair onto his forehead. "Your money is safe with my brother. He saved you as you lie dying on the street. His name is Ignacio Verona and I am Marquita Pena. You must be very rich to have so much money in your wallet."

Questioning her veracity, Americo started to scheme. "How did he know where I live?"

She answered intriguingly. "Circumstances were favorable to you last night, Senor Americo, they brought you to us and your life will never be the same."

His head spinning, Americo closed his eyes and pulled the light serape blanket over his shoulders. Focusing on the images of the hotel in Guaymas, he recalled being attacked with his wallet full of the cash.

Marquita held a cup of hot thin soup to his lips.

"There were four of them; they jumped me when I was walking to my jeep. I guess I was too drunk to fight back, because the last thing I remember was being thrown in the backseat of a car."

"It was my brother who put you in his car, Senor Americo. He found you lying on the street unconscious, but you weren't robbed of anything. The men were just part of the circumstances and now that the role they were to fulfill has been served; you will never see them again. Sometimes power moves in mysterious ways."

Americo became impatient with her ambiguous explanation. "I don't know what in the hell you are talking about, I just want my money back and I need to see a doctor about my hand. I think it's broken. Is there any way you can contact your brother?"

Marquita mocked him. "I can heal your hand with the medicines I use. Your hand isn't broken, only your heart is broken." Continuing to speak provocatively, she told him, "I am a curendera and I use the medicines from Terra Madre. I can heal your hand and your heart, Senor Americo. Your heart is full of love for a woman who has left you, and I can help you forget her."

Americo ignored Marquita, believing he was being conned. "How can I find your brother? I want to make sure he has my money, and then I'm going to the police."

"He'll be here very soon. He's bringing food for your kitchen and then we have an offer for you."

Americo instantly liked Ignacio Verona, a gentle man and a gifted carpenter. Although Ignacio stood a head shorter than Americo, his countenance was that of a powerful man. Americo struck a deal with them and offered to provide a place to live and food in exchange for help restoring the structure of the hacienda.

Three months later, Americo stood in the courtyard with his hands on his hips, watching as Ignacio and Marquita added a finishing coat of bright blue paint to the windowsills. In a few short months, the able carpenter Ignacio Verona had transformed Americo's two room living quarters into a place of comfort and serenity, and for the first time he looked forward to living alone, comfortable in his home. An adobe fireplace in the living room added warmth to the rooms and the white washed walls were brilliant in the sunlight streaming through the windows. Bright red flowers bloomed in the large clay pots on his covered porch, and Americo felt content, something he hadn't felt in over a year.

☪

Rarely a loser, Americo felt a wave of depression lapping against his soul as he drove home from the poker match, discouraged that he had lost seven hundred dollars to an opponent he had met for the first time. As he slowed his jeep to cross a deep, dry arroyo his heart longed for Lauren and his imagination haunted him as he visualized her waiting at home for him. "Lauren, I wouldn't give a damn if I were coming home to you tonight. I can just see you in my rooms at the hacienda. There would be flowers, the smell of your incense and candles everywhere." Americo imagined the scene he longed for. "I'd walk in the door, take you in my arms and let you hold me until this feeling I have left. I need you, Lauren." Smiling half-heartedly, he imagined drops of paint on her nose. "I really wanted you to be here with me, Baby. We could have had so much fun working on this old place together. If I only knew if you were safe."

The light from a kerosene lamp in his living room window frightened Americo. Fearing that he may be in danger again, he grabbed a flashlight from his jeep and stopped as a snake slithered across his path. Americo's heart raced as he approached the door. Seeing Ignacio's sister Marquita sitting in front of his fireplace, Americo snapped. "What in the hell are you doing in my rooms, Marquita?"

Marquita stood, shook her long black hair and walked towards him in greeting. "Americo, why are you so sad? I've watched you for many weeks now and so seldom do I hear you laugh?" Americo held the door open, indicating with a nod for her to leave. Marquita stared defiantly into his eyes, with a taunting mysterious grin on her lips. "Is it only because your heart is aching for a lover you have lost?" She walked toward the fireplace, sat down and opened a woven bag. "I can help what troubles you; I know many ways to help a broken heart."

Americo yelled at her. "Hey lady, I told you before I don't want to forget about Lauren, now get the hell out of here, I want to be alone. You can't come in here uninvited and if you do it again I'll throw you off the property."

Marquita ignored his outburst, laughing slyly. "You are too young to live with your heart broken, and I will show you how to feel happy again if you will let me. But first, I have to know that you want to be happy, because what I do will never help unless you have desire."

Americo slammed the door and threw his hat on the table as Marquita continued to tempt him. "I held your sadness in my heart as I prepared the plants provided by Terra Madre to heal people of sadness. I help people die, so they can live in happiness when they return from their journey. Does what I say frighten you, because it should? If you let me help you, you will never be the same and some people fear that."

Becoming fascinated, Americo watched as she mixed ingredients in a small clay bowl.

"I will help you for as long as you want me to, Americo Rios, the handsome young man from Arizona."

Americo heard the suggestive tone in her voice and saw a look of desire in the raven-haired woman's dark eyes. Smiling softly, Marquita lit the small pipe in her hand and refused to acknowledge Americo standing at the door. Frustrated, Americo pulled her from the floor and then heard the truth in his words as he tried to explain. "Hey, Marquita, I appreciate your offer to help me. I do love a girl who doesn't love me, but I honestly don't think I want to change that. It's far too complicated for you to understand, but I still haven't given up hope for us. Now come on, get out of here."

Marquita held the pipe to his lips. "Goddamn it, Marquita, get away from me. I've taken acid enough times to know what this stuff is all about. It's a fun trip and I've opened a few doors with it, but I decided to stop doing drugs when I moved down here. I'm not in the right state of mind anyway, you shouldn't fuck with that stuff when you're down."

Americo floated above his body, lights flashed and as the smoke from the powdered mushroom plant saturated his mind he put his hands on his neck as if strangling. Trying to answer the monotone female voice, his lips were ashen as he spoke. "I see a ladder with doorways on it. The ladder's swinging, it goes on forever and my arms won't reach that far." Americo tried to reach with his right arm. "The doorways don't line up, the ladder's spinning and so am I." Still reaching, Americo screamed, "God, it's Lauren who's spinning. Lauren, hang on to my hands, Bruja, I won't let you go, I promise, here's my hand, I'm reaching as high as I can, can't you see my hand? No, No, Lauren, focus on me, don't leave." Stopping, Americo saw Lauren standing under a threshold.

Her hair turning to twisting strands of gold, he waited and Lauren paused. "Lauren, there's something shadowy following you and I don't know if it will hurt you, Baby. I can't climb the ladder, it keeps twisting and turning, I want to save you and if it would just stop or go in a straight line, I could reach you." Tears fell from his eyes as Lauren closed the door. "Why do you keep closing the doors? Damn, Lauren, stop it. Slow down. Please don't go so fast. Open your eyes and turn around or you're going to fall. No, Lauren, don't go through that door, no, not that one, please. How can you stay on the ladder while it's spinning? You're running so fast and the ladder is spiraling into the unknown. I can't see you anymore. Did you fall? No, Lauren, No, No."

Americo reached for someone close to him, laughing in relief. "Lauren, you're back, I thought you had fallen, but you were here all the time." Americo held her close, looking into her opaque eyes. "You're back with me, Bruja," he laughed with tears running down his face. "After you took my hand, it wasn't so bad was it? Kiss me like you did that first night, and then I'll hold you so you don't feel so cold. Princess, I didn't think you would ever come back to me. Let me hold you closer, so I can take care of you forever. Doesn't that feel good?"

An expression of profound awe crossed Americo's face. "Look at this, there's a strand of gold connecting us like an umbilical cord, see how it stretches and how it contracts. Lauren, lie down on the rug and let me look at your body again, I never want to forget how you look tonight." Lauren arched her back and Americo made love to her, whispering, "Bruja, your breasts are so beautiful, let me kiss you below again, I loved the taste of you. Here let me kiss you so you can taste you too. Lauren, I can see into your body and I can see threads of light in your belly. They look like the strand of gold connecting us. I love you so much, please don't go, I want to hold you again like I did the first night we made love."

Lauren left Americo as quickly as she appeared. Americo

tried to stop her from stepping onto the spiraling ladder. "Lauren, stay off of that spiraling ladder, you're so reckless, you're not holding onto anything and it's going to kill you."

Hours passed before Americo woke to sunlight in his eyes. He looked blankly into the eyes of the nude woman leaning over him. "Where is Lauren, who in the hell are you, and where in the fuck are my clothes?" Americo tucked his white shirt in his Levis and Marquita, without embarrassment, looked in his eyes as she slipped her simple cotton dress over her body.

Believing that Lauren was deeply in trouble, Americo questioned Marquita if he had really been with her. Having witnessed that Lauren had no regard for what happened to her, Americo needed to know if he could maintain the connection by taking the plant medicine Marquita offered him. Speaking with quiet dispassion, Americo addressed Marquita slowly and deliberately. "I need to know if I was making love to Lauren or to you last night, Senora Pena? I need the truth, so I can decide if I'm going to do any more of this shit with you or not."

Marquita answered with more forthrightness than he expected. "Honestly, Americo, I brought Lauren's energy into my body. The lights you saw inside of her are still in her body. You must have put them there when you made love to her. It was my physical body, so in a way you made love to both of us, but it was her face you looked at with your eyes of a puma, and I knew that. It doesn't matter to me that you love your Lauren; it isn't your love that I want." Marquita stared with bold intensity at his tall, lean body and took her time before continuing with a hint of intrigue in her voice. "I can help you, Americo, especially since a golden thread of energy connects you to her. I can help you keep that connection if you choose to, but you should know the consequences." She further enticed him. "There is a lot for you to learn, and I can take you into worlds you have never known."

☾★

There is a land of Wizards and Witches, Magicians and Mystics. There is a place on Earth where anything is possible if one is willing to see both natures of reality. It is a vertical world, where one can touch many ecozones in a single day, a land of contrast and change, from the mother ocean to the mighty apus. It is a land where people walk softly on the Earth. It is a place where people slip through the crack in the world with ease and where, if you look very carefully, you will see sloe-eyed magicians fly up the mountains, grabbing the filaments of Apu Asungate as they navigate their way to the stars. The ancients have not left this land; rather they walk side by side with those still carrying their corporality. It is a land that vibrates. The vibrations of the rain forest are languid, slow, mysterious, and filled with revolution. The midland, the agricultural valley, vibrates with the heartbeat of the mother, Pachamama. When one stands under the stars on the mist-enshrouded mountaintops, they experience vibrations that are crackling, sparkling, and quick like the footsteps of Wizards and Witches. Filament dances to the rhythm of the cosmos and on the mountaintop, there is love. The vertical world is divided in half, half to see and half to know. The right side is the world we live in, the island of our daily experience, the world of knowledge. The left side is the mystery, the larger self, the witness, wisdom, and the nagual. There is not a contradiction, only a reversal of perception. Life is lived in ritual, there is no separation between meditation and daily experience. It is a world of energy, heavy and light. It is a world of filaments, connecting all aspects of life together in a perpetual story. It is a place to learn of circumstances, perspective, and how to turn worlds upside down.

The hour flight from sea level straight into the sky, weaving between the folded lips of the Andes, alters one's perception in an instant. The air sparkles ever more brilliantly as one approaches the ancient Inca city of Cuzco, the junction of the four suyus, or regions that comprised the Inca empire. Cuzco was the axis and the center of the cosmological order of the Inca world. The energy of the city is vibrant, and the colors are vivid as the modern world weaves itself into the weft of the Quechua Indians. The Coricancha, the Temple of the Sun, the foundation for a cathedral, reminds each passerby of the conquest, the overlaying of a tradition not born of the land. The ambiance is surreal. It is a world of hyper-reality. It is a world that must be entered in a state of trust, with an open heart, a heart open to the unknown.

The driver wove his way along the crowded streets filled with honking horns, pedestrians, and spirits that gently moved to the left to allow the vehicle to negotiate the traffic. Lauren sat between Benito and Feliciana, secure in their concern and enraptured by the stories that Benito started to unwind. Benito pointed at a large statue in the center of an intersection, "Pachacuteq is known as the earthshaker. You will probably feel tremors of terramotos, earthquakes, while you are here, Lauren. Our world is always trembling; it trembles because it knows the consequences of turning upside down, both physically and culturally. We also believe we are at the beginning of a time when all perceptions will be reversed."

As they drove through Inca Square, Lici pointed out the marketplace. "Look at our marketplace, everyday is a festival, a festival of survival. The marketplace in the square and along the Avenida Sol is the hub of our society. We will take you to many marketplaces, in many towns in the campo while you are here. I love to listen to the women tell their stories as they work. Like all women, Lauren, the women of the Andes love to gossip."

Lauren's eyes were big with wonder, having entered a world of magic. As tears filled Lici's eyes she promised Lauren a special night. "But now I want to take you to our home and tonight I'll cook a special dinner before you sleep your first night under the Southern Cross. I have been so homesick for my pacarina; I know how you must feel being so far from your land."

Lauren blinked her eyes when the winding street terminated suddenly at the top of a slight incline. The mist lifted, the van stopped and they were parked in front of an enchanted cottage nestled in the trees, guarded by a gate that Benito opened with a wave of his hand. Sunlight reflected from the many large windows as Lauren stared at the small adobe home protected by a red clay bar tile roof. Benito stood at the entrance to his home with the dignity of an Inca prince. "Lauren, you have entered this experience based on trust alone and it is a journey into the unknown. One day, it may be tomorrow or it may be thirty years from now, I do not know, but you will become aware of the importance of your experience. Your life will have been changed at that moment."

Curious, Lauren looked at the symbols on his door. "What do the symbols on the door mean, Benito? I know what they are, but what do they mean?" she asked, pointing to the bolt of lightening and cauldron made of red-tinged gold metal.

Benito chuckled as he told his favorite story. "My last name means lightning and that is my calling card. The cauldron is for my woman," he said patting Feliciana's belly, "because she carries one in her body. With a flourish he opened the door. This is our home, Lauren. Please enter. Welcome my sister of the heart, for as long as you wish to stay with us."

Benito Yupanqui searched the world looking for Feliciana Mora, the woman he wanted for his own. Benito, son of a high priest, a Kuraq Alleq, walked off of the mountain at age fourteen. He had a calling, a calling from his ancestors the Inca, to spend his life working with the most precious metal, gold. Gold is his channel for the mystery. Trained in mystical practices of his people from an early age, he stands with his feet in two worlds, the traditional and the modern. Benito is a master of the right side, the seen, the pragmatic, the world of precision.

Benito saw Feliciana's face in a dream and in every city where he exhibited his art, he watched for her. He found Feliciana Mora in Madrid where she was a student doing research on her paternal ancestors. Feliciana was dancing in a club, enjoying being a young student on the town when she felt a light tap on her shoulder, a tap that jolted her back to the time when she was a young girl living in a small village. When she looked in his eyes she saw the Andes, her home.

Feliciana is the daughter of the Andean high priestess, Yoci Cela, and Javier Mora, an attorney of aristocratic Spanish ancestry. Yoci was a peon seasonal laborer on the hacienda. Javier was the heir apparent with a suitable fiancée, waiting for him to finish his education. Feliciana, a technician of left side, the mystery, will one day assume her mother's position in the village of the brujas and she is the keeper of the secrets of both sides of her lineage.

Benito brought Feliciana home, and one year later she pulled him into her suyu as her mother and his family celebrated the festival of Qolloriti, an annual Andean celebration held in a glacier bowl high in the Andes. They live gracefully in all worlds, the left and the right, the mountains and the city, the modern and the traditional. They flow freely back and forth, carrying the best of both on their backs.

Benito looks like the Andes, he looks like the Earth that has sustained his people for thousands of years. He is a short, dark, intense man with long, black, straight hair and coal black sloe-eyes. He is reserved, somber, and implacable. The planes of his cheeks are broad and severe, and he walks like a puma in his sandals with soles of tire rubber. His muted tan and gray poncho is alpaca wool, and he is never without his hat, a felt hat that carries the blessings of his father.

The quiet grace of Feliciana Mora is incomparable. Her regal carriage, oval face, and high cheekbones remind people of her paternal grandmother, the aristocratic wife of a wealthy, tyrannical hacendado. She is taller than most women of her culture, slender, elegant, and exudes a quiet sensuality as she moves softly throughout her life. Her slanted, blue eyes reveal her paternal heritage. Feliciana lives in the mystery, she knows the past and sees the future, and she knows that one day she will retreat to the village of her mother to save the secrets for women who understand.

Lauren stood alone in the simply furnished living room feeling the enchantment of a large patterned weaving hanging over the fireplace. Overwhelmed by dizziness, she closed her eyes, steadying herself by placing her fingers on the mantle, listening to Lici speak. "Ah, my sister of the soul, the altitude has affected you. Let's have some coca tea to help you acclimate and then talk about our ancestors. We both come from a lineage of weavers, so we truly are sisters. The weavings record the stories and every woman knows that, don't we, Lauren?"

Feeling dizzy, Lauren merely nodded in agreement.

"The men talk about the earthshaker, the great Pachacuteq, but women, well, we know what women talk about. The men talk about the turning over of the worlds, but women know that everyday is the eternal, and the eternal is rearranging itself all of the time."

"I know what it feels like to have my world turned upside down, Lici," Lauren said sadly. "It happened to me when I left home and couldn't go back."

"Si, Lauren, and it will happen again and again. Not to worry, my young sister, your destiny is already in place." Lauren asked about the weaving above the fireplace. "The weaving you admire was made by my mother when she carried me in her womb and it has been with me all of my life. She said she channeled the threads of my story into the cloth as she wove it. Yoci wrapped it around me and cradled me on her back until I was old enough to walk. She said the vibrations that were made as she walked resonated my story into my body."

A gifted listener, Feliciana hoped to find the key to help Lauren to cry. "Tell me about the satchel you carry, Lauren."

Feeling sleepy, Lauren told Lici about her Grandmother.

"I thought so. The patterns remind me of many that the women in the Andes incorporate into their designs. But most of all, I'm curious to see what you carry inside."

Lauren pulled her satchel closer, feeling insecure as Lici chatted with her like a long lost sister. "There is nothing more revealing than the contents of a woman's bag. In my culture the women

carry their lives on their backs. In yours, you hang them from your
shoulders. Regardless, we all do the same thing."

Lauren shyly asked Lici why she didn't carry a purse.

"I wear a lliklla rather than carry a purse, but my mesa is
very much like your satchel. Our mesa is a woven cloth that represents the cosmos and when we travel we fold the mesa around
our earthly treasures, just like the skies surround us like a blanket. The objects I carry in it are more precious to me than Benito."
Lauren looked at her with aghast on her pale, tired face.

"Don't be surprised," Lici laughed softly. "He wouldn't have it
any other way."

Entranced by the dreamy sound of Feliciana's voice, Lauren
closed her eyes feeling the pressure from the tears she couldn't
shed. "Why can't they understand that I'm dying inside? It's so
hard to sit here and pretend I'm happy. Do they have any idea how
far away from home I am and what I've been through? My arms
feel so heavy and empty, and I keep expecting something to happen. I feel like everything's building up inside of me, and I think I
might explode if something doesn't change."

Sensing what troubled the younger woman, Feliciana
touched the gold charm bracelet on her arm. She spoke gently to
Lauren as she felt the sincere vibrations emitting from the delicate gold links. "Did your young lover give this to you? Si, I
thought so; I can feel the love it has absorbed. In our culture we
believe that gold is the metal of the Inca, of the sun. It's precious
to us but not in the way others value it. For us it carries the light
that has been embodied in the gold. He loves you very much,
Lauren, are you certain you don't want to contact him? He sent his
light to you in this bracelet."

Lauren felt panic rising in her body, and her first impulse was
to escape. She screamed inside. "I can't deal with this," and then
snapped in frustration, "I'm here to forget him."

Lici considered the pain she heard in Lauren's voice. "Her
womanhood has already enveloped her, but she doesn't yet understand what that means."

Smiling mysteriously, she held Lauren's pendulum in her
hand. For a moment she looked at the crystal ball. In the crystal,
Lici saw many doors that would be closed to Lauren for a very long
time. Not wanting to tell Lauren, she infused the crystal ball with
her energy before quickly setting it aside. "I rarely ask to touch
another's sacred articles, but I want to know you very well, and I'll
show you how to clean it of my energy if you should want to do so."
Lici touched the red rock to her forehead as tears came to her eyes.

Carefully she picked up the small white pearl button that Lauren had been reluctant to show her. "Does this belong to the father of your son?"

When Lauren nodded yes, remembering that she had found it on the floor of the Casino the day after they had made love, Feliciana carefully placed the button in the small crack in the red stone where the crystal was exposed. "This is your world," Lici said dreamily, "hold it close to your heart and yet let it go. It isn't time for you to go home yet. The doorways you will walk through back to your home are out of alignment. One day, when you see footsteps walking away from where you are standing, you will know it's time."

Almost hypnotized by Lici's melodic voice, Lauren found the words to describe her feelings. "Lici, I feel your words spin and weave a story that surrounds my body like a rainbow."

Lici smiled softly offering Lauren some words of wisdom. "Lauren, when you decide to tell your lover about your son, make a cloak of your story, gently put it over his shoulders and surround him with love."

Lauren sighed and smiled, wondering if she would grow up to have the wisdom of the woman speaking to her.

"Before we join Benito, there is a question I want to ask you. What does the father of your son call himself?"

"Americo Rios," Lauren said very quietly. Lauren watched as Feliciana and Benito greeted each other and feeling lonely, she became very aware of their affection. "Oh, Americo, we were just too young to know." She didn't yet know what she and Americo didn't know, but she felt something rise in her awareness. "They're making planets the way they look at each other." She thought back to the look in Americo's eyes when he held her face in his hands. "We didn't make planets, we made a baby, but maybe there's not a lot of difference."

☾★

With quick whisking motions, Lauren swept the floor in front of the picture window framing the view of thousands of bar tile roofs. She gazed over the mist-enshrouded ancient city, feeling that she might be living in a fairy tale. Rows of trees enclosed the yard, shielding the cottage from view. Lauren leaned on her broomstick. "From here Benito and Feliciana can see everything, but nobody else can see them. It feels like I'm in a magical kingdom, and the king and the queen have adopted me."

Feeling rested and secure, Lauren giggled as she sat down at her workbench next to Benito's. "Benito, why do you say that spirit needs an alpaca to ride? Where I come from we would probably say a horse to ride."

He grinned at her, sharing his philosophy on art and its purpose. "No difference, a horse and alpaca, it doesn't matter because the spirit is the same. Spirit needs a channel, and art is the most direct line between spirit and human. When you work on your art, you are opening yourself up to the events of time and place. You are the conduit, and it is a matter of cooperation between spirit, you, and the material, and from the agreement that is made, stories are recorded. Spirit appreciates having a ride and an invitation."

Earnestly, Lauren asked another question. "Benito, why do you always call Feliciana your woman, instead of your wife? Haven't you heard that some women don't like that?"

He answered so tenderly Lauren thought she would melt. "Lauren, she is my woman and I mean that in the deepest sense of the word. She is my complement, my equal but different counterpart and my love for her knows no boundary. She is not my mirror; I do not see myself when I look at her. I see her for the priestess that she is. She is not my wife, because we approach the matter of marriage differently than your culture does. We may not marry for years, but we are mated for life." Knowing that Lauren had witnessed the passion between them, Benito wanted to help Lauren make sense of her decision not to disconnect from Americo. Benito spoke to her in a brotherly tone, as he took her hands in his own. "Lauren, you made a brave decision when you decided to keep Americo's filaments in your body. I wasn't certain that you made the right choice and there really are no wrong choices, just different choices that lead to different paths. But I'm told how you are willing to be empowered by the filaments of your first lover, and that tells me you are in touch with your womanhood and that you have great courage."

Lauren stared into the distance; her eyes no longer focused on her work. She stopped polishing the gold earrings and thought back to the letter Americo sent to her. "He said he wanted me to be his woman someday, and I told him he shouldn't say that to girls. It was probably the greatest thing a guy could say, and I told him he was old fashioned. Oh well, I can't be his woman anyway. Someday, he'll say that to another girl and she'll say yes." Lauren's energy body retreated from the expansion Benito witnessed earlier. Dark clouds gathered around her abdomen, having touched a place of profound pain. "I think I understand what you mean, Benito, but sometimes I have to think about things for awhile."

"Lauren, you have heard the words and they have vibrated into your body. That is all that matters."

Lauren sat in silence, afraid to speak.

"You have a gift, but with that gift will come your greatest challenge. You are highly absorbent, very receptive, and I mean this as a complement. Your Grandmother has encouraged the female attributes of your being and I hope you never lose them, but the challenge for you will be to discern the energy you absorb. If you don't, you will be the victim of seeing yourself through others eyes. You want to please people, and you have been conditioned to want the approval of others. Be careful whom you honor with the privilege of imposing their expectations on you."

"Daddy always expected a lot from me, and I always tried to please him."

"You absorb knowledge easily, and your receptive nature is your chariot into the mystery. That is the gift, and the gift will make you a great artist."

Lauren giggled. "Oh Benito, you're just teasing me now."

"No, my sister, I don't tease," Benito said firmly. "You also absorb the pain and doubts of others. You have found a way to cope, however, when you are ready, you will use the energy for power, not coping. Time, Lauren, this will take time."

Benito's words made sense to Lauren as she remembered times when she experienced what others were feeling. Benito pierced a lightning shape piece of gold to solder on a bracelet. "When you absorb the expectations of others, they build up layers around you and soon the core within you will become invisible, and you won't remember who you are. You will have become a mirror for those around you."

"I had a dream that I was a mirror, but I was looking at myself looking at myself. It really scared me."

Benito saw into the mirror Lauren dreamed of and shook his head sadly.

Lauren tried to imitate the deft movements he made with his hands, talking somberly and openly. "I like to be invisible most of the time. When I'm invisible I don't get yelled at or criticized. That's why I didn't tell anybody about..."

Benito had opened one of the doors. "Lauren, listen to your words, you are already using a technique that has two edges. Like an animal, becoming invisible or harmonizing with your environment can prevent you from becoming prey and it is an extremely important tool. But, I think you are using this technique to keep from revealing yourself because you don't want to disappoint others. You have given them your power and I'm afraid that someday you will have to reclaim it at a very high cost."

"I don't think I understand. Besides, you haven't heard my mother and father yell all of the time."

"They must be very unhappy and frustrated, but they are on their own path, and you cannot let them define yours."

"I'm trying to remember everything you tell me, but in a way it's like a dream. I remember then I forget."

He smiled at her efforts, realizing her insight was coming at great cost. "When the time is right you will hear my voice saying them to you again, just as if you were still sitting here with your brother, helping him make his art. At that time you will remember that I told that circumstances dictate and you will tell the father of your son with no apology, knowing you acted out of love."

"Benito, in a way I'm nervous about the ceremony tonight. I don't know what to expect from the experiences I'm going to have. Maybe we should wait." Lauren looked reluctant and excited at the same time.

Benito placed his hand on hers and spoke directly to her heart. "You must know, once you start down this path there is no going back. You are taking the first step tonight, and your life will never be the same."

"I already know what it's like to start down a path where there isn't any going back. My life hasn't been the same for over a year."

"Do you think the paths could be one and the same?"

Lauren tilted her head to the side, crinkled her eyes and spoke with a slow Arizona drawl. "Reckon so, brother."

Benito laughed with gusto. "You are a handful, Lauren. I wonder about the fate of the men who will love you."

Lauren giggled. "You already know the damage I can do. Are you sure you don't want me to pay you for what you're teaching me? I have the money, you know that already."

"Lauren, I explained our system of anyi, reciprocity. When the time is right, you will return to us more than we could ever give you. Not to worry, sister."

C★

The lively atmosphere of the city at night thrilled Lauren as they drove through the crowded streets noisy with honking cars. Benito pointed to the south where a large political rally was being staged in front of a stately cathedral. Lauren spoke loudly, trying to be heard over the speakers and horns, hoping to find out what they were protesting. Knowing the dangers of mass hysteria, Benito expertly turned the old van onto a windy narrow side street and quickly took a shortcut to Sacsahuaman, the ancient Inca fortress overlooking the jewel city of Cuzco.

Benito stopped his car at the entry gate of the fortress. "Lauren, I waited until the quality of light was perfect for our time together. I have a particular fondness for the time when the veil of darkness falls." In silence they waited for darkness. Lauren was nervous, not having experienced a ceremony of rebirth before. Benito took her hand, offering comfort. "We have already taught you many ways to clean your energy body and that was a beginning, but tonight your experience will be greatly intensified. I want to prepare you, by telling you that tomorrow you may feel more tired than usual, or you could find yourself feeling extremely energized. It will depend on how both your physical and energy body responds to the work. You are now in a container that I will provide for you, and you don't have to be concerned. You are under my protection and will remain so until you leave Peru."

Wondering what secret Benito carried in his large leather shoulder bag, Lauren followed him as they entered the courtyard of the mysterious edifice. Lauren, captured in the moment, failed to follow him. Benito did not intend for the night to begin by sightseeing and led her firmly towards a giant monolith. Lauren stopped again when she passed a giant outcropping of rock. "As grand as you are, I think you pale by comparison to the red rock formations at home."

Benito interrupted her remembrance and directed her towards an opening in the monolith, explaining the ceremony. "You will discover that I will not be teaching you anything while you are here. I will provide circumstances, and they will be your teachers. If you have questions, hold on to them for a time and see if the answers present themselves as you move through your experience." Standing at the opening, Benito seemed transformed, appearing as an ancient god relaying a gift to a young pilgrim.

"Now I want you to experience once again your first physical journey, the one you took before you were presented to this glorious world. The opening goes all the way through the mountain and I want you to use your body to find your way through the boulder."

"Alone?"

Benito understood Lauren's fear of birth after hearing about her reluctant delivery into the world. "Think of this as the passage you took from your mother's body before you saw the light of our sun at the end. Nobody gave you directions, it was dark and you were alone. You felt her body try to hold on to you while at the same time deliver you. You were reaching, and the journey was painful. The passage from this boulder will provide your birth from the body of Pachamama and that is the only birth that really matters." Benito walked towards Lauren and placed his index finger near her shoulder bone, transmitting energy into her body. Feliciana remained silent, walking soundlessly, listening to Lauren and her responses.

"Mother Earth is the only mother that should concern you because she is the one who has ultimately birthed and mothered all of us. Our relationship with her is the one to nurture, because it is the only one that is eternal, and she should always be our reference point. All other relationships are temporal and like the snow when it melts, they are transient and will pass quickly. If you will trust me, I would like to have Feliciana hold your satchel and clothes while you make your journey. When you came into the world you were naked and you had nothing to help you, and being exposed is the manner in which you should make this birth journey, as well."

Feliciana held her finger to her mouth and with her eyes made Benito aware of his voice. Benito nodded his gratitude to the stars for the moment. "I want you to notice the silence. It is rare that there is a moment like this." There was a pause while Lauren became aware of the sound of nothing. "The last time there was silence for you was the second before you were conceived. You have been experiencing sensory input from that instant and all of the input is now deep inside of you, but it is not you. After your birth passage you will be closer to your essence."

Lauren stepped to the opening of the boulder trying to peek through to the other side. "Why did he tell me to dress warm, if he wanted me to take off my clothes?" Shaking from cold and fear, Lauren looked to her teachers for assurance. Before disappearing into the dark, leaving her alone to find the other opening of the passage, Benito gave her a salute and told her he would be there to deliver her on the other side.

Lauren braced her hands on the cold rock as she started through the dark tunnel. "I feel like I'm being squeezed to death, maybe I won't fit through this narrow part and I'll have to go back." Out loud, she said with her voice shaking, "I can't feel the walls now, what if I get turned around and get lost? It's so dark, and I can't see a thing. What if there's a wild animal in here?" Lauren got on her hands and knees, crawling slowly, shaking with dread. "Maybe I'll just disappear, and nobody will ever find me. I could get trapped in this boulder. What if somebody else is in here with me?" Feeling trapped, Lauren experienced fleeting memories of her birth journey. "Maybe I didn't even want to be born. I don't think I want to see the light at the end of the tunnel, maybe it's too bright."

Waiting at the opening with a look of an expectant parent on her face, Feliciana received Lauren with open arms and a motherly smile. Lauren saw the light emanating from Benito and pale and shaken, she fell into his arms. Holding the limp young woman to his chest, Benito felt her trembling diminish and spoke softly and proudly. "Welcome to our beautiful world, Lauren. Muchas gracia, Pachamama, for delivering my sister to me."

Feliciana held a cup of coca tea to her lips, stroking her hair as Lauren sipped the hot fluid. Lauren basked in the after delivery ceremony as Benito withdrew a condor feather from his leather bag and gently stroked the light emitting from her center. Feliciana sprinkled sacred aqua de florida on her body. Requesting that Lauren select a kintui, three leaves of coca, from the woven chuspi around his neck, Benito read the leaves as he turned to Lici for guidance. The leaves had been read, they knew Lauren's future and under the light of the millions of stars they offered their gratitude to the Earth and the heavenly bodies spinning in the sky.

Later, safe in her warm bed, cuddled up under the colored alpaca blanket, Lauren gazed out the tinged with blue window glass at the moon high in the sky. With a heart that felt lighter, she spun back to the moment she had become aware of Benito chanting as he cleaned the heavy energy from her body. Almost drifting off to sleep, she could still hear the beautiful toning in the ancient Quechua tongue and felt again the vibrations of his words as he wiped the heavy filaments away.

The palm of Lauren's hand rested on her belly, protecting the space her son had lived for nine months of his life. She cried without tears as her heart longed for Americo. "Oh, Americo, you would have loved holding him in your arms. He smelled so good, and his hair was so black. In a way he looked like both of us, but I couldn't see his eyes, and I never will."

It was then that she saw Americo's face looking at her the night they made love. She felt his penetrating amber eyes staring deeply into her being, and then she remembered what he said. She heard his low husky voice as if he were saying the words. "Lauren, this will keep us connected forever. Nothing will ever be the same after tonight. You can't forget me now, Bruja, not ever."

Lauren sent a prayer that the filaments given to her when they made love would keep them connected forever. "Americo, please let me keep the connection we made that night. If someday you should want to disconnect from me, I'll hate it, but I'll understand, but you'll have to be the one to do it, because I won't."

Grief has a life of it's own, and it was birthed in Lauren's sleep. Maternal love overwhelmed Lauren in the middle of the night, leaving her with a feeling of irreplaceable loss. Holding on to her pillow, she pulled it close to her chest trying to fill the empty place where a baby would have rested his head. A pain so deep it couldn't move settled into her heart, a pain that caused her to feel constant tears she could not shed. "Americo, I don't know who else to talk to, you're the only one who ever really listened to me. I lost more than our baby in the clinic. I feel like I lost myself. I remember the spinning feeling when he was born, but when the nurse took him away from me, I felt a part of myself disconnect and follow him." Hugging her pillow for comfort, she squeezed her eyes seeing her baby's face. "He was so pretty, Americo. His skin was dark like yours, and his fingers were so long for his little body. I just know he would have looked like you, and maybe he would have had your sexy walk when he grew up. Oh God, why do I keep tormenting myself? You can't hear me." Rummaging through her satchel Lauren retrieved the photograph of Americo she carried with her, and held it softly to her lips. "I've pretty much decided that I'm going to tell you, but I'll just have to see what it feels like when I see you again."

Lauren pondered the experiences Benito and Feliciana were planning and felt the goosebumps on her arms. Rediscovering a lost part of herself, Lauren made a vow. "Well at least being nervous is better than not feeling anything and I've been numb for months. Maybe if I take chances and do everything in the extreme, I'll feel like I'm alive. The highs and the lows, it looks like that's where it's at for me. Everybody always said I was reckless, but at least I won't be like a zombie."

Lauren stood under the sweet, freezing waterfall as the river flowed slowly like the time since she said goodbye to her home. She shivered, knowing she had to endure the pain, and sent a message with the river. "I still have your filaments inside of me, Americo." Tenderly, she touched the gold bracelet on her left arm. "If you can feel me reaching for you, El Jugador, please let me know. If we are connected because of what we did, then maybe you'll know I love you. At least I can give you that much after all I've taken away from you." She felt an explosive sensation in her belly and remembered having the same feeling after they made love. "Did you receive my thoughts? Is this how I'll know when you feel me reaching out to you?"

Vibrations from Benito's words penetrated her body, causing her to rejoice with sudden lightness in her heart. She remembered him saying, "Fear is the opposite of love. When you feel fear, it's because you don't feel love. If you are ever afraid, go to the place in your body where you hold your love." Carefully looking at the river Benito told her could claim her life, Lauren wondered if she could harmonize her energy with the water and prevent herself from becoming prey to the possible dangers. A feeling of peace lifted her eyes. "This water flows by the cave of the anaconda." In her vision, Lauren saw the eyes of the anaconda Feliciana told her lived with the moon. Lauren lifted her chin and looked at the sun. Standing at the edge of the river, Lauren dropped her eyelids and then stared until the water melted into pure frequency. At that moment, she knew without any fear that she could survive the swim. Slowly and deliberately Lauren slid into the water without making a ripple. She didn't know if hours or minutes passed, all she knew was that she had to swim until she saw the large out-cropping of boulders. Lauren ceased to exist for the duration of the swim and became one with where the water and sky met. She didn't think, because then she could fear, and the vibrations of fear could mean the end of her life.

Walking onto the rocky shore, she saw their smiling faces. Feliciana held a blanket for Lauren, and again swaddled her as if she were a precious child. She had found her way without help and without thinking, relying on her feelings and instinct. She radiated as Benito looked into her face, greeting her with pride. "Bonita, bonita, Lauren, my sister. I've never seen anything so beautiful. Do you now understand what love can do?"

Lauren laughed wildly at the river, knowing she had won. She giggled when she remembered that she could have been trashed in the formidable water and when she rubbed the gooey black mud over her body, she knew she could do anything. She felt a rush of power and sent a message to Americo. "It won't be so bad, Americo. I'll tell you about this when I get home and maybe, after some time, we can laugh together again. You would have loved seeing me do this, I just know it."

Benito had final words for Lauren, the most important words he would offer her on her first journey into the Andes. Standing in front of her, clasping her hands to his chest, he told her to listen carefully and to follow his advice. "Lauren, you must cry. If you don't cry, someday you will hurt yourself or somebody else. Don't carry corpses, Lauren, if you do, you'll get stuck and be unable to move forward. Hurry home, tell your lover the secret, and then return to your soul brother's home as often as fortunes allow. I love you and I'll watch over you from high on a peak in the Andes."

Lauren left Peru two days after a Andean priest placed his hands on her head offering her a blessing to take back to her pacarina. Not understanding Quechua, Lauren didn't know the profound gift she had been given. Feeling strong and loved from her time with Benito and Feliciana, Lauren closed her eyes as the plane departed Lima, fully intending to tell Americo about their son as soon as she saw him. She had discovered an art form she loved and looked forward to earning a degree in art at NAU. Many of the ghosts that haunted Lauren had been cleared. She had survived a near death experience during the birth of her son, met a woman in Crete who furthered her connection with the Goddess, and her soul brother and sister had gently guided her through many soul retrieval experiences. Still carrying the ashes of her son's body, Lauren hoped that she and Americo could release them on the rancho together.

When Trey and Sunnie met her at the airport a few days before Christmas, Trey gave her the news from home. Americo's parents had been killed six months earlier in a tragic car accident. Americo had not been back to El Rancho de las Estrellas since their funeral and had sent the message that he didn't want to see her if she ever came back to Sedona. Jake Auldney continued to spend money recklessly on horses, not seeming to care if he won or lost in the game called the sport of kings. In deep depression over the loss of his brother and best friend, Jake had turned increasingly to alcohol, distressing his mother and Lydia. Excitedly,

Sunnie showed Lauren her wedding ring. Following the death of America's parents, Trey and Sunnie decided to forego a large wedding and eloped to Las Vegas over summer break. Sunnie was now attending a small college near Stanford to finish her teaching degree.

Lauren's bubble of confidence and hope burst before she ever saw the red rocks of Sedona. She had failed to be in Sedona to celebrate the lives of her aunt and uncle, her father was on a path of self-destruction, her best friend did not want to see her, and her brother and Sunnie had a bright, promising future, with each other to hold every night.

Although she tried, Lauren could not hide her heartbreak from Rita and Zack when she sat at the dining room table during Christmas dinner. She sat in silence, feeling alone, and did not share the stories she had planned to tell her family about her year of wandering.

Jake, although happy to see his daughter, was more concerned that she adhered to the plan he had for her. "Lauren, I hope you're paying attention to how your brother is conducting his life. Trey married a nice girl, stayed in school, saves his money, and has a plan. I hope to see similar behavior from you. You need to get in school, find a promising career, marry a nice man, and give your daddy some grandkids. Make me proud of you, Lauren, show your daddy what you can do." Trying to be agreeable, she let Jake talk her into attending Arizona State University in Tucson and moved there early in January, gaining late admission with Lydia's help.

Driving her new used, red Volkswagen, Lauren left Sedona with her dog, her clothes, a bag of pot, the stolen money, and a heavy burden she could not release. She felt numb, there was a perpetual black tunnel distorting her vision, and she still had over 450 Demerols in her satchel. Chewing coca leaves had been Lauren's drug of choice while in Peru, keeping her pain pill supply well intact.

Looking back at the rancho as she started to drive away, Lauren remembered the night in Peru when she had decided she liked the thrill of extreme highs and lows. Popping two Demerols in her mouth, she laughed hysterically while looking in her satchel for the needle she always carried. "To hell with it, Lauren, you better spin it girl, because you've got a lot to do and it looks like you'll be doing it on your own, just like you said you would."

☪

Eighteen months later, high on pain pills and alcohol, Lauren eloped with a handsome, preppy premed student, determined to take a respectable husband home. Jim Reese fit her criteria perfectly. He fell in love with a wild girl that he was certain would clean up her act after their marriage. He didn't know about the pain pills until much later after Lauren had found a way to buy more. In spite of her drug use, Lauren had a job at a small boutique, earned excellent grades and when she took her husband home, her father breathed a sigh of relief thinking his little girl had finally grown up.

Although Lauren was capricious in her studies, there was a constant theme. Within every discipline, if one is able to make connections readily, there is a path to the Goddess. Lauren wrote brilliant papers, regardless of her major, on the influence, past and present, of the role of the woman in society. Her inspiration was fired by her personal identity of a sexual mind and creativity. Eagerly Lauren explored the relationship between women and nature, reading every paper and book and integrating the theory into her daily life. The environment became a passion for Lauren. Participating in Earth Day celebrations and working on local concerns with her husband gave them common ground to hopefully build a marriage.

Two months later Lauren held a razor to her wrist while her husband watched in horror. Screaming in a haunted voice, Lauren, without tears in her eyes, taunted him with her plan. "I'll do it; you know I will. By the time the ambulance gets here, I'll be dead. Don't come near me or I'll slash you too." Her body was slashed with cuts she made with needles, there were holes in her skin she made with tweezers, she had lost more weight, and Lauren didn't care if she lived or died.

☪

Don Esteban Madera came into Americo's life seemingly by accident when they met each other in a bar in Guaymas. Sitting at his table in the corner of the bar, don Esteban Madera had quietly observed the countenance of a young man telling his amigos stories of his lost love. As the fishermen returned from the sea don

Esteban gazed over the busy harbor from the window, no longer watching Americo but listening to his tales of Lauren. It was early in the afternoon and Americo had won big at the tables the night before. He had felt more gregarious than usual and sought the company of some friends.

"Hell, I'm still waiting for that damn woman I love to realize she loves me. You know me, can't give up on a lost cause." Machismo reeked in the smoky restaurant as Americo bragged and showed them a picture of Lauren getting on her horse. "Did I show you the picture of her in my wallet? Si, Si, long legs, firm, round butt. My love's eyes look like a hurricane or a twister, especially if she is angry or hurt." He paused as the men visualized his words. Americo spoke wistfully, knowing the men were deep into commiseration with him. "Or, her eyes can be as soft and gentle as an eddy. But they are always like a deep whirlpool and I could never get tired of looking at them, mis amigos, especialmente if I ever make love to her again."

Knowing he had entertained them with the story many times before, Americo, eating his shrimp with gusto continued describing Lauren to his captive audience. "No, no, amigos. Lauren isn't beautiful como a movie star; pero ella is muy naturale y muy especial. Si Pilar, you remember what I've told you before; her skin is like velvet." Americo played the role of a jilted lover expertly, rolling his eyes as if remembering. "Her hair is soft like silk. That's absolutemente correcto, Rafael, she is very quiet y muy seriouso and also very funny. She wants to be an artist and when she was a little girl she was a dancer. Si, she moves like a ballerina and she makes my heart laugh with her chistes, her jokes. My Lauren is muy complicado, ella no esta facile a comprende, she isn't easy to understand."

Jesus asked a question, and Americo, imitating Lauren's scowl, continued the fun. "No, no, my love doesn't yell. She glares at me with her intense eyes of green, and then I go ouch." He laughed as if her eyes had pricked his skin. "Lauren is muy intellegente, muy listo, very bright, my amigos, but remember," Americo spoke in a hushed voice as the men leaned closer, "she is also a bruja and her magic is potent." Americo spoke honestly with remorse in his voice. "No, lo siento, I'm sorry, she doesn't love me, but no problema." He winked at his friends who were enjoying listening to the sad love story. "Pero, maybe una dia before I disappear into nada she will let me make love to her again." Americo pretended to stab himself in the heart. "She ripped my heart out with a dagger, amigos, but still I love her more than any other woman."

A waitress delivered a message to him. "Si, Flora, I see the man sitting over there." Americo turned to look at don Esteban. "Who is he and why does he want to talk to me?" Americo acknowledged the man with a tip of his Stetson. "Tell me again, Jesus, you say he's a sorcerer, a Nagual. Absolutemente, I'll be careful, but he doesn't look dangerous to me." Americo ground out his cigarette. "Buenas tardes, mis amigos. I'll go see what he wants, and then I'll go home and shovel the manure out of my corrals." Americo did not go home until late in the night after spending hours walking with his new teacher.

☪

Americo had successfully completed his plans. The hacienda was restored and his bank balance, due to his winnings and inheritances, was considerable. He now owned half of El Rancho de las Estrellas and wanted to return to his home in the red rocks. Americo felt alone in the world and longed for the comfort of Sedona, his grandparents, and even Jake, who along with Lydia had offered unyielding support at the time of his parent's death. After learning of Lauren's marriage, Americo went on a month long binge. Drunk and angry following a poker game, Americo stood in front of his friends, took a joker from his pocket and ripped it apart, telling his friends, "Tonight I'm throwing the fucking joker away."

Don Esteban Madera had become Americo's friend and father figure, as well as his Nagual. Americo seemed a natural for the world of sorcery, and don Esteban guided him with wisdom and example. Together they had taken a journey into Copper Canyon, walking deep into the gorge and living there for two weeks. Americo had made the decision to return to Sedona and as he walked with his Nagual, he tried to explain his reasons.

Don Esteban did not believe that Americo should leave Mexico. "It doesn't matter if I understand or not, Americo. You are gifted in the practices I've taught you and what you do is up to you. There is a great deal you still don't know, and you continue to indulge in the love you feel for your Lauren."

Americo protested, often contradicting himself. "I'll be back often, don Esteban, and you're welcome to use the hacienda anytime. I haven't seen Lauren for five years, and she's been back in

Arizona for more than half of that time. I made up my mind to avoid her, and I have, but that doesn't mean I don't love her, some of the time." Americo stopped to chew some Tums.

"Americo, you haven't yet learned how to turn your love into power. You continue to allow energy to dissipate from your body, making you sad and weak. Notice the area in your body where you feel pain." Don Esteban knew Americo did not make the connection. As they stopped to drink from their canteens, he tried once again to help Americo recognize the energy draining from his body. "You need to enfold your love, let it feed the energy you have, rather than spend it in useless mourning for a love you may never have. Love her if you must but don't dwell on it like a child, just love her and let that be enough. Don't indulge in what she doesn't give you. You're still saying the same things I heard you say in the bar the first day I met you. You are in love with a broken heart, and a jilted lover has become your disguise."

Defensive and tired, Americo became argumentative. "You don't know her, don Esteban, or you would understand. I feel something between love and contempt. I don't know."

Don Esteban Madera knew. Speaking sternly to Americo, don Esteban drew patterns in the dirt with a stick. "I know enough, Americo Rios, my friend. I have traveled with you, and I have seen her power. Your energies are entwined like strands of the dna, like the two snakes you saw in your vision the other night. You have a lot to learn about this woman, and I regret to tell you, it may take many years before you fully understand her. She has a double edge; I saw it in my vision."

Americo stomped away, only to be summoned back by his teacher. Don Esteban spoke gently, seeing the hurt in Americo's eyes. "I've shown you how to break the connection between the two of you, yet you have chosen not to do so. You have been given three choices. You can break the connection that ties you to her or you can block the energy that flows between you. The best decision would be to transform it into power. You will have to decide. A sorcerer needs a purpose to be an impeccable stalker, and perhaps your love for this woman is your purpose."

Don Esteban laughed knowing Americo wouldn't understand his words for many years. "It is a difficult thing to contain a woman, because she already carries a container within her. This gives her the freedom to live with abandon. You must learn to pull your power toward your purpose, whatever that may be. For now I'll be happy if I can keep you from dying from the power that pours from your body like sweat."

☾★

In the world of academia, Lauren's insatiable mind guided her into many worlds other than art. While fulfilling most of the requirements for a major in art, Lauren changed her focus several times, exploring the disciplines of art history, dance, religious studies, and philosophy. As soon as she completed most of the required classes in a department, she changed majors, once again. Consistently unfocused in all areas of her life, she changed jobs and apartments often.

Her husband graduated and had been accepted in medical school in the south, and Lauren was faced with a decision as to whether she wanted to continue in the charade of her marriage or live by herself. A fear of being alone had crept into Lauren's soul. She worried constantly about everything, often creating circumstances so she would have to worry. Lauren lived in fear of being committed to a hospital by her husband, yet she feared abandonment more.

The small apartment close to the university was trashed and at 5:00 in the morning Lauren grabbed her head in agony recalling the violent fight with her husband the night before. Fearing for his life, he had not slept at home and when Lauren got out of bed she deliberately smashed three tennis trophies on his desk. Standing in the middle of the small living room, Lauren looked at the cushions from her rattan furniture she stabbed with a steak knife when her husband threatened to call an ambulance or the police.

Wishing she had stabbed her husband instead, the pounding in her head drowning out the noise from the street, Lauren moved like a sleepwalker as she picked up pieces of filling scattered around the room. Robotically returning thrown books to the shelves; Lauren struggled to remember what they argued about, and as she swept up the broken glass from the kitchen floor, she remembered.

Brown Dog sat attentively on the corner of her bed as Lauren set her chin with determination and packed her yellow duffel bag. "At least he can't threaten to commit me if I'm in Sedona. If he would just stop hassling me about medications, I wouldn't flip out like I do." Lauren giggled at her frazzled appearance in the mirror. "Besides I can find plenty of medications on my own." Giving a picture of her husband the finger, she told him at least she wouldn't have to see him for three weeks. Lauren had been summoned home by Rita to help care for Zack, who was failing. As she meticulously packed her clothes, Lauren pondered what it would be like to see Americo again after five years.

Lauren's hands were clammy, her knees shook, and her legs stuck to the vinyl seat when she took a deep breath while looking at Cathedral Rock. "Now that Americo's back on the rancho there won't be anyway to avoid him." Lauren twiddled her fingers on the steering wheel, remembering saying goodbye to him at the airport. "God, what will I say to him?" Lauren arrived on the rancho straight, having made a promise to Rita not to be high when she arrived home. "I'll probably have to see him with a girlfriend, but I always knew that would happen someday. If I'm lucky, maybe it will be like when we were kids. We can play poker and talk like nothing ever happened, after all, it was one time, one night, we were both stoned and it's been a long time."

Still wearing his running shorts and cap, Americo sat by the bed where Zack rested while recovering from a heart attack. Holding a glass of water to Zack's lips he noticed that Zack kept glancing out the window, seeming to be listening for something.

Telling him to move quietly, Rita motioned for Americo to follow her into the living room. Feeling the loneliness in his heart, she tucked a lock of his hair behind his ear. "Americo, I'm so grateful to you, I don't know what I would have done without you for the past two days, but Lauren is on her way and if you don't want to see her you better go home."

Americo took her in his arms and rested his chin on her head. "Grandma Rita, it's going to be good to see Lauren again. I probably still love her, but that's my problem." Americo heard the unmistakable sound of Lauren's car and saw Zack open his eyes, looking around, seeming confused. Clinching his fists, Americo closed his eyes, trying to imagine how she would look. He heard Brown Dog barking at the hens in the yard and felt his legs go weak when he heard the sound of Lauren's footsteps on the porch.

Relieved that Lauren had arrived safely, Rita fussed over her granddaughter. "Lauren, sweetheart, you're soaking wet. Do you want some lemonade? I have a message for you from Jim. He called about an hour ago saying he was on his way to the airport and wants to talk to you before he flies back to Tennessee."

"I'm glad I wasn't here yet, Grandma. We had a big fight last night, and I don't know where he slept, but he wasn't home when I got up this morning. I want to see Grandpa. If he wasn't awake when I got here, he probably is now with all of the noise Brown

Dog makes."

Rita started to tell her that Americo was in the bedroom. "Lauren, you should know...Never mind, it was nothing."

Americo listened carefully and noticed a change in her voice. He felt his heart pound when he heard Rita and Lauren walking towards the bedroom, and saw Zack look at him with reassurance in his tired eyes. Lauren walked through the door and Americo was stunned by her appearance. "She's so skinny."

Lauren's long hair rested on her shoulders, and her eyes opened wide with surprise. With a tentative smile on her lips, she looked at Americo, not knowing what to say.

Americo saw the charm bracelet on her wrist. He stood with a stabbing pain in his left side when Zack urged him with his hand to go to her. Seeing the sparkle in his eyes, Lauren held her hands on her cheeks. Americo crossed the room with long strides. The shadows in her eyes met the light in his. Lauren whispered, 'Jugador." Americo took her in his arms, whispering, "Bruja." Lauren had not shed tears for five years. "Don't cry, Lauren."

Weak, old, and tired, Zack laughed as he interrupted their reunion. "Now come and give your Grandpa a hug, it makes me damn happy to have both of you here with me. Lauren, don't you worry about me, I can't die yet because I've got a beautiful young wife and she still wants me to hold her all night."

Rita noticed that Zack held their hands clasped tightly together in his grip.

Zack stopped Rita from leaving the room. "Rita, my Darlin', the weaving you've started for Lauren is perfect. Don't change a thing. It's time you started on Americo's."

Rita smiled mysteriously when she saw the smile on her husband's ashen face. "If Lauren's weaving is perfect, why do I need to make one for Americo?"

A porch is a portal, a passageway to enter or leave a home. Americo stood on the porch watching Lauren, wondering how he could bridge the gap between them. The passageway to the sanctuary of Lauren seemed impassable, impossible, and without solace to one who had lost.

The small, pink flowers in the fabric of Lauren's dress shimmered in the setting sun as she stood on the porch looking over the rancho. The screen door closed, then Lauren heard the sound of his boots on the deck as he walked towards her. Shivering from the breezes carrying away the afternoon monsoon, she pulled her white sweater closer for protection. Americo stood behind her, boldly wrapping his arms around her as he rested his chin on her head. Americo closed his eyes, feeling the empty space to his left fill as they stood silently looking at the setting sun, each one waiting for the other to speak.

Americo broke the silence. "That was a great dinner, Lauren. The table looked so pretty with all of the flowers and Rita's china and crystal. You have a way of making things seem really special." Lauren didn't respond. With emotion in his voice Americo no longer held back his feelings. "I love having you home, Princess. I've missed you so much."

Lauren swallowed, trying not to cry again. "I've missed you too, Americo. I didn't realize how much until I saw you. I haven't cried for five years until this afternoon when I saw you." With Americo's arms still wrapped around her, they talked softly, never looking at each other or moving.

"Why not, Lauren?"

"I'm crazy. I think I've been afraid if I ever started I wouldn't be able to stop."

"You've always been a little crazy."

"I know, but I sometimes do things I don't know I'm doing. Only, I do know, it's like watching yourself in a dream."

"Are you happy?"

"Don't ask that. I never know. I am right this minute, but I don't think I deserve to be."

"Why are you so skinny? You're skinnier than when you were a little girl."

"I don't know. I eat all of the time, it's like I never get full."

"I heard you fighting with your husband on the phone. What's he like?"

"You wouldn't like him. He's a preppy. He say's he's going to commit me to an insane asylum."

"I'll kill him if he does."

"He wants me to act normal."

"Don't let anybody change you, Bruja. Why did you marry him?"

"I didn't have anything better to do over spring break. He's so normal and I wanted everybody to think I was normal. Americo, I keep waiting for something."

"What?"

"I don't know. I just always feel like something's going to happen. Do you have a girlfriend?"

"Not really. I date a little. How's school?"

"Good, my grades are good but I keep changing majors. I've got tons of hours, but I don't know when I'll graduate."

"I'm going back to NAU later this month. I'll graduate in December."

"Lucky you. Are you going to law school?"

"Nah, I'm a gambler and I don't want to live away from the rancho ever again. This is my home. I don't have anything else."

"Yes, you do."

"I want to be here when you decide to come home."

"I won't come home, Americo. I can't."

"Yes, you will. I'm learning to be a sorcerer. I find you when I enter into dreaming."

"I think I feel it when you do. Sometimes I get a feeling... I had a dream one night that you were making love to me."

"It wasn't a dream. I'll tell you about it sometime. There's a connection between us."

"I know. Why didn't you want to see me? Trey told me you hated me."

"Trey knows better. I was hurt, and I guess I wanted to hurt you."

"I had something really important to tell you."

"Tell me now."

"I can't, I think I've kind of forgotten about it."

"I always knew you'd turn out to be a real beauty."

"You're crazier than I am."

"I'm glad you liked the bracelet, Princess."

"I wear it all of the time. I've never taken it off."

"Why?"

"It makes me feel safe. I think about killing myself all of the time."

"Don't. Come to me."

"I'll tell you before I do it, I promise."

"There's something different about you."

"I change all of the time. What was I like before?"

"Don't you remember?"

"I think I'm remembering right now."

"When are you moving to Nashville?"

"Right after Christmas. I'll be back here for Christmas and maybe for Thanksgiving if I don't have to go to my in-laws. They hate me."

"Why?"

"They think I'm too unstable and wild for their son. They wanted him to marry a debutante, not a crazy country bumpkin."

"That's bullshit, come home."

"I can't."

"Yes, you can, I have a lot of money and I can take care of you."

"How did you get so much money?"

"My inheritance from my parents and grandparents, insurance, my winnings. I have a plan."

"Americo, you've always had a plan. I have a list, but it isn't a plan. I made it a long time ago, and I made a promise to myself to do everything on my own. It has to be that way."

"You don't have to."

"I've done some terrible things."

"You were just a kid; they don't matter."

"They matter, believe me. Did you get my presents? The ones I sent you from Greece and Peru."

"Yes, but I haven't opened them."

They stood in silence watching the startled deer jump over the fence. The ravens swooped and cawed as they flew overhead, and the coyote watched, calculating his next move as he watched the rabbit dart across the lane.

"I liked the way you smelled when I saw you today. It reminded me of, oh, you know."

"Good, I felt the same way."

Americo felt Lauren's body quivering. "I shouldn't say this, and I hope you're happy, but I didn't think it would end up like this. I thought we were just getting started as a couple when you changed your mind. Why?"

"I didn't have any choice."

Feeling her body start to tremble he knew she had started to cry again. Pulling her closer, his tears started to fall. "Will you come to my house tonight? We can play poker, listen to music, whatever you want to do, Baby. I can feel your body saying yes, Bruja. Don't put a no between us, not tonight."

Lauren waited to answer, feeling the vibrancy of his body, comparing it to the bland, benign energy of her husband. His tears fell on her hair, breaking her heart. "I've made more wrong decisions than anybody could ever know. If this is a wrong decision, what difference will one more make?" She answered with no guilt or remorse. "I shouldn't, but I will. I'll be there as soon as I can sneak out of the house." Lauren smiled and crinkled her eyes, for an instant reminding Americo of the little girl he had so fiercely guarded. "It won't be just tonight, Americo, if you want me, I'll be with you every night I'm here. Just don't ask me any more questions. Our time is our time, nothing else matters. OK?"

"I love you, Lauren. I always have."

"I love you too, Americo, but someday you won't love me. You'll hate me."

"Why?"

"Just stuff I've done. But no questions."

"Here's a key to my house, you can come to me anytime, I mean it." Lauren dropped the key in her satchel. "I still have the hair you cut off at the airport in my pocket. I carry it in a little silver box."

"Will you let me cut off some of your hair so I can keep it with me?"

"Sure, maybe you can give me a haircut while you're here."

"I want to do everything for you, I want to shave your face, I want to clean your house, I want to cook for you, I want to iron your shirts, I want to read your cards, will you let me?"

"God, Lauren, I love you so much."

"The feather left a scar."

"I'm glad. I'll make tonight special for us."

"I'd like to feel special, in fact, I'd like to feel anything, because usually I don't."

"You will."

"Someday, maybe."

☪

Lauren stood on the landing of Americo's porch listening to the soft music. She touched the door, but she didn't knock nor did she use her key. Waiting was sweet, because she knew that he knew...

Americo was prepared to welcome his Princess back into his arms. Quart jars and glasses were filled with sunflowers, the fireplace was lit, and a bottle of champagne chilled in the refrigerator. A freshly rolled joint rest in the ashtray, clean sheets were on the bed, the music had been selected, and he had two new charms to give Lauren.

Americo opened the door; they looked at each other hesitantly and then suddenly started to laugh. Holding each other's hands they laughed at a joke that neither of them had told, yet they both understood. Speaking softly, they danced and talked without reservation. "Baby, I want to feel you in my arms just like you were at your graduation dance. Do you have any idea how in love with you I was that night?"

"Help me remember, I've forgotten who I am. Wake me up from this nightmare, it's like I'm in a deep sleep and I'm afraid."

"Stay with me, Lauren, please."

"I can't. Please don't say that."

"Will you stay with me whenever you're home?"

"Yes, and somehow I'll figure out a way to come early for my visits. We can have days and nights alone together that nobody else knows about."

"I'll send you a ticket no matter where you are."

"Thanks, I don't have very much money."

"Can I come and see you?"

"Maybe, or maybe we could take trips together. Let's just see how I am. I don't know what I'm doing all of the time, but we can call and write letters to each other."

The fire dwindled as they drank champagne, talked, and got high. Leading Lauren by the hand, Americo took her into the bedroom and lifted her onto his bed. Stopping to look at Lauren's face he lit the candles and incense, and then standing at the foot of the bed, Americo removed his shirt. Lauren knelt in front of him, holding his face with her hands as he unbuttoned the tiny, white pearl buttons on her nightgown. The candlelight was dim and Americo didn't notice the many scratches and cuts on her body as he started to make love to her. For two hours, laughing and crying, they made love as they rewove the connection that had been damaged almost critically. As they felt their filaments reconnect and weave together, they made promises and vows neither had the right to make. Lovingly running his fingers over Lauren's body, Americo noticed a difference. "Your body looks different; it's so womanly."

Lauren giggled as she kissed his chin. "I'm all grown up now." Touching a bruise on Americo's neck, Lauren questioned him. "Why do you have all of those bruises on your arms and neck?"

"I don't know what happens to me, but I get in a lot of fights when I've been drinking. I feel frustrated, like there's something I'm not seeing." Americo wondered if Lauren's husband hurt her. "Why do you have those scars on your arms and legs?"

"I pick holes in my skin just so I can feel something."

"You couldn't do that with your fingers. What do you use?"

"Needles, tweezers, scissors, blades, anything I can find."

They held each other in silence, Americo feeling helpless as he realized her unhappiness. He was desperate for her presence and desperate for her safety. "Hold me, Lauren, there's always an empty space to my left when you're gone."

For years Lauren occasionally felt a warm spot on her cheek for no apparent reason. "I know what you mean. When I think of you I feel a warm spot on my right cheek." She held his finger to the spot. "Right here."

"How can we stand this?"

"When we're apart, we'll still feel the connection between us. Think of me standing beside you all of the time."

"I know. I'll try, but it hurts."

Although Lauren planned to tell Americo about their son when she came home from Peru, she realized that to lose him now would probably cost her life. "I know, but I have too many problems right now to give you more. Maybe someday."

"Promise."

"Promise. Let's open your presents. I know you'll like them, because you have the first rug I gave you on your wall just like you said you would."

"Get a few hours sleep, I'll see you a little later at Rita's. I love you, Lauren."

"Not as much as I love you, Jugador, and someday you'll know that. I promise."

☪

The day was too perfect for a funeral. The relentless heat of the summer retreated for a day, the clouds danced lightly across the sky and a soft warm breeze wafted through the valley as Rita scattered Zack's ashes in her spiral garden. The guests had left El Rancho de las Estrellas, leaving the family to say goodbye to Zachary Tanner Auldney in private. Trey raised his glass and offered a toast to his grandfather. Sunnie and Lauren held hands and cried. Americo stood by Lydia, and Jake helped his mother scatter the ashes around the spiral.

Trey spoke for the family. With his grandfather gone and with his father spiraling down, Trey now believed he and Americo shared the role as the guardians of the rancho and the women in the Auldney family. "It's the end of an era. The days of cowboys, gamblers, and the old southwest has ended. Zack Auldney was one of the last. The Arizona gambler is dead. He was unique for his breed because he didn't carry a gun. Rather than use a gun, he dueled with his skills. He had a full life. He loved one woman madly for over fifty years; he lived on the land he loved and rode good horses. He was a magician with his cards and with his wisdom. We will miss you Grandpa Zack."

# The Unspinning Begins

*All acts of love and pleasure are my rituals. Starhawk*

*The ancestors are always with us. They speak
through our blood. Martha Graham*

As they walked the path foretold before the world began to
spin, the tale of Lauren and Americo grew rich with feelings and
memories. According to destiny, their energy threads remained
powerfully connected as the faithfully spinning Vortex provided a
self-contained pattern. Americo lived in an axis straight line and
Lauren spun around him, trying to find her way home. He climbed
his ladder to the stars, and Lauren often stopped, but couldn't
stay.

Lauren and Americo, like the spiral and the ladder, together
formed the pattern of duality, the dynamic aspect of unity. The

ladder represents space, ascending and descending, touching the heavens, the terrestrial, and the underworld. The spiral, holding the axis within the eye of her belly, is pure motion and like time, inexorably unfolds towards the future and contracts the past within itself. Time unfolds and space expands, and true to the biologic imperative of their physiology, Lauren and Americo embodied and lived in the embrace of this essential duality.

As the Great Weaver wove perpetual stories of Lauren and Americo into the land of the red rocks, the Vortex spun Lauren close to Americo, and then cruelly flung them worlds apart. Spinning wildly, Lauren lost control. Spinning wildly, Lauren found her art. Spinning wildly, Lauren found her way home.

☪

Sybille Ginot committed suicide. Dressed in a stunning Dior gown, wearing full makeup, with her affairs impeccably in order, Sybille swallowed a bottle of sleeping pills. Didier Chesnel discovered Sybille dead in her bedroom, notified her family, and executed her will. Her children did not benefit from her estate, and inexplicably she returned her divorce settlement to Jake Auldney. Sybille was not mourned; she was forgotten.

Lauren laughed hysterically, stoned out of her mind. "I wonder if she would like me to have a lovely cocktail in honor of her demise?"

"Tough break," Trey said reading the telegram on his way to teach an undergraduate class.

"Poisonous, predatory bitch," Jake said writing a check for another racehorse.

"It was her destiny," Rita whispered as she wove a pink thread into Lauren's weaving.

☪

Lightning, descending from black, pregnant, swollen clouds, danced menacingly on the red rocks over El Rancho de las Estrellas on an August evening during the late summer monsoons. Safe in her Grandmother's home, Lauren hypnotically stirred homemade chicken soup on the stove. Taking a little break from life, Lauren spent two weeks in August on the rancho, riding horses with Americo, spending nights in his bed, trying to figure out how she could rewind the Vortex of time and live her life with him or without him. "Grandma, I know I don't love Jim, but I don't think I hate him either. In a way he scares me because he wants me to be so perfect. I'm trying so hard to do things right, but the harder I try, the more frustrated I get."

Rita stood next Lauren, mixing a bowl of dumpling mix for the soup. Adding some sprinkles of chives Rita stopped to look at Lauren's strained face. Behind her glasses, Lauren's eyes were sunken and ringed with dark circles from lack of sleep. Her skin talcum pale, she seemed fragile, about to crack. "What is it that would make your heart sing, Lauren?"

Listlessly, Lauren stirred, staring into the bubbling pot as if an answer would magically appear. Tears ran slowly down her cheeks as she turned to Rita. "I'm just so mixed up, Grandma, more than anything I want..."

Lightning struck. Lauren froze when she felt the cold, fierce bolt of energy blast through her body. Only a second passed but when Lauren opened her eyes, the stove, the pan, knobs, and drip pans had melted. Lightning had followed a pathway through the wiring, into the house, and into Lauren. Returning to awareness, Lauren turned, stunned. "I guess I was just given a sign."

Rita waited.

Lauren misread the sign.

Due to her perpetually bizarre behavior and at the insistence of her husband, Lauren saw a therapist. After submitting to brain wave tests, personality tests, physical examinations, and talk therapy, the therapist diagnosed her with Borderline Personality Disorder. This is a condition characterized by a pervasive pattern of instability in interpersonal relationships, fear of real or imagined abandonment, identity disturbance, impulsivity, recurring suicidal behavior, affective instability due to marked reactivity of moods, chronic feelings of emptiness, along with inappropriate, intense anger. Lauren was also diagnosed with an accompanying acute Dissociative Disorder called Depersonalization, wherein a person experiences a change of self-awareness such as feeling detached from their own experience, with the self, the body and the mind seeming foreign. She also exhibited all of the symptoms

of a condition known as Derealization, wherein the world surrounding a person feels unfamiliar and unreal.

However, the therapist also offered her an alternative. It was
discovered that Lauren could alter her brain wave patterns at will
and could enter into deep meditative trances with startling facility. The therapist, a grandson of a Native American shaman,
encouraged Lauren to embrace her qualities and consider them a
blessing. Based on Lauren's childhood dreams, he explained to her
in mythic terms, that her mind and soul were fragmented. This
provided her with an opportunity to rearrange the parts of her
being in a more harmonious order. This made sense to Lauren.

Feeling understood Lauren made the announcement that she
was not alone in her madness. "My heart, mind, and soul have
already been broken into a million pieces. Now I just have to put
humpty back together again." Lauren laughed at the look of fear
on her husband's face. Lauren liked what the therapist said,
threw her medications in the garbage and rudely gave her husband the finger, but not before throwing the chocolate malt she
held in his face.

☪

Standing nude before the High Priestess Lauren felt the
wand tap her on the shoulder. The full moon, casting silver brilliance over the coven of thirteen Witches, opened a portal for
Lauren to enter her destiny. In the North Carolina Blue Ridge
Mountains, Lauren solemnly made an offering to the circle. Slowly
opening her eyes, she walked to the cauldron and deliberately
removed the small gold wedding band from her finger. "I'm not
coming home, Jim," she said to the flurry of bats flying overhead.
"For seven years you've tried to kill the only good part of me I have
left, and I better leave before I kill you." Cringing as she recalled
the fear of her husband's constant threats to commit her, she
vowed to never give anybody that kind of power over her again.
Remembering the night she left home after slashing his entire
wardrobe with a pair of scissors, Lauren wondered what awaited
her when she told him of her decision. "I've got my dog, my
Volkswagen, tons of hours at the university and no degree, a few
thousand dollars, and nowhere to go. This ought to be easy."

It was easy. Lauren got a job designing jewelry for a world-
renowned establishment. With a gale force the doors of her career

blew open. Lauren got her degree, forgot to get a divorce, tried to stop loving Americo, and within three years fell in love again with a married man fourteen years her senior. From her home base in Atlanta, she made contacts, spent weeks at a time in New York City, and traveled with wealthy clients to their homes around the world. All the while Lauren expertly carved her body, cleverly hiding the wounds so few knew of her secret.

☪

Gaining consciousness, Lauren surrendered to a pair of intense, loving blue eyes. When he took her in his arms, carrying her into the hospital, although almost thirty years old, Lauren felt truly safe for the first time in her life.

"It's a sunstroke," the doctor told Wyatt Kirkman. "She's been partying all night and playing tennis in the heat of the day. She's dehydrated, her temperature is dangerously high, her pulse is racing, and she needs to rest. Are you family?"

"Not yet," Wyatt smiled, patting Lauren's hand. Wyatt spoke to the doctor in private. "But I assume responsibility for anything she needs."

Lauren's annual visit to Sedona was cut short that year by a call from Wyatt asking her to meet him in Aspen. Standing in the snow wearing her sandals she knocked on the door of Americo's home, determined to end their affair and spend her life with Wyatt. "I can't do this anymore," Lauren told him coldly. "I'm not honest with you, and I've kept secrets I can never tell you. I know you don't understand and neither do I." Setting her chin, intent on not crying, she told him before walking away, "Find a nice girl, get married, and have those ten kids you want. Believe me, if you forget about me you'll have a happier life, because I'm a murderer, a liar, and a thief."

Furious, Americo cracked open a new deck of cards. "You, Lauren, are a fucking fool."

Lauren was fired from her position as a designer when she defied protocol and went to the chairman of the board to renegotiate her contract. The head of the design department demanded an apology. Lauren said, "Fuck you," picked up her portfolio, settled her account, and left the imposing building on Fifth Avenue.

Lauren and Wyatt cuddled in front of the fireplace in the small cabin she purchased from him in the hills of North Carolina.

"Wyatt, I agree, let's have a baby. No," Lauren said sweetly while scratching his shoulders with a needle and tasting the blood, "if you get divorced I'll leave you. I'm too crazy to be responsible for your happiness. I love you, and I want our relationship to stay just the way it is now."

Lauren screamed. Wyatt called the ambulance and as he held her in his arms in the emergency room, Lauren lost their baby. "I caused it to happen," she told Wyatt when she awakened. "I told you that someday I would have to pay for what I did to the guy from home. I don't deserve to be a mother, so go home to your wife and two daughters."

Wyatt didn't agree, and within a week he had tools, gold, and stones delivered to her door, encouraging her to contact the agent in New York who wanted to represent her. Lauren was frozen. She spent hours looking at the studio space in her house, wishing she had the energy and courage to pick up a tool. Packing her bags himself, Wyatt then drove to his plane and took her to the Yucatan for two months to heal her body, soul, and mind with a woman who became her teacher and guide for many years.

Again Lauren's career flourished. The agent she hired was brilliant, and she was paid enormous amounts of money for designs and finished pieces. Life was too good, and once again Lauren yearned to wander. Lauren's life was sweet and doubting that she were truly alive, Lauren carved open a window. "Wyatt, I've hurt myself. Please hurry," she screamed into the phone, "I can't stop the blood." Wyatt paled when he rushed into her house and saw blood on the towels, bed, and carpet, wondering how she could still be conscious. Refusing anesthetic, Lauren reeled in the pleasure of the pain as the doctor stuck a needle in her leg.

"She needs help," the doctor told Wyatt, as he made small precise stitches in Lauren's leg. "This behavior can lead to suicide."

"Bullshit," Lauren cursed life in general as she hobbled out of the hospital refusing Wyatt's help. "Wyatt, I'm leaving you and I want to sell my house." Glaring at him, defying him to try to stop her, she told him, "Don't try to talk me out of it, because I've made up my mind. I'm not going to some fucking therapist and let those idiots turn me into another robot."

☪

Sitting alone in her apartment Lauren opened the envelope she received from Americo in October, expecting to see an announcement of his engagement. When an airline ticket fell to the table, she started to cry. "Jugador, I am such a bitch." Reading the note he enclosed she felt sick, knowing she would return to his bed without telling him the truth. The note was short and emphatic, but in the background of his words, she felt his love. Again, she read the note.

> *Lauren, I'll see you in December. A deal is a deal, Bruja, and we made a promise no matter what. A*

The ride from the airport was silent. Americo gripped Lauren's hand, staring ahead at the road. Hardness had set in, his lips were tight and his eyes had lost their sparkle. Retreating to his home, for two days they held each other, barely saying a word. On the second night Lauren prepared a bath for Americo.

With the grace of an experienced courtesan, Lauren dropped lavender, lemon grass, dried citrus peels, and honey into the steaming water. Tens of candles lit the small sunflower filled bathroom. Silently leading him by the hand to the large claw foot tub, Lauren looked into his eyes, asking him to surrender. She undressed him slowly, licking his body, stopping to touch him, not wanting him to forget. Three times, Lauren rang a bell and with a pass of her hands called in their magic. Massaging his chest with a soapy sponge, she crinkled her nose giving him a sheepish grin. Relaxing, Americo tiredly mussed her hair. "Whatever you're doing, Baby, please don't stop," Americo said closing his eyes. "Ring the bell again, Lauren. I felt the vibrations move through my body."

Lauren instructed in a hushed tone. "Just be. Don't try to think or feel, just be."

When he opened his eyes he saw soft sparkling energy surrounding Lauren and tears rolled down his cheeks.

"See," Lauren said touching his cheek with her finger. "I told you to never ever give up on us. There will always be hope if we keep it alive, Jugador."

"Promise?"

"Promise."

The next wave of magic rolled in as Lauren stepped into the tub. "Close your eyes and let me shave your face. Oops," she said as she nicked his skin. "Let me lick the blood, Americo." Waves of ecstasy moved through her body.

"I find this an interesting way to have a conversation," Americo said sitting in front of the bathroom mirror while Lauren, wrapped in a pink fluffy towel, trimmed his long black hair. Looking at her in the mirror he said, "It's like our reflections are having a conversation at the same time we are." Shaking his head he continued, "Actually it's a little disconcerting to me. I keep wondering, whom am I talking to, and who is talking to me?"

"Does any of it really matter, my love?"

Lauren's glasses rested studiously low on her nose, her willing subject submitting to her serious effort. Snipping each lock with precision she crinkled her nose mischievously, tantalizing him with the scissors when he teased her. "Be careful, my little vampira, or it'll look like I've been abused, not pampered beyond my wildest expectations."

"You haven't seen anything yet," Lauren promised him. Listening to the chime of the bell on her charm bracelet, Lauren whispered. "Let's go to bed and make love. In the morning we can open our presents and pretend we're having Christmas together in our home."

☪

Sipping creamy eggnog, Lauren sat on the floor by the Christmas tree holding her baby niece. Carefully avoiding Americo, Lauren pretended she had just arrived the afternoon before. Jake looked up from the painting of a stallion Lauren had given him and scrutinized her, feeling there might be more to Lauren's story. "Lauren, come over here and tell me what my little girl does with her time."

"Oh, Daddy, I make a little jewelry and try to sell it. I play tennis and golf, but mostly I just hang out and go dancing with friends. You know, no big deal."

Disappointed in Lauren's career choice, Jake encouraged her to change courses and criticized her as he walked across the room for more eggnog. "I never thought a daughter of mine would end up doing work like that. It's not too late to earn your Ph.D. and then teach at a university. It seems that what you do is rather like working in a factory."

Silently Lauren's small bubble of confidence burst as she smiled, keeping her secrets. Thinking of her small studio space decorated with special treasures, paintings, and candles, Lauren couldn't understand why he didn't understand the beauty of her work. "I'll get my Ph.D. someday, Daddy, but I don't want to ttt-teach," Lauren stammered. "I love what I dddo."

"Are you still stuttering, Lauren?" Jake said sarcastically. "Stop it. No wonder you don't want to teach."

Rita looked at Jake with anger in her eyes. "Stop it, Jake. Don't you know you're hurting Lauren's feelings?"

Americo stared at Jake, fiercely gripping his hands together to keep from attacking Lauren's father. He felt Rita's gentle touch on his arm, unaware that she had seen the savage rage in his eyes. "How can he say those things to her?" Wanting desperately to comfort Lauren, he smiled at her thinking, "Why can't he tell her what an incredible artist she's becoming?"

Lydia watched as Lauren squeezed her eyes trying not to cry. Confusion clouded Lauren's mind and with her hands shaking she sat down next to Trey and Sunnie. "Don't let it get you down," Trey said wondering why she always overreacted. "He doesn't mean anything by what he says."

Picking up her baby daughter and motioning for Lauren to follow her into the kitchen, Sunnie hissed at Trey, "Trey, he better not talk to our daughter like that or I won't stay here."

☾★

Americo stormed out of the hacienda, feeling trapped. Marquita Pena had just told him she was pregnant with his child. "I knew you were trouble," he yelled back at her standing in the door. "You know there's no damned way I'm going to marry you." Reminding her of the boundaries he established from the beginning, he grabbed her by the arms and shook her. "You did this on purpose; I know you did. I bought birth control pills, and you didn't take them. Admit it, Marquita." He stared coldly into her frightened eyes.

Earlier in the day he had put Lauren on a plane. Plans had been made to meet in the summer and Americo's heart was breaking.

"Americo," Lauren said to him at the airport with her head resting on his chest, "we have no choice. I love you and I'll always love you." Holding his face in her hands she whispered to him softly, "You are my light, but someday you'll hate me. I care too much about what you think and until I don't, I can't come home. Leave me if you have to, I want you to be happy. I'll hate it," Lauren said brushing lint from his hat, "but I'll understand."

Marquita protested, but not too much, as Americo escorted her by the elbow into the dark back alley abortionist's office. "I'll wait for you," he said gently. "I'm sorry, Marquita, but you knew from the beginning that I love Lauren."

"Someday," Marquita thought as she acquiesced with a small pained smile, "someday you'll both pay for this. I'm going to hell for murdering a baby and I'll take both of you with me."

☪

Stoned again, with pure abandonment Lauren danced wildly under the stars. Deep in the Smoky Mountains of Tennessee, she shook her tambourine trying to forget her son, her lover, and her home. Now in her thirties, Lauren had flowered into a beauty. Her body was luscious but slender, her facial features were delicately carved and her eyes spoke of the deep mystery held within her. As she learned to trust, she fascinated people with the many contradictions she reluctantly revealed. Without meaning to, Lauren became a teacher.

Lauren returned to a small craft school that she had attended to help teach an intensive session in precious metal fabrication. She didn't like to teach, but she loved the life. Thirty artists gathered and lived in primitive conditions to devote three months exclusively to their art. Reveling in the cold outdoor showers, Lauren greeted every morning hours before others reluctantly crawled from their beds. Often working late into the night alone in the common studios Lauren found her artistic voice. Sipping warm scotch and eating cheese and crackers, images came to her mind. Soon, she had the courage to expertly craft them into extraordinarily bold designs. Her work lost the quality of shy restraint, became erotic and devoted to the female anatomy. Holding a detailed, gold, labia-shaped pendant to the light, Lauren sighed, "Yes." Smiling as she sketched more erotic designs in her book, she said, "This I understand."

☪

Within a year Lauren took the new understanding of her art to Monaco, and true to her list, Lauren lived simply, and did it on her own. For ten of the years Lauren remained in exile, the Mediterranean Sea, the bluest water on Earth, was the view from her living room window. Always living simply, Lauren lived alone in a small caretaker's cottage owned by Didier Chesnel. Hours passed as she looked at the water with her eyes defocused, remembering eons ago when the red rock castle of Sedona emerged as the inland sea receded.

The vow Americo and Lauren made to love each other and have a relationship was honored, and each year she returned to Americo's home in late December, remaining in Sedona until mid January. Most years, they met at his hacienda for a month in the spring, and in the summer, Americo left the cruel heat of Sedona to find shelter for a month by the Mediterranean Sea. There were camping trips, vacations to remote places, letters, phone calls, and visits in dreamtime. In her deepest knowing, she acknowledged she had sacrificed her life with Americo to a secret and the expectations of others, and she knew that if she returned to Sedona to stay, Americo would have to be told the truth.

Making certain her life was portable she chose an art form that took little space. She worried about security, yet her attachments were few. Self-destruction became a way of life. Lauren earned money and spent money, not believing she had a future. Her instability waxed and waned, and the scars on her body increased as the secret she carried became heavier. Lauren's arms felt emptier as she kept waiting for something to happen. Numbness overwhelmed her sensibilities and while alone she scarred herself, trying to feel something, anything. At times she lived dangerously, drug use was light but constant. She married on impulse and looked to dangerous men or impossible relationships to reinforce her feelings of worthlessness. Lauren understood her art, her craft, her love of being a woman, and her gypsy lifestyle, but she did not understand why she chose the men in her life. In the book of her men, there was a rich racecar driver, a young artist twelve years her junior, a football superstar, jet setting playboys, and a shy, bookish poet. The only constant among the men in her life was their propensity to seek altered states, rarely legally. Her career flourished, relationships foundered, her material needs were few and Lauren thought she was free.

Through it all she had a touchstone to the girl she had been. Some souls hide and some surrender. Lauren cracked rather than submit. Through defiance she protected the wild self, never again surrendering or complying with the expectations of others.

The wrinkles grew deeper, the flesh began to soften, hair grayed, veins started to show, love deepened, the heartbreak remained, and the number of disappointments grew. Many promises had been broken, but with the ripening of age the heart lightens, and the soul remains eternal.

☪

Ten years later, Americo perused the deeds on his coffee table, wanting to discuss the investments he made with the money Lauren brought to him over the years. "I've matched every dollar she brought to me with two of my own, and she never wants to discuss finances." He shook his head at her lack of regard for money. Checking to make certain all of his preparations were ready, he started watching for lights of the car. Long before he saw the lights, Americo felt Lauren traveling towards him. He lit the candles by the tub, felt the charm in his pocket, and readied the champagne glasses. "Baby," he said greeting her at the door, "you look so tired. Let me carry you across the threshold, I've been so lonely without you." Thanking Ignacio profusely for delivering her, Americo locked the door, locked out the rest of the world and took Lauren in his arms.

The sky was clear, the stars hung close enough to feel their vibrations and on their last night together, under the light of the moon, Lauren and Americo planted the new tree. After making love on the oversized chaise lounge, Americo lit a cigarette wanting to discuss his plans. Speaking in a low husky tone Americo told her the bad news. "Your Dad's in trouble," he said solemnly. "He's broke, and he's mortgaged his part of the rancho."

"I'm not surprised." She responded hesitantly, slowly kissing his fingers. "What's going to happen?"

"I can bail him out." Americo turned his face to look into her eyes. "I just wanted you to know about it first."

"What about his house?"

"He'll still have his house and a small amount of money from the equity to live on."

"Thank God."

Lauren put her arms around Americo, asking him, "Why do you want to do this?"

"For you, for us, for a promise I made to myself a long time ago."

"Why for me? The only regret I'd have is having strangers live on our rancho."

To Americo the landscape was a woman, and the woman was the landscape, and he loved his land like a man loves a woman. Throughout his life, he surrendered to the receptive, absorbent red sandstone labyrinth, making himself a part of the land and the land a part of him. He attuned himself to the red rocks, discovering the correspondences and thus created an extended identity with his environment far beyond himself. Receiving, not grasping, he had climbed the rock faces, held his hands on the body of the Earth, ventured deep into crevices, found hidden caves, waterfalls, and rock walls stained by the ages that contained his story.

Americo could not separate the land from the woman he loved and holding her face in his hands, he saw the landscape through the filter of Lauren. "Bruja, I want to do it because to me the land is eternally female, and I see the replication of our rancho and the Vortex in your eyes and in your ways. When I look at you, Princess, I see the female essence of the red rocks, the spinning, the relentless motion, the turbulence, and the passion of the Vortex. You've spun around me just like the Vortex; sometimes coming close and other times wandering so far away. When you were born, this land was imprinted on your body, mind, and soul and someday you'll know you can never escape."

Lauren closed her eyes, seeing a ladder to the stars, an axis mundi in the center of the Vortex, revealing the stack of his experiences. She saw herself spinning around him, containing him within the hollow center of her soul, and Lauren knew that she had never escaped the power of the red rocks or the pattern of the Vortex. "The rancho is all you've ever wanted, isn't it?"

Americo tweaked her nose, laughing. "I have a degree in philosophy, and I've read Heidegger regarding the importance of dwelling in place." He laughed wryly once again. "Hell, Baby, I know the value of your place, your home, the horse you rode in on, and the cards you were dealt. Do you want me to loan you the book?"

One by one, the plans and dreams he made as a young man were coming true.

Five years later, when Lauren left Sedona after the holidays, she boarded the plane with a star-shaped garnet ring on her finger, Rita's blessing, and the words she could not ignore. "Lauren, the Vortex is pulling your filaments home." Rita made her demands one evening while spinning by the potbelly stove. "Destiny is summoning you and you have no choice. The time has come for you to end your exile, complete the circle and return to our red rock paradise. You can no longer continue creating paths to nowhere in your life, my garden, or in your heart."

Rita handed Lauren pink silk from her baby dress, gold thread and a needle, telling her to make holes in the silk representing her heartbreaks, mend them with the thread, and then release the memories to the past. "Complete the task I'm giving you, and I will see your footprints in my garden before this year ends. The doorways that you closed while wandering are now aligned on the spiral path of the Vortex, and if you do not pass through them now, you may never have another chance."

Often, just before it slows, life spins the sweetest. Lauren sat in the garden she tended talking with Didier Chesnel, telling him that she had decided to move home to Sedona within the year. "Didier," she told him with tears in her eyes, "I appreciate that you kept my secret. It seems that life is kindly allowing me to reflect and acknowledge with honesty the path I've taken."

He answered with fatherly regard in his voice. "Lauren, we've been friends for a long time. It's a gift to become aware in a moment of clarity of what one has done." Pouring Lauren another glass of wine, he said solemnly, "Becoming aware is a moment of profound poignancy, and it is a moment of truth that each living being must face if they are to live within the authenticity of their lives."

To a friend, Lauren described the past year as the time a soft pink veil of peace covered her life. "I'm not afraid anymore," she said leisurely over a glass of wine and bowl of vichyssoise at a small café by the harbor. Crinkling her eyes, now lined from years of experience, she smiled thinking of the January morning Americo put her on the plane. "When Americo put this ring on my finger, he told me that it could mean anything I wanted, but for him it was a formal commitment. I don't feel guilty anymore, I won't apologize, I've accepted that I did the best I could, and when I wrap the warm cloak of our story around him, I think he'll understand." In answer to the question her friend posed, Lauren answered, "I'm not going to tell him until I'm back in Sedona, because believe or not, I'm moving home for me, not for him."

The year flew by, not a month passing that Americo and Lauren didn't see one another. Unexpected, Americo arrived just in time to escort Lauren to the opening of her show in March. She laughed when she unpacked a tuxedo he had custom made for the occasion and swooned when he walked out of the bedroom. "Americo, don't we look gorgeous for a couple of country bumpkins from Arizona? If my old classmates could see me now."

The hacienda was a haven of domestic bliss for them in April. They took care of each other as they cooked, cleaned every room in the small dwelling, and gave all of the walls a fresh coat of white-wash. After painting the trim on the windows a bright chili red, Lauren planted flowers in the window boxes, while Americo made repairs on the bar tile roof and trimmed the honeysuckle vines. Quiet, balmy evenings were either spent alone, riding their horses in the moonlight, walking on the beach in San Carlos, or in the company of Americo's friends at a local cantina, where they held each other close and danced to the sensuous music of the guitar.

In May, on the Greek isle of Crete, Lauren set up camp for them near the Matala caves where she lived after running away. Under the moonlight she danced for him on the beach in the same place she danced with her heart broken, thirty years before. Holding his hand, she showed Americo the farmers market where she bought the first small carpet for him. Much to everybody's delight, she cooked a meal complete with fudge cake for dessert at the home where she worked as a housekeeper. They left Crete with each other's names tattooed on their butts, having drank too many beers over a long lunch at an outdoor café. At the airport, Americo made Lauren blush when he held her fanny, proclaiming loudly for all to hear, "Mine, Lauren, this is all mine."

In August, just as Lauren finished eating cream puffs and sipping coffee on her balcony, they kissed hello at her door, Americo arriving by taxi. Arriving in Monaco to escort Lauren to an opening and spend his month by the sea, he possessively held her by the elbow as she showed him the display she created with her hand-painted brooms, jewels, dolls, and soil from Sedona.

Lauren glowed with pride at her exhibit of her dolls standing by the brooms encircling a large mound of red soil. "As you can see, Darling, I've swept up my life just as a good Witch should. I've swept everything up and mixed it with the red rock powder I had you ship to me last February."

Sipping champagne on the beach Lauren took his hand and kissed his fingers one by one. "I'm all grown up, Americo. I've come to terms with my life, and I'm ready to start a future without apology. I'm moving home to Sedona after my time in the Andes."

Americo spoke huskily, holding her breast, starting to make love to her on the sand. "I'll buy you a one way ticket from Lima to Phoenix tomorrow." Americo left Nice with a packed suitcase for Lauren that he would bring to the airport when he picked her up.

"Darling, I want to go somewhere so we can be alone and talk as soon as I arrive in Phoenix, I don't want to wait until we get back to El Rancho de las Estrellas." Holding her arms out to show how free she felt, she told him, "I can only carry a backpack when I'm trekking in the Andes, so I'll need these clothes when you pick me up. Please find a place where I can get some massages for my old aching body and where we can spend a few days talking about what I have to tell you."

Hugging goodbye at the airport, after spending days packing Lauren's belongings, Americo assured her once again, "I'll love you no matter what your secret is, I've always told you that." Americo lifted her chin with his fingers. "Lauren, promise me again that you didn't take the gun, it would kill me if you hurt yourself with something that belonged to me."

"My God, Americo, I promise. This has been the happiest year of my life, why would I want to kill myself now? Haven't you noticed that I'm not cutting my body anymore?"

Americo gently touched the faint scars on Lauren's chest, reminding her that he always checked her body for signs. "I've noticed, but I worry, and you know I couldn't live in a world without you in it."

With her head on his chest Lauren started to cry. "Have a wonderful time at the hacienda and with don Esteban. Will you make certain the flowers I planted are being watered? Please give my horse some extra apple treats, and I can't wait to cook dinner for you on the new outdoor stove."

"Lauren, tell Benito and Feliciana I send my love and tell them to take good care of my woman. Don't cry, Baby," he said softly running his fingers through her messy hair, "I want this to be the last time you're away from me for so long. Americo whispered through his kiss, "Believe me, I'll stand by you no matter what." Americo had often wondered if Lauren had committed a crime, hurt somebody, or loved a man she hadn't told him about.

"I will, I promise," Lauren said holding her tearstained face in her hands. Lauren stood on her toes, giving him a hundred quick kisses. "Please guard these things with your life, other than you, I really don't have anything else in the world."

Americo turned and waved, once again in awe of how deeply

she trusted him. In his care she sent her design books, special tools, her personal jewelry, her collection of gemstones, and inventory of completed pieces of jewelry.

"Read your letter. I love you."

☪

As the plane crossed the Atlantic Ocean taking him from his Lauren, Americo enjoyed a stimulating debate with a New York investment banker discussing the potential real estate market boom in rural America that Americo had anticipated for years. Cocktails and dinner were served, the conversation became livelier, and the time passed quickly before Americo closed his eyes under the first veil of sleep. He stretched his long legs into the aisle and slept more soundly than he had for years. Americo was content, the empty space to his left, the lonely place he held for Lauren, was filled with her presence and commitment. He woke briefly, looked at his watch and smiled. "It's the witching hour so it must be Lauren I'm feeling next to me." Just as the plane began to descend into Kennedy Airport, Americo remembered the letter. Catching the eye of the banker seated beside him, he winked when he opened the scented envelope and a small, pink vaginal shaped seashell dropped into his lap.

"A love letter?" the man next to him asked.

"Yes," Americo answered proudly. "It's from the woman I'm going to marry in a few months." Reading the letter Americo laughed with gusto, causing the flight attendant to smile at the unusual sound of such pure delight. He read with amusement as he looked at Lauren's scrawled handwriting and tried to decipher all of the lines, dashes, curlicues, and hearts she drew in the margins. Americo grinned to himself when he translated the erotic drawings on the back of the page, knowing he was being reminded of the rainy afternoon when they stayed in bed for hours, much to his great pleasure.

> *My Dearest Love,*
> *This will surprise you. I'm full of surprises at this time, aren't I? I told you years ago that I knew how much money I owed you from our poker games. I've kept track since I was eleven years old and as I write this check, I realize that I should*

*have stopped playing long ago.*

*I'm giving you this check because I want to come home with all of my accounts paid in full. I'm planning to start a new life, and I want to start from the beginning. Don't worry, because the check will clear my bank. I can see you laughing, Jugador. As you know, I had a great show in March and this one was even better. I want you to do something very special for yourself with the $17,382.97.*

*By the time you read this letter, I will be leaving for Peru in a week and you will be traveling to Mexico. Darling, we've had the best year together. My wandering is over, and I come to you a wiser, although admittedly more wrinkled and crinkled woman than the one who left you so long ago. Americo, please bring our photo album when you pick me up at the airport. There is only one more thing I need to do to reclaim my life, and I pray that after that we can receive our future, blessing the past for what it taught us. Do you think we should keep it a secret that we've loved each other for thirty years? I love you, my Americo, and I'll see you at the airport in less than a month.*

*Your Lauren*

"Baby, the veils that surround you certainly enhance your oh so mysterious ways." Americo laughed again. "But at times I can almost see right through the almost transparent, shimmering, silky, multicolored veil you put between us." Taking long confident strides down the corridor of the airport Americo patted the letter in his pocket. "Yes, our outdoor lives have aged us. Experience shows and we've both had plenty of that, but I love every line, scar, bruise, bump, and wrinkle on you." Americo grabbed his bag from the carousel and made a plan. "Lauren, I don't know why you did it, but I'll cash your check and buy myself the Indian motorcycle I've been looking at. We'll talk about it later, but for now get that fabulous fanny of yours home," he smiled thinking of her curvy body, "and start taking care of your lonely man."

☪

Holding a small piece of paper in her hand, Lauren stood outside of the doctor's office, not knowing if she wanted to laugh or cry. Remembering the afternoon that Americo looked at her calendar and asked why she hadn't started her period, she laughed softly as tears ran down her cheeks. "I wonder if he thought I was pregnant."

Americo had looked at her with questioning eyes, hoping that another of his dreams would be realized.

"Honey, I'm just late, aren't you glad I'm not getting my dot until you leave town?"

"No, Lauren, I'm not," he answered, kissing her, "you know how I love it."

Lauren shivered as she recalled his face, wild with primal passion, as he smeared the blood from her womb over their bodies.

The pharmacist filled a prescription for hormone replacement, and Lauren stood alone in her kitchen, crying when she took the first pill. "I'm really changing in everyway. I never realized it before, but a small part of me always thought Americo and I would have another baby."

Lauren laughed, popping the little blue pill in her mouth. "So, I'm going home a crone. What the hell, life begins at fifty."

☪

Dreading the humid blast furnace, Lauren checked her fanny pack for documents, smiled at a woman staring with amusement at the red laces in her hiking boots and walked into the hot, sticky Lima dawn. Greeting Lauren as she inhaled the salty ocean air were haunting, abandoned planes, neglected and imprisoned with barbwire fences.

Three hours later, with hundreds of dollars worth of soles in her money belt, Lauren held her breath as Aero Peru flight 752 began the step ascent from sea level to 14,000 feet towards Cuzco, the jewel of the Andes. Flying straight into the air above a cushion of clouds in a plane filled with pilgrims, tourists, and native Quechua, Lauren exhaled as she gazed at the mist blanketed valleys and ravines of the Andes. Lauren sighed, hoping her state of mind would remain as high as the ascent, for in less than an hour she would see her soul brother, Benito.

☪

The Cuzco marketplace, vivid and rich with color, seemed a vibrating tapestry. Empty egg cartons stacked several feet high stood next to bagged coca, a mountain of fresh cut flowers, piles of ripe bananas, and mounds of sensuous green avocado. Clutching her satchel Lauren followed Feliciana down a narrow alley into a dark building and quickly closed the door behind her. A wrinkled face peeked from behind a woven drapery, and Lauren squealed with delight when a wrinkled, bent woman emerged to greet her. Wondering what mysterious treasure the owner of the Witches Market had to show her, Lauren followed the grandmother into closed private chambers.

In the darkened, dusty, musty, smelly room, shelves were filled with seeds of every variety, skeletons, monkey tails, dried llama fetus, bats, and dead birds with their wings spread as if in flight. Lauren jumped when she felt a spider web on her hair, making the old woman cackle with glee. Slyly she opened a box and motioned for Lauren to peek inside. Lauren's hand flew to her mouth when she saw a stone perfectly shaped like an owl. The owl stone was smooth, the color of midnight, and fit perfectly in the palm of her hand. Lauren rubbed the owl gently not wanting it to leave her touch and looked at the grandmother questioningly, hoping it was for sale. The old woman put her hand between Lauren's breasts, chanted a blessing in Quechua and indicated for Lauren to open her satchel. With a kiss from the elderly woman on her cheek, Lauren knew she had been given a gift of great power, and with tears in her eyes, hugged her friend hoping it was an omen to accompany her hope-filled heart throughout her journey.

Visiting with the grandmother and young woman preparing the despachos, Lauren watched carefully as gifts for the brujas were created. She appealed to the women, "Por favor, please make my future a sweet one. I need all of the help you can channel into the despachos." She then radiated a warm smile and presented them with gifts of Rita's small weavings.

A despacho is a gift to the Earth and the stars offered in ceremony under the heavenly Andean skies. Deep in her task the young woman wrapped varieties of seeds, candy, paper money, heart-shaped plastic ornaments, claws, wings of butterflies, cats whiskers, pieces of fur, sprinklings of soil, small rocks, leaves, and star-shaped stickers in meticulous small bundles of newsprint, tying them with short pieces of colored yarn. The small bundles were then wrapped into a larger one. The bundles are protected until those who believe in magic join together in an ancient ritual performed on mountaintops under the Southern Cross. The individual bundles are opened by an elder, sprinkled with sacred flower water and liquor, and then arranged according to information received from Pachamama and las estrellas. The story told by the arrangement reveals the future, with the past firmly absorbed into the present. Following the reading the despacho is burned, sending the energy to the heavens and the remains returned to the Mother. Having shared a kintui of coca with their friends, the three women left the small mysterious shop with eight despachos, four bottles of agua de florida, blessings from the grandmother, and a promise to return when back in Cuzco.

☪

Lauren peered fearfully over the ledge and feeling the heaviness of her backpack and satchel, she questioned if she had the strength to carry the burden on the narrow rutted path to her destination. Following a steep descent, the path was uphill, and there were few hours of sun before darkness descended from the high folded mountains. Seeking a comforting farewell, Lauren touched the divided trunk of the magnificent tree and absorbed the vast wisdom contained in the texture of the skin. Three friends and fellow travelers stood at the opening gazing towards the path. Proud of his women, Benito hugged each of them as he bid them buena suerte and goodbye.

Hand in hand Feliciana and Lauren stood under the divided trunk, while Lici spoke to her in a reverent voice of the journey ahead. "This is a silent journey, my little sister." Pointing to the mountaintop Lici asked Lauren to prepare a kintui of coca and offer it to the grandmother tree. "Since you have walked this way many times before, you know this path will take you to my village and to my mother. If," Lici said with emphasis, "you look carefully while you walk this long and winding path, you will see that there are many places to hide. The path makes many switchbacks, and there are many crevices. These present choices that could deter you or entice you from your destination." Placing her finger on Lauren's lips, Lici refrained her from speaking. "If you should wish to stop, it is your choice," Feliciana told her coldly. "I will continue on and wait for you at the village. You can find your way on your own power later. If you should become deterred or enticed away from our walk and wish to continue later, just follow the clearly marked path and it will lead directly to the village."

Excitement coursed through Lauren's mind, leaving her breathless. "Maybe I'll try to do it on my own this time. Maybe I won't follow Feliciana, after all I know the way to the village, I've been there a dozen times before." Her eyes glazed over, the landscape turned to frequency, and then suddenly she saw the tolerant expression in Lici's eyes. "You don't know the markers yet," Lauren realized surrendering to Lici's experience. "That's what this is all about. Just like Benito said, I step in every trap that gets set for me."

Feliciana smiled, pleased that Lauren had spotted her trap. Putting her finger to her lips and leaning towards Lauren, Lici shared the code of the Andes. "Once we step through the opening, we will walk in silence. I'm pleased," she said lightly touching the tightly woven fabric, "to see that you wear the poncho Benito gave you, because the cloak will keep you warm. You may use the time we walk to reflect on what you are leaving behind, or you may disappear in silence into the body of Pachamama." Lici touched the Earth with her hands. "It doesn't matter; the choice is yours. You might think of what awaits you, or you may feel the presence of your lover, or you may fall off of the ledge and if you do, I'll hope you can fly. Regardless of your choices," she said slightly raising her voice, "I will continue to walk with the power of Benito's love stirring within me."

The magnitude of the journey overwhelmed Lauren as she realized she was leaving behind a secret that had separated her from reality. She paused, knowing the potential loss was the greatest test of her life. "Am I really willing to sacrifice my relationship with Americo, to save my soul?" She pondered, chewing on her thumbnail. "Can I really go home if he isn't going to be a part of my life? Yes, I can," she resolved, "I can do it."

Trying to focus, for a second Lauren saw the world as she had as a child. The colors were brilliant, the light was intense and she saw clearly what she wanted and desired. She felt light, free, and happy. She became attached and clarity left as quickly as it had arrived. "I can't see the same as I did as a girl, my vision is different." Lauren remembered how her vision had changed when she handed her dead son to the nurse. "It's as though I've fallen into a hole, and I can't see out. I look this way and that way, I turn and sometimes I see some light, but I can't stop spinning and when I spin, I lose my focus."

Lauren remembered what Lici said about choices, choices she
could make along the exposed root crisscrossed path. "At this time
in my life I don't want to be deterred, and I don't think I'm any
longer easily enticed," she thought introspectively, "and I certainly don't want to fall off the ledge again." Lauren giggled, looking at
the ground and behind her to see if she had unconsciously missed
something. "But I better watch where I step, because the traps are
everywhere."

Feliciana waited for Lauren at the crumbling adobe arch
marking the entrance to the village. A fleeting doubt crossed her
mind when she pondered Lauren's willingness to face her most
difficult journey. "Congratulations, Lauren, for making the long
and difficult journey. I have been watching you struggle to carry
your satchel, your backpack, and the heavy energy in your heart.
We are now passing under a doorway to another world," she said
mysteriously.

Feliciana pointed to the terraced fields in the near horizon.
Standing near the circular adobe brick wall enclosing the village,
in the horizon Lauren saw a tapestry of various patterns and colors decorating the hillsides. Lauren exclaimed, sweeping her arm
over the horizon. "I'll never get used to the beautiful patterns on
the hillside. It looks like somebody took threads of many colors
and wove them through the Andean mountains." Staring in awe,
Lauren stepped back. "When you stand back and look from a distance, the mountain looks like an enormous weaving." Staged
against the muted horizon, her red poncho contrasted dramatically with the rocky, tawny brown Andean soil. Feeling proud of her
journey, Lauren stood on the overlook taking deep breaths of
mountain air, restoring her life with refreshment from the
Goddess. Opening her eyes slowly, the tapestry revealed dozens of
women on their knees working in the fields. From the distance it
seemed the small homes were stacked on top of each other, like
building blocks soaring to the sky. They appeared so close, Lauren
reached out to touch each of the sharply angled thatched roofs
that seemed to grow out of the one below. The courtyard was silent
except for the fluttering of a robin-sized hummingbird, the
guardian of those who walk in the Andes. With smoke in the air
tickling her nose Lauren heard someone excitedly calling Lici's
name.

"Hola, Hola, mi hija," the woman called with delight in her
voice. "I will never recognize you when you are dressed in men's
clothing." The diminutive woman asked mischievously, looking at

Lici's canvas trekking pants, leather shoes, and heavy sweater, "Why do you dress like that, when you could wear beautiful hats and skirts like you used to wear when you were a girl?" Feliciana and Lauren laughed as they hugged the child-sized, elderly woman, remembering that Yoci always greeted them with the same questions. Shocked at Yoci's uncharacteristic boldness, Lauren wondered why Yoci put her hands on her belly, chanting words that she could not understand.

Lauren could not stop observing the women, once again noticing their silent communication in the vocabulary of process, the language of Pachamama. She became aware of their tired bodies, and their quiet joy, and watched them spin threads of light into strands of gold. "Observe the women very closely," Lici reminded Lauren, as they waved greetings to the women with round brown faces and mysterious deep black eyes, "because they are the happiest women in the world. Their happiness is potent and profound because they spend all day in communication with the Earth, affirming by their loving touch that they are indeed sisters."

Feeling revealed and vulnerable, Lauren took Lici's hand, telling her how exposed she felt under the gaze of the women in the circle. "Lauren, your frequency has been altered and the women are aware of the change in your energy body. They're not looking at you; they're seeing you, seeing if there is a new hole in your weaving, or if your energy is heavier or lighter. They're checking to see if your right and left sides are balanced and where your filaments are attached." Lici dropped her voice ominously. "Also, they need to know if somebody could be robbing you of your power with their tentacles deep inside of you."

Pretending to be nude Lauren faced them, opening her arms and turning in a circle. With trust on her face she offered them a smile of acceptance and as her heart opened, she received the understanding women offer one another.

"Now," Feliciana said with what sounded like sweet relief, "I want to go change my clothes. I want to become a woman of the high Andes again. Let's take your backpack into my small room and again, I hope you won't mind sleeping on the floor, because we need to sleep with our ear on Pachamama while we dream. We have many alpaca blankets to keep us warm and if we get cold we can snuggle up together," Lici said excitedly like a young girl. "We'll be like roommates, so maybe we can talk all night and share secrets."

Like a bouquet of wild Andean flowers that bloom only in the night, the women emerged from their houses donning fringed hats and dressed in colorful hand woven shawls. Honoring each woman Lauren offered gifts of Pisco and flowers, bowing slightly in their presence.

As assistant to the High Priestess, Feliciana consulted her mesa, and following instructions from an unseen source she ran her hands over the woven square of cloth, stopping for several moments, holding a knotted ball of yarn. Holding the orb of many strands to her eyebrows she murmured soft words, looking at Lauren with a prayer on her lips.

The silvery crescent moon dipped low in the sky as Lauren stood in the center of a circle of women. Surrounded by faces with piercing black eyes, Lauren felt her body dissolve into pure light. Surrendering to sound of quiet footsteps as Yoci and Feliciana wrapped strands of colored yarn around her body, Lauren absorbed the muffled chanted vibrations in the background.

The chanting stopped, the sounds of footsteps ceased, tension rose, and Lauren heard the snapping sound of strands being broken.

An overburdened custodian held the discarded pieces of yarn, each piece containing the heavy energy absorbed from the left side of Lauren's energy body. Holding the heavy energy before releasing it to the river, the woman's face sagged, her arms were heavy, her head was bent, and her shoulders stooped.

Feeling lighter and lighter, Lauren heard the snap between her brows. The final thread broken, she was free at last. Lauren shot to the stars on the chariot of the silver crescent moon. Straddling the silver chariot Lauren spiraled high into the dark blue sky, finding peace in a soft spongy pocket between folds in the galaxy. The gentle rocking of the crescent moon reminded her of riding her horse on a perfect day. She saw her brother and Sunnie riding together and Americo riding by himself, looking for something he seemed unable to find. Not surprised to find that she had taken a side trip alone, she felt profound relief when the soft red Earth trail led back to Americo.

Later, in the chilly damp night, with starlight peeking through the uncovered window, Lauren and Feliciana whispered softly to each other. "I'm losing something," Lauren sighed as she rested her head on her elbow. "I feel something deep inside of me changing." Lauren's voice dwindled, "Everything that was in the despacho tonight reminded me of something I've lost."

Lici felt the tears behind Lauren's words, knowing that loss had been a constant theme in her life. "Loss has become your friend," Lici offered, accepting the design of fate. "Loss is the path circumstances designed for you many years ago, but oftentimes when we lose something, it is the most profound gift."

Lauren squinted, holding back tears, yet feeling the truth in Lici's words.

"Sister, it's the way of life to offer gifts to the cosmos." Feliciana lit another candle, knowing the conversation would continue long into the night. "Throughout our lives we offer gifts of love and life to the universe, just as we offer despachos during ceremony. A despacho is an offering, just like our experiences are offerings to the Earth and the stars. The gifts we receive from Pachamama and las estrelllas are not for us to keep, so we offer them to the cosmos with the energy of our prayers."

Watching Lauren run her finger back and forth through the flame Lici became concerned that she may hurt herself. "Lauren," she said as she moved the candle, "one must never stop the flow of energy that is created by our thoughts, actions, or when a ceremony is performed." Lici confided in Lauren, "These teachings were learned over thousands of years, from many generations of women, and to honor them we hold them close and treat them with great respect. Our way of life permits us to call in our power with these gifts from our grandmothers. The despacho is like your womb or your art, for after you reveal the creations you carry, you must release your gift to the world."

Lauren caressed a finger-sized rag doll made from cloth the village women wove, remembering the night thirty years ago when Lici presented her with the gift. "I could never explain the comfort this doll has given me. I carry it everywhere, and I know it carries the spirit of my son."

Lici tenderly brushed Lauren's hair from her eyes. "I knew the doll would help you find strength from the unspeakable loss you suffered when you were so very young. I know you talk to him, and he now tells you he wants to go home where he entered your young body in an act of deep love."

"I've missed him every moment of my life." Lauren opened her arms to reveal the emptiness she felt. "Do you have any idea how empty your arms feel when you release a baby to the stars?"

Lici understood Lauren's grief, yet did not. She pondered, knowing in her world, although heartbreaking, it was a most profound gift to offer a baby's body to Pachamama, his soul to the Apus, and his spirit to the stars. Feliciana hesitated knowing the words Lauren needed to hear to find courage for the next part of her journey. "Lauren, remember always, when your tears fall because you miss him so much or when you retreat from others because of your guilt, that he was the one who opened the gates of your mystery." Feliciana opened her eyes wide, looking deep into the abyss. "First, your lover opened the door a little, but never forget, the magic happened when your child opened a passage for your energy to flow. It isn't the particular child that's important, although you may find this difficult to understand. As wonderful as a child is, it is still a fleeting experience and like the leaves on a tree, one day they all leave their mothers arms for another." Lici patted her belly with the palm of her left hand. "It doesn't matter if the child stays with you, leaves this Earth, or leaves your arms; the important thing is that you delivered him to the world. Remember this, when your child left you, he also left you with his power. You carry the power of two, and it is an enormous responsibility."

Lauren laughed through her tears. "Lici, you know I have enough trouble managing the power of one."

Pointing her finger to the stars Lici spoke with excitement in her low mesmerizing voice. "Your gates are open, and you have lived the magic of female experience. The experience joins you with all other women who have felt the contraction and expansion of their body as they delivered their gift to the Earth. Only then does their energy fully merge with that of the cosmos in the inhalation and exhalation of a continuous birth. The woman who has given birth becomes one with Pachamama, for she has taken into her body filaments from another and delivered them back to the gaze of the sun, transformed."

Lauren grasped the small doll in her hand and holding the treasure over her belly, she remembered the long, painful delivery that left her alone in the world with empty arms.

Lici fluttered her fingers in the air like hummingbirds flying freely in the sky. "Feel blessed, for nothing else in the world will do this for a woman. It was a gift your lover gave to you, and he gave it to you to keep."

☾★

Lauren woke to the sound of Lici's melodic voice. "I want to say this to you while the comfort of sleep still protects you. Remember love and you won't feel fear," she whispered tenderly. "I will be leaving in a short time, but you will be staying here without me. If you wish you can leave at any time, nothing is holding you here but power." Feliciana tapped her fingers on the cold hard earthen floor emphasizing every word. "Don't try to speak," Lici shushed her with her fingers. "While you are here, you will work with the women, you will dig in the fields, you will cook, and you will wash clothes in the river. Then you will carry water to your room. You will feed the alpacas and herd them to their corrals. You will sweep the floors of my mother's small casa, and you will carry your world on your back. You will sleep on the cold floor with only an alpaca blanket to keep you warm, and you will walk to the tops of these mountains, and later, you will be alone with only Pachamama to hear your cries." Lici continued to chant as Lauren screamed silently within herself.

Lauren looked at the face of her friend and no longer saw the delicate expression she knew. "Stop, Lici, please stop. I feel like you're hitting me on the head with a hammer." She saw a woman with rage on her face. "Why are you leaving me here? Why can't I leave with you?"

"Because," Lici continued in a firm voice, "each one of us is really alone in this beautiful world and you need to learn that. There is a difference between being alone which is when you touch the divine and being lonely, which is indulgence. You feel loneliness and loss because you haven't shared the secrets of your heart. Now you will share them with Pachamama, because she will be the only one who will understand you." Feliciana's face softened as she gently took Lauren's face in her hands. "Lauren, I have asked my mother to give you this lliklla to carry on your back. I am going to take your satchel with me," Lici said emphatically, not opening the door to protest. "Yes, even the picture of your lover. I will leave only the needle and silk thread your Grandmother sent with you, everything else you need to survive you will carry in this cloth. Just remember this, the woman informs the content of the burden she carries, and the content of the burden reveals the woman. When you leave you can take this beautiful lliklla with you or bury it in Pachamama, it doesn't matter. But, you will have carried it while you work."

☪

Alone in a hidden valley, under the watchful eye of an old crone, with only the Earth to listen, Lauren cracked again. She cracked wide open, her heart broke, and again she stepped in every trap. Tentatively placing her footprint on the next stepping-stone of her journey, Lauren learned the meaning of the circle. The sun beat relentlessly on the land as Lauren raised her arms overhead and held the pointed stick towards the Earth. She looked pitifully at the sun, so close yet so far away, and as she pierced the rock filled dirt with her digging stick, she called dejectedly for help that would not come. "Americo, I don't know what's happening to me. They tell me to keep the dirt on my skin to keep the germs away, and I feel dirtier than I ever have before. I want to dig the dirt off with this stick, the one I hold while I work." Reaching into the deep hole with her hands, she cried pitifully. Finding determination, she removed a large rock. "I'm on my knees, and I'm tired. My hands are dirty because they make me work in the fields. They won't talk to me, and I can't understand them. When I say something, the women walk away."

Lauren threw the rock not caring if she hit anybody or not. "I couldn't forget you, Americo. I couldn't forget the way you felt, and I couldn't forget the feather. I couldn't forget the spinning, and I couldn't forget what you said to me and how I left you. I never forgot the first explosion in my body and for so long; I couldn't feel anything at all. When the darkness falls it scares me," Lauren cried to the deep rich humus, black and gritty on her hands.

"What do you want from me?" Lauren spoke sharply to the sloe-eyed woman staring at her. "I know you can't understand me, but could you at least have an expression on your face?" Standing tall, dwarfing the diminutive woman, Lauren put her hands on her hips, challenging her. "Am I doing this right? You could tell me how I'm doing, you know. That would be the polite thing to do. How am I to know the way if you don't tell me?" she asked with a raised brow. Lauren watched the particles of soil dissolve under her falling tears. "If I just keep my head down, maybe they'll leave me alone. That's the way to leave here," she realized. "I'll dissolve myself with tears and sink into the Earth. I'll disappear and then no one will ever find me. Even the soil has no mercy here, it's so hard to dig and all I have is a stick."

The copper skinned old woman watched with glee as Lauren pounded the compacted soil with her digging stick. She listened carefully to the low frequency vibrations coming from Lauren's lips. When Yoci felt the waves of agony leaving Lauren's body, she knew the chariot Lauren needed was to dig deep and dig hard. "She needs to dig into the body of Pachamama. Lauren needs to pierce the skin and turn the stick in circles until the hardness of the soil is released into a soft rich bed for our potatoes. She doesn't know it, but she's digging into her own remorse, her indulgence, and her own heaviness that she carries like a corpse on her back. She needs to make a good bed for our potatoes," grinned the rigid taskmaster standing over Lauren. "Maybe I'll plant sweet potatoes, beautiful big sweet potatoes, that I can take to the market and trade for something pretty."

Lauren became angry when the old woman picked up a rock hard clod of dirt and threw it in front of her. "So I missed one. How can I break up every one of these hard pieces and what does any of this matter anyway? I'm stuck on a mountain in Peru, and I have no place to hide." She hoisted her stick and dug more furiously, hitting another rock with her stick. "Damn, another rock," she cursed. Lauren dug viciously around the rock, finally freeing it from the tomb of its capture. "Well, fine, that's the least you can do," she said to the rocky hard dirt as she felt many smaller rocks tumble away. "It seems once you get the big ones out of the way, the digging is easy."

Lauren spoke to the crone, even though the crone couldn't understand her language. "If I were a slave, you would probably beat me with my own digging stick. This digging stick is a very stupid thing, why don't you call the men and have them plow the terrace? I'm so tired, and I need to rest," she protested throwing the stick over the adobe wall. "I'm a Princess, and I shouldn't have to work this hard, at least that's what my father told me." Irately Lauren picked up a clump that had fallen from the crumbling adobe wall. Throwing it on the ground she stomped it back into the Earth with her feet. "I should feel safe here, after all, the mossy wall surrounds me." Lauren stared at the wall and as another clod fell to the ground she thought, "This fucking wall is falling down. I wonder if they can see that."

With her dirty, gnarled hand the old woman pointed to the pile of dark brown, powdery compost and indicated for Lauren to put it in the basket. "What now?" Lauren yelled at her. "What do you want me to do?" The old woman continued looking at the disintegrating woman and stared as if she didn't care. Lauren noticed cracked, dirty fingernails as Yoci picked up a handful of the moist rich ingredients, slowly sifting it through her fingers as though it contained magic. Yoci honored the musty smelling particles with a whisper and with a touch of her fingers to her heart.

"What in the hell do you think it is, stardust?" Lauren growled at the solemn face. "I can't do this," Lauren yelled at the sky. "I've got to get out of here before I crack up. There won't be anything left of me if I don't walk through the gate and find a place to hide. I'll disappear." Lauren schemed of a way to make her way down the difficult trail by herself.

Yoci held her ground, demanding Lauren with the movements of her eyes to fill the basket in front of her. Belligerently Lauren grabbed two handfuls of the compost and threw them in the basket. With spite Lauren tipped the basket over spilling the compost on the ground. "Oh bullshit," Lauren thought, "no fucking way. Take that, you old Witch," she said with hate. "You can't make me do anything. Nobody's ever been able to," Lauren stated emphatically looking at Yoci with vengeance. Instantly, Lauren regretted yelling at the tiny old woman and remembered her Grandmother saying, "Lauren, your life will be so much easier if you listen to what I say."

"My hands are tied," she cried. "I can't even speak up for myself," she thought as she felt the stare of Yoci's demanding eyes. "Why all the rules? They're like ropes around my arms. I couldn't hold you if you were right in front of me, Americo. You're going to have to kill me," she yelled again. "If you don't, I'll do it myself. Won't you be sorry then?" she said accusingly. "You'll be in so much trouble," she said shaking, "for what you're doing to me up here in your little haven."

Standing in front of Lauren, Yoci placed her hand on her shoulder. Lauren saw worlds spinning in the wrinkled face and spun into them in defeat. Lauren's defenses crumbled, she went limp and fell slowly to the ground in front of the compost pile. Yoci walked away without looking back at the destroyed woman lying on the ground.

"Who's there?" Lauren called with fright in her voice. "I can feel you looking at me. Don't you know it's rude to stare at somebody who's in pain?" she called, thinking Yoci hid behind the stinky corral. "If you have any guts, you'll come out," she snarled. The silence scared her as she grabbed the basket to throw at the intruder. With a vacant look in her green eyes Lauren gazed into the interior of the tightly woven container. Her thoughts spinning back to Americo, she remembered the small basket she had found in the cave. "I can still see your eyes that day, Jugador." She turned the basket over, and his face disappeared.

"Maybe if I just stay here, Yoci will leave me alone. I need to consider my next steps very carefully. I need to decide what's important to me and what I want to keep, because I feel like I'm being stripped down to my bones." She put her hand over her heart and carefully paid attention to the warmth. Lauren touched the moist brown powder, pulling back when she felt the intense vibrations. Dropping deeper into the compost she pondered, moving her finger as if stirring. As she pondered she saw an opening in front of her eyes. "It takes a long time to make compost and stardust."

All she could see were the women on their knees in the fields, but still she felt like somebody was watching her. "They're praying," she thought as she saw the women offering coca leaves to the Earth. Slowly, Lauren picked up handfuls of compost and filled the basket with the rich powdery substance. Defiantly she looked at Yoci and pulled the basket to her breast. "I filled it up, and you aren't going to take it from me." Lauren ordered, pointing to the stack of baskets leaning against a wall, "Fill your own basket, Yoci." Sternly, with her hands on her hips, Yoci looked at Lauren with intense scrutiny. Yoci held out her hands and indicated for Lauren to give her the basket, offering a small acknowledgement with the nod of her head. "But it's mine and I want to keep it," Lauren cried. "Why do I have to give up everything? This is my gold, and I know what it took to make it. I know the secret, but you probably think this is just fertilizer."

Yoci took the basket and put it on her head. She watched the tiny old woman walking with short, quick steps ahead of her. "That cloth on her back looks full but it must not be heavy or she couldn't move so fast. I wonder what she's going to do with the gold," Lauren thought as she walked.

In her child-sized hand Yoci held a large handful of compacted dirt and offered a prayer to Pachamama. While Lauren watched, she took a pinch of the golden brown powder between the fingers of her left hand and looked at Lauren with a gleam in her eye. She held both hands to the sky looking at the bright rays of the sun and then solemnly mixed the gold powder into the dirt.

"What now?" Lauren thought as she stared at the mixture. "So what, it still doesn't look like the soil in my Grandma's garden. Nothing will ever grow here."

Using her hands, Yoci told Lauren to mix the ingredients together. Lauren surrendered. "I'm here to learn, so teach me, old woman, how you make your garden grow. I didn't fall of the ledge, and I didn't turn around, yet all you've done is make me work hard. So give me a break, damn you, I've earned it." The fields in Lauren's vision were covered with green leaves, convincing her that plants did indeed grow in the garden. "It does work," Lauren smiled in awe of what she saw. "It only takes a little pinch of magic to make the garden grow."

Lauren accepted the walking stick Yoci offered. She looked

down at her feet in tire rubber sandals remembering the flip-flop
sandals in her backpack, and laughed. "The mountainside is so
steep, how does she walk so fast?" She looked ahead at the line of
women proceeding in front of her. Holding the walking staff in her
hand she followed the women as they walked on. "It seems they've
made a circle. I can see their homes from here. What was the purpose of the walk? All I've done is hurt my feet, broken my back,
sweat until I'm weak, and I still end up where I started? Is this
what women do with their lives, walk in circles, ending up where
they started, happy to have made the journey? Well, isn't it interesting that I'm doing the same thing with my life? The only difference is, my circle was a little bit larger and it kept spinning."

Lauren held a staff decorated with feathers and ribbons.
"What is this, Yoci? Why are you giving this to me?" she asked as
she twirled the staff. "Do I really see a smile on your wrinkled old
face? Is there really some humor behind your opaque black eyes?
What should I do with this wand?" Lauren walked around Yoci,
tapping her on the shoulder with the wand. "Should I cast a spell
on you so you'll disappear and at the same time carry me home?
Muchas gracias for the gift," she said sweetly, remembering her
manners.

"Yoci," Lauren shrieked loudly, with shock in her voice. "I simply don't believe you're going to make me do that. I thought you
loved me, now we've come full circle again. Last night at the celebration you were so nice to me. You want me," she said pointing
her finger to her chest, "to clean the manure out of the corral. I
don't believe you. I never had to do work like this when I was a little girl. Daddy said that was men's work." Seeing the determination in the old woman's face, she knew she had no choice. "But
why should I clean up the shit? It's not mine," Lauren said with
contempt for the overly small old woman. "Yoci, don't think you
can stare me down because tougher people than you have tried to
tame me and failed. At least you could help me," she challenged as
she grabbed the rake from Yoci's hands. "Give that rake back to
me," Lauren screamed as Yoci retrieved the tool from her hands.
"What do you expect me to do, use my hands?" Lauren picked up
the shit, laughing all the time. Stomping her foot into a large pile,
she giggled hysterically. "Yeah, I've stepped in this trap before.
Somebody else's shit has always been right in front of me."
Submitting to Yoci's demands, Lauren accounted for her work.
"Now, I've cleaned your house and helped you spin your yarn. I've
swept your dirty floor, and I put flowers on your windowsill. Are
you happy now?" Lauren asked as Yoci stood in her doorway and

smiled. "I must admit, I didn't mind doing it as much as I thought I would." She stopped and glared, "I'll bet you think that's funny, you mean old bitch. Why do you stand there smiling? Do you think you've won?"

Lauren stopped, took a breath and realized she was in one of her best spins. In fact, she spun back so fast she could hardly breathe. "Jake, now you get to listen to me," Lauren demanded. "You used to call me your silent wonder. You used to brag about me, telling people that still water runs deep. That was real cute, Jake. Well listen to what I have to tell you now, I decided a long time ago never to tell you anything again. I've gone places, loved people, and done things that you know nothing about. So the joke was on you, wasn't it? I didn't give you the chance to tell me if I did something wrong. You wanted me to be so perfect, well, you ought to know what your little girl has done in her life."

She stopped spinning again and said quietly with a disgusted look on her face. "Sybille," she spat, thinking of her mother. "What could I ever say to you? You weren't even there. I couldn't see past the mask on your face to even know who you were."

Stopping for breath, Lauren kicked dirt into the air, put her hands on her hips and started again. "As for you, Americo Rios, did you ever once wonder...?"

Late in the night, by light of the candle, Lauren completed the task her Grandmother issued in January. Lauren didn't bother to address the individual heartbreaks; rather she recognized the nature of the traps. "Yes," Lauren said as she charged the gold needle by the light of the moon, "I stepped into this trap, the trap of wanting to please in order to earn love." Cutting a jagged hole in the soft silk of her baby dress she recalled another. "I felt guilty because I didn't accept everybody's rules." Giggling, Lauren told her naughty secret. "I always knew other peoples rules sucked and that the people who made them weren't as smart as I am to begin with." Sewing with quick sure stitches, another fatal step reminded her of her naiveté. "I kept a secret, thinking I was protecting somebody I loved. I put myself in prison and numbed myself because I was afraid to tell the truth. I cared what others thought of me, and I started seeing myself as an evil person."

Looking at the stars, she told Americo, "If you can't accept what I did, then I'll make a life for myself without you. But, I won't hide myself from you anymore. If the choices I made kill your love for me, then so be it." Lauren weakened as she finished her task. "Just one scratch, she promised holding the needle to her wrist. "No," she said recognizing another trap. "I don't need to hurt myself anymore."

Feliciana stood at the gate motioning for Lauren to join her. Pale and wan, with lips chalk-white, Lauren walked slowly with her eyes cast down at the unrelenting Andean soil. Walking towards Feliciana she carried the staff decorated with ribbons and feathers, twirling it like a maypole. Over her shoulders Lauren wore the colored lliklla. Her burden was light. She smiled shyly, her task was completed, and Lauren knew she could do anything. The scars on the baby pink pieces of silk were strong, and the traps were identified. Her gold needle was used only for sewing, her doll carried her secrets, and nearing the completion of the circle, she felt free.

☪

Deep in the belly of Mother Earth, in the inferno of Copper Canyon east of Guaymas, Mexico, Americo Rios was confronted by his Nagual. Having never doubted that his love could save Lauren, Americo laid miserably in his sleeping bag with his head on his backpack, listening to the soft spoken man admonish him for underestimating the power Lauren carried. His stomach rumbled, his head throbbed, and his confidence was shattered as don Esteban released him to face Lauren and the story she would bring to him.

A gambler and a cowboy, loving one woman his entire life, Americo believed himself to be a throwback to the days of the old west when a man protected his woman with the accuracy of his fist, the security of his money, and the passion of his love. Always believing Lauren needed him, Americo listened with astonishment as don Esteban informed him that Lauren's power had been the shelter that protected him as he efficiently designed his life in the safety of his home in the red rocks.

The universe is female, and in the world of sorcery the power of a woman is acknowledged, but not revered by all. Don Esteban is the exception. Because of their femaleness, a woman has the facility for enhanced awareness and she journeys through the seen and unseen worlds with a constant infusion of natural female power, unencumbered by the expectations of cultural accountability. Women are fierce, intense, and have rhythmic, cyclical, physical manifestations that are magical doorways between the worlds. For thirty years, don Esteban endeavored to mend the hole in

Americo's energy body, the hole in his weaving that prevented him from crossing into full awareness. Americo was trapped, unable to move past the intense belief that his love for Lauren was his greatest gift to her. Sitting straight-backed and cross-legged on the hard ground next to Americo, don Esteban spoke, "Americo, in spite of your training and your expertise, you are still just a man just like I am just a man, and we follow our promise of power with love." With a look of implacable serenity on his lined face, the Nagual revealed more to Americo than his usual short, cryptic comments permitted. "You took an event and you allowed it, wisely or unwisely," the old teacher said with kindness, "to become the guiding pattern for your life." Patting Americo on the shoulder, don Esteban refused to indulge Americo in his perceived illness. "You have loved this woman in a never ending, always changing continuum. You have at different times loved her body, her mind, heart, spirit, and soul." Don Esteban stopped speaking wondering if Americo had ever considered another perspective. "Have you ever considered that perhaps she made a decision out of love for you, a love so great that she altered her life for you? A warrior must notice everything and the glow of your awareness failed you. Your woman is powerful, not fragile like you think she is, or want her to be. Your Lauren learned the fine art of the enigma in order to disguise herself for many reasons. You were caught in a moment, never seeing that she had grown or found her own way."

Americo paled catching a glimpse of himself as a young man. The face in front of his eyes was familiar, the expression more relaxed, yet the face contained a mystery he could not understand. The eyes transformed from amber to green, the complexion lightened and the features were enhanced by a refinement that seemed familiar. He looked again, the smile was warm and as he felt a wave of fear grip his gut, he saw a freckle above the upper lip of the young man in his vision. "I'm afraid, don Esteban," Americo whispered.

"Forget your self, Americo," was all don Esteban offered.

The hour of power passed, yet the heat relentlessly tormented Americo as he felt his rib bones, now gaunt from the twenty pounds he lost in ten days of fasting and wandering alone in the countryside of the interior. Don Esteban served water to Americo from a tin cup as he watched the man he respected indulge in self-pity and denial. "You have honorably loved a single woman for all of your years, and you have done everything you could to keep her from traveling her own very necessary path. You have made two mistakes, and I fear you are not ready to quit indulging in them."

"How can loving someone steadfastly and completely be a mistake?"

"I've told you many times that until you surrender to a worthy woman you will be incomplete. You have not submitted to this most receptive, supple woman. You wanted to design her life with the same precision you have organized your own. A nagual women carrying brilliant energy cannot be tamed, especially a woman in touch with the power of her womb, the organ of magic in her center. A woman who passes freely between the crack in the worlds is one who is pitiless but enchanting, shrewd but pleasant, enduring but dynamic, sweet but deadly."

"That's my Lauren," Americo chuckled heartily as don Esteban flipped a flour tortilla in a dented metal pan over an open fire.

Don Esteban chewed slowly, watching Americo reach for Lauren, seeking strength by the touch of her hair that he kept with him. "Americo, you have given her your love, but you have not given her your respect or surrender because you indulged in the romance of rejection. The woman you love is whole and she is formidable because of the path she has taken. You," he said while waiting for Americo, "only think you know the nature of her journey and you have assumed many things, without giving her the respect of a simple question."

Feeling genuinely confused, Americo confessed, "I don't know what in the hell you're talking about, old man." Splashing cool water from the stream on his face Americo felt his strength returning. Losing patience, knowing Americo understood more than he would admit, don Esteban opened his small bag of tobacco offering it to Americo.

Americo declined, the smell of a cigarette disgusting him. Squatting on his heels, don Esteban pointed at the owl that followed. "Don't look so confused, you'll understand what I'm saying soon enough. She will do what you were unable to do because she is strong, but perhaps not as ruthless as she will become. The depth of her feelings surpasses yours for she has grown on her own, unyielding to the dictates of society and has established an order of her own accord."

Americo leaned against a tree, folded his arms and stared at his Nagual, thinking perhaps the old man had lost his edge. "Tell me more, don Esteban," Americo said as he coughed repeatedly.

"The woman you love," don Esteban continued as he started to walk back to the campsite, "has the gift of two wings of power." Americo walked closely, letting don Esteban's words become markers on the trail. "Just remember my words when you receive your gift. You haven't lost anything, because she still carries the power and the edge I spoke of. Know what you are doing, or you could lose everything and find yourself lost in the wilderness, wandering alone. When you do return, if she will still have you, please bring your strong woman who is blessed with two edges. I have always been delighted to have the company of the beautiful, twice powerful, ever-enchanting Lauren."

Revived and healthy, in the bedroom of his hacienda, Americo dressed to return to Sedona to close a real estate transaction before meeting Lauren. The words of his Nagual had penetrated his mind, but Americo failed to embody the wisdom presented to him. Arrogantly he looked in the mirror still believing Lauren needed him. He disregarded her words and also those of don Esteban as he buffed his ostrich skin boots to brilliant high shine. A silver framed photograph on his bureau, taken of Lauren at the hacienda over twenty years ago, caught his eye, puzzling him. The expression in her eyes had changed from that of a lonely young woman, to that of a mature woman unafraid as she confronted him with her gaze.

"How do you do it, Lauren?" he said carrying luggage to his SUV. "Sometimes your face is fresh as a young girl's with dancing freckles on your nose, and in introspection, you look like a wise old crone. You are endlessly fascinating to me, Bruja, but most of all," he leaned his head on the rest missing her terribly, "I love your green eyes and how they rest so deep beneath your brows." The rutted dirt road brought Americo to attention, reminding him that he might be overlooking something. "But what frustrates me is that internal swirling sea of yours that nobody but you is allowed to enter."

Rebuffed by her former lover, peering from the window in her small room behind the cocina, devilish Marquita Pena schemed as she watched Americo drive away. Not trusting his housekeeper, as always before leaving, Americo vehemently instructed her to stay out of his private rooms in his absence. Locked safely in a trunk in his bedroom were Lauren's belongings and as Marquita turned away from the window, she called his hand by retrieving a small key from the pocket of her skirt. Laughing at Americo's stupidity she lit a candle. Holding the flame in front of a small mirror she began to chant and as she chanted Lauren's image appeared. "You silly woman," Marquita cackled. "Now that you're old, you think you can come home to Americo and keep him." Admiring her own smooth olive complexion in the mirror, Marquita hexed Lauren with doubts. "Someday he'll see your wrinkles and not see the pretty young girl anymore. Then he'll leave you, like he left me." Imitating his instructions, Marquita scoffed at his self-importance. "He told me to water your flowers and not to use your new oven because he wants you to cook the first meal in it for him. Ha, you can't cook tortillas."

Making plans to torment Lauren, Marquita anticipated Lauren's reactions. "What will you say when you see that your soft pink sheets have been used by another, and what will you say when you see another woman's clothes in your chest? Silly Lauren, my power is stronger than yours." Marquita laughed as Lauren disappeared.

☾★

High noon with twelve hours of travel ahead of him, Americo stood smoking in front of the local cantina where his amigos waited to wish him farewell. A vision of his bandito grandfather, Saul Rios, came to Americo when he saw a dignified, white haired, Mexican man with a cane walking slowly along the side of the dirt road.

"Grandpa Saul." He saluted a greeting to the man who would not release Americo from his gaze. "Power moved many years ago for myself and Lauren, long before we were born. Make it happen, Saul," he implored the spirit of the past, "make it happen for two bad asses, the granddaughter of an outlaw and the grandson of the greatest bandito of them all."

Brushing the dust from his immaculate khakis, Americo checked the front of his soft white t-shirt for ashes. Striding towards the swinging half door, he waved adios to the vision of his grandfather and entered the cantina to the welcoming cheers of his cronies. "Si, si," he said with his arms held wide, "my woman is coming home to me. In one week, una semana, I will have her in my bed." Between the lewd remarks and macho gestures, the men realized that Americo vibrated with genuine happiness for the first time in the thirty years they had known him. "The next time you see me, my friends, I will have Mrs. Americo Saul Rios on my arm."

☪

In the familiarity of domesticity, Trey and Sunnie spent time talking in the privacy of the cozy bedroom. Sunnie sat in front of the antique oval mirror brushing her hair while watching her husband's reflection. Trey reclined on their bed, sipping his bourbon, pondering the state of his marriage. Smiling back at Sunnie in her reflection in the mirror, Trey wondered when passion had left their lives. "I like seeing your freckles, Sunnie. I wish you wouldn't cover them up with your makeup. That was some pretty bright red lipstick you had on tonight."

Pursing her lips, she looked at him in the mirror, "Trey, do you want a kiss?"

Trey ignored her and threw his socks across the room defiantly. "Dad looks like shit, doesn't he?"

"Lydia said he had a lot of tests last week and we should know something on Monday."

"Looks like Americo's going home, he sure as hell doesn't spend as much time hanging out on the porch if Lauren isn't here, does he? Talking on Rita's porch is quite a tradition those two have had over the years. What do you think they talk about all of the time?"

"Besides all of their esoteric and intellectual stuff, who knows? Maybe they talk about the drugs they take to have hallucinations. I know Americo takes them all of the time, and I think Lauren's done her fair share, too."

Trey wondered if he had missed something in life. "It's true, we've always been so conventional and those two have always been the outlaw and the bandito. How is it they ended up being the renegades and we ended up being boring small town people?"

"I don't know, but I'm glad it ended up like that. Do you remember at Lauren's going away party last January when they got high on champagne and pot and called themselves a couple of bad asses? It's like they're proud to be wild."

Trey scoffed. "Americo might think he's wild, but he's a man with a plan and that's not wild. In the world of the wild, Lauren's a natural and Americo is a wannabe."

Trey finished his drink, took off his gray sweats and black t-shirt and turned away from her. Sunnie looked at her husband and wondered when he quit offering her a bedtime dessert.

☪

Thursday in the late afternoon, Ignacio saddled Americo's horse, checked his watch and headed for the creek. Irritated since morning when he learned of Lauren's homecoming, Ignacio rode quickly towards the canopy of willow branches lining the stream. The afternoon sun was brutal, parching the already dry land. Stuffing a wad of tobacco in his cheek, Ignacio visualized Americo surprising Lauren at the airport in Dallas. "That bitch is going to kill him someday," Ignacio cursed as he spit on the ground.

"I'll never understand why he made my beautiful sister abort her baby, and I'll never understand how a fine man like Senor Jake sired la puta mas bonita en todo el mundo?"

Removing a packet from his shirt pocket, Ignacio's anger intensified. "Americo is too fine of man to put up with her bull-shit." Following Marquita's instructions to the letter, Ignacio dismounted the mare and dug slowly and methodically with his knife in the soft, red soil by the river.

☪

Twenty-four hours a day the Dallas Airport is full of cowboys. Lauren had been traveling for a full day, with a twelve-hour lay-over in Lima. She was exhausted and as she walked out of customs she wondered how to spend the next four hours. "Call me if you ever come to Sedona," she told the man handing her his business card. "No thanks, I need some time alone before I make my connection."

Having arrived in Dallas to surprise Lauren, Americo stood with his hat tilted watching her rebuff the stranger. Mildly jealous that the man handing her his card believed Lauren was available, Americo smiled wryly thinking of Rita. "It runs in the family," he thought starting to walk towards her. "Some women's charms diminish with age, but Lauren's charms keep accumulating, always enchanting those who meet her. I don't blame the son of a bitch for trying, she's a devastatingly beautiful woman."

Not taking her in his arms, or stopping to kiss her, Americo knelt on his knees pinning a sunflower corsage on her sweater. "Lauren, my Princess, will you go to the dance with me? I see all that you are and all that you will become and I'll kneel before you everyday of my life if you'll have me."

The days alone Lauren had asked for were put on hold. The chemotherapy Jake was undergoing was drastic, and Lauren wanted to rush to the rancho to help care for her father. Holding her hand on the drive from Phoenix, Americo made a plan. "Baby, Lydia can't take care of Jake by herself, so I think we better be put on hold for a month or two. We'll both help, and the family can assume we've just fallen in love. We'll tell them when the time's right, but to tell them now would take the focus from Jake, and he needs us all."

Once again, Lauren felt strangled, frustrated, and stifled. "But..."

"Shhh, Princess, take a nap because we've got a rough road ahead."

☪

The lantern flickered as she stopped in front of Americo's door. Looking at the copper panel she remembered seeing for the first time twenty-five years ago, she shivered pulling her father's old jacket closer. "Tonight," she promised herself, running her fingers over the design she engraved the first year she returned to his bed. Engraved on the door was a circle with two dots connected by a spiral in the center. In the center of the spiral was a ladder with seven rungs, each different. One rung looked like a serpent and another was broken. One had a handhold and other sagged slightly to the left. The engraving was delicate, mysterious, and below it were her initials. "I wanted everybody who crossed through his door to feel that I had been here," she smiled as she put her key in the lock. Listening to the owl hooting softly in the gnarled branches of the cedar tree, Lauren felt possessive of their sanctuary. "He doesn't know how fiercely I've guarded his home, our home, for so many years."

Americo waited, sitting on his chocolate brown leather couch in front of the fireplace, knowing that she was at his door. He took a sip of brandy from the snifter, followed by a drag on his cigarette. Americo, as the custodian of their memories, thumbed idly through the photo album documenting their affair. In the album of photographs was a black and white photo of Lauren lying nude in the orchard basking in the moonlight. Shadows of the barren branches cast black lines across her body as she extended her arms toward him. Her lips were parted, and her fluffy hair fanned invitingly over her head. "You're early, Bruja," he said looking at her tired face. "Let me fix you a drink, Absolute on the rocks OK?"

Lauren blew out the candle, slipped off her red cowgirl boots, and cuddled beside him on the couch. "I feel so happy here, Americo. Let me put my head on your shoulder," Lauren smiled softly pulling an afghan around her. "The sunflowers are so beautiful."

"I'm glad you came early, but I'm surprised. Jake must be feeling a little better."

"Let me look at the photographs in our album," Lauren laughed softly. "We've had some beautiful times together, haven't we?" Lauren turned the pages slowly. "Every year we took pictures of each other and I always wondered where you had them developed. Somebody certainly knows my body almost as well as you do."

"Not even close, Princess," Americo laughed. "Let's go look at the pictures my Dad took when we were growing up. My parents loved you so much, I think my mother thought you were her daughter the way she worried about you all of the time."

Tomas Rios chronicled life on the rancho with his photographs. Over the years he decorated the long hall leading to the bedrooms with framed memories of his family. The hallway was haunting, memories reflecting off of one another, blending the past into the future and cycling it back again. Over the years Americo changed his childhood home into the home of a single man, but the picture wall remained untouched. They stood, Americo's arm over Lauren's shoulder, looking at the hundreds of photographs in front of them.

"Americo, we were so young," Lauren giggled when she looked at the picture of him bowing at her at the dance the night of her graduation. "I felt so pretty that night."

"I was the first," Americo said quietly. "I want to be the last, Lauren. I want to grow old with you like Zack and Rita. They were still madly in love the day he died. Do you remember?" he asked pointing to a picture of them taken on the porch the day Zack's ashes were sprinkled in the spiral garden.

"I could never forget. It was because Grandpa was sick that I came home, and we saw each other again after five years. I still loved you so much, and it was the first time I'd cried for so long. "

"Do you remember this?" Lauren pointed to the picture of her on her first pony.

"I remember what I felt that day. I didn't understand it, but I knew something happened between us. I'll never forget how you smiled at me after I helped you onto your pony. Do you see the faint outline of the energy between us?"

"Yes, I wonder why I haven't noticed that before."

"What about this one?" Americo asked looking at a picture of him pushing Lauren in the swing. "You always wanted to go faster and faster, and higher and higher. You were such a wild child, in so many ways."

"Americo, we've already had so much together, a whole lifetime really. I wonder if I've tempted the fates by coming home."

"It was time," Americo whispered in her ear, holding her close to him. "Let's go look at the new apple tree we planted yesterday. I'll get the camera, then we'll go to the Casino."

"Americo, I think I should tell you...tonight."

Americo hushed her, and teased as he slipped his hand inside her red satin bra.

Lauren ran her fingers along the inside of his thigh, moving her body against him.

The winter solstice and once again, in the sweet comfort of a long time love Americo and Lauren made love slowly in the light of the fire, him watching the flickering shadows dance in tandem with her body. Reliving the first night they made love, Americo slowly tickled her body with the raven feather and not asking this time, he tasted the sweetness of Lauren. Remembering the first time, he kissed her again, reminding her of the many firsts they had shared. Whispering as he held her in the afterglow of love-making, Americo decided, "Lauren, we'll tell the family we're engaged on Christmas day."

Like a serpent Lauren rose from the bed. "Now," Lauren shuddered, "tell him now."

Desire surrounded Lauren, desire for truth, desire for rebirth, desire for freedom, and authenticity. Quivering, she felt the burdensome skin of her secret start to crack. Like a seed opening to fulfill its destiny, the exhalation of freedom teased her, she could feel the pulse and see the bright light, and she was no longer afraid to grow towards herself. The thin, fragile, and dry layer was no longer needed and as she moved towards her truth, she moved away from the frail bondage of secrecy, once more powerful than ropes, chains, or shackles. Her eyes seemed focused, yet they were not; she was not seeing Americo or what might have been. She saw the Vortex rearranging her perceptions and wide-eyed she stared at the man she knew would fail her. Her heart pounded, she prayed to be wrong, and offering him not a needy girl, but an experienced woman who had made a decision based on love, she faced him.

Her pause lasted only seconds, but a second of light will instantly and completely wipe out thousands of years of dark. "What is it, Baby?" Americo asked slipping on his Levis.

Perhaps it was the moonlight filtering through the patterned fabric, perhaps it was the dwindling fire, or perhaps it was Lauren's light shining from within, but when Americo looked at Lauren, what he saw frightened him with its brilliance.

Lauren pushed forth from the skin of her secrecy, she felt fully alive, hopeful, and she had never loved him more. With a life-time of love for him, she let her heart break open and with the vibrations from her core, she offered him protection. Lauren remembered Feliciana's words and like a radiant, translucent rainbow, she gently surrounded him with a cloak woven with the threads of their love, their story, and their destiny. Lauren's emotions, grounded in the tentative, fragile new flesh were now revealed to a man who said he would stand by her in spite of anything.

"Lauren, are you feeling alright?"

First birth is long, arduous and often painful. Rebirth is intensified, and the stakes are higher.

"Americo, please just listen to me before you say anything. Did it ever occur to you, Darling," she paused, almost unable to go on, "that you put two of us on the plane, the morning I left for Monaco thirty years ago?"

Taking the cigarette from her hand, he looked at the new light in her eyes. "I'm confused, Lauren," Americo said as fear gripped his heart. "Be more specific."

Lauren searched in her satchel for a small faded purple silk bag. Looking directly at Americo, she handed it to him with shaking hands.

"What is this, Princess?"

"Don't open it yet, please," Lauren said starting to cry. "I've got a story about a lost princess that I have to tell you." Lauren took a deep breath, and leaving nothing unsaid, she gripped his hands, transmitting the story through touch as well as words. "I was so afraid. Sybille said Daddy would have you arrested, I lost my courage, I almost killed myself with a razor, I remembered how much Daddy expected of me, I lied, I stole a diamond ring and sold it, the pain was so terrible, I wouldn't have an abortion, I threw the adoption papers in my aunt's face, I died, I tried so hard to hang on to him when he left, I had a part of you inside of me for nine months, I stole pain pills, I couldn't see because of the black tunnel, they told me to cry, Sybille told me I didn't have any reason to cry, I was lost and parts of me are still lost, I looked in the mirror and asked myself if I would change anything if I could, I said no, I ran away because I couldn't face you, I knew you would hate me, I wore your bracelet everyday, I had the chance to disconnect from you and I said no. Americo, say something...anything."

Holding his throbbing head in his hands, unwilling to look at her, Americo listened to each word Lauren said. The words of his Nagual pounded into his consciousness. "You didn't give her the respect of a single question. Did you ever consider that she made a decision out of love for you that changed the course of her life?" Rita's words swept hauntingly through his body. "Be kind to her, Americo, she has done so very much out of love for you." Remembering the many times he felt her loneliness and saw the shadows behind her eyes, Americo cursed himself. "You stupid bastard, why didn't you ask when you knew something was wrong with her?"

"Is it time for me to open the bag?" he asked, feeling years of fatigue overwhelm him. Rita's words came to him. "Americo, you are going to be given such a special gift." Holding the threadbare silk bag in his roughened fingers, Americo asked her what it contained. "Tell me what it is first, I can't take anymore surprises tonight."

Opening the bag for him, Lauren answered. "It's his hair, Americo. It's our son's hair. I cut it off when they brought him to me in the clinic. It's just like having the person with you, you know."

Slowly taking the locks of soft, black baby hair from the bag, Americo saw the image of his son. Looking at Lauren, he again saw the small freckle above her upper lip, wondering when he had last noticed. "I've seen him," Americo said softly reaching for her hand. "He came to me in a vision when I was with don Esteban."

"Tell me what you know about him," Lauren said clutching

Americo's hand.

Americo stood, pulled Lauren to her feet and led her to the bed.

"Christ, Lauren, you didn't have to go through it alone. You knew how much I loved you."

Lauren answered without apology. "Americo, you have to believe that I did the best I could under the circumstances and I can't regret my path, because if I made other choices, possibly I wouldn't be here now. God, who knows where our lives would have taken us, you, me, TJ? We were so young, Americo, the chance of a marriage lasting were so remote, regardless of how much we loved each other. We play the cards we're dealt the best we can, don't you agree?"

Unwrapping the afghan, he rested her head on a pillow. "I need to hold you, Baby. I need to feel your skin next to mine." Frustrated, desperately wanting to be inside of Lauren, Americo gave up. "I can't do it, Princess, I just can't do it," he said angrily pushing the covers away. Looking at Lauren as if he didn't recognize her, he said blankly, "I'm going back to my place; I need some time alone."

Alone in his home, Americo cried. He cried for all that Lauren had suffered. Imagining her alone in Paris, young, frightened, and almost dying, he looked at the phone. "I shouldn't have left her by herself, she probably needed me tonight more than she did then." Visions of his son growing up on the rancho tortured him as he imagined teaching him to ride his first horse and how to play poker. The pictures in his mind were those of Lauren and himself taking their son camping, honoring birthdays, other babies, building a home, sitting together on the porch, waking every morning in each others arms, Lauren pursuing her art, and him following his dream to become an attorney. He saw Rita holding TJ, Jake playing with his first grandson, his parents still alive to celebrate and stand by them. Americo wondered what it would have been like to see Lauren nursing TJ, walking the floor with him, and teaching him to see the same magic in life that she beheld. His remorse turned to anger. With pent up rage he kicked holes in the sheetrock and tore pictures off of the wall, breaking the glass as he threw them across the room.

"How could you, Lauren? I told you I hoped you were pregnant. He was us, the two of us, and your lie killed our son."

All vitality left Americo, and a feeling he had never known descended. Numbness. He could no longer afford to feel. And he was afraid of the shell that grew quickly over his emotions.

"Alex, Americo here. Just checking to see if you were home. Want some company?" he said coldly to the sleepy woman on the phone. "Yeah, I've got something I want to ask you. See you in fifteen minutes." Still in shock, Americo hung up the phone. As if sleepwalking he splashed water on his face, brushed his teeth, and drove away, not seeing the candle in the window of the Casino.

☪

Pegasus flew on fierce red wings, and Americo thought he had found a way through his grief. Hatred, an emotion that betrays one's integrity and best interest, had arrived at his door. He should have refused delivery. Screeching to a halt next to the spiral garden, his amber eyes narrowed to a slash in disbelief. When he saw Lauren wave, he was incensed that she worked in the garden seeming as if she didn't have a care in the world. He penetrated her with his stare, detesting the woman he had loved for over thirty years.. "I ought to kill that bitch for what she did to us." His rugged fists gripped the steering wheel, aching to brutally strangle her.

The steady rain pelted his windshield as the back and forth motion of the wipers reminded him of the relationship he was about to end. Sadistically he punched three holes in a box carelessly tossed on his front seat. "That's just the way it's always been for us, back and forth, here and gone, not now, maybe sometime."

His rarely displayed dark temper out of control; Americo grabbed a fist size red rock and hurled it through the car window. "It would serve her right if she got struck by lightning. What the hell, she's been hit by lightning before and survived. Maybe it's true that nothing can kill a real Witch."

Clinching his fists Americo kicked the gate and threw his cigarette on the ground, smashing it with the toe of his cowboy boot. Aiming at Lauren, one by one, Americo hurled the boxes over the fence. Her tiny dolls shivered and looked desperate for shelter from the brutal assault of being scattered over the unfinished fieldstone path. "Get your ass over here, Lauren, I've got a few things I want to say to you. You're a lying, crazy little bitch," Americo said gritting his teeth. "I knew when I couldn't make love to you, that the dance is over, and you might as well know that after I left you last night, I went to Alexandra Kingston's house and asked her to marry me."

"Americo, I did the best..." she started to say as she twisted the garnet ring on her finger.

He shouted at her shaking his finger in her face. "Don't you dare say a word to me, you flighty Aquarian Witch, until I'm finished talking to you. I don't know how we'll do it," he gritted his teeth, "but we're going to have to be civil to each around the family."

The midnight black raven huddled under the leafy branches as the coyote watched from behind the house. The branches a deer pulled from the willow tree seemed as lost, wasted, and helpless as she felt seeing the deep angry prints of his boots in the wet, red soil. It was dark enough for the owl in the gnarled Manzanita tree to open its eyes and stare at her in disbelief.

Wrapping her arms around herself, Lauren bent in agony as she twisted her body from side to side. "How could you, Americo? You promised that you would always love me no matter what," she sobbed. "Everything I did, I did because I loved you." Surrounded by clumps of iris that would burst into a riot of purple in the spring, Lauren collapsed to the ground remembering the words Benito Yupanqui spoke to her when she was eighteen years old.

Her arms wrapped around her knees; Lauren could hear his haunting voice speaking to her in melodic Spanish. Closing her eyes she could see herself as a broken young woman listening as he offered her the opportunity to change her destiny, if she chose to relinquish her connection to Americo.

"The mysteries between a man and a woman are many, and they are profound." Benito looked solemnly at the pale ashen face of his young soul sister. "You are young and just learning of their power. There are times," Benito spoke sadly to Lauren who was standing in the drawing room of his Cuzco home, "when we have the opportunity to determine our own destiny. Usually, we do not." Standing directly in front of her, he challenged her with his piercing black eyes and intimidating words. "You have chosen to keep a secret, and I am giving you the opportunity to change the course of your destiny that was determined at that time," he said turning his hand to reveal his palm. "I can help you disconnect from your lover. The choice you make after considering what I say will dictate the rest of your life."

He spoke kindly looking into her sad eyes, "Young Lauren, when a man gives you his filaments while making love to you they will remain inside of your womb forever, unless you take measures to remove them." Placing his fist over his heart he whispered thoughtfully, "This can give a man a great deal of power over a woman and most men do not understand or respect this. I am not familiar with your lover. You refer to him as a boy," he said shaking his head. "If that is true, he may not understand the responsibilities or consequences of what he has assumed. It's up to you, Lauren. Do you want to remain connected to him forever in this way?"

Taking Lauren's shaking hand in his he told her, "You were receptive to his filaments if they were given to you under the appropriate circumstances, and I believe you received them in love. There are times to be receptive and times to transmit. If you choose, you can transmit his filaments back to Pachamama, Mother Earth."

Benito gestured to the sun filtering through the paned window, "There are consequences if you choose to remain connected to him as a result of your lovemaking. Every choice you make will be impacted by the presence of his filaments inside of you. Don't consider the romantic nature of your encounter." Recognizing Lauren's romantic naiveté, Benito chided her softly. "This connection can also work against you. You say you love him, but do you? If you should want to forget him, you will be unable to."

Benito whispered ominously, "Lauren, it will not matter how many other men you love, your first lovers filaments will always be there. Every relationship you have, he will be there. Each lover you have will feel his presence." Benito continued speaking, assaulting Lauren's consciousness with the rhythmic cadence of his words. "His filaments will help you choose the men you love. Do you want to give him this power over you?" He asked her the question with a raised heavy dark brow. "Is he worthy of the responsibility?" Shrugging his shoulders he said somewhat indifferently, "I'm not saying he isn't. The question is, do you want to forget him? These are questions that should be asked before making love, but there are ways to turn worlds upside down, and this can be accomplished also."

"Oh my God, Americo," Lauren whispered softly watching the spiral in the garden start to spin. "What have we done to each other?"

☪

Christmas day was not postcard picture perfect. The sky was crystal clear, snow failed to frost the red rocks, and Santa Claus didn't come to Lauren's house.

"This is good," Lauren said as she checked the length of her skirt. Dressed simply but beautifully, Lauren put the finishing garnishes on the dinner wearing a luxurious black cashmere sweater, a leather mini skirt, and black, patent boots. A wide gold cuff bracelet adorned her wrist, and dangling garnet earrings accentuated the black pupils in her eyes. Defiantly, she wore her star garnet ring.

Pouring water from a pitcher into the goblets on the dining room table, she heard Americo and Alexandra laughing together as they walked up the steps onto the porch. Americo held the door open for his fianceé, catching sight of Lauren as Alexandra kissed him on the cheek.

"Fine," Lauren fumed, "you wanted to go to the dance, let's dance."

"Merry Christmas, Alex," Lauren said warmly extending her left hand showing her garnet ring. "Americo, you look handsome today. Santa Claus must have been very good to you this year, Darling." Lauren stood on her tip toes giving him a friendly peck on the spot Alex had just kissed him.

For the first time in twenty-three years Lauren did not sit by Americo during Christmas dinner. Congratulations were offered as Alex, flaunting her victory, showed everybody her perfect three-carat diamond engagement ring.

"Yes," Americo bragged, "I took Alex to a little resort in Scottsdale the day before yesterday. We needed some time alone, and I wanted her to select an engagement ring."

"It was marvelous," Alexandra insinuated suggestively, "we had massages, a fabulous dinner, and after we got up at noon, Americo bought this ring for me at Tiffany."

"I suppose," Lauren said sarcastically knowing Americo would know what she meant, "the ring cost a bit more than $17,000.00 and change."

Lauren stared, hypnotized as she looked at Americo's hands. Jealousy, an emotion that Lauren considered indulgent, felt unfamiliar and confusing to her. "I know what it feels like to have those hands on my body, and I hate you for where they've been, Americo," Lauren felt uncharacteristic jealousy racing through her body. Looking at his lips, Lauren felt a deep stirring. "I know where your lips have been too." Lauren knew the look. Alexandra looked satiated, over loved, and blissful. Unable to stop it, an orgasm shook Lauren's body.

Americo laughed crudely, licking his lips, knowing by the look on her face what had happened. Taking Alex's hand to his lips he kissed her ring, looking at Lauren with contempt.

"Will this dinner ever end?" Sunnie whispered to Trey.

"What in the hell is going on here?" Jake wondered as Lauren shivered.

"Have you got any new real estate deals in the works, Americo?" Jake asked trying to neutralize the situation.

"A few," he answered vaguely.

The champagne talked, and Lauren decided to plunge a sword in Americo's direction.

"Interesting word, deal," Lauren slurred looking at Americo. "Tell me, do you always keep your deals, Americo? Personally, I've learned that a deal is a deal, no matter what." Twirling her ring on her finger for all to see, she continued, "It seems to me somebody wrote that in a letter a long time ago."

Nobody missed the look of pain that crossed Americo's face as he stood up and demanded that Lauren meet him on the porch. Uncrossing her long legs, Lauren defiantly waited, not responding to his demand.

"Damn you, Lauren," she felt his words. Taking her by the arm Americo drug Lauren outside.

"I guess he wants to dance with me," Lauren giggled over her shoulder. Standing silently together Americo handed her a gift.

Lauren opened the box and looked at the charm, a silver owl with amber eyes.

"It's over, Princess," Americo said with sad finality, looking straight ahead. "I know you're hurting, but let it go, for both our sake."

Lauren giggled again. "It's only over if he says it is, Americo," Lauren whispered solemnly holding her hand to capture filaments sent to her from the figures contained in Cathedral Rock, "and only if the Vortex disconnects our energy threads."

☪

# A Time to Consider the Spinner

*"There are things we know, and things we don't know...
and in between there are the doors."*
*Jim Morrison, The Doors*

Sadness descended slowly, falling softly and sweetly as daylight licked her lips, tasted the sadness, exhaled, sighed, and surrendered. Reluctantly Earth rotated and wiggling her reptilian toes, she bid her lover, the light, farewell. For a moment the land savored a delicious longing, pausing long enough for Lauren to accept the inevitable. Intersecting the zenith and nadir, a flaring ball of fire exploded, as the Sun implored Earth to postpone her journey. The south wind blew, a door opened, the Vortex hesitated and Lauren received. The Vortex hummed softly, vibrating the words into Lauren's awareness. "Lauren, if you forget the stories of the land, you will have forgotten the dream."

"Please tell me the stories again," Lauren entreated the messenger wiggling her fingers to the sky in union. "I can't see what I don't know." Lauren slipped into the gap, the space between the words describing the dreams. Lauren closed her eyes and like roots beneath the surface of the Earth, threads of connection ran everywhere. Nurturing analogues of breast-like clouds emerged over Cathedral Rock, and Lauren surrendered to the opened doorways.

"The Earth subsumes, transforms, and reveals," the spinning strings of energy manifested. The formation in the distance revealed Earth in process. The spiraling threads spoke again. "Erosion exposes the old, then covers the new." With a quick reversal of perception, Lauren saw the other side. "The new covers the old and the old is made new through revelation," the spinning Vortex explained. "Neither is superior or inferior, because all is revealed in its own time."

Lauren giggled, thinking of her secret. "Don't you get it, Americo?" She sighed. Inhaling deeply, his face appeared in her vision. Lauren exhaled, still wondering why.

☪

With cheerful abandonment a hot summer wind gust gently from the south, undermining his grief with the torture of latent happiness. Alone on his veranda, surrounded by the sweet scent of honeysuckle vines, Americo grieved. Without warning, Americo took a breath. As the effervescent breath flowed through his weary body he felt his heart open knowing the breath was hers. Willing her form to present itself, in a hoarse voice, he told her, "We live in an undivided universe, Lauren. We'll always be connected, yet one unto ourselves." Looking into her eyes, he confessed. "I'm starting to get it, but it takes time. Fight your best fight, Baby." He watched her disappear on a sliver of smoke.

☪

Absorbing the message, Lauren turned to the group of quivering sunflowers and nodded her head in agreement. Both separate and multiple realities presented themselves as Lauren stepped into the spinning Vortex. "Please tell me more about my journey," she requested with the trust of a child. Feeling a wind stir in her belly, Lauren heard the Vortex spin. The soft humming continued, "It is the nature of a woman's life to make many descents. You must submit to the process, regardless of the pain. When you descend, the Earth will subsume you, transform you, and then reveal you once again. When you submit, you die, and with death there is descent. A descent is a doorway waiting to be opened. A descent is always a gift." The Vortex offered a promise. "The longer the door waits to be opened, the more rust you will find on the lock. You have the key, use it."

"Hmmm," Lauren matched her vibrations with the Vortex, "if descents are doorways, I must have walked through a lot of them. Why didn't somebody tell me descents into hell were gifts from the Goddess? What is the key?" she petitioned the Vortex. "If I ever had it, I must have lost it as I wandered."

"You know the answer," the Vortex sighed as she spun faster creating heat in Lauren's body. "Every woman holds the key where you feel the wind stirring. You speak of your wandering," the Vortex said, expanding the cone. "It is the nature of a woman to expand and contract. You expanded your perceptions and aware-ness as you wandered." The Vortex concentrated into a spinning cylinder. "They are now contracting as you move closer to your center."

Standing with her arms wide, Lauren turned slowly, offering herself to destiny. "I surrender," she called to the forces. "I trust," she whispered dropping to her knees.

"You now fully understand the Vortex and what you must do next," the spinning body said as it harmonized her filaments.

Lauren relaxed, seeing beyond the field of wonder as she summoned the reluctant gentle rays of last light to her breast. Once again, she accepted the nature of a woman's life. Stepping softly, leaving her footprints on the oracle beneath her feet, she submitted to the rhythmic order of nature, embarking on her next descent. Touching the moist, humus filled soil in her Grandmother's spiral garden; Lauren tasted the promise of her task. "Yes," Lauren sighed as the evening star presented itself to the night, "stars are forever, but on Earth we live trying to balance ourselves within a state of constant process."

☪

Gold discs from Americo's concho belt were lined perfectly on his dining room table. The ashtray filled with twisted butts, the brandy bottle empty and alone in his grief, his cheek rested on the leather belt. Americo was a scarred man with deep indentations of the gold conchos on his stubble cheek. For hours Americo had arranged and rearranged the conchos, trying to find order in the lines, dots, and symbols delicately engraved on the exquisite twenty-four carat discs. Failing in his drunken state, he had tried to find meaning in the small colored stones set within the patterns. Now he could not remember the order in which Lauren had given him the discs, and he wondered if it really mattered. Mumbling in his drunken sleep, Americo had a dream. He dreamed of his grandfather and mentor, Zachary Tanner Auldney. In the dream he saw himself as a young boy being trained to play poker with the finesse of a sorcerer. Zack told Americo about the night he almost lost it all.

Zack appeared to him as a much younger man, perhaps thirty years old, and seemed lonely as he walked into a saloon and ordered a drink. Zack sat alone at a table, considering the game with the implacable countenance of a warrior. His relaxed impeccable bearing could have been described as regal without ostentation. Zack did not feel under siege despite the fact he was soon to enter the game of his life. His face was calm, almost serene, but when he opened his pocketbook Americo saw that his funds were limited. It was obvious to Americo that this stand could be Zack's last, and he was ready. Zack, having the wit to know what his surroundings were, had chosen the battleground for the high stakes poker game. Simplicity was Zack's personal code, never wanting complications when he made a decision about the game. His brown wool jacket was finely stitched, but not flashy. His boots were of the finest quality, but well worn and unadorned. Zack was relaxed as he greeted his opponents. Although well dressed they appeared fearful. Zack did not.

The game ran late, and stakes were high when Zack called a break. He retreated outside, stood alone in the cool evening smoking a cigarette. His mind wandered, but he knew the precise moment to return to the game. He had to make a decision. Without a brilliant maneuver, Zack would lose it all. With efficient intensity Zack stopped the circle of time. Expertly, before raising the stake, he spiraled time back into itself, to a game he left a winner. Nobody noticed until Zack swept the money off of the table that he had captured the big prize.

Although powerful, Zack never stood out. He preferred

anonymity to notoriety and subtlety to flamboyance. Zack laughed knowing he could lose it all tomorrow. He stayed late, patiently waiting as his friends drank at the bar. Knowing he did not yet have the money to buy the ranch property, he sat quietly, improvising a way to accomplish his task.

Zack spoke to Americo in the dream. He put his hand on his young apprentice shoulder, reminding him of a teaching revealed by a shaman. "Did you see that?" Zack asked. "Power only comes once, Americo. You would be well served by reversing the circle of time, opening your eyes, and extending your hand before power gets away."

Americo awakened and slowly put the discs back on his belt. They were out of order, and he didn't remember having the dream.

☪

Stalling the Vortex, Rita created a portal for her husband. Smelling the sweet fragrance of his pipe tobacco, she rested her head on his pillow and felt his hand gently touch her hair. She whispered, "Soon, my love. Very soon."

"What a long and lonely journey it's been for our loved ones."

Rita hushed him, knowing he couldn't stay. "The frequency is in place, and like ours, their filaments are entwined for all eternity. If they can survive the next descent, all will be well."

Zack assured Rita with knowledge from the other side. "Our Lauren's light is bright and her soul is ready to come home." Visions of Americo as his young apprentice came to Zack. "Americo's candle is low, and he needs my help."

Rita felt him leaving. "The parts of herself that Lauren sacrificed are now reaching for her, but there is so much yet for her to face. Hold Americo and Lauren in your love, we all need you more than ever," she told him as he slipped away.

☪

In every age, there are signs and markers that identify the times. Lauren Auldney spun into young womanhood in the age of miniskirts and hotpants. Lauren was a dancer with great legs, and she wore hotpants, although not always visibly. As a girl Lauren preferred pink, when she got a little older and wiser, she realized pink doesn't quite get the job done.

Wyatt Kirkman thought he saw an opening. Feeling adventurous, he decided to take an unexpected trip to see Lauren, his damsel in distress. When Lauren opened her eyes that morning following a restless night of worrying about her current problems, she thought her eyes looked particularly open and receptive. Later, as she hung her lacy red satin panties on the clothesline, she wondered if her eyes were open, or if she had opened her eyes.

Flying to Sedona in his Gulfstream private jet, Wyatt decided to take Lauren dancing. "The poor girl needs to let off some steam." Wyatt felt noble, rather gallant and knightly. "I'll take her out to rock and roll." Wyatt, being a bit older than Lauren, decided to take a nap.

The Vortex spins really fast in Sedona during the scorching hot month of July. The key ring she carried looked remarkably like a mushroom and as Lauren inserted the key into the ignition of her sports car, she was really feeling the heat. "I sure hope this heat is building up to something." Lauren put the top down on her convertible, speculating about the coming monsoon season. "If it gets any hotter, the tops going to blow off something tonight."

Wyatt's plane landed on time, screeching to a halt on runway number two. He stood on the platform looking like a handsomely rugged sixty-two-year old man. His steel gray hair needed cut, the nap had rumpled his dark blue cotton shirt, and he had the look of a man about to take a tumble. Wyatt could have taken time to get a haircut, but his only concern was landing his plane.

Running to greet him, Lauren stumbled. As she gracefully got up from the runway, she bent over to tie the lace on her red canvas running shoes.

"Hmm, Lauren still wears red panties."

Lauren saw the gleam in his eye.

"Scarlet, my love, you look as luscious as a sweet chocolate cookie right out of the oven." Wyatt held his arms out to hug her.

"Well," she thought giving him a warm kiss, "if he likes what he sees, maybe I'll let him see what he likes."

Later in the evening, about 7:30, getting ready to go dancing with Wyatt, Lauren polished her weapon. "Style is everything," she thought polishing her red cowgirl boots. Everything Lauren wore to go dancing that night had style. Her style was developed over years of wandering the world. She didn't glean it from fashion magazines, and the editors of fashion magazines wouldn't have approved of her style. Lauren believed style begins from the inside and spins its way to the outside. Layer by layer, Lauren got ready to go dancing. Lauren knew that if a woman wears great lingerie, fabulous jewelry and noticeable shoes, nothing else really matters. Thinking what a great jewelry collection she owned, Lauren looked in the mirror. "You've got some really hot stuff, Lauren." She then slipped her just tight enough jeans over her fanny.

She clasped three gold bracelets of her own creation on her right wrist. One bracelet had a little rattle on it. From another bracelet, many dangling fine threads of chain shook when she wiggled her wrist. On the third and final bracelet, a little channel set gold ball rolled back and forth. Lauren was ready to shake, rattle, and roll. After putting on a white silk tank top, red cowgirl boots and tying a woven Andean belt around her waist, Lauren was ready and she looked like hot stuff.

Traffic stopped as Lauren and Wyatt got out of her Audi in front of the nightclub where all of her problems began. "Wyatt, do you remember when that nasty woman told me that one day I'd be old and ugly and traffic wouldn't stop for me?" Putting the lipstick tube in her handbag, Lauren hoped the big Mercedes hadn't stopped on her account.

Wyatt motioned for the Mercedes to go ahead. "Scarlet," Wyatt said while Lauren combed her hair with her fingers, "there have always been a lot of women who don't like you."

"I don't understand that, Wyatt," Lauren said taking his arm. "I studied women artists in art history, I worship the Goddess, the concept of woman is endlessly fascinating to me, and I know how to keep a home, cook, sew, and grow flowers. The womanly arts are really my thing." The keeper of the door gave her a look of recognition. Thinking of one final thing before going into the bar, Lauren, with a look of innocence on her face, told Wyatt, "All in all, I like women."

At that moment Lauren heard the keeper of the door telling a patron. "Here comes trouble. The last time she was here, she went home and tried to kill a man." Sticking her tongue out like a snake, Lauren gave him a little hiss.

"Hey, cold fish," Garry Baker said loudly over the music, "The other day I thought about those hotpants you wore when we were in high school. You sure fooled everybody."

"You fool, you never did learn how to cook a fish," Lauren sassed back at him. Lovingly wiping the sweat from Wyatt's forehead, she walked away.

Wyatt wondered why anybody would call Lauren a cold fish.

Wyatt hailed from Georgia. He was a country boy who had made good in the world. That night when the lights went out in

Sedona, he had Lauren Auldney in his bed for the first time in almost twenty years. That's the night Lauren tumbled a not so innocent man.

The task given to Lauren took most of her time that summer, and truthfully Wyatt was a very married man, who was also very busy. Regardless, Wyatt found many reasons to visit Sedona; after all, he was funding her defense. The golf courses in Sedona are challenging and beautiful, and Lauren needed to get away from the rancho occasionally for a little change of scenery. Lauren needed money, having never saved very much. A very generous man, Wyatt thought his wife, two daughters, and four granddaughters needed some new jewelry for Christmas. They struck a deal. Wyatt sealed the deal with a bouquet of sunflowers, a magnum of champagne, and a lovely room at a very nice inn.

"It makes sense to me, Wyatt," Lauren said charmingly spinning a tale over champagne at a local resort. "I have needs, you have needs, and maybe we can help each other. I certainly don't have any other deals going at this time."

☪

The deafening sound of a slamming door startled Lauren from a night of restless sleep. An owl hooted its departure and urging her to leave the cocoon of her bed, the first rays of light filtered through marred panes of glass. Drifting back to sleep, Lauren felt a hand clasp her own. The hand felt familiar, a young man's face appeared and Lauren smiled. "Is it you, my little boy?" She brushed a lock of black hair from his forehead. "I've missed you so very much." Lauren saw the tears in his gold-flecked green eyes. "I'm sorry that I didn't bring you home to your Daddy," she said clinging to his hand. "He would have loved you so much."

She felt his hand on her shoulder. "I've been watching both of you," he said with a hint of Americo's deep gravely voice. That was my destiny. Living with you on Earth was only one possibility. I've never left you, and I never will." He smiled at her with Americo's slow grin.

A veil floated in the light as Lauren felt a burden lift from her back. "Please go to your father, help him understand," Lauren beseeched her son. "TJ, he needs you now, more than ever."

"I'll travel with him to the beginning," her son smiled, making the freckle on his upper lip dance. With a sassy tilt to his head much like her own, he assured her with confidence. "I'll teach him the story."

☪

Lauren lingered in bed staring at the dolls on the shelf. Slowly, meaning came to her. Each of her creations, with the exception of one, was a mother holding a child. Madonna-like, each doll contained the poignancy of profound maternal love. Now fully awake, she had another awareness. On the back of each mother, there was a burden filled cloth, bag, or satchel. "I've always wondered why women wept when they saw the dolls I made." Lauren comforted herself with a hug. "I've been processing my love and grief without knowing it." Feeling the burden of her pain diminish, she came to realization. "If only we could scream our grief to the universe, rather than try to be strong, the burdens wouldn't have to be carried for so long."

Lauren smiled at her childhood dolls, *"You have listened to my stories over and over."* Looking at dolls of her own creation, she solemnly thanked them for carrying life on their back. *"You, the issue of my hands, heart, and soul, have carried the burden with me."* Lauren, acknowledging that women have carried culture and family as well as personal pain on their backs throughout all time, made a vow. "When this mess I'm in is over, I'm going to make a series of dolls called 'On Her Back.' Laughing without restraint, she designed the final piece in the series. In her mind she saw a woman reclining on her back, with her legs bent and spread, ready to receive a man. "On our back, or on our backs, that seems to be the way of the woman." Lauren stepped out of bed, feeling a renewed sense of purpose. "I totally love being on my back waiting for my lover," she giggled, feeling risqué as she felt the hot water in the shower tingle her breasts. "But I'm sure as hell going to lighten the load I carry on my back."

☪

Later in the morning Lauren spent time by the creek dangling her feet in the water, remembering when she used to go skinny dipping as a rosy cheeked, wide-eyed, too eager to please, bare butted, cracked, sitting on the border girl. Too much time passed, and Lauren remembered she had to do her hand laundry. Standing over the sink in the laundry room, Lauren sprinkled fluffy, white flakes of soft soap, thinking how great it would be to be a bubble. "I wonder," Lauren said watching a cluster of bubbles, "if that's the way the galaxies stick together. Hmmm, guess I'll go check it out later when I have time. Who needs a map?" One by one she washed her delicates, carefully rinsing the last of the bubbles. Some of the bubbles went down the drain, some floated in the air, some were little and some were big. They all had one thing in common; they were translucent little balls that caught the light.

Clothespins in her hand, Lauren stood under the circular clothesline in Rita's backyard. Five satin bras of different colors shimmered in the early morning sunlight, heralding their purpose and place in life to the raven flying overhead. Sending a message to the raven, Lauren carefully pinned her lacy red panties on the next row. Next came the soft, pastel colored camisoles and silk teddies. "You're as pretty off as you are on," she told her lingerie, feeling light of heart.

Carefully buttoning her delicate linen blouses, Lauren recalled with melancholy Americo's fingers tenderly touching the lace-bordered collars. Three pair of jeans, two summer dresses, two cotton skirts, four pair of running shorts, and six white tank t-shirts joined the others whipping in the breeze like flags of luscious female power. "Ymmm," she said sniffing the already drying garments, "there is absolutely nothing like sunlight and a soft summer breeze to freshen your life."

Rita knocked on the window, disturbing Lauren from her musing. Pointing with her cane, Rita invited Lauren to join her on the porch for coffee and cream puffs, sharing Lauren's passion for sweets before lunchtime.

Surprised to see Rita peeling an apple, Lauren sat down on the porch to give her grandmother's six cats their daily brushing. Rita's namesake, the self-declared goddess who helped Rita spin the Vortex, took her time before allowing Lauren the pleasure. Readying herself to explain Lauren's task, Rita offered a silent prayer petitioning the Goddess. The temperature rose quickly foretelling a scorching day, and Rita was perplexed. "You haven't said a word about him, Lauren."

Lauren cupped her chin in her hands, resting her elbows on her knees. "At this point, Grandma, I don't know how much this has to do with Americo. I know I've said this before, but I really feel what I need to do is a response to me and what I need, not a reaction to what Americo thinks or feels." Lauren felt another veil lift from her vision. "I know, I know, Grandma," Lauren waved her hand in protest, "the worst is coming, maybe many worsts are coming, but I'm ready to take the first step."

Rita smiled. "Finally, Lauren has learned to be detached."

Lauren started to laugh, quickly covering her mouth with her hand. "Rita, you're a mean old Witch." Lauren laughed slyly. "You banished Americo, just like in a fairy tale."

Rita cackled with delight. Becoming serious, she sipped her coffee looking at Lauren over the rim of her cup and then held the apple for Lauren to see. "Lauren, when do you suppose the apple stops being an apple?"

Stunned by the question, Lauren held her breath, looking wide-eyed and puzzled. "That's the eternal question isn't it, Grandma?" Lauren stretched, and then bent at the waist to touch her toes. "Does the apple quit being an apple when it decays on the ground, when we take the first bite, make it into sauce, or dry the slices in the sun?"

Lauren recalled pestering Rita with a similar question. With fluffy white cream smeared on her upper lip she told Rita she had finally figured it out. "I remember you telling me that even though we grate the chocolate for the cake, mix it up in the batter, bake it in the oven, and eat it with tea, the chocolate is always chocolate."

Rita smiled remembering the many afternoons she spent with Lauren in her kitchen and garden. She listened indulgently as Lauren tried to articulate the answer spinning in her mind.

"I guess if we use the apple as a metaphor for Lauren, it goes something like this." Lauren took her time forming her answer. "Like an intelligent fool, I fell from the tree, not waiting for somebody to pick me. Whoever found me polished the skin until it was bruised. Oh, Grandma," Lauren resigned contentedly, "it doesn't really matter, because no matter what happens to it, the apple is always an apple, just like in spite of everything, I will always be Lauren." Laughing at her own ineptness, Lauren confessed. "I just have to figure out who in the hell that is, don't I?"

"Don't forget," Rita brought her back to thoughtfulness, "the apple, if combined with other ingredients, can be transformed into gold."

Rita stood, forgetting to use her cane and directed Lauren's gaze to the garden. "Think of the compost pile and the rich trans-formation that takes place by combining the remainders of our life, love, fairy tears, and sunlight with the eternal soil. Consider your experiences in the same light, because you are now ready to compost your experience with your original self."

"Do you mean I'll be transformed into gold, Grandma?"

"Possibly," Rita said with a devilish wink, "but don't forget, the apple, regardless of the transformation, will always live on in a new form."

Rita held her hand in the air, tracing a spiral with her finger. "First you are going to clean my house and yard. Then," Rita intended to provoke Lauren, "I want you to spin the spiral in the garden the other direction."

"But won't that confuse the Vortex?" Lauren said with aghast.

"My Dear, the Vortex tells me that its time for all of us to change the direction we spin," Rita whispered, initiating Lauren into her task.

☪★

Rita revealed the task, hoping Lauren would understand that any act we take with our bodies, we are also accomplishing the same in our minds and souls. Telling Lauren to consider the house to be hers, she set forth her expectations. "Lauren, you will start in the kitchen, only because your heart is broken and the kitchen is the heart of the home. I want you to empty every cupboard, wipe off the contents, polish the copper pots and pans, wash the china and crystal, and organize the ceramic bowls I've collected." Rita issued orders like the cruel stepmother. "I want you to organize the spices, clean the refrigerator and oven, restock the pantry, and then," she paused, "you will wash the walls and scrub and polish the floors until the old tile shines."

Room by room, Rita walked Lauren through the old ranch house telling her what to do. "You know how to sew, Lauren, so make new curtains for the bedroom windows." Rita suggested something light and airy. "The bedrooms are where we make love, rest our bodies and talk with the spirits in the dark of the night." Walking into one of the bathrooms, Rita instructed her. "This is where we refresh ourselves, see ourselves in the mirror first thing in the morning, and soak in a hot tub when we need to return to the womb. I want you to paint the walls bright yellow, then paint flowers around the door." Taking Lauren by the hand into the living room, Rita gave her carte blanche to pick the paint color. "The only rule I have is to never disturb your grandfather's chair, boots, or cigar table." Rita stood with her hand on the potbelly stove. "I want you to paint the walls, shake the rugs, clean the stove, stock the copper washtub with wood, organize my yarn according to color, and polish my spinning wheel." Into the dining room they walked as Lauren heaved her breast, feeling overwhelmed by the task. "This is the room where our family and friends gather to celebrate our life on El Rancho de las Estrellas," Rita continued, sitting down at the head of the table to rest. "I want you to hang new wallpaper, something in a soft pink. Then," Rita instructed her with a flourish, "wax the furniture, polish the silver, and reupholster the chairs with weavings I've made. Be sure to clean the credenza, Lauren, you never know what you will find," Rita added with a note of intrigue. "Lastly, my dear, you will clean the attic. This is the most important part," Rita hesitated, becoming misty eyed, "because in the attic is where the dearest memories are stored."

☪

Lauren served lunch to her Grandmother on a small table in a shady corner of the yard. The table was impeccably set with an embroidered cloth, everyday china, and jewel red glasses from Mexico. Expertly Lauren sliced cucumbers paper thin to serve with the juicy tomatoes from the garden. Trimmed slices of bread were spread with a special dressing Lauren invented on the spot. Purple rings of onion, black olives and iced tea were carried on a tray from the kitchen, completing the array of food. Rita took the first bite, nodding her approval to Lauren as she nibbled on a seasoned cucumber slice.

"Tell me about the yard, Grandma," Lauren inquired spreading more thick sauce on a slice of bread. "What do you want me to do?"

Rita had a list ready and pointed at the tall hedgerow. "You will need to trim the hedges, thin the groundcover, and haul all of the debris to the compost. Also, I'd like to see some flowers planted next to the house like I used to plant when you were young."

Lauren swept her arm across the horizon. "Grandma, I'm going to have so much fun doing this work. I felt like I was grounded when they took my passport away, now I feel like I'm on retreat and I might even lose the five pounds I've always meant to."

Rita napped after lunch, giving Lauren time to make a list.

Sipping sherry on the porch Rita and Lauren watched the sun drop behind a red rock cliff, announcing the arrival of the hour of power. Rita completed her instructions, "After you harvest the garden, then you can spread the compost, mix it in the soil, and at that time," Rita added the final touch, "you can reshape the spiral in the garden." Rita stopped at the door, after having said good night and gave Lauren one additional piece of work. "Lauren, my dear," Rita said blowing her a kiss, "before your task is finished I expect you to complete the paths to nowhere you've created on the property. I don't care where they end or if they connect, but make them lead to somewhere."

Lauren sat on the porch long after darkness had fallen, making a plan. "This is a first for me," she said in awe of the relief it provided her. Absent-mindedly stroking the back of Rita's namesake cat, Lauren felt content. Rocking into the night, sitting on her grandfather's chair, in Lauren's dreamtime Americo walked through the gate. She heard the bells chime, and she saw him nod in greeting. The moonlight reflected starkly from his white shirt and as he strolled closer, the scent of cinnamon tickled her nose. He held her hand and kissed her palm. He motioned towards Cathedral Rock, and Lauren responded with a smile, "I'll be there, Darling, wait for me."

☾★

A man of enormous appetites, Americo Rios no longer had zest for life. For months he had been disinterested in sex, food, or making plans for a future. His vitality, once high and vigorous, was bleeding from his body, rending Americo impotent. Without the regular infusion of Lauren's wild, random energy, he would continue to dwindle. His love of life would die unless he gave up living by a plan. Random living had never been his strong suit, and hidden in Americo's unconscious was the awareness that he made a dreadful mistake the night he threw the joker away. Americo had put himself in a box without a key. He had dishonored himself by becoming engaged to a woman he did not love or desire, and his belief that Lauren tried to kill him had not diminished. His Nagual was not available to him, leaving Americo lost and alone in the now haunting quiet of his remote hacienda in the barren countryside. In despair, not having the strength to ride, Americo sold his favorite horse, at the same time finding another home for Lauren's mare. He dismissed his housekeeper, no longer visiting her for companionship, and desiring only the solitude of his own company. When his friends called, he listlessly opened the bar and long before the conversation ceased he retreated into the small, dark room where he slept.

Waiting for the messengers Rita warned him about, Americo neglected his hacienda, allowing the weeds to overtake the flowers and the vines to climb predatorily under the clay bar tiles on his roof. Lauren's new outdoor stove remained unused, the flowers she planted died, and Americo placed her photographs in the trunk with the rest of her belongings, planning to send them to her when he became motivated. The Indian motorcycle he brought by trailer to Mexico sat in the courtyard, not having been ridden since his arrival. Unwisely Americo had not followed Rita's mandate to go to his orchard to pray and take inventory of his life before leaving Sedona.

It was a moonless night, the night Americo went to the small private cemetery where his and Lauren's ancestors were buried. Sitting on a meditation bench in the center of the graveyard, Americo wept for what might have been. "My son," he said in barely a whisper. "I had a son. He cried, and I wasn't there." A column of light appeared, lighting the stepping stone path leading to the gate. The light pulsed, commanding Americo to heed its presence.

The face he had seen in the desert presented itself and Americo heard a voice that sounded like his own. "It was a choice I made," the young man with sparkling green eyes told him. "The circumstances of my birth had nothing to do with my choice. I was conceived in love and that was all that mattered." Standing with his hands on his hips, TJ Rios challenged his father. "Dad, don't you remember me, don't you remember the last time?"

Looking at his son, Americo felt old. His hair had started to gray and as it fell loosely around his face, he clinched his fists and leaned his elbows on spread legs. "I had so much to give you, son," Americo said quietly. "I had the time to spend with you, I loved your mother more than myself, you had a home on our rancho waiting, and I needed you both so desperately."

"Don't you remember me?" TJ asked his father again.

"I don't know," Americo answered honestly. "I feel something in my body that tells me I do." A flash of remembrance came to him. Americo looked to the left and saw Lauren holding a baby, standing next to the cave where she found the basket. Screaming, Lauren ran for shelter, fiercely clutching the crying baby to her breast. Lightning struck in the distance and then the fire raged through the forest. "Did we make it?" Americo asked TJ, listening to the owl in the distance.

TJ laughed, extending his hand. "Dad, come with me, I want to show you how brave my mother is."

Earth is round, however, like a weaving, the grid of frequency is flat. Experience is somewhere in between. Deep in the night, father and son stood together in the shelter of Cathedral Rock. With a pass of his hand, so like Americo's, TJ Rios turned the world to frequency. Defocusing his vision, Americo started to see. The grid vibrated and as he saw past the present, into the past, he found Lauren standing on a mesa against a backdrop of red rocks. Behind Lauren he saw a crippled man, his leg mangled and his body scarred.

"My Mom saved us both," TJ said as his image emerged from the grid of frequency.

Americo dropped to his knees and witnessed the ferocity Lauren invoked as she pulled him from the fire after a falling tree had broken his legs, leaving him unable to save his woman and son. Americo saw his son in a small sheltered cave, his legs wiggling in the air, crying as Lauren left him to save her mate. TJ forced Americo to face the truth. "She saved me first, just like she always did." As if layers of an onion had peeled away, Americo's vision cleared and he saw Lauren, courageous, independent, and willing to do anything for her man and child.

*A woman weeps as she digs in the unforgiving soil, searching for bulbs to feed her son. Her hands are dirty and her hair stringy. She sweats hauling water from a flowing creek to a hillside enclosure of earthen bricks. With a handmade broom, fashioned from the branch of a tree, the woman sweeps a dirt floor. Agave plants roast in the pit. With a cactus quill needle she stitches their deerskin clothes and weaves threads from agave into sandals to protect their feet as they walk on the rocky path.*

*Too tired to sleep she tenderly wipes the brow of her mate, who lies dying in their bed. She holds his hand to her lips, her breast, and her cheek, before kissing him goodbye. His body prepared for burial, with all of the strength in her body, the woman digs a hole deep in the Earth. From the cloth she carries on her back, the woman removes their collected treasures, sending the power they contain with him to the next world. Her son helps her cover the body of her beloved sleeping man as tears fall from her eyes, dissolving the red soil beneath her feet.*

*Now a widow, she tends a sparse garden while her naked grandchildren play with sticks under a tree. She sees in the distance as her muscular, dark skinned son returns carrying a small deer. In a trance, standing in front of a red rock wall, the woman draws a spiral of entwined threads. By the fire, sitting in a deep alcove, the woman, old and bent from toil, tells stories about her beloved mate to her four grandchildren, using her hands to describe the pictures.*

*A decade later, she tells them with wonder in her eyes, "I would have sacrificed anything for my man but my life." Adding more wood to the fire, she smiles at her family, revealing her toothless mouth. Her son's widow asks, "Would you change anything about your life?" The woman, in this life Lauren, answers with conviction, "No."*

Responding to their call, Lauren joined Americo and their son standing within the belly of Cathedral Rock. Her son took her hand as they walked towards Americo. "My Mom has carried me on her back her entire life," TJ told his father. Joining his parent's hands, TJ told them to watch. First, he reminded them of the Spinning Game they played as children. "You stood on a point," he told them pointing to the spot Lauren had chosen for their spinning. Moving his finger in a large circle, he painted the picture with his words. The point began to rotate, creating 360 degrees of possibilities. "The first time you played the game, you stopped here," he said moving in the direction they had faced. "Our destiny was determined in that instant." With a quick pass of his hands, he showed them all other possibilities. "You know," he gleamed with Lauren's green eyes, "the other choices didn't fall into the gap and someday you'll see them all."

Lauren and Americo stood in the rotating spoke of gold rays. Flashes of other possibilities appeared, other lives together, and other outcomes of their choices. "How many other lives have we had together, TJ?" Lauren asked moving closer to Americo.

TJ prepared to leave them. With a look over his shoulder, he answered Lauren. "We've had one hundred and thirty-two lives together on the red rocks and until all possibilities are realized the three of us will keep returning to our castle."

Americo stood behind her, encircling Lauren's body with his arms. Resting his chin on her head, he whispered, "I love you, Lauren." He placed his hands over the cauldron within her and with his rugged veined hands, protected the precious core of his woman.

"Someday we'll remember this." Lauren glanced at him over her shoulder. "Like I told you, it isn't over, unless he says it is."

Together they faced Cathedral Rock and with awe for her courage in his voice, Americo asked, "Why can't we see it now, Baby?"

Lauren pointed to the figures protected by the walls of red. "Because, my love, you are still looking up at the stars, seeking the ideal." She made him face the truth by seeing the tilt of the man's head. "And, I'm still looking within, trying to remember who I am." Lauren saw the reality of her life in the female figure staring at the wall of red. "But, he's with us, Americo."

"We've been looking the wrong direction, Lauren," Americo said as they parted. "We should have accepted ourselves and faced each other as we really are." Returning to give Lauren a last kiss, he summed up the trap. "I think we've been trapped in our perceptions."

"We have to remember how to spin together, Darling," Lauren giggled knowing they wouldn't recall this moment for a very long time. "Then we can realize all possibilities together."

"Someday I'll remember you, Bruja," he called as he disappeared into dreaming.

"Yes, Jugador," Lauren yawned as the sun kissed the red rock Earth good morning, "you'll remember me when the winds again blow my magic into your awareness."

☪

By the light of the silvery, rocking, crescent moon, the nimble fingers of the Great Spinner spun Lauren's fatigue into strength. Weakness left her body, leaving her taut and powerful. The summer moved past, beckoning autumn to appear. Slaving in the kitchen on her hands and knees, Lauren painted sealer on the old tile floor. As she peered into each organized cupboard, she felt a coherency of mind and heart previously unknown to her. Laughing as she charmed an appliance repairman on the phone, Lauren fixed two burners on the stove that hadn't worked for ten years. "It's all a matter of making the right connections," she decided with growing confidence that she could do anything.

She struggled and swore as she tried to move the refrigerator.

"Lauren, remember," she told herself groaning as she pushed, "use the method all women know. Move things an inch, a bucketful, a teaspoonful, or an ounce at a time. It might take longer, but by Goddess, we get the job done on our own if we set our minds and hearts on accomplishing a task." Bending over her sewing machine Lauren put the final touches on the new, soft, pink, gauzy curtains for her bedroom. "Now I can wake up in the mornings and see beyond the visible through rose colored light." Lauren swore when the hammer hammered her finger, not the nail, to the wall. "Hmm," Lauren said looking through her rose colored vision, "maybe things are not what they seem to be."

Lauren got tired of looking at the torn ruffled flounce on her bed. Searching in Rita's mending basket she found the exact needle she wanted. Sitting on the floor with her legs crossed, taking quick deft stitches, Lauren pricked her finger and finally discovered the purpose of a needle. "Well, for goodness sake," she told herself sucking the blood, "Lauren, you are so silly. A needle is for repairing wounds not making wounds." Proud of her acquired wisdom, she congratulated herself. "Well, it's a good thing you figured that out before you let your soul, creativity, and life force bleed out of your body." Holding her finger to stop the blood, Lauren pondered. "I wonder if there's a part of me that is bleeding to death, and I don't know it. Oh, I don't know," she finally decided, "I think my blood bleeds for something I'm always longing for. I wonder if somebody else bleeds blood that longs for me."

Blood is the mystery. It is warm, red, primal, viscous, frightening, essential, foundational, filled with a lot of good information, and it flows. Women experience blood flowing in their bodies and periodically, flowing out of their bodies. Not every woman loves blood, but Lauren did. Blood speaks to everybody if they taste it. The sight of blood had always fascinated Lauren. In order to find order in her disorder, she cut doors into her body to see, feel, and to taste her essence. Blood spoke to her in a vocabulary she could understand. Blood is eternal, it reproduces itself and it carries our family history as it flows through our bodies. Lauren knew on some level that it contained much more. She knew her blood contained only half of the ongoing story, and she knew she had tasted blood that told the rest. Now that she's younger than before, but old enough to know better, she thinks there are probably better ways to open doors than with a needle.

As she stapled the weavings onto the padded cushions of the dining room chairs, she pondered. "I wonder who will change these covers next time." Seeing into the future, she recognized a young, tired looking woman seated at the head of the table with a large family gathered for her birthday dinner. "You again," Lauren whispered to the eldest son sitting to her right. "Weren't you supposed to be an only child?"

Her handsome, black haired son lovingly patted her hand. "This is a good one, Mom. You and Dad have it all."

"Everything except time for each other," Lauren thought passing the creamy, buttery mashed potatoes to the girl on her left.

Late in the night Lauren drew trailing vines spiraling around red sunflowers in the freshly painted bathroom. The creamy light yellow paint was glossy and slick, providing the perfect background for Lauren's delicate brush strokes. "I will definitely be taking more baths and fewer showers," Lauren vowed as she stood back to get perspective, admiring her work. "You are just too good, Lauren Auldney," she bragged.

The words of her father came back to haunt her. "If you're so good, why aren't you rich and famous?"

"Sorry, Daddy, I love you tons, but fuck you," Lauren said feeling like a shit free little girl. "I'm not a gullible, naïve, not knowing woman any more. And, just in case you're listening, I don't see the world through your glasses any longer either."

Lauren had an idea. Tapping the little tacks into the back of an oval framed mirror, she caught a glimpse of herself. "Grandma, you may not have known who you were," she said to the reflection mirroring her aging self, "but you always knew precisely what you were doing." Sighing as the reflection revealed her life, Lauren spoke to her own image. "Lauren, not only did you forget who you were, most of the time you had absolutely no idea what you were doing."

Hundreds of skeins of yarn were scattered over the living room floor. Sorting them by color Lauren sat amidst a pile of reds and oranges. Dark red, Earth red, purple red, sunset orange red, hot pink red, orange, orange red, and bright red surrounded her. Feeling her first two chakras start to vibrate, Lauren experienced desire. "They tell me that because I'm an Aquarian, I live in my mind. Bullshit," Lauren whispered low enough for Rita not to hear, "don't they know that there's a hot, reddish orange wind that blows in the crack of a woman's body? Who cares what they say, I'm a first and second chakra person who happens to have a few too many brain cells and a heart that won't quit loving Americo," she giggled lasciviously.

Lauren then laid wood in the potbelly stove for the first fire of the season. Cleaning out a drawer in the desk, Lauren found a Christmas card from Sybille. "Oh, Sybille, you killed yourself because you couldn't bear to get old and wrinkled. Well, you ought to see your daughter now, because I'm older than you were when you died." Lauren pondered the paradox of mother love. "It's OK, Sybille," she sighed with forgiveness for her mother, "just like all women, you had your own burden to carry. You just didn't carry it very well."

Stewed apples were bubbling on the stove as Lauren prepared the quart jars for applesauce. "It'll be alright little apples," she assured them, as she tasted a teaspoon of tart sauce. "Just don't forget that you're an apple, even if somebody calls you a pear." Sniffing the fragrance, Lauren formed a perfect question. "Am I seeing everything that lurks behind the door of what I'm seeing?"

The attic. "I'm not looking forward to this part of my task," Lauren told herself in the mirror while she counted the gray hairs on her head. Dusty, cobwebbed, neglected, and eerie, the attic hadn't been cleaned in over forty years. Lauren tied a bandana around her hair and climbed the rickety steps, carrying a broom, dusting rags, and dustpan. "Oh no," she sighed with exasperation. "Does anybody have any idea what is in here?" A box marked, do not open until my death, caught her attention. "You old rascal, Grandma," Lauren giggled affectionately. "Is this my weaving?"

Lauren sorted and reboxed old clothes, dishes, souvenirs, and forgotten memories. Trying one of Rita's old dresses on for size, Lauren had a glimpse of herself as a housewife. "Doesn't fit, does it?" Lauren asked the unknown person in the old cheval mirror from her girlhood room. She surrendered to sadness recalling the night of her graduation and how she had twirled in front of the mirror before descending the staircase to Americo. Blushing just a little, she remembered admiring her body after making love in the Casino. "I thought I was so devastating in my no longer virgin body. I didn't know it then, but my life was about to become devastated." For a while Lauren sat by herself with cobwebs in her hair, crying.

An old gilded birdcage that she had never seen before needed to be moved. Thoughts about freedom filled Lauren's mind. Thinking about how imprisoned she had been by keeping a secret, she wondered how she could have ever been so naïve. "I thought by not telling Americo and Daddy about TJ, I gained my freedom. Now I know," she quietly accepted, "I imprisoned myself in a cage of my own design." Thinking there might be more to the story,

Lauren thought of something else. "I'm pretty sure I know something I wish I didn't know."

"Whisk, whisk, wisk," went the broom, sounding like little mouse feet running across the floor. Lauren swept up the glass from a broken art deco gold lampshade. Lauren made a promise to the dancing woman on the base, a promise to make something lovely from the broken parts. "I know what you feel like. I've been broken and imperfect myself, only I didn't have the courage to show those parts to certain people. Now I think the broken parts are the best parts, because they give us a chance to rearrange them according to our own ever changing perceptions." Looking out the window, deciding to take a day off when she finished the attic, Lauren had an epiphany. "Perfection is boring, impossible to maintain, and reeks of death. Embrace your imperfections; after all, they reveal your unique path. To hell with the ideal," she called to the dove cooing in the yard.

Spending three days thumbing through old scrapbooks, Lauren found a wild, carefree little girl who knew exactly who she was. There was a picture of Lauren lying spread eagle on the lawn, looking at the sky. Trying to recall the moment, she supposed she was counting little sperm like filaments that were floating from her star. There was another picture of Lauren standing on the porch, entranced by the fluttery moths flying in front of the light. Lauren wondered if she had spent too much time pondering the unknowable. "I remember exactly what I was wondering. I was wondering if the moths had a path to follow or if they just flew randomly." Awareness came to Lauren with ponder lines forming around her mouth. "It doesn't really matter, because the moths only cared about being close to the light. Guess I should have paid closer attention," was her next thought.

The day she finished cleaning the attic, Lauren skipped down the stairs a happy woman. As Rita listened from the living room, she heard Lauren singing in her off key voice. "Row, row, row your boat, gently down the stream, merrily, merrily, merrily, life is but a dream."

Rita smiled.

Incensed by his friend's banishment, Ignacio Verona watched Lauren with his binoculars as she meditated under the tree "Lazy, spoiled, no good puta," he spat on the ground. Ignacio packed his bags in Americo's truck, tucked the mail he was delivering in the glove compartment, and dropped the keys to the house and barn at Trey's house. A local man had been hired to feed and ride the horses, and Alexandra had custody of Americo's cat in his absence.

"Hey, thanks man," Trey said shaking Ignacio's hand at the door and quickly hanging up the phone. "Sorry you went to the trouble because I've already got keys. Americo and I have always kept keys to each other's homes and cars."

Ignacio fumed, thinking he was the only person Americo trusted.

There was a knock on the door. "Lauren, what's up, Sis?" Trey gave her a quick peck on the cheek. "As skinny as you're getting, I have to think Rita's making you work too hard."

Lauren gave Ignacio a warm hug, while telling Trey he was wrong. "Actually, I'd call it hardly working," Lauren giggled. "I feel like I've been on the best retreat of my life. I feel so relaxed and refreshed." Walking away from Ignacio, Lauren laughingly answered Trey's question. "I'm not even close to being finished, so who knows, I'll probably feel like I've been massaged, manicured, and pampered before it's over. Rita's house has always been filled with enchantment, so living there has been pure delight."

Giggling at her naughtiness, Lauren sent a message to Americo. "Give Americo a little kiss for me, Ignacio." Lauren then scratched a mosquito bite on her fanny.

☪

Sitting at his massive pine table, Americo sorted through his mail, indifferently throwing most of it in the garbage. He quickly scanned a letter Alexandra sent, only to read amusing stories about his cat. Ignacio stood, waiting to be offered a drink. Pointing to the bar, Americo told him to help himself as always. "So tell me, Ignacio, what's going on at the rancho? I'm homesick as hell."

Calculating his moves, Ignacio set a trap. "You shouldn't be away from the rancho, my amigo. The one who should have been sent away is Lauren. For her own good," he told Americo cleverly disguising his disdain.

"Have you seen much of Lauren?" Americo wondered why he

cared.

Ignacio laughed snidely. "I've seen her many times. I've seen her sunbathing in the yard, driving her sports car to town, having dinner with her lover, and spending the afternoon visiting with her brother."

"I'm glad she's got Trey and Sunnie. Can't help it man," Americo confessed with embarrassment, "for some reason I don't want her to be alone and sad while she works for Rita."

"Ho, don't you worry about that." Ignacio opened the door wide. "She told Trey she hardly works at all. She also mentioned something about going on a delightful retreat at the Enchantment Resort to get massaged and pampered."

Slyly he waited for Americo to respond.

Americo couldn't help it. The thought of Wyatt Kirkman made his gut wrench. In a weak moment Lauren had told him about her affair with a married man and Americo knew without question Wyatt was Lauren's current lover. In front of his eyes flashed a picture. He could see Lauren with her head thrown back in ecstasy as she held her breasts and rocked her body over Wyatt. Americo's ears throbbed as he accepted that she no longer cried out his name. When Americo averted his eyes knowing Wyatt must be providing the luxuries, Ignacio brought the message. "The most beautiful Ms. Lauren sent a message to you, my friend." Ignacio walked to the bar for another shot of whiskey.

With his heart pounding, Americo felt more alive than he had for weeks. "What did Lauren have to say?" His voice quivered slightly.

Ignacio paused, wanting full effect. "Lauren looked very beautiful the morning she gave me the message. Her hair was shiny and curly, and her eyes sparkled like she was in love. She wore red sandals, she is more slender than ever, and her red shorts were so short," Ignacio paused, wiping his brow, "it was almost too much for this old man. She looked at me so sweetly and then told me to tell you..." Ignacio took a deep breath, "to kiss her ass."

Americo laughed uproariously. "I can just imagine she did say that." He continued to guffaw with tears running down his face. Wondering which way the words had been spun and remembering passionate nights of sex with Lauren, Americo didn't care if the words had been converted and inverted. "I'll bet that wild, crazy Witch would like that." He chuckled scratching his head and walked into the bedroom he hadn't slept in since his arrival.

☪

The voice of process is slow. Change can occur quickly, like a flash of light that illuminates something instantly. Process takes time. Process can be horizontal or vertical, but ultimately it is circular. Process follows its own path, each step is essential and the words are chosen very carefully. Process moves with intent, not intention. There is no goal, for it merely follows its natural inclination, choosing its own path and its own vocabulary, with no end in sight. Magic resides in process. All of life is in process, if it is not, it is dead. Every living thing grows toward the light, but there is always a moment when a longing sets in to the soul of process. It is a longing to return to the dark. The dark interior of the mother calls. She needs food.

Eve was dying. Her dry, cracked bark ached from years of birthing new growth in the winter, pink blossoms in the spring, and luscious juicy red apples in the late summer. The one hundred year old apple tree sighed in anticipation, knowing her life force would follow Rita to the other side. She resigned herself to her fate, dreading that some time would pass before she could release her vitality to the Vortex and reenter the eternal spin. Eve loved her name, and she loved the girl who bestowed it on her on a happy summer day decades ago. Remembering Lauren swinging from her branches and climbing high to pick ripe apples, Eve welcomed sharing time with her friend. Eve struggled to push forth the final issue of her branches as Lauren gathered heavy tools and walked towards her. Eve was the witness. Rustling her leaves in the soft breezes, she absorbed the stories of the lives of the Auldney-Rios clan and held them safe in the contours of her graceful, sensually curved body.

The garden spiraled as Lauren walked across the ground toward her beloved tree. The red soil crunched under her footsteps as the first light of day again awakened life on El Rancho de las Estrellas. Lauren stood under Eve's canopy, holding her hands on the rough bark, channeling love into the grandmother apple tree. The pulse had slowed, the vital energy had diminished and they both knew life was changing. "You know everything, don't you, Eve?" Lauren asked as she pressed her lips to the bark to feel her temperature. Eve quivered, causing the brightly colored ribbons Lauren hung on her limbs to writhe like serpents reaching for the ground. Chimes on her branches rang like bells, welcoming

Lauren to her bosom.

"It's been almost a year." Lauren shared memories with her friend. "I returned home because I wanted to be here when you take your last breath, and I want to eat the last apple to fall from your branches so you will live on as a part of me." Lauren fantasized, hoping that one day before Eve died, Americo would push her in the swing so she could fly with the ravens once again. "Eve, I'm going to plant a new apple tree close by so you can teach her your stories. My Grandma teaches me everything and I want you to do the same for your granddaughter."

Offering tobacco to Mother Earth, Lauren petitioned permission to open her body. She offered the gift of a tree for Earth to love and nurture. The Earth exhaled, gave permission and prepared herself for short term but essential pain. Swinging a pick over her head, Lauren broke through the rocky soil, digging a hole for the new tree.

Rita, watching Lauren from her porch, invoked the Vortex with a twirl of her hand. Pleased with Lauren's progress, Rita reviewed the efforts made over the summer. She sipped her morning coffee alone, wondering if Lauren realized the many paths to nowhere she spent years creating, had been connected to the somewhere of her heart.

The brick path connected with the red flagstone path. A red cinder block path led the others around a bend. Random flat rocks, interspersed with purple flowers, called footsteps to follow behind a tree. Ripple rock, woven between the manzanita forest met the pea gravel path at the well. "Well, well," Rita clucked. "I wonder if she knows that the well is on the former property line separating the Rios land from the Auldney land. Americo, my dear blind grandson," Rita scolded him from afar, asking repeated questions while shaking her finger. "Lauren has met you half way. Tell me, what are you doing besides indulging in your loss? Have you implored don Esteban to guide you back to the beginning? Do you realize now that you can never tame Lauren, in spite of your good intentions? Do you realize yet that she has been nurturing your wild soul and that you need her far more than she needs you? Do you realize that she has, what you do not?"

On her knees Lauren gripped a tiny trowel and with every scoop removed more of the loosened soil from the hole. Clawing with her hands, she moved more. Holding each handful as a gift from the Goddess, Lauren offered gratitude before releasing the soil to be scattered to higher ground.

With a pointed tipped shovel piercing the ground, Lauren

pounded it with her foot, for she had entered into combat with a large determined rock. She forced the tip of the shovel, loosened the rock and felt a rush of power as the rock tumbled from its lodging. The rock teetered and tottered before falling off the shovel. As she watched the rock tumble, Lauren had a funny, fleeting thought. Experimenting, with her vivid imagination running wild, she picked up a pitchfork and stirred the loosened soil in the hole. Pretending the fork was a shovel, she giggled out loud as the powdery fine rock flour soil slipped through the tines of the fork. "Isn't that just like life?" She stopped and observed. "Some times you try to move a boulder with a teaspoon, knowing at the beginning that you will fail. You try to eat raw sugar with a fork and it slips right through the tines. It's sort of like my life," Lauren thought with amusement. "I have the right tools and I know how to use them, but sometimes the two just don't line up." Looking at the array of tools lying on the red ground, she smiled and drew the conclusion. "It's one thing to have the tools, but to use the appropriate tools for the right job is something else. Imagine, trying to eat vichyssoise soup with a fork, or cut a bone with a demitasse spoon. It just wouldn't work."

Moving with the euphoria that flowed through her body, Lauren spun high in the blue morning sky, feeling ecstatic from her newly discovered insight. So she spun and while she spun she talked to the fairies, saw the magic, and heard the Vortex calling.

Rita called to Lauren from the gate. The wild spirit twirling with her wavy hair flying, her arms extended and her eyes closed in joyous foolishness, didn't mind the interruption. Rita called to her, but not before noticing that Lauren was spinning the opposite direction. Looking into Lauren's hazy eyes, Rita saw serene, glorious madness in her soul.

Dizzy from the spinning, Lauren saw her Grandmother in a special light. She saw a woman of two worlds with her feet securely planted on the ground, held fast by roots sunk deep into her place. Lauren heard her Grandmother transmitting wisdom, without saying a word. "Home is the place where you never lose your way while wandering." Rita did not utter a word as she pushed her roots further into the underworld.

"No wonder Grandma never loses her way, her roots are so deep that she could survive a flood, hurricane, or blizzard. It's true," she reasoned while opening her eyes, "you never have to worry if your roots are securely attached within the Earth." Turning a little to the left to balance, Lauren saw something else. She saw Rita receiving from afar. Lauren saw the light, rich with images and spirit, hovering around her Grandmother. Like a conduit, Rita received the bigger picture, moving it into her heart space. With a whirling wind in her center, Rita wove that from above with that from below, into the whole story.

"And they tried to make me believe I was crazy," Lauren said, feeling pissed off. "They wanted me to quit spinning and to see things from one point of view. Don't they know the woman who receives, moves, and combines magic consciously while she spins in place, has really caught the wave? I just had to get back to the place where my roots sink deep within the Earth."

Scrutinizing Lauren, as Lauren scrutinized her, Rita became aware that in her maturity, Lauren now fully embodied the dual nature of a woman. "The outer Lauren, the Lauren we think we see, is matchless in her ability to move in the world we know," Rita said with pride.

Seeing out of the corner of her eye, Rita caught a glimpse of a raging, fearful man hovering around Lauren. "But, my dear, your inner being, that which we do not always see, is wild, knowing and fierce and must rise to the surface in order for you to vanquish the predator who believes you need him. Thank the Goddess that you never relinquished that part of yourself as you grew yourself to wholeness by making poor choices." She also saw what was there and what wasn't there. "Sweetness and niceness will not be the tools you need to accomplish this task."

Lauren walked towards Rita with long certain strides. Her teeth were bared, she had an unwavering look in her eyes, and prepared for anything, she held a shovel in her hand. "I just figured out that life is about using the right tools at the right time. Grandma, do you think I've got the right tools to make a happy life by myself?"

"Of course you have the right tools. After all, I'm the one who trained you."

"Grandma, you look about a million years old." Lauren grinned with their secret well intact. Putting her hands on her hips, she stared into Rita's eyes. "Are you feeling upish or downish today?"

Rita smiled knowingly. "A little in betweenish, Lauren. Somewhere in the middle."

☾★

Rita always told her heirs that the world is undivided, yet divided. Successfully Lauren had completed her task for the tamed, domesticated part of her soul. "The home is a part of culture," Rita explained carefully to Lauren one day about twenty-eight years ago. "The home is tame, but hopefully not too tame," she whispered so the boys couldn't hear.

The garden, the place where we dig in the soil with our fingers, looking for the ageless, every age, all age woman, is the transitional zone where the tame meets the wild. In the garden there is a magical mixture of both. "In the garden," Rita indicated with her hand full of compost, "you learn to let go, keep, nurture, and destroy." Rita squished some mud in her hand. "Don't you just love the feeling of gooey, wet mud in your fingers?"

In the garden, one makes choices. We decide what to plant, what to move and often spend time pondering what is a weed and what is a flower. If we like it we keep it and if we don't, it lives on in the compost pile. "You have some choices to make," Rita told her pointing to the basket in the middle of the spiral.

Lauren leaned on her shovel, listening earnestly as she pondered the questions whirling around in her mind. She adjusted her bandana, raised her sunglasses and listened as Rita, who seemed younger now that she was older, made suggestions. Lauren, who knew she had been older when she was younger, stretched and yawned. Seeing directly and knowing some of the answers, Lauren made a decision. "I'm going to spin it, Grandma," she announced, sounding like she knew what she was doing. "I spun counter clockwise this morning and although it made me a little dizzy because I couldn't find my focal points, it felt great."

"As you reverse the spiral, I want you to turn the beds. We need to see what has been beneath the surface," Rita added mysteriously, knowing that the wild woman spends a lot of time underneath in the dark.

Putting on her black sunglasses, Lauren took a sip of water, waved at Sunnie and dug passionately with her small tools, hands, and soul.

☪

Dolls carry soul and Lauren had always trusted her dolls with her soul secrets. Dolls also carry signs of the times, they are historical documents and this part of Lauren's history needed to be recorded with an offering from the Earth. Considering the ball of sticky red mud in her hand, Lauren couldn't resist. "I think I'm going to need some help with this part of my task, maybe even a guide." Lauren squatted down to form her companion. Digging a little deeper for some dry soil to mix with the wet, her fingernails lost their polish. "Oops, there goes another layer."

Slowly the doll came to life. It was a fat, bodacious, little doll with arms spread wide and strong, stocky legs. Lauren wanted to know the doll a little better, so she asked the doll about her personality. Enthusiastically the doll wiggled her toes, hinting at serpent power. Sorting through seeds, she made a mosaic on the body. "Now you look like serpent woman. Take me with you to the underbelly," Lauren told her as she prepared herself to follow. Not quite finished, Lauren decided she needed a crown.

First, Lauren had to pee. Having always been a nature girl, Lauren quickly ran behind a tree and hoped she wasn't again revealing her bare butt to an unknown spy. "This feels so good," she said squatting, watching a blue jay watching her. "Why not give a little bit back?"

Lauren gently cut some quills from a pear cactus. Like a halo, the quills made a half circle on the head of the doll, but that wasn't enough. The doll needed to see. Running to the house, Lauren decided which of her stones would make eyes to see in the dark. "Opals," she decided quickly opening the protective papers, "brilliant, beautiful, glowing opals."

The eyes glowed flashing brilliant sparks of color back at Lauren. Suddenly the eyes changed, they lost their many colors, became dark, evil, and menacing. Lauren stood back, feeling threatened. The eyes looked familiar; Lauren felt like she was choking and she gasped. "I told you not to fuck with me," she said intimidating the person behind the eyes. "Don't say I didn't warn you. I'm a good Witch, and white magic always wins." She paused thinking of one more tool. "I'm not only a good Witch, I'm a menopausal Witch. That makes me a crone and you know what they say about us. So there."

Thinking the doll needed to see from another direction, Lauren had another idea. Looking in all directions, Lauren found what she needed. She snipped several needles from a pine tree, sliced a gash between the doll's legs and gave her another head of hair. Lauren spotted an old packet of seed. "Let's give you some teeth." Lauren emptied yellow corn seeds on the ground. The doll got two sets. Now the doll could really chew the dark, moist underbelly where all possibility resides.

Lauren followed the doll, and slowly the garden started to spin. The soil turned upside down. Now, with the right side up, the doll was not the only one who could see. Lauren took a little pinch of red soil and put it on her tongue, thinking red dirt is pretty tasty stuff. Soil is the result of process. It requires millennia to create one inch of topsoil. The break down of rock, the decomposition of animals and plants, sunlight, and water, all contribute to the creation of this magical byproduct of process. Process follows its own path with intent; however that does not mean it is without order. In the soil, with her guide, Lauren saw process and order. She saw the nematodes, the insects, the dead buried bodies, and she also saw the light that is emitted by internal process. She also heard the high pitch frequency, communicating between units of information that speak in signs and patterns. There were crystalline structures within the soil, willing to emit and receive the information required to move process forth. Lauren saw the light, as well as the dark. Growling and hissing like a wild creature, Lauren vowed, "Look out world, because you haven't seen anything yet." Wondering who would dare try to tame her, she told them, flickering her tongue, as she returned the above to the below. "Don't even try to stop me, because I've felt it. I've changed directions and there's no going back."

Relieved of her constraints, the spiral in the garden spun with joy. It spun with renewed relish, the other direction. In awe, the Vortex liked what she saw, thought it was a very good idea and spun on. She spun into autumn, looking at another point of view, enjoying a new perspective.

Lauren took a nap.

Rejected again, before light broke over the horizon, Americo started to walk. He did not walk alone as he crossed the forbidding land, but he was not aware of his companion. Americo was markedly lean, his cheeks were gaunt, his olive complexion had lost its luster, and the swagger to his walk no longer identified him. With his hands clasped loosely behind his back, his head was bent in dejection, and his once spirited eyes were averted to the ground. Americo did not want to see what was in front of him.

A chance encounter with his Nagual the night before had dissatisfied him. Heeding Rita's instructions to ask don Esteban to take him back to the beginning, Americo had solicited don Esteban's assistance. "The shine I recognized in your eyes the day I met you is gone, Americo," don Esteban said to him with no pity. "You know the shine I speak of, my friend. Sadly, because of your loss, you are no longer in touch with your intent." Before leaving Americo alone on the street in Guaymas, don Esteban bid him, "Walk, Americo, maybe then, if you are lucky, your assemblage point will move and you will rediscover the tool you cannot afford to live without."

He no longer moved with the grace of a cat, his footsteps were heavy, and Americo stopped. "When did I lose it?" he asked, lighting a cigarette. The shine in his eyes had dwindled slowly, deceiving Americo that he still mastered the most important tool to stalk power. Self-pity had set in, sobriety had faded into harshness, his edge was gone and in his self-pity, he had become self-important. Americo was no longer ruthless.

Americo hitched a ride. As he started to walk again, behind him he heard the familiar rumbling of a beat up pickup truck. A friend from Guaymas stopped, told Americo he was going fishing and convinced him a morning on the sea would revive his spirits.

In the small boat rocking rhythmically on the waves in a cove near San Carlos, Americo felt his energy start to shift. Out of the corner of his eye, he caught a shadow. The shadow persisted, it did not flee, and Americo knew he was being stalked. Americo did not catch any fish that morning, but swaying in the belly of Mother Ocean he did catch a promise of hope. "Follow me, Dad," TJ Rios beckoned as they docked the boat in the slip. Americo felt a calling to the lava formed hillside overlooking the bay. "Walk with me and I'll take you back to the beginning of our story."

"I'm going to walk back," Americo told his amigo who had been looking forward to an afternoon in the local Cantina. "I'll catch up with you later."

For two hours Americo climbed over the swollen, frozen lava flow. He followed an unknown bidding, he was driven and compelled to reach his goal. He scratched and blistered his hands reaching for handholds on the sharp, porous ledges as he followed a yearning to reach a cave on the distant mound. He bled, wiped his hands on his pants and as he sweat, he climbed.

Defying harsh circumstances, small, determined cactus grew from fissures in the gray-black lava. Unknown to Americo, when the molten lava flowed red and hot over the land, it had carried an old story from the serpent oracle sleeping deep within Earth. The once old story was reborn as TJ Rios prepared to guide his father back to the beginning.

Reaching his goal, Americo leaned against the wall of the cave, stretched his legs and rested. Protected in the womb of the story, he drank water that he carried in his backpack. He decided not to smoke and closed his eyes and drifted into unconsciousness.

Squatting next to Americo, TJ stroked his father's brow. He looked deeply into the man he would have grown to resemble and saw the void. TJ, with the love of a son, touched the lines of concern between Americo's brows and feeling his father respond, touched his forehead, his heart, and navel, opening the centers of reception. Americo's body shuddered, he felt a breeze, then felt it cease. He saw a cloud and then saw it dissolve. He felt a warm touch, and then he tumbled backwards into no time.

"Dad, now you can start to remember."

☪

Before the beginning there was the void. Nothing.

In the beginning there was pure potential. Potential is merely possibility held captive until disturbed by the implosion of desire. Desire moves energy, causes change, drives forth evolution, and creates life. Instantly and simultaneously urge was born, eros was born, love was born and then, in an expression of passion, the stars were born.

The stars, born of love and desire, gave freely. Burning from the love within them, they sent forth more love. Eternal love, constant love, forgiving love, selfish love, and passionate love rode on strings of light, writhing and swaying into the cosmos.

Lauren stretched, arched her body, and then returned to sleep.

Americo rolled over, dreaming of pushing Lauren in a swing.

For eons the long strings of light floated freely in the cosmos, randomly existing. They acquired desire, then searched for coherence and meaning in their existence. They were charged by the passion of their origin and desired their likeness.

Lauren dreamed of the first night she made love.

Americo felt desire for Lauren.

They formed pairs. They danced. And as they danced to sounds of serpentine movements, they became coherent, alike, and bonded in attraction.

Lauren moved her feet, dreaming of dancing on the beach.

Americo reached for someone, wanting to hold them.

The attraction grew, and they could no longer dance freely. The strings felt the pain of tension and bondage. They were entwined. Unable to writhe and wriggle, they withdrew from the dance, coiling into dense, compressed dots.

Lauren huddled in the fetal position, feeling restrained.

Americo wrapped his arms around himself, wanting to be close to someone.

Wings of light escaped capture, and the dots flew through space, summoned by destiny.

There was a heavenly cloud-covered orb circling a star. The orb had a magnetic core. The dots felt the attraction. They submitted. They landed. The landing was forceful. The landing caused a small recession in the dot. Inside the dot, a fissure occurred. It was invisible. The fissure was a void.

Lauren tossed and turned, bumping her head on the brass headboard.

Americo jerked, bumping his arm on the wall of the cave.

The dot rested from flight.

Lauren sighed.

Americo smiled.

Desire filled the fracture. Desire wiggles and writhes. Desire shines. Desire receives. Desire looks like a crystal. Desire pushed forth.

Lauren wiggled in her sleep, knocking the red rock geode Rita had given her from the nightstand.

Americo raised his arms over his head and stretched.

There was an urge. The message was received. The internal pressure rose. The fissure widened. The dot cracked open. The entwined strings started to uncoil.

Lauren yawned, almost awakening to the light.

Americo blinked, the sun in his eyes.

Tasting freedom, the strings continued to uncoil. They yearned for the beginning. They started to divide.

Lauren stood, twisted and turned, stretching from her nap.

Americo tossed and turned, afraid to be alone.

The serpentine strings separated slowly, cautiously, and finally.

Lauren cried without warning, not knowing why.

Americo screamed, the haunted sounds echoing from distant hills.

The writhing strings followed each other, alone and lonely, circling the orb, looking for each other, not knowing the other followed.

Lauren wept looking out the window, her heart broken from loneliness.

Americo sat up and looked behind him as tears started to flow.

The first string stopped. Looking the other direction, the other string writhed to its side. They made an agreement. They changed while remaining the same. They each duplicated, connecting the new other with rungs. The rungs split, the strings bonded, creating a third. They did it again, and again, and again.

Eternal soul mates were born.

Lauren felt the presence of her son, extended her hand and smiled.

Americo felt the touch of his son as he opened his eyes and saw.

With her hands shaking, Lauren picked up the geode. A perfectly formed hexagonal crystal had fallen from the cluster of crystals in the center.

Americo's heart opened as he turned to his son and thanked him.

Holding the crystal, Lauren extended her hand to Rita. With tears in her eyes, Rita clasped Lauren's fingers around the crystal. "You found it again, Lauren. You brought the desire crystal from your star so very long ago."

With love pouring freely from Americo's heart, he said to his son, "Son, I see you again. I lost you so very long ago."

"Someday," TJ imprinted his words on his father's soul, "you will see my mother again as well."

Lauren heard words from a familiar voice. "Someday he will see you for all that you have been, all that you are, and all that you will become."

☪

Beyond the garden is the desert. Some call it God's country because at times he makes himself known there. Every woman knows that a man can't take the harsh nature of the desert for long, just like they know a man would perish if they gave birth to a baby. They know that's why God appears in the desert, only occasionally. The Goddess and women spend a lot more time in the desert, because they can take the heat. Rita knew, as all mystics know, that there is something else about the desert, the wilderness, and the mountaintop that is often felt, but not often enough recognized. There is silence. And in the silence of the desert, the mountaintop, and the wild, one goes feral, natural, crazy, and back to their original wild, untouched self. In the wild, natural silence of potential, the real is born again.

Having summoned Americo home, Rita sent Lauren on a quest in the desert.

Flippantly offering her brother a chance to have mid-life crises, not knowing he had been considering the same, Lauren tossed him the keys to her sports car, borrowed his SUV, and started to pack.

Rita admonished her for packing her tent, camp stove, solar shower, design book, drawing pencils, and lipstick. "Leave all of this behind, Lauren." Rita set the record straight. "In the wild there are no choices. In the wild, one must simply be."

"I know that, Grandma, I just thought I'd do a little work until I really get into the experience."

Rita looked at her grimly, knowing that more important work already awaited her. Watching Lauren unpack the car Rita advised Lauren to take candles, wire, string, a blanket, matches, and good sturdy shoes. "By the way," she told her sternly, "you should take plenty of water, because that's all you will have." Lauren pointed to the red, felt Andean hat she wore, wondering if that too would be forbidden. "Yes dear, you may also take a hat."

Holding her parasol for shade, Rita gave Lauren final instructions as she watched Lauren load gallon sized jugs of water in the back of the car. Lauren pled, remembering that when she lived out of a backpack she at least had some essentials. "Not even a brush, washcloth, or toothbrush?"

"No," Rita said taking them out of her hand. Tapping her cane on a large flat rock Rita finished her list, clicking it off by memory on her fingers, speaking in staccato rhythm. "If it's scattered, gather it. If it's buried, unearth it. If it's broken, repair it. If it's dirty, clean it. If it's alive, kill it."

Lauren tilted her head, considered the list, knew she could do anything, and answered, "No problem, Grandma, I can do that."

Rita continued, ignoring Lauren's overconfidence. "After you finish, light a candle. After you light the candle, put it aside. After three days, blow out the candle. Sit by yourself in silence, until you no longer hear the silence." Lovingly, Rita offered her a small picnic basket for the road. "Then you should come home, because your task will be complete."

☪

Lauren followed the nests; markers on the trail left behind as transient birds stopped, birthed and nurtured their young, and flew unto their destiny. The sign presented itself as Lauren readied a secluded area near where she, Trey, Americo, and Sunnie had camped as teenagers. It was an out of sight corner of the forest and the integrity of the haven was undisrupted, leaving it pristine and intact.

A deer followed Lauren, stopping to watch with large doe-eyes as Lauren beckoned protection. The doe stepped quietly closer as Lauren petitioned the directions, the elements, and the spirits for help completing her task. Pine needle filtered light cast lacy patterns over her skin as Lauren cast her circle around a disk that captured the light, the dark, the up, the down, and the around. A glow of power surrounded the disc; silver, soft, pulsing power. The silver disc absorbed and emitted the vibrations of the cosmos, purifying and channeling them in Lauren's behalf. With its eyes glowing, an owl shaped black rock guarded the disk, hooting, "You feel no fear."

Years of fallen leaves had created a soft forest floor, the new covering the old as the old disintegrated into the new. Sniffing the musty, rich odor of decomposition, Lauren shivered as she felt the spirit of the forest in the desert flow into her body. As one arrangement of dna decomposes, it is recomposing. The dna remains. The mother tree puts forth her issue, providing food for herself as she lives. When she dies, she surrenders to becoming food for the next generation. It is a self-contained system of life, nurture, consumption, and death. It is process. It is compost. Composting ingredients have a particular fragrance. If tended properly, it is sweet. Nature knows how to compost properly. Only humans fail to tend this and other cauldrons of transformation tenderly.

As the afternoon shadows grew longer, small flowers growing in red rock outcroppings opened their petals, having selfishly protected the soft, moist centers from the beating midday rays. Having lived under the loving protection of her Grandmother, Lauren now felt alone. Lauren recalled the words of her teacher. "Feliciana, if you could only see me now. I'm alone, but not lonely. I'm alone, but no longer in exile. I'm walking, but I'm no longer wandering."

Lauren's soul had been entrained to the desert as she grew to young womanhood within the Vortex of Sedona. She had not been

called to the desert, for she was a part of it. The mystery of the
desert had been imprinted on Lauren's appearance, her finely
formed bones reflecting the pared down minimalism of the desert.
The mystery of the desert was evident in her humor, offering just
enough levity to lighten the moment, without the lush overgrowth
of sentimentality. The brilliance of her eyes spoke of the jewel like
flowers spaced far enough apart, allowing just enough to survive.
Most life survives in the desert by remaining underground and
Lauren had survived by protecting her authenticity deep within.
Her authenticity stirred, the process had begun, and Lauren
tripped over the first bone barely hidden under the blanket of
leaves.

Lauren was always stepping ahead of herself. "Grandma, you
sly old Witch," Lauren hissed, having ripped a hole in the knee of
her jeans and badly cut her hand. "The bones. That's what this is
all about, a little journey to see my old girl buddy, Erishkegal.
What do you want me to do, hang my old, bloody skeleton on a
cross?"

Flesh cracks and when it does you often find the best parts.
The same goes for a mind.

Red rich blood ran profusely and there was a crazed, wild
longing in her eyes. Spinning, a raven fell to her feet, dead.
Lauren cawed. The raven cawed; then flew away. A snake coiled.
She uncoiled it. She couldn't stop it; she wanted more. Lauren
sucked the blood, urging it forth. Ripping off her t-shirt, she
howled loud and long. She saw patterns, circles, squares, trian-
gles, hearts, and spirals. She jumped through each one and decided the spiral fit the best. "Let me spin right in, baby," she giggled.

A root wrapped around a rock caught her eye. "Good catch, I'll
trade you one of mine for one of yours."

A blood drop fell on the Earth. "Cool, you feed me, so I'll feed
you."

The moon fell as the sun rose with a roar. It was a cloud sun.
You always see what you expect to see and seldom expect what you
do see. Then she heard a star fall. "I'll probably see you in about
3000 more lifetimes." She felt a rush of power, and it sounded like
wings. There was nothing in sight.

Seeing beyond the stars, past the void, past potential, she
saw the Stickman. "Get your ass out of bed and quit making a
plan," she yelled to him. "Go help Stickwoman with her work.
She's making bubble babies, and she needs you to hold them
together before they crack apart." She checked the red light. "You
better hurry, Stickman, they're leaving you." Then she changed

her mind. "Oh hell, Stickman, you stay put and study, analyze, count, measure, and arrange something." She thought of something else. "Stickwoman needs to wander, because it's very much like spinning. Look out, because she's putting on her red shoes." Lauren had some advice for her friend. "Follow the dots, girlfriend, unless they go in a straight line. A spiral path is the best path."

Minding her manners, Stickwoman sent a lovely dinner to thank Lauren for her advice. A big potato landed at her feet. "But Grandma said I have to fast," Lauren pouted. The big potato made a dent when it landed on its noggin, and suddenly, Lauren knew she better act fast. Tossing the potato back in the sky, she cried, "Hey, Asteroid, go blow up another planet, I've still got work to do and I don't have time for a dinner date."

Looking out over the horizon, Lauren got a new perspective. The trees in the distance seemed to grow from the top of the one in front of them. Looking down and looking up, she saw them growing out of the ground toward the sky. "Which is right? Which is wrong? Who in the hell knows, because it's all a matter of where you're standing."

"Live wild or die," she cried to the wumpus lurking behind a fallen log.

Lauren heard a bang, a big one. The whirling galactic pinwheel of possibilities caught her eye. Rushing away from the bang like a bunny from a coyote, the pinwheel called the Milky Way caught sight of Lauren. Stopping to chat, Lauren reminded her of a visit they had a while back. "Hmmm, I've seen you before, in fact, I've stood in your center rolling my dice. Wonder what my life would have been like if I had spun three degrees to the right instead of the left."

Lying on her back, Lauren had to make a big decision. "Should I spiral up or spiral down?" With the fiber of her being, she felt the being of fiber, in the compost under her feet.

Lauren crossed the line in Nogales and wondered why she kept thinking about cracked versus crumbled cookies.

She heard the footsteps of an old friend with legs of gold. Standing over Lauren was her friend Haefustus, god of goldsmiths, restoration, love, magic, the cracked, the broken, and the split. Lauren and Heafustus had spent a lot of time together over the years, and she really loved the cool gold stuff he made to repair her body and soul. "Hey, Brother, neither one of us had parents who were worth a damn, did we? Aren't we lucky! Now we know how to fix cracked cookies for ourselves and others too."

Before bidding her adieu, her soul brother handed Lauren a gift. The gift was a small silver vessel filled with powder of gold.

"Rub this on your body when you go before the Judge," Lauren heard him say. "Shine, Baby, shine, whether they like you or not, never forget to shine." Lauren liked the gift, a lot!

With perfect vision, she looked at the stars. She saw them spiraling from deep within as they sprinkled light meant only for her. Wanting company, Lauren called, "Come on girls, let's spin."

The bats whooshed by in the night. She saw their eyes and ducked, hoping they weren't looking for her. She needed to move. Holding her arms above her head, she swayed her body in rhythm with the pulsing hum of process.

Lauren climbed down, brachiating from root branch to root branch, following exposed roots to the end of the story. Spotting Erishkegal, Lauren jumped right in. "Hey, Girlfriend, having a good hair day?"

She rubbed the blood from her cut hand on her face, her arms and her breasts. A snake writhed by wiggling its tail. Lauren flickered her pointed tongue and hissed. She hissed again. A visceral woman appeared. Lauren made love to her beauty. Blood covered her hands as she hurriedly gathered wood for a fire. "Water, I need water," Lauren yelled frantically, searching for the vessel. Using the fluid to dissolve the soil, she made fierce black circles around her eyes with ash from a long ago fire. Lauren was the mask.

She filled a bag with her personal history to take to the creek later.

"A century plant in bloom, cool." Lauren followed a beetle around a spiral path to the top, yelling to the world, "Spin it."

Looking out over the horizon she saw two breast-like peaks, with a mons veneris nub in the center. "Hmmm, so that was my first sight in this world. I thought it was a really cool looking black haired man."

The box. Lauren spotted the box. It was well hidden under an ant pile full of big, red, desert ants. She jumped up and down, and squealed. "Ohhh, Pandora, let's play together. I always thought the stuff you had in your box was the best stuff!"

Lauren turned herself inside out, and looked at the world from the outside in. "Wow," she said, checking out her womb, cervix, and birth canal. "I have paintings of bison, spirals, wavy lines, priestesses, and hands right here. Why did I bother going to the caves in Lascaux?"

Standing on a composted leaf, Lauren saw Bell Rock. "Not a bad name and I do love bells, but Lady, you need to lift your skirt and show us your secret."

Lauren lit a candle, and the light from below met the dark from above. "Interesting world upside down, now will somebody send some starlight?"

Lauren polished a red rock, turning it into a faceted diamond. Looking at herself in the diamond, she saw her own many facets.

The mist sent smoke to Stickwoman. Lauren blew chains of perfect smoke rings at the moon. "It's so wonderful to be an Aquarian," she blew words to planet Uranus. "Air can enflame and extinguish. Not only that, air can carry water, Earth and starshine. I've got it all," she cried with joy.

There was a border, and she jumped it.

"I want to feel whole again," Lauren cried becoming afraid and lonely. "I still feel like half of me is missing."

Lauren took a sun shower, running to catch the rays before somebody turned off the faucet.

"My heart still needs a little protecting," Lauren confessed to the sacred spirit of the deer. Darkness was falling, falling, falling. Lauren built a small fire for protection. Wrapped in her red, patterned Pendleton blanket, curled up by the fire with her head on the ground, she heard a story. From a very old book, that not many people take time to read, the six billion year old storyteller picked a chapter to tell Lauren by the light of the fire. Bright strings of filament surrounded Lauren as she first dreamed of dots with wings floating from the stars. A dot landed on the skin of the Earth, and the story began.

The storyteller began to whisper, speaking slowly and rhythmically, so that Lauren would not forget the most important words. In the story, as a fire roared through the forest, there was a young woman who saved her son and mate from perishing in the desert. The woman called on power deep within, to provide and care for those who could not care for themselves. The fire that roared through the forest was powerless compared to the fire that burned inside of the woman. Lauren sweat. She felt her bones and found the cave. She found the opening to herself. Deep in the night she heard the voices of the light, the dark, the water, the air, and the fire, all telling Earth stories in pictures.

The deer continued to watch, cleverly blending into the surroundings. Gently Lauren retrieved the porous rib bone, dusting the particles of composted leaves from cracks caused by years of dehydration. Wondering if a hunter had wounded the deer, leaving it to die alone and afraid, Lauren held the rib-bone protectively to her heart, knowing that at one time the rib had protected the heart of the deer.

Becoming in touch with the ongoing process, she attuned to the deer. Lauren felt a very young gentle girl within her emerge. Two days passed, and Lauren remained in a state of gentle understanding. She was safe. She was safe, covered in her own blood, guarded by the clan of ravens perpetually flying overhead, the coyote that scurried by looking for leavings, and the owl that lulled her with soft hooting in the night. She never saw the dapple coated deer watching as she gathered the rest of the bones. For the first time she could remember, Lauren felt truly needed. The dead deer and Lauren needed each other as guides back to the bones, the eternal, and the story. "That's what we both have to do, Darling," she whispered sending her understanding to Americo. "We need to get back to the bones. We need to remember the story."

She heard Americo answer, "I need you, Lauren. I lose my fire without you."

Lauren shed tears as she accepted their journey. "You have to find it within yourself, Americo. You have to meet me halfway, because I can no longer reflect back to you what you want to see."

Discovering the pelvis, she wondered if the deer had been carrying a fawn when it fell to the ground, surrendering to the inevitable. A tremble from deep within shook Lauren's body as she identified with the mother deer. Unexpected tears meandered down her cheeks from a well that she had never divined. Nature often marks experience with serpentine lines, like veins, crinkly gray hairs, and wrinkles. Looking at the little wrinkles on her belly that signed the fact of her pregnancy, she placed her hand protectively on the squiggling little lines. "God, I remember how alive I felt while fearing death, as I gave birth to a child that didn't live." Lauren spent her grief as she identified with the mother deer. "When and where does a life stop and another begin?"

Slowly, Lauren recapitulated her life. She took her time, without fear or remorse. Her only intent was to again see the traps, reverse them, thus reconstructing some integral experiences in her life. Some experiences and behaviors were forgotten, others were made new, and she discovered a power available only to those who face their lives, present, past, and future, without fear.

Holding a thighbone she marveled how deer move through the forest with efficient grace, never making a sound. The smooth rounded hipbone, gracefully contoured with the suggestion of a spiral, reminded her that the deer has no habits, but moves freely with caprice, need, and whim.

A shaman will wave a stick, but a Wild Wise Woman always rattles the bones.

All but one, the bones were accumulated. Tired, sweaty, and bloody, Lauren knew once again she had to figure it out for herself. "Anatomy never was my strong suit," Lauren laughed feebly, feeling giddy. By the afternoon, she had found an order. The skeleton began to speak by showing her the form of function. Lauren asked the rest of the ribcage, "Do you do things because you have a reason?" Holding the cage, with arms outstretched, she turned the present world upside down. "Or do you reason because you do things?"

Lauren figured it out. She also figured out the wavy, spirally tendrils on the tips of agave plants worked better than string or wire to hold the past together. Then she discovered she was still missing something. She had a headache from all the figuring, but she found the skull. She found the skull rather close to the cave, but not before stepping in a pile of juniper berry loaded coyote shit.

Like desert flowers that conserve their moisture by blooming only at night, Lauren could see in the dark. She had cat eyes. Childlike, Lauren held the skull to the light. Her dancing snake earrings shimmered, wiggled, and spun. Separated from those she loved, Lauren indulged in pure delight as she danced nude with rapture under the moon, with a candle lit skull to witness her joy. She had been initiated on her path to innocence. She submitted to the process, the process of life, death, and rebirth that continued without comment, criticism, or expectation. Desire was the only fuel and as the candle burned for three days, the silence diminished, and then there was nothing.

In the wild, in the silence, in the nothingness, there is nothing.

Carrying the skull on a walking stick she fashioned from a fallen branch, Lauren left the forest. She left wiser and wild in the way of the undomesticated. She expected nothing, feared nothing, and hoped for nothing, and once again she was just Lauren. She was just Lauren in love with life, not worrying about a thing.

☾★

There is an objective truth to everything. It is the truth of the wild. It usually doesn't last very long because something, or somebody, always wants to interpret, make aware, discuss, alter, or change it. Usually, the something is a human. The objective truth of the matter at hand is straw is very good material to use to build a house. Another good thing to remember is that Earth, especially sticky clay red Earth, mixed with water and a little love, makes a very good covering for the straw.

Livvy Auldney was hoping to become pregnant, filled with love and wanted to help her Aunt Lauren build a dollhouse.

Long ago, over thirty years ago, Lauren promised the Pequenacita's at Ollantaytambo in Peru, that someday she would build her dolls a house. Lauren had been very busy stepping in traps, traveling, making baubles, making bad choices, paying for them, wondering why me, wandering in red shoes and red-hot hotpants, keeping secrets, having fun, and telling Americo, maybe next year. Finally, she had the time to catch up on a few things. Her task was complete, and she didn't go on trial for her life until next week.

Livvy popped the question. "Have you ever been pregnant, Aunt Lauren?"

"It had to happen someday," Lauren sighed, resting her behind on a bale of straw. "You don't see me taking care of grandkids, do you, Livvy? I've never changed a poopy diaper in my life." Lauren danced some fancy word steps in her red cowgirl boots. Luckily, Trey stopped by to help Lauren stack some straw bales for the house. The house didn't have to be a particularly sturdy house; after all only little dolls would be living in it and only part of the time. Flimsy houses are good houses too.

The house rose out of the ground looking as if it had always been there. Ancient looking, the house appeared to have been crafted by nomads as they rested in the land of the red before wandering to a high alpine region to the north. Livvy and Lauren smeared the red, sticky soil, making their handprints and footprints in the mud before it dried. Then, they placed little rocks around the doorways, arranging them in patterns channeled from the stars. With sticks they made ladders to rest against the windows. "Hold that ladder steady, Livvy." Lauren climbed to take a peek in the interior of her mind. "Wow, the ladder is starting to spiral, now it feels familiar."

With another stick they carved spirals in the red clayish mud, one right side up and the other right side down. They just couldn't agree on which was which. On a whim Lauren scored the house into four parts. It looked like an upside down teacup, divided into four equal servings. "Livvy, let's go underground and see the house we didn't build." Lauren squealed, jumping across the abyss.

For a very important reason, Lauren ran to the house to find some little perfectly round marbles she thought looked like dots she saw somewhere, some time. Livvy stuck the marbles in the mud just as it was about to dry.

Then it was time to address the truth window. In most straw houses the builder makes a truth window. The window opening is there to reveal and tell the truth that the house is really a straw house. It serves to warn the person standing in front of the window that the house could fall down at any time. Or perhaps it could go up in flames. One never knows with an unstable commodity like straw. Lauren lit a match. Or maybe she had an idea. Lauren was good at the power of saying something and not saying it, at the same time. We must remember that Lauren is literal, speaks in metaphors, and talks in circles.

Back to the house Lauren went to fetch a doll and a pail of nails to prop up one of the ladders. Hurrying back, she carried a rag doll wrapped in swaddling cloth. The cloth was woven of many colors and was well worn. "I think this little boy looks so cute wearing the blanket his mommy made, don't you, Livvy?" Lauren didn't tell Livvy that she had woven the cloth when she took lessons in Peru. Also, she didn't tell Livvy that she had imbued the clay doll with the spirit of her son. Livvy didn't understand why Lauren cried when she placed the doll in the truth window, tenderly placing the panel of glass in front of the opening.

Lauren patted Livvy's tummy, telling her that her soon to be conceived daughter would be the fourth of four. "What do you mean, Aunty Lauren?"

"I mean this, Livvy. Your daughter will be an Aquarian, just like us and Grandma too."

Livvy sighed. Lauren was always forgetting things. "Grandma doesn't know when her birthday is, Lauren. That's why she celebrates it on New Years Day."

Lauren sighed. Some people didn't remember anything. "She doesn't know that I know," Lauren said taking Livvy back to the house to have some tea and chocolate cake. "But I know some things she doesn't know."

Two Auldney Witches, plus one in waiting, walked to the house to greet the fourth on the porch, waiting with a pot of hot tea, chocolate cake, love, and words of wisdom. "Lauren, my dear," Rita said in admiration. "I'm amazed at what you know."

☾★

Intentionally avoiding each other for several weeks, despite good intentions and hard work, attraction won. Americo and Lauren had an encounter. As if pulled by a magnet, Americo, lonely and with something on his mind, made a plan. Autumn had arrived seven weeks earlier on a cold wind from the west. Times were sad and trying. Lauren was preparing for trial and Americo wished he could come up with a plan to make it all go away. Although he still believed she tried to kill him, he, at this point, was willing to dance with her again.

It was early evening and after meeting with Lydia to plan strategy, Lauren was relaxed, comfy, feeling safe, and loved by her Grandma. Looking quietly luxurious following a long soaking bath, wearing soft, gauzy, red, cotton shorts and a white t-shirt, Lauren yawned. Her Grandmother's cat pawed at the window trying to attract the attention of swooping, darting blue jays in the yard. It was one of those evenings when a woman takes the time to condition her hair, shave her legs, do her nails, and play with cats.

Lauren has great toenails, and they were painted blood red, topped with a coat of gold glitter. As she started to paint little yellow snakes on the canvas of her toenails, she heard the knock on the door. Hoping the noise wouldn't wake Rita; she hurried to the door with a towel wrapped around her wet hair. Thinking it was probably Lydia, she opened the door without looking at the caller through the paned glass door. To her surprise, she saw Americo Rios with his hand resting on the threshold and a mischievous grin on his face.

He handed her a single mammoth sunflower. "Lauren, how are you, Baby?"

The towel covering her wet hair fell to the floor. "Americo, how dare you come here? You know I don't want to see you," Lauren fumed while handing the sunflower back to him. Americo smirked, continuing to stare unwaveringly at Lauren ranting very quietly. "Why do you keep hovering over me, watching everything I do? Aren't things bad enough for me right now without you stalking me like a coyote? I don't want you to wake Grandma up, so just leave."

"Lauren, I won't wake Rita up," he said pushing her aside, "but we have to talk. I probably shouldn't be here, but since you were charged last June I've had a few months to think about things. Damn it, Lauren, why did you want to kill me?"

Americo sat down casually by the old pine table in the kitchen and lit a cigarette. He looked at Lauren boldly, scrutinizing her face for a sign. Looking deep into her soft womanly eyes and openly admiring her tall, curvy body, he smiled remembering what a handful she had always been. Lauren stood with her hands on her hips and hate in her heart. "Americo, whatever you have to say to me, say it to Lydia. I don't want anymore of your interference, and I mean it. Without your interference my life would have been a lot different, in every way." Americo frustrated Lauren. "You really think you're cool, Rios, sitting there like a big macho man in your biker boots and vest. What are you doing, reliving your easy rider days or wishing you were back at Woodstock?"

He didn't say a word.

"You look stupid holding a flower." Rudely, she yanked his ponytail. "Why don't you cut that ridiculous ponytail off? It's so retro. What happened, did you get caught in a time warp? Now get that stupid smile off of your face and leave."

Americo grinned, loving the feel of her fingers on his hair. "Lauren, I just want to say a few things to you." Holding his hands up in mock defense, he told her laughing, "I'm not here to fight, wild child. I just want you to know that it's the State of Arizona prosecuting you for what you did, not me." Weighing the risk and benefit, Americo continued laughing. "I actually thought it was pretty funny being hit over the head with a Witch's broom, but why in the hell did you try to kill me?"

Lauren couldn't decide if she had found danger or opportunity and was undecided as to which she preferred, or if there was a difference. She remained silent, letting him lay his cards on the table.

Americo was about to drop the joker again; he just didn't know it. "I'll always love you, Lauren," Americo told her with tired sadness in his eyes. "I'm sorry we can't be together, but I think you understand why I had to let it go, my little runaway." Americo sat the flower down on the table.

The oven temperature continued to rise, readying itself for the cake Lauren mixed earlier. "Oh don't you start that, you asshole," Lauren hissed. "I don't run away anymore. I don't even have my passport."

"Lauren," Americo said as he stood to leave, "you're way out of line. I just wanted you to know how I feel."

"I hate you, Americo Rios," Lauren said venomously as she

clutched the gold spindle hanging around her neck. "You might think of yourself as being deliberate, pragmatic, and calculating, but I know you're just plain cold. I feel sorry for you. In the end, you'll be the fool, because I'm innocent and I'll probably end up saving your ass in court as well as my own."

Lauren was on a very good spin. Months of soul work were forgotten, and she felt the separation between them widening. "Why don't you just get on one of your spotted ass horses and ride away from the ranch you stole from Daddy? Or here's a better idea, Mr.Starwalker, why don't you start climbing one of those Hopi ladders you've collected and when you get to the top, just keep walking until you disappear? That way I wouldn't have to lay my eyes on you until the next life."

"If I remember correctly, Bruja, you're the fool, but I am glad to see you're still wearing the charm bracelet."

Ignoring his comment, Lauren addressed an issue Lydia planned to discuss with Americo the next day. "By the way, Americo, what happened to all the money I gave you to invest for me over the years? You just never bothered to account for it did you, my big hero? Maybe I'll sell the damn bracelet or melt it down for the gold, so there."

Lauren's new convertible sports car had irritated Americo from the day she drove it home. It wasn't practical, it was too sexy, and he knew it attracted attention. What he didn't know was that it wasn't any of his business. "You must have some money, or you couldn't have bought that sports car. Or did Wyatt buy it for you," Americo said sarcastically wiping his hands on his leathers, "like he put up your bail?"

The response is usually stronger than the stimulus. "Piss off, Rios." Something else was on her mind. She had an idea, but she hadn't been able to prove it. "Did you ever stop and think maybe your fiancée did it? Maybe she followed you to the Casino. You know how Alexandra hates me, and maybe she overheard you saying you still loved me. I'm surprised she didn't shoot me."

Americo hadn't thought of that. However, he did think Lauren looked rather charming with a chocolaty wooden spoon in her hand. "I can't speak for Alexandra. I wasn't with her after your show, but you know I've always suspected you stole my gun, and you've already admitted that you had it in the Casino."

"I want my money as soon as possible, or I'll sue you; I mean it."

Standing by the kitchen counter, Lauren gave the cake mix another quick spin, thinking it looked pretty tasty. Her good manners failed her as she stuck her finger in the gooey batter and stuck it in her mouth, giving it a good licking without offering a taste to Americo. The heavy red crockery bowl was one of her favorites and as she savored the rich chocolaty mix, she thought she felt a ball hitting her in the back of her head.

Americo was really pissed. "You don't have the balls to sue me, and I know it."

Lauren looked at the sudsy water in the sink, thinking she had a lot of bubble balls.

Sometimes the lighter the ball; the greater the impact. "Hmm, hmm." Lauren licked her lips as she thought of something else.

Americo was always licking his lips.

Lauren wasn't about to let him have the red crockery bowl, knowing he had always wanted it, but she did think he might need a dose of these little balls. "Take a dose of these balls, goofballs," she giggled tossing him a ball of ovary power.

It was time to reconsider, considering. "I'll have Ignacio bring a check over for your half of our investments. You sign the deeds, Baby," he told her with his temper boiling, "and you'll get the money."

"Well, Rios, you've got the money, but I've got the time, sweet time."

He just couldn't let it go. "By the way, you forgot my birthday this year. Let me remind you, I'm a Leo, and I don't like to be forgotten."

Lauren had been carrying his gift for thirty years. "Oh, I didn't forget your birthday. Maybe when I go to jail, I'll give it to you." She had absolutely no intention of going to jail, and she was very certain he no longer deserved the gift.

Puffy clouds in the Sistine Chapel sky were backlit by the setting sun, casting pink light over the red rock landscape. A small deer jumped over the fence into Rita's spiral garden while a raven circled overhead. A coyote watched the deer from behind the Casino as Americo stood on the rickety wood porch, hesitating before leaving on his motorcycle. Lauren stood in the doorway with her hands on her hips, wishing him dead. "Hey, Lauren," he said excitedly, forgetting the estrangement between them. "Do you see the deer? Come and look, you'll love it."

Not impressed by a raven, a coyote, or a deer on this particular evening, Lauren spun it another direction. "No way, Americo, El Jugador," she told him angrily twisting the garnet ring on her ring finger. "I'm not about to stand on the porch with you again, not ever."

Having had enough of Lauren's sharp tongue, Americo bit his tongue following one more comment. Although bitter and angry at her turning the tables, he wanted to remind her of something she told him long ago. Americo checked his temper, but Americo didn't check his pocket and didn't notice that he really had dropped a joker. "That's too bad, Princess, because you used to be pretty good at following the signs."

Lauren stood on the porch watching the reverse sunset after Americo rode away on his Indian motorcycle. She didn't feel guilty in the least that she wished the bike would fall over and break his leg. Gently watering the scarlet begonias in the large terra cotta clay pots, she noticed the deer still in the garden and heard the raven cawing overhead. Lauren spoke to nobody and everybody as she picked up her broom. "You have some nerve, Rios, talking to me about following the signs." Sweeping every inch of the already swept porch, she hoped to remove any trace of his presence. "If you had followed the signs thirty years ago," she thought sadly, "things would have been much different." Laughing as she picked up the card he dropped, she tucked it in her pocket. "Lucky me. Just like a cat, the Fool always lands on her feet." The card had landed face up.

When Lauren curled up in bed trying to go to sleep, she talked to her dolls. Every night she told them her secrets, while others are praying their secrets are never told.

*"Dolls, are you tired of the fairy tale yet?" she asked the collection on her dresser. "This story just gets more complicated all of the time, doesn't it? The Princess and the Poker Player, what a pair we are. Do you remember the first night I told you about him? The story didn't exactly end up like I thought it would, did it?"*

☾★

# The Knots, The Ravels, The Frays, and The Mends

*"There is a crack in everything, that's how the light gets in."*
Leonard Cohen

*"Blessed are the cracked...for they shall let in the light."*
Author *Unknown*

Shadows licked their lips, savoring little juicy drops of anticipation, while Princess Lauren, perched precariously on her jewel
encrusted spinning ladder teetered and wobbled, offering hope to
the shadows. Would she stumble or tumble? When asked, even
Spinny and Weavy declined to comment. The Vortex really
hummed, in fact, it was buzzing the morning of show time in
Yavapai County. All over Sedona you could hear the buzz as witnesses called for the prosecution prepared for trial. The buzzing
was so insistent it almost buzzed Lauren awake.

Waking early, Americo Rios deliberately weighed chance versus skill. He held a ball of each, one in each hand, tossing them back and forth.

Tim Richmond, the prosecuting attorney, had placed Americo first on the witness list, knowing he had a big, powerful gun and he knew how to shoot it. Tim knew without any doubt that Americo's reputation of credibility and stability would take the little Witch down.

Americo, with a ball in each hand, settled on chance. Still with one ball in each hand, trying to decide if the shape determined the content or if the content determined the shape, he decided to shape the content with his own spin on things. Deep down he knew better but...Americo Rios also had charm and he knew how to use it sublimely. So he took a chance. He felt princely, noble, and looked handsome and refreshed. "I didn't fold for thirty years. I stayed in the game in spite of Lauren." So, needing to take a shower, he folded everything up and put it away, for the time being.

Wyatt Kirkman had arrived the day before to escort Lauren to trial. Having been summoned as a witness as well, he decided to land on runway number one. Unfortunately, runway number one was still under renovation. Wyatt had power, money, and influence and he knew how to use them. "I better pick up the ball and roll this renovation along a little faster," Wyatt decided, feeling the pressure.

Lauren had already told him that she wanted to drive her own car, so Wyatt agreed to meet her on the steps. He knew she needed him to make an entrance.

Garry Baker woke up thinking he better take a package of important papers with him, just in case he had to wait before testifying. He prepared the package carefully, hoping everybody would notice that he is an important, busy man. Sometimes when you're a little guy inside, big packages make you look important.

Now, Alexandra Kingston didn't take any chances and the only package she took to trial was Americo. True to her character, she packaged herself very beautifully that morning. The night before trial she went to bed early, knowing that as you get a little older you need more rest to appear ravishing and alluring. She really wanted her package to look better than Lauren's. Alex gloated when she sculpted some cheekbones with a brush of good fortune the Goddess failed to use. "God knows what Lauren will wear to the trial; she has absolutely the worst taste." Deep down she knew Lauren has very good taste in men, after all Wyatt

Kirkman has deep pockets and Alexandra knows many ways into deep pockets.

Graciela Ybarra, looked in the mirror talking to Marquita Pena. They were both exotic, very enchanting women, each in their own way. Marquita was devilish, calculating, and disguised her razor sharp mind very cleverly with her voluptuous, swaying body. Graciela looked razor sharp, cleverly disguising her incredibly devilish body with a classic Chanel style suit, new jewelry, and the weapon of her casual friendship with Lauren. Graciela carefully wrapped her tools in a pretty, soft, pink, slinky package.

"Marquita, you were so clever to get your hands on these. If you wait long enough, an opportunity always presents itself. Somebody dropped a ball and you were smart enough to catch it." Marquita, with help from her brother had caught the ball and Graciela was taking the ball to court.

Ignacio had been asked to stay behind to manage affairs on the rancho when Americo went to trial. Thinking Americo a fool, Ignacio turned to his task. Months ago, Ignacio had buried an object of power belonging to Americo in the soft, red river bank under a willow tree. It was an object that contained the hope that had dwindled in Americo's heart. It was now time to retrieve the object. As the river flowed by it had washed away the power. It had washed away the power, the hope, and the dream.

Unashamedly, Ignacio started to dig, knowing nobody remained on the rancho to witness his betrayal. His small fang-like teeth were yellowed from years of chewing tobacco and as Ignacio placed the object in the bag, tying it closed with a yank, his heart filled with hate. Wishing he had taken revenge, he hacked and spit, muttering, "Ms. Lauren, I should have shot you with the gun when I had the chance."

☪

On a dark night in February almost two years ago, Ignacio watched as Jake Auldney, having first learned of his cancer, held a gun to his head. For a time, Jake didn't think he had the courage to face the slow dwindling of his life in pain and suffering. Courage fluttered to Jake, and he reconsidered, returned the gun, and took the first step to facing his death.

It was Americo's gun, an heirloom that a gunsmith had just reconditioned. Jake had stolen it from under the seat of his car while looking for a pack of cigarettes. Ignacio then took the gun and with an ulterior motive, hid it in the garden shed knowing that Americo would forever believe that Lauren had stolen it from him. He knew the shed was seldom opened now that Rita, in her old age, tended her garden with other tools. Ignacio didn't know that Lauren was a gardener, albeit a wild one. Having never seen Lauren tend to Americo's house or twirling in the orchard, he considered her a spoiled hothouse rose.

Failed by Americo, Lauren started cleaning out small spaces. First, she cleaned, painted, and made the Casino her home. She was alone, felt guilty, did not feel worthy of spaciousness, and as a woman facing life alone she tried to make what she had meaningful in small ways. Lauren found the gun while looking in the shed for flowerpots to adorn the small porch surrounding the Casino. The gun had been a gift to her grandfather from Americo's grandfather, a gesture of friendship, a collectible, and as Zack had gifted the gun to Americo on his twenty-first birthday, she knew the meaning it held for him. Estranged from Americo, she placed it on a table in the Casino meaning to ask Trey to return it and once again, Lauren forgot.

☪

Sunnie and Trey made love, at least they had sex, lately it seemed neither had been able to tell the difference. On the morning at hand, Trey felt uneasy about the trial and worried about his sister and best friend. Life on the rancho had been tense and to Trey, his perfect wife seemed less desirable and his perfect marriage now seemed less perfect.

Lately, Livvy seemed withdrawn, having started to keep her feelings to herself in spite of the seeming sweetness of her life. The young man she lived with was a graduate art student with a promising future and loved her deeply. More and more, avoiding her parents, Livvy sought Lauren's company when home on the rancho.

Trying to ignore his conflicted feelings, Trey took Sunnie in his arms. Feeling divided loyalties and still considering the midlife crisis Lauren so flippantly offered him, he surrendered to the warm, safe space of his wife. Trey was unable to get the crises off of his mind. "Sunnie, Lauren's going down and I still have a feeling she's guilty."

Sunnie sighed, looking forward to getting on with life. "Trey, don't be too hard on her, Lauren's got an incredible bag of tricks." In spite of their close friendship, Sunnie, like others in the family, had not seen Lauren land on her back in times of crises and pondered why Lauren always seemed to land on her feet in spite of the chances she took. "She'll pull the Magician out of the bag, just wait and see."

At age one hundred, Rita was wise beyond her years and had prepared Lauren for a descent as her life unfolded before the court. Lauren had cleaned her house, spiraled her garden the other direction, and found the wild woman in the out of sight forest in the desert. Rita spun as she sat on her porch, knowing that she had given Lauren the tools to climb down the cold, lonely, moist, forbidding steps, carved into the deep underground of self-acceptance.

Seeking the approval of others, and seeing herself through other's eyes, had exacerbated Lauren's natural hypersensitivity. At the time of the death of her baby, her already damaged psyche cracked. Although Lauren suffered soul loss, depression, euphoria, dysphoria, manic and psychotic episodes, and self-abuse, she instinctively refused to surrender to parasitic forces and expectations of others.

Oftentimes, the princess who wore hotpants and miniskirts went too far. She spun way out there, seeking people and experiences to feed her wild soul. Very often she ate food that wasn't good for her. Drugs aren't good for the wild woman. Relationships that undermine one's authentic self are poison for the wild woman. Keeping a secret, not for the sake of mystery, but for the sake of what others consider to be acceptable, is almost like strangling the wild woman. Wearing other people's glasses can really mess up the wild woman's ability to see.

"But," the Baba Yaga tells the young girl lost in the forest, "wearing red-hot hotpants and miniskirts when you stay out late can save a mixed up girl's life." On second thought, she might have said, "Have hot pants, stay out late and show the men what you have under your skirt." Sometimes the Vortex spins so fast you rearrange things with your perceptions.

Defying convention, breaking other peoples rules, and ignoring authority figures are all very good paths to the wild woman, if done within the context of awareness. Lauren did them all, often without awareness. Instinct, mustered from the brain and soul, will often rise up in our behalf. Defying temperance and moderation covered Lauren's fanny, until she opened her own eyes. There are many foods to feed the wild woman that will nurture and keep her alive. Art, spiritual practices and the good sense not to come home before curfew, were the good foods that Lauren fed the Baba Yaga. Art is soul food. Art is a channel for soul. Spirit, both Earthly and heavenly, cleanses and intensifies. Staying out late is magic. It defies everything, and it also gives a woman a chance to fool around with the man in the moon.

Lauren had a sense of humor and although dry and mysterious, on a deep level it kept her from taking life too seriously. Because of the teachings of her Grandmother, Lauren's wild woman was intact, if not always fed good food. The problem of not taking your problems seriously; is that others do not always take you seriously. Lauren's family, other than her Grandmother, did not take her seriously at all. Although Lauren did everything on her own, they thought she was a ball of fluff, because in their opinion, she had not reached the potential she had within her. They saw her as an irresponsible, flighty, secretive, and far too fun loving woman. They perceived her as such because she had not lived up to their expectations.

Rita forgot something as she spun away the day in front of the fire, sipping first coffee and tea, and later in the afternoon a small glass of sherry. Lauren Cubera Auldney is a sassy smarty panties. Lauren thought she had already made the descent very successfully and was now ready to rock and roll.

Lauren stirred.

The beautiful little cauldron Lauren kept by her bed needed stirring and a clever Witch never forgets to stir her cauldron. Stretching luxuriously, as if she didn't have a care in the world, Lauren stirred, gently, slowly, and with purpose.

Thanks to all of the other activity in the Verde Valley, the Vortex had already been stirred and was spinning nicely on it's own steam for the day.

Lauren, although literal, saw the world through the eye of the metaphor. But since she literally experienced the metaphors, the metaphors were literally real. Lauren could see over, behind, in between, and under the veils that others called reality. It had been said that she lives in a state of derealization at times. Lauren stirred the cauldron very tenderly. "Is the real, the realization? Or," she sighed in relief, building up to the big answer, "is the realization, the real? Sometimes, there's nothing like a little private time with the Goddess."

Having stirred the cauldron, offering her morning gratitude to the Goddess, Lauren experienced the first step of descent.

Awakened by the stirring, from within her deep warm cauldron rose the wild woman. Lauren felt a roaring, a thundering. The wild woman hissed like a snake and growled like a bear. "Remember your hotpants, you smart little cracked cookie."

Altered, Lauren was not altered. "You've still got it." The drawer of her bureau flew open and as if by magic, before her eyes, were new red panties. Only this time, they were thong panties, trimmed in lace, with a little pink dot right where it counted. Things get a lot better as you get older.

Some people have class. They can't help it, it's something you're born with or you're not. It's a karmic thing. It's the style you carry your karma. Other people have taste. They develop it. Everybody can have taste. Usually, it means that you taste something that somebody else cooked up, and you like it. Very few people have style. Style is something that cannot be described. You know it when you see it, but if you try what you see on for size, it won't fit. Some people enjoy being around people with style. Others are discomforted by style, because it doesn't have any rules, and you can't get it out of a book or a magazine. It comes from the soul.

Lauren Auldney had all three. Her father was proud that she was born with class. He gave himself credit for having good breeding. Lauren had taste, but she only tasted stuff she liked, and she didn't care what anybody else tried to feed her. Style, Lauren had tons of it and not just one style either. She knew how to use style as a disguise, a weapon, or a tool, and at this time she was stalking her life. Today, going to trial, she needed them all. She knew one thing without question, when you go into a courtroom, you can't show your stylish, red thong panties.

Lauren dressed accordingly, for day one. Lauren was and was not looking forward to this day, because Americo Rios was going to testify and although he didn't think she had balls, she knew very well he did. She just didn't know if he was going to use the ball of chance or the ball of skill. Both balls served him very well in the game of poker and life, but you can't take many chances when you're juggling big balls in a glass house.

☪

The Great Weaver paused, considering what color to use for the next string of yarn in the story. The focal point is critical when constructing a work of art and this weaving had to be perfect. The Great Spinner had given her many colorful choices, this life had not been bland or neutral, and the outcome was yet undecided.

A mistake some artists make, as well as some people, is that they too rigidly follow a plan, forgetting that serendipity must enter the channel. Time and space, although real, are unreal and never constant, especially when you're trying to weave in a Vortex. However, time, space, perspective, awareness, and circumstances must be considered before the creator surrenders to the inevitable outcome. The Great Weaver considered the focal point, was a little tired of red, so therefore, turned to pink for the beginning.

Wyatt Kirkman was a Knight waiting to escort his lady into the historic county courthouse, just as he promised to do. Despite his circumstances, Wyatt believed that Lauren should have stayed with him and raised a family. Had Lauren done so, Wyatt believed at this time in their lives, they would be deciding where to send their children to school. Wyatt stood on the steps, handsome in his cashmere sports coat and soft wool slacks, looking like a man satisfied with his success, his life, and his ability to be with Lauren when she needed him.

Only recently Wyatt's wife asked him about the little bite marks on his chest and shoulders. Wyatt was rather clever. In a flash, he saw Lauren's cat like eyes. "I'll be damned, didn't I tell you, Sweetcakes," he drawled, oozing southern male charm. "I was trying to catch this great looking wild cat, thought I'd try to tame it for the grandkids, but when I caught it, it bit the hell out of me." Wyatt's wife had never before seen cat bites, so it worked out fine. Three days later, she wondered if it was the same wild cat Wyatt had been unable to tame several years ago. Wyatt knew more than that about feral cats. He knew that you leave them in the wild, even if you do love them.

Lauren knew now, just like she did many years ago, that with Wyatt to rescue her she would never learn to rescue herself. Wyatt was over protective and under the secure, warm blanket of his love, Lauren knew she would have smothered or withered from too much care.

Fresh and innocent were the words to describe Lauren as she ascended the stairs to take Wyatt's arm. Nothing in the world will make a woman appear fresher and more innocent than a distinguished looking older man at her side, offering protection. Wearing a long, pink and brown flowered skirt and a floppy brimmed hat, Lauren was a sophisticated flower child. Only two people in the courtroom would know the pink cashmere sweater she wore was thirty years old.

Detesting the new and shiny, Lauren learned the beauty of the well worn and well cared for. She knew that old boots, well polished, carried more aplomb than a shiny new pair with no scars. Small stitches made to repair a seam in an old silk blouse, add to the character. Sometimes called the bag lady, Lauren had bags of all shapes and sizes, all of them used, not abused. The sheen of cashmere garnered from time and wear is exquisite. Pink cashmere sweaters have the finest sheen of all, and Lauren knew this. At the door of the courtroom Lauren stopped, taking a deep breath. From the corner of her eye she saw a shadow. The putrid smell of burning hair lingered. Lauren stepped closer to Wyatt. "Wyatt, do you smell that?"

He shrugged his shoulders.

Graciela Ybarra was the first to meet Lauren's gaze. The two women smiled in greeting; Lauren puzzled that a casual acquaintance would be in the courtroom.

A woman with style understands the mystery of the unveiling. Although it is something that is learned, it is not contrived or planned. The art becomes the charm of the woman. The entrance, although not planned, had been effective. Wyatt held the door, scanning the room for something that could harm Lauren and when satisfied, he further opened the door and in strolled the Princess. As Lauren entered the courtroom, the unveiling began. With great care, Lauren removed her satchel from her shoulder. She pondered the satchel for a moment, as if considering something. Smiling at Wyatt, Lauren handed him her shawl. Lovingly, seeming to hold a priceless object, Wyatt put it over his arm and patted it. Her gloves were removed one finger at a time, then deliberately, as if under great consideration, she looked at her fingers and centered her garnet ring. Next came the sunglasses. First, peering over the tops, Lauren looked at the crowd, slowly. Carefully putting her sunglasses in a case, she then dropped them somewhat nonchalantly into her satchel. Turning to look out the window, Lauren removed her hat with one hand resting lightly on her hip. The lines were serpentine, graceful, and seductive. Knowing others watched, Lauren set up her small altar and although it could have gone unnoticed, Lauren offered it the respect of non-disguise. Reverently, she opened a small weaving and rested the silver disc in the center.

Americo Rios also knew how to enter a room. He paused, surveyed the territory, established eye contact with familiar faces, and focused across the room before taking a step.

Lauren couldn't help it. She liked what she saw and took a quick inventory of his attributes. Smiling to herself, she checked out his rust colored leather jacket and black turtleneck. "He's still a tasty treat for the eyes." Admiration. Boldly she continued to stare. Only Americo Rios could make a pair of Levis look like dress slacks and his Ostrich skin boots had always been her favorites. Lauren felt the heat. Furnaces work very well in sturdy old buildings. Lauren wiggled provocatively in her seat. "He's so tasty I'd like to lick his handsome face and taste the sweetness on my tongue." Americo swaggered Sam Shephard style, reeking testosterone, enjoying Lauren's admiration.

Glasses have a language of their own. Glasses make a statement and a person gifted in the employment of their glasses, employees a mighty tool. One can hold them in their fingers, tap them on a table to make a point, or hold them steady as if musing about something pleasant. A person can peer over them in disdain, or look down, appearing coy. One can also casually wear them on their forehead, bringing into question whether you need them or not. Lauren's glasses were expressive, used tactically and she knew without question, even if she didn't need them, she would wear them. "Too bad I can't see your lion-like eyes, Mr. Leo. You really ought to take your sunglasses off, that look is just a bit too cool." Americo reached for his glasses. Holding his glance, Lauren looked at Americo's eyes, wondering why his usual clear eyes seemed clouded and unfocused.

Americo didn't see what he should have seen, but he did see Lauren. "You are such an audacious little Witch, but you certainly look sweet today. Only you would know that the sight of that pink sweater would drive me crazy. You are a cauldron of contradictions, Lauren."

Lauren knew how to send a signal. She knew about cauldrons as well.

Americo had revenge, hate, rejection, and charm, all on his side. He smiled evilly. "I'm going to take you down, Lauren, you just wait. How dare you sit there like you haven't got a care in the world? Don't you realize you're going to jail for a long time?"

Lauren caught the thought and had no intention of going to jail.

"Hell, she probably thinks Wyatt Kirkman will save her ass."

Lauren won that round.

Americo saw another familiar face, he thought. Unable to recognize Graciela Ybarra, he took Alexandra by the hand and guided her to a seat behind the prosecutor's table.

Graciela had a right to feel smug. "Americo, mi cara, I can fool you so easily."

Americo had dropped a little ball, but he had another card to play and tenderly cupped Alex's face in his hands. "Are you sure you want to be here for this, Alex?"

Alexandra lost composure, being unused to Americo's concern. "No, No, I'm not leaving here! Now that everything is so perfect between us, I can stand hearing it again." Kissing Alexandra's cheek, he met Lauren's cold stare.

☪

Americo walked to the stand appearing poised and sophisticated. Nobody in the courtroom could see his body quake or know that a pain stabbed the left side of his gut. With his hand shaking as he rested it on the bible, he took the oath. Usually composed, Americo glanced at Lauren out of habit and briefly saw the look in her eyes he once considered to be his. His emotions betrayed him, and he rubbed one of the gold conchos on his belt, remembering that Lauren's hands crafted the museum quality belt that an appraiser told him would buy a small house in a respectable neighborhood. He tossed Lauren a question with his eyes. "Damn you, Lauren, can't you see how much I need you?"

Lauren got it and tossed it back with a defiant nod. She was ready to play energy ball. "You're on your own, Americo. You loaded their gun, and now you have to be the one to pull the trigger, not me."

Retreating behind his tough exterior, Americo recovered his seemingly natural charm and disarmed the jury with his openness.

Feeling loved and protected by Wyatt, Lauren listened carefully to Americo's voice, while her mind protested at the conflicting meaning of his words.

The prosecutor addressed Americo as if they were old friends. "Americo, will you describe to the court what happened the night you were so brutally shot and almost killed?"

Americo answered with his gravelly voice, giving the spectators in the room a small engaging smile. "Of course, Tim, I'll be glad to." Americo played his hand, charm. "I took my fiancée to the opening of Lauren's show at the Langdon Gallery. I wanted to support a friend, especially since she had been going through difficulties because of her father's illness."

Lauren arched her eyebrows. "You are one great, great guy, Americo."

Tim continued. "You took the time, out of courtesy, to support a friend. You're a busy man, Americo, and I'm impressed. I understand the show was a success so it must have been a pleasure to see her art."

Americo knew where to stab the knife. "I've already seen enough of her work and," he paused cruelly, "in all honesty, I find too much hand evident to suit my taste."

Lauren was disgusted. "You mean you like the high polished manufactured look, Americo. Your taste has certainly deteriorated due to the company you keep."

Americo liked the ghost of hurt feelings he saw on Lauren's face.

Tim Richmond had an eye for subtlety and saw the exchange.

Wyatt had not taken time to eat breakfast before leaving his hotel room. Not caring if he defied protocol, he reached in his coat pocket for the sweet roll that had been left in a fruit basket, delivered compliments of the establishment. Americo saw him take the first bite and he also saw the look. He didn't know why, but it made him think of fresh bread. It pissed him off, but he licked his lips anyway. "Wyatt looks like Lauren's been wrapped around him like a tortilla." Alexandra never ate bread because it made her stomach puffy, but she was thinking she might like to have a bite of Wyatt.

Tim called Americo back to court and out of the bakery. "Americo, if it's alright with you, I'll let you tell the story without interruption from me, unless a point needs clarification."

Americo sounded innocent and charming and his eyes were sparkling mischievously. Revenge is sweet. "Hell, I don't know what happened to me, it was like a spell had been put on me." He had no idea. "Lauren is what you would call a natural Witch, and believe me, she is very capable of rearranging a person's perspective. I guess I forgot how powerful she is because I fell for her all over again."

Lauren mocked him with a grin and an arch of the brow. "At least I don't have to take drugs to cast my spells."

Americo stared back, provoking her more.

Lauren crossed her legs, reminding him of other things. "I'm a natural and you're just a wannabe."

"Go ahead, Americo," the prosecuting attorney said as he glared at Lauren.

Guy talk. Americo needed empathy from someone who would understand the plight of a man smitten with a Witch. With a help-less look on his face, he shrugged his shoulders as if to say, "You understand, don't you, Tim?" To the attorney and the jury, he spoke as if in the clutch of romance. "I watched Lauren talking to her guests, and I realized I still had feelings for her. Lauren is very mysterious and much like the crescent moon she worships, she keeps most of herself hidden. I must say there's always been something about her beauty that overwhelms me, and I guess I fell under her magic. Something akin to temporary insanity," he laughed a little. He looked apologetically at Alexandra, who returned a look of understanding.

"Temporary insanity, my ass," Lauren thought. "You've been obsessed with me for years."

"Anyway my fiancée became very angry with me for watching Lauren at her show."

Americo paused and then spoke slowly and thoughtfully. "I drove by the nightclub and saw Lauren's car in the parking lot and when I got inside Lauren was dancing with Garry Baker."

Garry Baker sat straighter, arranging the package of papers on his lap.

Americo noticed, pretended he didn't and continued painting the picture. He wanted everybody to know he had always looked out for Lauren's best interest. "I don't know how it happened, but somehow when we were children I became Lauren's protector. When younger, Lauren was a tease and more often than not I had to step in and solve her problems."

"You stupid, stupid jerk," Lauren thought. "Don't you know the guys called me a cold fish?" Then, the red thong tickled her fanny.

Americo wondered why she kept wiggling in her seat. The broad strokes had been painted, now Americo picked up the fine brush of his charm and smiled at the women of the jury, hoping they would understand how brotherly his intentions became as the night wore on. "I sat down at a table by myself and had a cou-ple of drinks while I watched her dance with Garry. She was on one of her terrors that night, high as a kite on life and cham-pagne." Implying she may have been high on something else, he said, "At least I think it was champagne."

Lauren folded her arms, plotting.

Americo couldn't forget how she looked that night. "Lauren looked fantastic in her short, black dress and she definitely want-ed to be noticed. You should have seen her show off with wild abandon on the dance floor." The way he shook his head, the witnesses couldn't tell if he was remembering Lauren wearing a short dress, or if he was insincerely surprised at being jealous. "I'll admit it, I was jealous and when she left with Garry I followed them to the parking lot. I knew Baker was pretty drunk, and I also knew that Lauren always crashes pretty hard when she gets so high."

"This is such bullshit, Rios. You never had the right to interfere in my life. I told you that a long time ago. That was one of the rules."

Americo was good at following a plan, not necessarily rules, and he wasn't bad with a paintbrush either. "I told Garry not to take advantage of her. I explained to him that Lauren had been going through a rough time and was vulnerable. Lauren mentioned something from the past; he started yelling, so I punched him. Anyway, it got pretty ugly, so after hearing Lauren admit she had a gun, I said to hell with it, got in my Land Rover and drove home."

Lauren giggled a little louder than she should have. "Hah, you don't want to tell the jury you were a failure in bed."

Americo licked his lips, and then shook his head like a broken-hearted lover. "I went home and had another drink and wondered if I should ask her again about my stolen gun. It was a difficult night, I was jealous and hurt, but I couldn't get her off of my mind."

Wyatt looked at Lauren, understanding.

"I saw her car in front of the Casino, and I suppose I could say it in poker lingo, I was ready to lay my cards on the table."

Lauren remembered the night she laid her cards on the table.

Americo had more to say. He had a lot more to say about the candles, incense, and champagne in the Casino. He helpfully suggested she might have been waiting for one of her many lovers. He then appealed to one female juror in particular. She looked needy, and he had a big gun. "The emotions between us have always been very intense, and we were once deeply in love."

Sometimes even a gentle stimulus doesn't get a response. Lauren didn't look up.

Americo relayed the rest of the events, chuckling softly and charmingly when he told the gallery about being hit on the head with a Witch's broom. He sounded understanding, implied it could have been hormonal; all the while sounding hurt and stunned. "Thank God, I got to the hospital and in the hands of good surgeons or I wouldn't be here talking to you."

Giving credit to the doctors hurt Lauren's feelings. "The surgery didn't save your life, you stupid ass. I saved your life by channeling love into your body. Why are you so blind, Americo?"

The prosecutor was sympathetic. "So all you are guilty of is trying to protect a woman you thought you loved, a woman you had protected for years, a woman you describe as a tease. Did you threaten to hit her?"

Americo looked shocked that something so insignificant would have been addressed. He acted a bit guilty, hung his head, looking contrite. "No, I told her I was so frustrated I felt like hitting her." Americo was adamant. "I have never hit a woman. I can give you a long list of women's names who would testify in my behalf."

"I'll bet you could, you jerk." Lauren sulked with her arms folded. "You're nothing but a he whore."

"Americo, explain to the court why you thought you had to protect Lauren when you were younger." Tim encouraged his damaging testimony.

Americo had his list ready, a list his mother would have been proud of. "Lauren seemed to have a problem of some kind, somewhat like a princess who got lost. I remember a morning when we were kids and planned to go horseback riding. I was very frightened because she didn't recognize me, and I had to take her to her Grandmother's for help. She was a real pest, always bugging me to do things with her. I must have what's called a rescue complex, because I went along with many of her crazy ideas." He shrugged like he was a great guy and helpless to her needs. "Hell, I even worried about her as an adult."

"Rescue complex," Lauren thought sarcastically, "that's a big concept for you, isn't it, Americo? Somebody should have rescued me from you years ago." It was getting ugly. Lauren was reacting, not responding.

"She didn't have a lot of friends, so I offered to take her to her graduation dance. I guess it was sort of a sympathy date," he chuckled wryly.

Americo held the sword over his head, getting ready for the kill.

Lauren squinted her eyes, seeing light reflecting from the blade. Americo was telling too much.

Americo licked his lips.

Graciela Ybarra carefully plucked a hair from the skirt of her suit, smiling.

Sunnie wondered when she would learn the name of her

problem.

Alexandra fussed with her purse, wondering why Americo seemed hungry.

"I had a very pretty girlfriend at the time, but I felt so damned bad that Lauren was going to have to go to the dance by herself. Poor kid, without me she wouldn't have had any friends."

Lauren started to steam. She smelled smoke too.

Americo had taken a chance. Lost.

Lauren wiggled her reptilian toes. "Is that right, you ass? I can't believe you're calling me a pest. You hovered over me all of the time."

Charm is a two-edge sword and Americo had cut both ways.

"My protector you say. Like you didn't want to be. You called our date a sympathy date. Oh boy, Rios, you've gone too far now."

Americo was always asking Lauren to go to the dance.

"You want to play a little game. Let's dance, you arrogant boob."

Americo dropped the ball with a little help of somebody else in the courtroom.

Lauren dropped the lids of her eyes, keeping very close eye on the ball.

He turned to frequency.

She found the leak. Big one.

She acted quickly, not giving a damn if he lived or died.

He lost sight of the ball completely.

Lauren manipulated her fingers very gracefully.

"You took your eyes off the ball, Americo."

Americo grabbed his throat.

Tim Richmond didn't want to lose Americo. "Do you need some water?"

Holding his throat, he started to stagger and heard Lauren's wicked little laugh.

He stumbled to his knees, all color draining from his face.

Alex rushed to his side miraculously, losing all poise.

Lauren thought Alexandra looked like an overdressed miracle.

Lauren didn't figure, she knew her skills were better than his and she didn't even have a plan. Well, she did, but she hadn't bothered to share it with Lydia.

"I thought you were better at the game, Americo."

Alexandra saw the smug expression on Lauren's face and the maniacal look in her eyes.

"You did something to him, you Witch."

Every person in the courtroom looked at Lauren, not Americo.

Alex screamed, bending over Americo as he struggled to breathe. "Help, hurry, I think he's having a heart attack. Somebody please help him."

Lauren was pretty certain Alexandra was not the medicine he needed. "Somebody better help him or I will kill him." The commotion in the courtroom spun out of control. Lauren laughed hysterically. Ignoring Lydia's efforts to calm her, she put her head on the table and congratulated herself for work well done. Americo rolled by on a stretcher. She felt a tug on her abdomen just below the navel. No problem. Witches know how to handle things like that. All restraint had been lost. Lauren jumped on the other side of the border and took another step into descent. "OK, Americo, now the fun really begins. We'll see who has the best control of power here, you or me. What you don't realize is that I kept my edge and I have double power. Spin it, Rios." Lauren jumped back to her side of the border, with double power. Power like charm, can be two-edged if not used wisely or with honor. Lauren had just violated the Witches creed. Oops.

Lydia had a problem. Lauren. For the sake of showing good intention to the court, Lydia decided to get Lauren into real, very serious therapy, now.

Lauren heard the thought. "Fat chance."

"Your honor, I have no more questions for Mr. Rios," Tim Richmond said after the court session resumed. "We can continue with the next witness."

☪

Witches do have some problems, especially after lunch. Every good Witch knows that if you've designed your life right by working smart not hard, after lunch is when you settle in for a sweet little nap. Lauren had been chastised by Lydia at lunch, didn't get a nap, and it wasn't a good afternoon. As Judge Pyron entered the courtroom to commence the session, Lauren rang the bell suspended from her bracelet.

Garry Baker walked towards the stand like a bandy hen, a very colorful bandy hen. His short stature was compensated by a muscular physique. His expensive clothes gave him the appearance of a man sitting in a country club having a drink after a long afternoon on the golf course sharing lewd jokes with friends.

Garry carried himself with confidence, knowing he was considered an outstanding member of the Sedona community, and the depth of his pockets added to the arrogance of his posture. He had waited a long time to take Lauren down a notch or two. The sweetness of the moment created a look of eagerness on his face that caused one person in the gallery to wonder if he would start frothing at the mouth.

Tim Richmond and Garry were friends.

"Garry Baker, did Lauren ask you to follow her home?"

"I told her I would be there in forty-five minutes. I was pretty happy that after all of these years Lauren and I might get together."

Lauren pinched her cheeks together.

"But did you follow her?"

"No, I changed my mind and I didn't want to tangle with Rios again. He seemed pretty out of it and was jealous as hell."

"What do you mean by after all of these years you and Lauren might get together."

"Oh, Lauren and I went through school together and I always kind of liked her. The guys called her the princess of Sedona because she acts a little royal. I think we probably could have gotten together a long time ago if Americo Rios hadn't always interfered. Man, nobody could get close to her but what he wasn't all over them."

Lauren had an answer for everything. "Don't you know that royal means real?"

Thinking it a good business maneuver, Garry offered his condolences to Americo, telling him that he had served the community well by keeping Lauren under control when they were younger. He didn't disclose that he was trying to buy an easement from Americo in order to build a cookie cutter, faux stucco, and imitation bar tile roof housing development near the rancho.

Yes, Garry summed up Lauren for the prosecution. He considered Lauren to be available, wanton, and not stable enough to be out alone at night. He had second thoughts, and knowing it would damage Lauren's case, he confessed the real reason he didn't go to the Casino. Garry said he was still concerned for his safety and revealed that Lauren had threatened to kill him with her gun if he arrived at her home. And, he emphatically told the jury that she had been violent all of her life, himself being the victim of her abuse on several occasions.

Lauren felt sick to her stomach. Karma can come around pretty fast.

The glasses Lauren wore while listening were glasses with mirrors. The mirrors are helpful if you want to see yourself. You can't escape seeing yourself, because you are right in your face, with nowhere to hide. Green eyes looked back at green eyes, and Lauren didn't like what she saw in the mirror. She saw a worried shy girl with a vortex wound so tight in her soul that she threatened to implode from the pressure. She saw a report card in her hand; a less than perfect report card and she knew the consequences. If you're not perfect, nobody loves you. Lauren saw two girls: one inside of her body and the other watching. She saw a seemingly silly, lighthearted girl, but she knew this girl needed a disguise. The other girl could only avoid the impending implosion by escaping, leaving a sassy, aloof, flippant, and outrageous girl to face the fear. If those who should have watched over her had done their job, they would have seen the crack.

This descent was not one you take with your own time and speed. Lauren started to slide. She slid down and down, down a wet, mucky slide with sharp edges. Danger at every curve, she barely missed the hazards. Then she crashed. She crashed into boulders that brought her to attention. When you hit a boulder, awareness comes quickly. "Spin it, Lauren." With awareness comes forgiveness for others and yourself. "To hell with them all. They didn't know, because they didn't follow the signs."

Lydia didn't know that Lauren had altered a perception.

☪

Initiations are difficult, especially when you are being initiated unto yourself. Nighttime can be cruel. Sometimes the daylight disappears too quickly, and the darkness is relentless. Sometimes you walk in your sleep, looking for answers to questions you don't yet have. The morning can also be cruel, when you wake with your cheek on the blood of your beloved.

Americo returned to court in full health, after all, a little Witch lash can't take a good man down. Nodding curtly to Wyatt, Americo looked at Lauren and gone was the fresh faced, rosy-cheeked woman of yesterday. Americo was confused by her now shadowy, subdued appearance, having seen her in a shockingly short red miniskirt, dining with Wyatt the night before.

Tim Richmond gloated. A winter vacation with his wife and family was scheduled, and he wanted to leave with Lauren

Auldney in jail. Offering a confident nod to the jury foreman, he commenced the next interrogation.

Brushing his graying dark blonde hair from his brow, Jim Reese dashed to the stand appearing as if dashing onto a tennis court. He appeared young for his age, his tan was fresh and his button down shirt was impeccably pressed. Jim hoped Lauren wouldn't notice the slight paunch around his middle and sucked in a breath, holding it as he took the oath.

He looked at Lauren, remembering the girl he had fallen in love with, consoling himself that he had wisely escaped from her madness. A wife accused of attempted murder did not fit the scenario he had created in his life. He had a lovely, extremely sane wife who was involved in many charities, three perfect, tennis-playing children and an estate in Connecticut. He didn't know that his oldest daughter had recently started using crack cocaine.

As Jim nodded a greeting to Lauren, a sad awareness came to him. "There's something about seeing Laurie again that makes me wonder what kind of life I would have had with her. Somehow, when she left me I lost being enchanted with life."

Lauren leaned towards Lydia, telling her emphatically to not interrupt the testimonies of her husbands and lovers. "Lauren, I'll have to interrupt if their testimony is going to hurt your chances for acquittal."

"No, Lydia, I'm being acquitted from a lifetime of being in prison. Please."

"I don't like it, Lauren, and I won't let you stop me from cross examining them. There are some things that may need clarifying."

"That's fine, but I want to hear what they have to say. I'm starting to feel as though I'm watching a painting being unpainted, or a carving before the carver entered the scene."

Tim liked this guy. "How are you today, Dr. Reese?"

The handsome former preppy sounded casual, as if talking to someone across a net on a tennis court.

"Very, very good. I couldn't be better, thank you. I'm ready for anything."

"Will you tell the court about your relationship with the accused?"

"Certainly, Laurie was my first wife. We've been divorced for more than twenty years."

"How did you meet the accused?"

"It was on registration day, fall quarter of our junior year at the university. We were both in the honors program, and we met standing in line to register for a class."

"What was her major at the university?"

Lauren didn't expect this question. "Oh shit, this again."

"She changed her major at least six times, more if you count the times before I met her. I think at that time she was a dance major, but she always took art classes. Art is fine, but I didn't think it made a sensible career choice. She has an excellent mind, in fact she's brilliant and I thought art was beneath her ability. I agreed with her father that she should pursue a career teaching philosophy. Every time she took a class in a new discipline, Lauren changed her major as well as the way she acted and dressed. It was spooky." Jim shivered slightly, considering her behavior.

"What kind of marriage did you have, Dr. Reese?"

Jim brushed his boyish stray locks from his brow. "It was a pretty good one, especially in the beginning. I moved into her small apartment and the only car we had was her little VW. We were good friends, we had intellectual compatibility, and we were both involved in environmental causes."

Lauren couldn't remember it being a good marriage.

Americo was jealous. "Yeah, you stupid bastard, you really thought you had something. Obviously, you weren't getting the job done, because she couldn't wait to take a tumble in my bed."

"Was it love at first sight, Dr. Reese?"

Jim became patronizing. "I think every man falls in love with Laurie on first sight. It's her wistful, ethereal quality that attracts men. It's later that it becomes more complicated."

Americo had to agree. "I'll have to agree with you on that, Jim. When a man meets Lauren, something happens that makes him want to take care of her."

Jim disclosed everything. Looking as dignified as an old preppy with his shirt gaping open is able, he told them how Lauren had slashed all of his clothes, trashed their apartment, refused to take medications, considered a shaman to be smarter than a therapist, changed jobs, threatened to kill him with scissors, wouldn't earn her degree, and left for weeks at a time to spend time on the rancho.

"Then what happened?"

"She left me."

"That was one of the smartest things I ever did for you, Jim."

"Do you mean she divorced you?"

"No, I had to get the divorce; she said she forgot. But she left me."

Nobody in the family knew that. Trey rolled his eyes, wondering if he and Lauren were truly related. Lauren related very little to what her former husband had to say.

"Jim, I'm sorry to tell you this, but you made absolutely no impression on my body and that's where I do my best thinking." She almost giggled out loud realizing how that could be misinterpreted. Lauren felt the current and heard the pop. She saw the picture and the pattern.

☪

Power. Power is an illusive entity, until you learn how to catch it. It comes in waves, flutters, blasts, or bombs, but regardless of the form, it will come. Learning to recognize it, catch it, and live within it is another matter. Most people never learn to live in power. Wyatt Kirkman did not understand the language of energy, but he lived in power. Wyatt wanted Lauren, but he did not need her. Her caprice, whims, and moods did not alter his perspective. Loving her deeply, Wyatt would have done anything for Lauren, except surrender his power to her needs. When she needed him, he was there for her. However, he did not look to Lauren to provide what he already had intact within himself. This was one of the many gifts Wyatt gave to Lauren, a self-referred, whole man. Wyatt did not drain energy from Lauren through expectations or needs of his own; he merely loved her openly and unashamedly, for exactly who she was.

Wyatt Kirkman, a man fully in charge of his world, surveyed the courtroom. His six-foot body was straight as an arrow and with his confidence commanded the attention of every person in the room. His eyes were hard, hard like a man who has lived fast for many years. He looked seasoned, like a man who defeats his opponents swiftly and ruthlessly on a golf course, at a poker table, or in fortune 500 company boardrooms. His steel gray hair accentuated his suntanned skin, and the only warmth on his deeply lined face was directed at Lauren. He held her in his gaze, loving her beyond words. His slow lazy southern drawl was disarming, and he used it like a weapon as he confronted the prosecuting attorney.

Lauren returned the gaze of the most important man in her life, remembering an afternoon on a warm spring day when they were walking to his plane, leaving on vacation to Aruba. She could still feel his hand under her long braid as his personal assistant ran towards them with urgent documents in his hand. Never removing his hand from her neck or taking his eyes from her face, Wyatt signed the papers without looking at them, preferring to look at the smiling young woman by his side.

Lauren felt butterfly wings of emotion surround her. Over lunch, Wyatt had asked Lauren to consider becoming his wife after the trial ended. Lauren knew that she would not go back to him. "Wyatt, I'll always think of you when I drink champagne and if I go to jail, it won't be because you didn't try to help me. Remember this, Wyatt, because it's all I have to give you. My love for you was never second best, and with you, the secret and the gift were the very best."

A woman bent with age caught Americo's attention. Americo was keen, his skills as a sorcerer still intact, and he caught a glimpse of something he had not been looking for. As if a deck of cards were spread on a table, Americo started to connect the fleeting moments that had nagged him for many months.

Tim Richmond appeared too eager. He was too impressed, and he was out of his league. He knew Wyatt was a hostile witness, yet he was a witness Tim hoped would prove that Lauren lived her life unshackled by the dictates of society.

"Mr. Kirkman, will you please describe your occupation to the court."

"I own a little real estate here and there."

"What was or is your relationship with Ms. Auldney?"

"We had a love affair for almost three years and didn't see each other for many years until recently."

Tim withdrew, returned to his table pretending he had lost his train of thought. He wanted the jurors to understand the nature of the corrupt woman they were judging.

"You were married at the time, isn't that correct?"

"I'm still married and yes, I was married at the time."

"Is your wife aware of your affair with Lauren?"

"It has never been discussed."

"Did you intend to leave your wife during your affair?"

"Yes."

Tim Richmond did not expect this answer.

"Why didn't you?"

"Lauren told me she would leave me if I did. She said she didn't want to feel the pressure of a contract."

Tim was attempting to paint Lauren black, and he thought the jurors should know to what lengths immoral people go to hide their illicit affair.

"How did you keep your affair a secret?"

"I didn't try to. We were open, public, and I loved her unashamedly. I was proud that she loved me."

With a wave of his hand, Wyatt took control of the courtroom. As a powerful figure, Wyatt had controlled conference rooms around the world and when he started to speak Tim Richmond took two steps back. Dismissing Tim, Wyatt stood and offered the questions and the answers. When Tim tried to interrupt, Wyatt interrupted him. "Let me save you some time, Richmond, I'll tell you everything you need to hear."

"No," Wyatt said speaking rapidly, "Lauren was not my mistress; she was the love of my life. She bought her own house from me, and I was proud of her for doing so. No, Lauren was not kept on an allowance, her material needs were few and she preferred to own no more than she could fit in her Volkswagen. She made no demands on me at any time; rather, she refused all financial help that I was able and willing to afford her. Yes, I paid for all expenses when we traveled together and that was frequently. No, Lauren would not introduce me to her family, because she preferred to keep the best parts of her life a secret from them. Yes, I am fourteen years older than Lauren. Yes, Lauren was emotional and extreme in her moods, but that was part of her charm. She had a desperate need to feel safe, and I did everything I could to provide that for her. No, Lauren is not violent. A woman who cares for her dolls, her man, her art, her home, and her pets like Lauren does, is not capable of hurting another person physically. Yes, we tried to have a baby and both of our hearts were broken when Lauren had a miscarriage. Yes, she left me and my life has never been as happy as the years I spent with Lauren. Do I still love Lauren and do I want her to be my wife?" Wyatt paused and looked first at Lauren and then at Americo. "The answer is yes and if she'll have me when this ridiculous trial is over; I'll happily make myself available to the woman I've always loved."

Judge Pyron called a short recess and Americo left the room without a word.

Sitting by himself in the courtroom, Trey Auldney watched Wyatt and Lauren offering solace to one another. He saw Lauren in the arms of a lover, being comforted, with not a member of her family nearby.

☪

The silence in the courtroom was palpable as the jurors shifted uncomfortably in their seats. The testimonies given during the session had revealed a complicated woman whom they wondered if they should admire her for her audacity, or despise for her unconventionality.

Tim Richmond addressed the panel of jurors as if they were his neighbors sitting around a pool waiting for barbecued steaks to come off of the grill. "Jurors, members of our community, you have seen the material evidence. Lauren Auldney's fingerprints are the only ones on the gun. She fired the gun. There were two bullets fired. One of them was found embedded in the fireplace hearth, and the other was embedded in Americo Rios' back. Is there any reason to believe she didn't fire both of the shots? Perhaps she missed her target with the first shot and kept her composure well enough to fire the gun again. Americo Rios told the police she tried to kill him as he almost died on the floor of her residence. You have heard testimony from her former classmates, lovers, and husbands that she practices witchcraft; she's a tease, violent and destructive. She's an extremist, she has taken illegal drugs, she is secretive, she has a mental illness, and she had an illicit affair with a married man. I think the question for Ms. Auldney should be, is there anything you will not do?"

Lauren answered, silently. "Probably not."

"Disregarding the testimony regarding her character, the material and circumstantial evidence proves that she fired the gun that almost killed Americo Rios. She had the gun and the opportunity. Please remember, her prints are the only fingerprints on the gun. The prosecution rests."

Americo walked and smoked. When he turned the corner towards the mountains, he smoked again. The assault of testimonies against Lauren had taken their toll and sitting on a cold concrete bench, he stretched his legs, feeling the emptiness to his left. A lifetime of images reeled in front of his eyes as he remembered how frightened Lauren looked the day she cracked when eight years old. He saw her silly smile and the way she fluttered her fingers when she talked. He felt her body close to his, remembering how content he felt waking in the night and finding her head on the pillow beside him.

Americo touched the belt he wore and her pure female energy surrounded him, haunting him as he yearned for her natural ways. He saw her with her special broom, smiling as she swept out his barn after riding her horse. He felt her legs wrapped around his waist as he made love to her. The tears fell as he stood again to walk, and he knew what he had to do. "I'll help you, Lauren. Even if you did try to kill me, I still love you. I'll be reaching out to you, Baby, just like I always have."

Americo rented a car and made preparations to set a trap.

## ☪

Lauren did not feel like a princess as she and Wyatt drove towards Sedona. She was not crying, but constant tears flowed down her cheeks. Silently she looked out the window at the dusk shadowed landscape. The first star appeared as they were driving towards the airport mesa, seeming small and pale compared to the lights of the city below. Wyatt stopped the car and walked Lauren to the overlook. His plane waited to take him home to Atlanta for the weekend, but Wyatt needed to hear Lauren say the words. He put his arm over her shoulder, needing the warmth of her body next to him when he heard her again say goodbye. "Witchy, don't worry, I'll be back in time for court on Tuesday."

Lauren giggled softly with tears still flowing uncontrollably. "If you didn't believe me before when I told you I'm not any good, you certainly do now."

Resting his hands on the railing, Wyatt looked over the small town seeing the silhouettes of the red rocks. Speaking with his back to her, he confessed. "Precious, I meant what I said; I want to try it again with you."

Gently Lauren pulled Wyatt to her and rested her head on his chest. "Wyatt, go home to your wife and family."

He laughed heartily as he picked her up and twirled her around. "Scarlet, that damn Vortex will never let you go."

Lauren giggled before answering. "Wyatt, the Vortex has been spinning me around for about a million years, don't you think it's about time I surrendered to it?"

Giving her a passionate kiss, Wyatt handed Lauren a present and made a promise. "I'll see you Monday night."

☪

Make up sex is hot, intense, and often desperate with the needs of two people to reconnect their filaments and repair damage done to the weaving of their relationship. First, sex can be awkward, with too much concern about performance. Break up sex can be the sweetest of them all. It can happen once, or it can happen over a period of time, but it always involves a return to the transpersonal. For people long in love, there is a need for each to reclaim the filaments the other has held in their capture. One reaches deep into the other, retrieves the threads of their love and begins to reweave them into their own story. The sex becomes less personal and more transcendent. As one returns to personal wholeness, they begin to make love to the Goddess. The partner is still cherished, but the lovemaking is that of the hieros gamos. The partners, reaching for wholeness within themselves, not with one another, are now able to surrender to the act, not the subject of their passions.

Sunnie and Trey were silent as they left Prescott in the near dark late Friday afternoon. Trey drove determinedly, having turned his phone off to save Sunnie from hearing the phone call he expected. Trey's mouth had narrowed and with two patches of white tension by the corners of his mouth, Trey looked hard. Hardness had set in when he realized for the first time that he no longer needed a mother. Trey had not yet betrayed Sunnie physically, but he had betrayed her in a more profound way. Having always encouraged Sunnie to be conventional and conservative, Trey had now fallen in love with a wild woman.

Insecure and confused, Sunnie seemed younger, more vulnerable, and small as she huddled on the passenger seat with her feet tucked under her legs. Rolling the window down when Trey lit a cigarette, Sunnie wondered if the confrontation could wait until after the trial and the holidays were over. Her daughter and future son-in-law were coming to Sedona for Christmas and Rita's New Year's birthday, her school needed attention, and Lauren might be going to jail.

Without warning, desire for Sunnie overwhelmed Trey. It was a desire so fierce it frightened him. He felt a tightening in his gut and pressure in his belly. The feeling was primal, and he didn't know where it came from. The car was the first place Sunnie and Trey made love and to keep a tradition alive, occasionally they relived the passionate nights of their youth. Trey turned his car on to a country dirt road, not saying a word. Trey did not want to want his wife. "Get out of the car, Sunnie."

Sunnie was frightened because Trey had never been abusive to her during their long relationship.

He grabbed her arm and shoved her into the backseat pulling her boots off. Next came her sweater and then he ripped the buttons on her blouse. Nude, Sunnie watched Trey furiously remove his clothes, rudely throwing them on the ground. She then saw the steely look in his eyes that she had never seen before.

Something about Trey excited Sunnie in a way she had never felt before. She taunted him with her lips, unrelentingly holding his gaze. Sunnie wanted this sex to be faced by looking each other in the eye, with nothing held back. Trey squeezed her breasts, forgetting that after the birth of their daughter he had lovingly tasted her milk. Sunnie matched his ferocity with a bold scratch of her nail on his neck. Trey pulled her hair, making tears come to her eyes. Sunnie scratched his back, leaving traces of her acceptance.

Trey reached inside of Sunnie with a finger, then two. Sunnie took him in her mouth, taking back what she wanted. Inside of her, Trey felt larger. Once Trey was inside of her, Sunnie felt more receptive. Sunnie bit his lower lip and Trey answered by leaving bruise marks on her inner thigh.

As each of them started to cry, it was over. Trey had taken back what he needed and Sunnie had retrieved a part of herself. The weaving of their relationship was quickly unraveling and neither of them tried to stop it from happening. For an hour they held each other in their arms, each of them afraid to speak the truth.

Sunnie spoke first, having realized what she didn't have. She stroked his graying hair, wondering if this would be the last time they would be together. "It's over, Trey. I won't be your mother anymore. I'm tired."

Trey laced his fingers through the hair he had once thought of as a curly mass of angel thoughts.

"Yeah, Sun, if you say so, but we better wait until after the holidays to tell the family."

What Trey failed to appreciate that night is that Sunnie had a pair of red-hot panties of her own. They had just been hidden in the back of her closet, while she spent her time caring for a fifty-two-year old little boy.

☪

Americo Rios is a well-connected man in Sedona and he had heard rumors about the mysterious wife of a Mexican government official. After having verified that Graciela Ybarra was in the bar at Enchantment Resort, Americo made a room reservation for the weekend. Americo cleverly disconnected some wiring and told Ignacio that long overdue repairs needed on his house would begin the next week, thus disguising the reason he would be staying at the resort.

On the drive from Prescott, Americo made a plan to trap the woman who had tried to trap him. The old woman in the court-room had been a clue and when he saw a small corner of the miss-ing pink silk scarf carelessly showing from her tattered shoulder bag, he made some connections. In spite of the humor he had found in the first message, the messages delivered to him by Ignacio had irritated Americo. Rita's warning of false messengers became clear as Americo recalled the consistency of Ignacio's twisted words. Years of friendship were shattered when Americo realized he had been manipulated for months.

Americo dressed with design, a design to trap a trapper. Characteristically Americo detested wearing dress suits, but tonight he planned to stalk in disguise. In the candlelight, clasp-ing his gold and tiger-eye cufflinks, Americo noticed the container was missing. The container was small, silver, and it was gone from the table in his living room. The container held the hair Lauren had given Americo at the airport thirty years ago. In his anger, Americo had taken it out of his pocket and placed it indifferently on the table and could not recall the last time he noticed it. Having been told by Sunnie of Lauren's persistent nightmares and the smell of burning hair, another connection was made. Only three people had a key to his home, Trey, Lauren, and Ignacio.

Hair is not a symbol of a person, for it contains their entire dna structure. It is the person in microcosm and if fallen into evil hands, hair can be a forceful tool used against them. Black magic, properly executed by using hair can cause the victim to experience through their senses, dreams, or sudden visions, the perception the magician desires.

Americo packed a small bag and prepared to leave the house. With a flashlight in his hand, he stopped at the picture wall. Pictures of Lauren taken throughout her childhood inspired

Americo. He kissed his finger and rested it on his favorite. Feeling confident and alive for the first time in months, Americo said to the mirror hanging in the entrance, "Lauren, Baby, I'm going Witch hunting tonight." Thirty minutes later, Americo swaggered into the bar at Enchantment Resort. With his gray streaked hair in a smooth ponytail, wearing a suit and tie, he looked elegant, royal, and desirable.

Graciela Ybarra smiled at her good fortune. Americo Rios was alone, in need of company. Much later while pouring wine into her glass, Americo sincerely told her of a long time passion. "I look forward to meeting your husband, Graciela. I've become interested in politics and want to contribute to new legislation regarding the dreadful situation that divides our countries at the border."

Touching his arm with familiarity, Graciela suggested they keep in touch.

Taking her hand in his, Americo kissed it, checking closely for familiar marks. "That would be wonderful, follow me to my room and I'll write down your address and phone number in Mexico. I plan to visit a private home near your residence as soon as I help a friend solve a problem." With his arm over her shoulder, Americo held her too close for casual acquaintance. Feeling her body yield, he knew his trap would work. Americo's voice, naturally resonant, was intimate with promise. "Graciela, I most certainly don't want to lose track of you."

☪★

Lovingly, as Lauren sat at her Grandmother's feet, Rita brushed her hair. Women know how to comfort one another in many ways and a good Grandma, who happens to be a Witch, knows the best ways of all. Slowly Rita stroked Lauren's hair, feeling the heavy energy release from Lauren's body. The energy gathered, forming a halo before spiraling into the cosmos, taking food to the stars. The background music from the radio was felt not heard. The music was soft, it lulled her and as she drifted into trance, Lauren saw Wyatt. Missing him, Lauren held her fingerss towards his image. She smiled as she saw him sitting in his plane, relaxing with a martini, and smoking a cigar. By the gentle look on his face, she knew his thoughts were of her.

Lauren saw a bird spiraling through the air as if in a death dive.

The cat knocked a pottery bowl to the tile floor in the kitchen, shattering.

Lauren sighed, not wanting to leave her trance.

Lauren smelled smoke, believing it the same she had smelled often over the past months.

Rita's gentle strokes relieved her panic.

Wyatt returned to her vision. Looking up from his papers, he spoke to her. "Precious, I probably won't make it back until later, it seems I have something to do. Witchy, don't worry, I'll still take care of you."

A tear rolled down Lauren's cheek. Lauren's trance was interrupted when she heard the unexpected voice on the radio. "This is breaking news. The private jet carrying Wyatt Kirkman, a well-known real estate tycoon from Atlanta, Georgia, has crashed. There are no survivors."

Lauren couldn't scream.

☾★

Lauren didn't pray, and she didn't cry. Rather, Lauren got drunk, alone. Facing her loss with courage, she waited to get drunk until after Rita retired to her bed. First, before she could grieve, the potbelly stove needed wood and the cats needed fed. She swept the broken shards from the mixing bowl, and then Lauren needed a shower. Wanting to remove all distractions, Lauren moved robotically as if her life force had gone with Wyatt. She felt bitterly frozen, unable to feel the heat of her body. She dressed in her flannel pajama bottoms and a heavy sweater. She saw a pack of Wyatt's cigarettes in her satchel and lit one, sitting by the window in her room, blowing the smoke to a star.

Numbly Lauren opened a bottle of chilled Absolute Vodka. A small crystal goblet caught her eye. The crystal looked molten as the translucent heavy crystal captured the light. She saw colors of the rainbow and light diffracting from one surface plane to another. It held two shots of vodka, and Lauren started to drink. Her love caught the light. "Wyatt, that's love. The light captured in the crystal is my love for you and believe me; you got the best of me. Maybe I just didn't see the light."

With shadows of skeins of yarn bowing over her, Lauren sat on the floor in front of the fireplace and started to cry. "Wyatt, if I had asked you to stay tonight, would you? It would have saved your life."

Wyatt answered Lauren. "Witchy, I had an appointment and I know you understand what I'm talking about."

Lauren leaned back on the floor, resting her legs on her grandfather's chair. Patterns of behavior became clear as she felt the presence of her son. Closing her eyes, she saw his face and felt his hands resting on her sloped forehead, giving her a transmission of awareness. She smiled softly. "I'm going to miss him so much, TJ. After you left me, I started leaving everything behind. I couldn't help it; I needed to keep waiting for you. As soon as love blossomed or an opportunity got too close, I walked away so I could feel the waiting. I left home, I left your Daddy, I left Wyatt; I left everything that really mattered to me behind."

TJ's fingers stroked her broad cheekbones, wiping away the tears. "That's how you kept me close to you, Mom. You were never alone."

Hearing her son's words Lauren recalled the many ways she had honored his few breaths of life. For thirty years, her body had failed to release the blood from her womb in January, the month of his birth. Lauren had lived in a state of expectancy, always fearing fruition. The shock to her psyche had been so profound it set up a lifetime pattern of perpetual grief. Having never grieved openly or discussed her loss with friends or family, Lauren's body and emotions responded for her, usually without her awareness. As if punishing herself, she put herself in situations and relationships she knew would end, thus allowing her to experience repeatedly the loss of her child. Had she grieved properly, a lifetime of feeling numb, intense rage, hopelessness, vulnerability, shame, and remorse would have been processed, saving her from a perpetual state of feeling fullness and loss, over and over.

To become unattached to belongings, people, and desires, is often considered a state of enlightenment. Living in nonattachment is liberating; it sets you free from the fear of loss. However, Lauren had lost the gift of relationship. Having experienced the most profound relationship of a baby inside her body, to Lauren, relationship meant loss. Her mother had diminished Lauren's loss causing Lauren to doubt the worthiness of her pain, and she thereby continued the pattern of not feeling worthy to grieve. At seventeen, pregnant, afraid, and alone, she made the bad bargain of keeping a secret, the most potent numbing agent of all.

TJ had lived every moment of the journey with Lauren. "Mom, remember what you said when you asked yourself the question."

Lauren remembered the question and her answer. Looking at America's picture taped on the mirror in her bedroom, she had asked herself if she could go back, would she change anything. Her answer had been, no.

Her glass was empty and Lauren needed to feel full. Sipping the icy, viscous vodka, Lauren felt it warm her core, the place her body had earlier refused to open. She felt a slow teasing opening as the swaying, circular motion of the Vortex started to rock her into gentle ecstasy. Lauren took the bottle in one hand, the glass and Wyatt's cigarettes in the other, and went into the backyard to take a star bath. A bright light guided her eyes, extending an invitation, asking her to stand under the stars and dance. Holding the full glass of vodka to the light, she curtsied and accepted the invitation. Drinking the vodka in one swallow, she felt a hand connecting her hand to another's. The hand she felt was America's and with tears that matched the crystal glass, Lauren swayed serpentine to the music vibrating from a very brilliant star.

Lauren laughed with all of her heart as she stopped to honor the column of light standing slightly to the side. With love and respect for the life she led, in spite of the cold December night, Lauren slowly shed one article of clothing at a time and danced nude under a shower of starlight. With her fingers wiggling to the stars, Lauren offered her acceptance of loss and destiny.

"Wyatt, my love, I'll always dance for you, but I have to go to the dance with America."

Ecstatic, Lauren twirled with her arms open wide, her wavy hair flying, and her green eyes full of light. Closing her eyes, she became dizzy, laughing, spinning, and acting delightfully foolish. She had an idea. "I wonder if I can still do it? Hmm. Why not?" Lauren stood still, stretched her arms once again to the sky, took six quick steps and tumbled forward, doing a perfect somersault. Thrilled, she did it again, tumbling in the reverse direction. Lauren was always the fool. Landing flat on her butt, Lauren giggled when she felt the scrapes on her elbows and fanny. "If you can still do one perfect somersault, landing on your butt really isn't so bad." Lauren spun. And as she spun, she called into the night for Wyatt. "Spin it, Wyatt. Spin it around and come back fast, we need you in this crazy world."

C☆

Payback time. When the light beckoned, Lauren had a hangover. She had slept hard and been awakened by her own snoring in the middle of the night. Still wrapped in the ecstasy of her midnight release, Lauren pulled the hand stitched quilt over her head, hugged her pillow and fell deep into dreamless, cathartic sleep. The catharsis opened Lauren and she needed to talk to someone. Lauren didn't need a shoulder to cry on, but she did need to share her grief.

Still hung over, Lauren sat in her car as the reality of Wyatt's passing swept into her body with the short, sure sweeps of a cosmic broom. The broom brushed the cobwebs from her memory, reached deep into the corners of her emotions and with gentle circular sweeps, opened her heart. While waiting, she saw the look in his eyes when he said goodbye. She also recognized that the way Wyatt looked at her was different than anybody else in her life. In her clarity, she also became aware that Wyatt had seen something in her that nobody else had recognized. It had not been merely the way he looked at her, but what he saw within her.

Lauren hugged herself and smiled with contentment and courage. Savoring a few moments for herself, she looked at her reflection in the rearview mirror, seeing a woman's face showing the experiences of her life in the deepening lines around her eyes. She grinned at herself, wondering what her life would be like a year from now.

Expectantly Lauren rang the bell. When Trey abruptly opened the door he was wild-eyed with anger. Sunnie stood in the background in her robe, crying. Neither had slept. Breakup sex had turned into a long night of accusations and bitterness.

Lauren had not expected to enter the den of domestic nonbliss.

"Yeah, Dad called this morning and told us about the old guy. Tough break, Brat."

Stunned, Lauren turned to Sunnie.

Witnessing the hurt on Lauren's face, Sunnie screamed, "Trey, you're an asshole. You never listen to anybody. You're selfish and I wish I hadn't wasted my life believing I was married to a decent man, because you aren't one."

A lifetime of friendship rescued both women from Trey's verbal assault. Sunnie hurried to Lauren, putting her arms around her. "Lauren, how much more heartbreak can you stand?"

Trey yelled at them both. "Sunnie, quit boobing Lauren, going to jail would probably do her good. What's your problem, Lauren? You bring all this shit on yourself. You've never done anything right in your life. What's the big deal? He was just one in a long line of lovers. So you lose one, find another. That's what you always do anyway."

Lauren's lips quivered when a familiar feeling of failing her family stormed through her body. Looking at her brother, having never acknowledged that Trey was selfish, Lauren turned to Sunnie. "You're right Sunnie; he is a selfish asshole. Why don't you go riding with Lydia and me this afternoon, we need some girl time and you need to get away from my brother."

Infuriated that Lauren was comforting Sunnie, Trey yelled again. "Who in the hell's going to get the horse trailer ready for you? It won't be me."

Lauren stopped and looked Trey in the eye. "I'll ask Americo to do it."

Trey got in her face and laughed viciously. "Fat chance, sister. He wouldn't do a thing for you after you tried to kill him."

Lauren laughed in his face with tears in her eyes. "Spin it Trey, if you've got the balls."

Trey was livid. "Fuck you, you've never done anything but embarrass me."

C☪

The brown leather bound journal in Americo's hands had not been written in for six days. He stared at the empty page with a pen in his hand, wondering why he couldn't write. The whine of Lauren's car caught his attention and Americo waved spontaneously, surprised that she had already slowed. Lauren took the time to brush her hair and freshen her lipstick and before taking the first step on his path, she offered him a shy smile. Americo could hear the "flip flop" of her sandals on the lavender-lined brick path to his house, and when Lauren stopped to touch one of the remaining sunflower skeletons growing wild among the lavender, she smiled remembering the list of flowers she made for him to plant in his yard. Americo, believing this was the answer to the message he sent to her, felt the stirring of familiar desire when he saw her long suntanned legs below the pair of red plaid shorts. He stood to greet her at the top of the steps. "This is a surprise, Lauren, I'm sorry about Wyatt; I know your loss is enormous."

Surprised by his tenderness, Lauren opened up to Americo. "Loss seems to be my karma, doesn't it?"

"Lauren, don't."

She smiled. "It's OK, Jugador. I just have to learn to deal with my losses." Lauren had a funny thought, looked up at America and giggled. "Or, maybe I better plan on losing the things I deal with. What do you think?"

America laughed, motioning her to sit down on the step, then ruffled her hair with affection as he sat down beside her. "I think you're a funny, spinning nutcase, Bruja. Do you want a cup of coffee?"

"Just a sip."

America laughed, and remembering her propensity for eating food off of other people's plates, he offered her his cigarette.

Lauren crinkled her nose in disgust. "No thanks, I have a hangover. I got drunk last night and spun my wheels." Lauren walked to the copper panel on his front door and gently ran her fingers over the engraving she made over twenty years before. "I'm sorry, America, I shouldn't have been a bad Witch in court."

"De nada, you've been bewitching me in some way or another all of your life."

"Sunnie and Trey are having problems. The perfect couple with the perfect life..." Lauren's expression became wistful.

"I know, you're brother is one stupid son of a bitch."

"I stopped by their house a few minutes ago, and I couldn't believe the yelling and screaming. Sunnie was in her robe and it looked like she had been up all night. Trey was livid and said some horrible things to me and about Wyatt."

"Yeah, Trey seems to think he's missed something, but he has no idea how much he'll miss what he has now. I told him you and I came this close," America held his fingers together, "to having a chance and he flipped it off, saying our affair was brief and meaningless."

"I guess none of us escapes our turn in the barrel, do we?"

"Certainly not us, Princess."

Rubbing the whiskers on his face, America wondered if he should tell Lauren about his plan. He sensed an underlying nervousness in her demeanor, and knowing Lauren hated to speak in front of a crowd, he assumed her upcoming testimony was the cause. Silently America offered her another sip of coffee, watching his cat crawl onto Lauren's lap. Lauren cooed at the cat, making silly faces, then turned suddenly to America, blurting a question. "When are you getting married?"

"Lauren, don't."

Lauren blushed furiously, hating herself. "Oops, just curious."

Americo didn't want to tell her yet that he had no intention of
marrying Alexandra. "There are no plans."

"Lydia, Sunnie, and I want to go riding a little later. Can we
use the trailer?"

"Sure, where are you going?"

"Long Canyon."

"Wish I could go...but I have an appointment."

Americo couldn't tell her where or with whom.

"Tell me what time and I'll have the horses saddled and
loaded for you."

Lauren relaxed and felt hopeful that their friendship would
survive.

Lauren took the cigarette from his hand, their fingers touching, neither wanting to move.

She took the next step. "I didn't do it, Americo. I didn't try to
kill you."

Americo waited. "It doesn't matter if you did it, Princess, I..."
He stopped.

Tears started to form. "You don't believe me, do you?"

"No."

"That just kills me, I never thought this would happen."

Americo walked Lauren to the car and opened the door. When
she started to sit down, he pulled her up and put his hands on her
shoulders. Lauren hung her head, fearing she would cry if she saw
his twinkling eyes. "Lauren, it's not over until he says it is. Didn't
a very wise person tell me that?"

Emotionally spent, Lauren laughed wistfully. "I thought it
wasn't over until some crazy Witch tells a secret and then hits the
mans she loves over the head with a broom."

Americo shut the door of her car, leaving his handprint on the
window as if touching her face once again. "See ya at the barn at
noon."

☪

Sly and devilish, Ignacio let no activity on the rancho escape
his watch. Having seen Lauren and Americo standing by her car,
he suspiciously wondered why two adversaries seemed friendly,
almost affectionate. Calculating how he could find out from
Americo why he had been talking to Lauren, Ignacio met up with
Americo at the stable.

Americo was ready, having already set the bait with Graciela the previous night at Enchantment Resort.

"Amigo, did you sleep in this morning? I brought some coffee, but you weren't here." Ignacio already knew of Americo's night with Graciela.

Americo licked his lips and yawned, exaggerating his satisfaction.

Ignacio took the bait, adding his own trap. He grinned lewdly, slapping Americo on the shoulder. "Big night with your beautiful intended?"

Americo looked around as if being overheard. "Keep your mouth shut, Ignacio. I think I've met the woman of my dreams." Americo rolled his eyes, suggesting more.

"Ohhh. Tell me more."

"I didn't plan for it to happen, but I had a fascinating conversation with the most enchanting woman I've ever met." Americo shook his head in mock guilt. "I've betrayed Alexandra, but she doesn't have to know about it yet."

Ignacio wanted to know the level of Americo's interest in Graciela, the plan he made having taken a turn for the better. "Do you plan to see this woman again?"

"Sadly, she's married." Americo shrugged his shoulders, as if martyred.

Ignacio stepped in with honor. "You be careful, men can be dangerous if you sleep with their wives."

Timing is everything when trapping a devil. "Oh, I didn't make love to her, but I'm going to soon. I can't help it my friend, I have a calling to conquer this woman and make her submit to   all of my desires."

The night before in his room at the Enchantment Resort, Americo teased Graciela, taunted her with his affections, acted remorseful for almost violating the honor of a married woman, offered to apologize to her husband, promised his undying love and begged forgiveness for his weakness. With his extraordinary skills, he kissed and caressed her body, whispering that he was helpless in her presence. He even cried a bit, swearing he would do anything to have her in his bed once she was free.

Ignacio lit a cigarette, wondering how to bring Lauren into the conversation.

Americo was ready. "I had an interesting visit this morning from that little hot box Lauren."

Ignacio grinned, his yellow tobacco stained teeth seeming ready to bite.

Americo had the look of a man who had been rode hard and running his fingers through his uncombed hair, he leaned against the fence, trying to appear casual. "She made me an offer of that delicious body of hers, as if I'm still interested. She seems to think her problems are about over."

"Ms. Lauren tried to kill you, Americo. How dare she?"

"That cunning Witch would do anything."

Ignacio heard bitch.

Americo ground his cigarette angrily with the toe of his boot. Spitting on the ground, fire came to his eyes. Americo used his hands to describe the scene in pictures he wanted Ignacio to see. "Ignacio, I missed a perfect moment. I had my hands around her neck, telling her that her problems aren't over until somebody else says they are, and all I wanted to do was put my arms around her and crush her until I felt her crack wide open."

Ignacio saw the picture. He saw Lauren's ribs crushed as she gasped her last breath.

Americo tightened the claws on the trap. "She thinks that hole between her legs is lined with gold, but let me tell you something my friend, to me it's lined with silver just like the moon."

Ignacio tested the water. "Maybe you'll find gold with your new lady."

Americo smiled suggestively, arching his brow, looking askance at Ignacio. "I'm sure I will, but perhaps it will be rose gold." Seeming to ponder, Americo spoke deliberately as if making a plan. Without expression, he looked at the ground as he confessed. "Ignacio, I'm afraid that one day before too long, I'm going find a good soft rope and tie it around Lauren until she screams for mercy. The deep dark feelings I have for her are about to explode, and by God, she'll get the best of it. When she screams for mercy, I'll take my match and light her hair on fire. You know that's the only way to kill a Witch."

Ignacio grinned in full agreement, smelling Lauren's hair flame and smoke. "She's never been anything but heartache for you." Ignacio couldn't read Americo's thoughts.

"No, my enemy, you are wrong. My heart aches for everything she's been through."

☪

Lauren swore, kicking the spare tire as she struggled with the latch on America's horse trailer. A friend of Lauren's, a knight, a handsome, young cowboy knight came to her rescue. Flirting outrageously, Lauren smiled sweetly and batted her eyes at the obviously smitten man. She drawled charmingly, patted his cheek, and enjoying his admiration she looked into his bright blue eyes and thanked him for rescuing three damsels in distress. Lauren felt frisky and desirable. "Well maybe I've still got it, or, maybe it was the red boots."

Sunnie couldn't laugh, but she sighed at the incorrigible Lauren. "You just have a thing for cowboys."

Lauren stopped her horse. "You'll be fine, Sunnie, whatever happens to you and Trey. Hell, we'll just have an all girl's club at the rancho, you can move in with me and Grandma and let that stupid ass brother of mine find out what he's missing."

The pain was too fresh and Sunnie wanted to ride in silence. Everywhere she looked, there were reminders of camping trips, horseback rides, walks in the middle of the night, and making love by the creek. The sun dappled trail narrowed, intensifying Sunnie's feelings, compressing the past into the present as she rode solo on her journey, wondering what lurked in her future, with deep memories of her young womanhood in front of her. Memories of Trey and America were in Sunnie's thoughts as she saw them riding ahead on their horses, slowly picking their way deep into the canyon for a sleepover under the stars, making certain the path was safe for her and Lauren to follow. As Sunnie slowed, she recalled Lauren dancing in ecstasy around the fire late in the night to the sounds of coyotes howling in the distance. Blinking back the tears, Sunnie recalled how treasured and secure she felt knowing Trey had been there to protect her. The thought of America alone, starring into the deep sky, taking a magical flight into the unknown, reminded Sunnie that America had always seemed to journey solo.

Waiting under a tree, with lacy light weaving through the branches blanketing her hair, Lydia broke the silence. "I've made a decision to move to Sedona."

"Guess the Vortex finally gotcha, Lyd."

"Oh, Lauren."

Suddenly, Sunnie made a decision. "I'm going to sell my school and move to Hawaii. I'm going to do something I've always wanted to do and couldn't because of Trey."

Lauren's light went on. "I know what I'm going to do when I get out of jail."

Lydia sighed, shaking her finger at Lauren for giving up.

"I'm going to go to the "Best Friends Animal Sanctuary" in Utah and do volunteer work."

The sight of three tired women, stretching on an outcropping of red, is an invitation for the Goddess of sleep to join them in sweet repose. A nap descends sweetly when the red rocks are warm, the sunlight is filtered, and precious melancholy envelops your heart.

Lauren woke first, feeling revived. She peeked at the others, wanting to further enjoy a delicious banquet of time with friends, a red rock guardian, a small fairy circle of sapling trees, the scent of composting leaves, and delicate branches casting flickering light over her body.

Sunnie woke up from her nap, angered by the bad investment she made. "I'm so pissed that I wasted my life on your jackass brother."

Lauren agreed. "I'm pissed that I wasted my life by not coming home, marrying Americo, and having ten kids."

Lydia woke up and smiled. "I'm pissed because I kept my practice in Tucson and didn't marry Jake."

Laughing and crying, Sunnie spotted a group of hikers meandering peacefully down the trail. "I know, let's howl and show them what crazy, spinning women really do in the wild." Three women in full agreement that some time in their lives had not been spent wisely, decided to howl.

The hikers stopped. A man with two women looked stupidly at the crazy women howling at nothing but their lives. The man called to them. "Hey ladies, is there anything pretty to see if we keep walking down this trail?"

Lauren became hysterical, jumping up and down and laughing with tears running down her face. Sunnie and Lydia joined her, laughing at the absurdity of the question. Lydia regained her composure first.

"No Sir, if I were you I'd turn back now before it's too late."

Waving her arm over the horizon, she shook her head. "There's nothing pretty around here at all. That's why we stopped to howl."

Lauren, Sunnie, and Lydia laughed, cried, and then got on their horses, knowing that everything in their lives, regardless of their circumstances, would work out perfectly in a very pretty spinning place.

☪

Alone in his room at the Enchantment Resort the next night, having further set the trap for Graciela by inviting her to accompany him and Alexandra to court, Americo pulled a letter from his pant's pocket.

Americo's charm had served him well. Graciela believed that he wanted her by his side when a woman who had betrayed him testified in court. With skill he had persuaded her that he needed her presence, adding that his fiancée, whom he was about to leave, would be a good cover. He told her they would sit together and listen while Lauren strangled herself with her own deceptive words. Smiling to himself, he read the letter written to him almost thirty years before.

> *Dear Americo,*
> *Guess what, you've got a girlfriend, me.*
> *Please don't ever, ever, ever, ever, ever give up*
> on us.
> *I really, really, really mean this so much it*
> makes me shiver.

Holding the letter to his chest, Americo slept, knowing his trap had been set, his enemies would become careless, and that he would never, ever give up on Lauren.

☪

A man and woman, safe in the belly of Cathedral Rock, cast a watchful eye as the gentle blanket of darkness covered El Rancho de las Estrellas. As the reflected glory of the sun beckoned, Lauren peered through the rose-colored window coverings in her bedroom and exhaled. Touching the cool damp panes with her fingers she then sent a prayer, resting her fingertips on her lips. Transformed to pink by the window covering, silvery moonlight woven through the fabric softly blanketed Lauren with hope and courage. Lauren yawned, reached to turn out the bedside light and without warning or reason, Lauren shivered.

A messenger came to Lauren on Monday. A mushroom quiche Lauren whipped up for an early lunch with Rita was ready to take from the oven. When Lauren reached into the oven, she heard the doorbell ring. Lauren had been expecting the flowers, but she hadn't expected a messenger. When they renewed their affair, Wyatt had confessed that he had periodically sent flowers anonymously over the years. Recently, he had flowers delivered weekly to her door. Lauren tipped the delivery girl and remembered the envelope Wyatt handed her when he left Sedona. The envelope had remained in her satchel, forgotten by the tragedy. When Lauren opened the masculine, richly textured envelope she saw a small red felt jewelers bag. First, Lauren read the scrawled note written on the outside of the envelope.

> *Witchy,*
> *I want to see this ring on your finger when we*
> *go to court on Tuesday.*
> *Wyatt*

Lauren's hands shook as she unfolded the letter, dated ten years ago.

> *My Dearest Scarlet,*
> *Mother passed away last week and you have*
> *been on my mind even more than usual. I'll never*
> *forget how happy you were as you helped Mother*
> *till her garden.*
> *Lauren, I wish I could give you this ring in*
> *person, but I'll respect your wishes for as long as I*
> *can. This is my mother's wedding ring and I want*
> *you to have it. She loved you very much and missed*
> *your company after you left us.*
> *I don't know if I ever told you this, so I will at*
> *this time. Precious, when I looked into your eyes, I*
> *saw the same qualities I feel in my soul. I saw the*
> *fire, the passion, the courage, and the dream. Not*
> *only did I love you more than I could have ever told*
> *you, I respected your will, honesty, and tenacity. I*
> *know these attributes will have served you well in*

*your life. I've missed you terribly and will love you
always.*

*Lauren, please wear the ring for me and for
what we shared. I've never doubted that you loved
me, as I love you. I still don't understand, yet now
that I write the words, I think I do.*

*With all my love, Wyatt*

The gold ring was exceptionally small. Having been worn for
sixty years by a woman who had accepted and loved Lauren, the
gold was now thin and fragile. Warmed by the transmission of
Wyatt's love for her, Lauren held the ring to the light. Feeling the
warmth of sunrays filtering through the channel, Lauren slipped
the ring on her little finger.

☪

Good wishes were not sent to Lauren by everybody the night
before her trial. Two people were plotting to deny Lauren of her
energy and power, and the only reasons were jealousy and
revenge.

Above all, Marquita Pena hated her because she believed it
was because of Lauren that Americo forced her to abort the one
pregnancy of her life. Marquita believed that without Lauren's
presence, Americo would return, just as he left her when he gave
Lauren the garnet engagement ring. For months the powerful sorceress had inverted her skills and used them as a black magician
against Lauren. Lauren had been tormented by her dreams, the
smell of burning hair, flashes of light, sudden panic attacks, and
uncharacteristic emotional responses. For many months Lauren
woke in the night, believing that somebody was trying to strangle
her.

Ignacio and his sister Marquita, cleverly disguised as
Graciela Ybarra, were trying to strangle Lauren. They were trying
to strangle her with her own pink silk scarf that Ignacio had
retrieved from the lane leading away from the Casino. They were
also using Lauren's hair that was stolen from Americo's home.

In the world of witchcraft a person's belongings are believed
to carry their energy. A skilled bruja knows how to effectively connect with the owner, thus making the item a conduit to manipu-
late the energy of the subject. One must never underestimate the

power of another, especially another whose motivation is hate.

Although skilled in the management of energy, Lauren neglected to protect herself by shielding, blocking, returning, or breaking the energy connection. Lauren was vulnerable.

In ceremony, the two plotted. In the small room behind the kitchen in Graciela's rental home, the two affirmed their connection to Lauren and Americo, knowing that tomorrow was Lauren's only opportunity to contribute to her defense.

A symbol, as in a word or a flag, stands in place of a concept, person, or thing. A sign points the way, referring forward and backward, to the signifiers and signified. In witchcraft, a doll is not a symbol, it is a container of the victim's essence and is much more powerful.

As containers for Americo and Lauren, Ignacio and Graciela made small dolls that are often used by practitioners of magic. The hair of the dolls was made from hair collected and stolen from their victims. To insure the correctness of the context, Graciela then created a connection between Lauren and Americo with a gold thread.

Viciously Ignacio cut the thread, burning it over a candle, believing it could never be reconnected. "Puta. Whore."

Maliciously, Marquita spit on the photograph taken of Lauren in the garden. Cutting the picture in small pieces, one by one she cast them into the fire. "Lauren, you are so sweet and so funny; you make him laugh, and make him cry. You didn't give him a baby, but you did give him heartache. Now you will lose him and your freedom. He loves me now, not you. He felt my body, caressed my face, and he kissed me with his tongue. Soon, Americo will be mine again, even if calls me Graciela."

The stolen scarf was held over the smoke. Marquita chanted her intent into the silk threads where Lauren had lovingly painted a watercolor rendering of Cathedral Rock. After wrapping the doll symbolizing Lauren in the scarf, Ignacio sneered and with his hand squeezed the doll as hard as he could.

Lauren gasped for air, grabbing her chest.

Pain shot through Americo's chest.

Laughing wickedly, Marquita tied a black string around the neck of the now crushed doll. Dangling it from her fingers like a puppeteer, Marquita spit on it again. The doll was now pitiful, damaged, powerless, and at their mercy.

Lauren cried out, tossing and turning from a dream of being strangled.

Americo sat up in bed, his throat parched and burning.

As Ignacio, with pure hatred in his heart, threw the doll that contained Americo's energy into the fireplace, Americo woke up.

A warrior had returned. Instant clarity allowed him to see. He became calm and calculating. Every move had to be precisely planned, yet remain fluid enough to change in an instant. His disguise was established, his intent was strong, and the man in love with Lauren was ready to go into battle. He returned to sleep, knowing he was prepared.

Lauren sighed, rolled over in her bed and dreamed of a handsome, dark haired prince riding a spotted horse...

☪

The wrapping of a package often does more for the person doing so than it does for the recipient. The first morning of her testimony, Lauren was adamant that her package would accomplish both purposes. Red tights were stretched over Lauren's long legs and as she stepped into black, strappy, do me, heels, Lauren smiled in the mirror checking out the view from the rear. "The jurors think I'm nothing but a disturbed tramp, well, let them see this prize." Lauren had been painted black and in full agreement, she decided to give them what they wanted to see. The jurors expected to see black, but they were about to get red-hot red. An expert at adding just the right touch, Lauren decided to put the scarlet letter on herself, boldly.

Years of experience had taught Lydia that in order to win a case, the defendant should appear conservative and contrite, yet confident. When Lydia picked Lauren up to drive to Prescott, she was shocked by Lauren's chosen costume. Admonishing her severely, Lydia pleaded with Lauren to go back into her room and tone the look down just a bit. Offering Lydia a brief false reprieve, Lauren defiantly reached into the back of her closet and adorned herself with a vintage, red fringed, silk shawl that she discovered in a flea market in the south of France. Lauren knew without question, that a well-compensated woman, working in an expensive bordello a century ago, had worn the shawl.

The people in the gallery were stunned by Lauren's beauty as she stood unselfconsciously gazing at the spectators, surveying the faces, and absorbing the mood. Not a person could tell if she looked like a fresh faced country girl, a professor, a vixen, an international sophisticate, or an exotic artist. It just depended on the perspective of the viewer. Lauren knew the power of the gaze. Raising her black horn rim glasses, Lauren crinkled her freckled nose as if sharing a secret with a good friend. Aware of people staring boldly at her, she scanned the room, nodding politely to familiar faces with just a trace of undisguised disdain directed at former friends and classmates. It was when she leaned over to look at some notes that the audience realized her black miniskirt was a bit too short.

Her chin length hair curled softly around her face, with just enough unruly natural waves to perhaps look like she stepped out of somebody's bed, not a beauty parlor. Her lips were stained with wine-colored lipstick, not too much, but enough to make some of the people watching think she had been properly kissed the night before. Magic.

With her miniature altar in place, Lauren felt confident, peaceful, and ready. Support sent by a messenger and the friendly encounter with Americo had fed her belief that by disclosing her secret, she would gain her freedom. Just as she turned to ask Lydia a question, Americo Rios walked into the room. With an expectant look on her face, Lauren smiled at Americo, believing she would receive a warm greeting in return.

Arrogantly Americo looked past Lauren, accepting nods of greeting as if he were the center of attention. Dressed properly for an elegant dinner party, he looked smug, cocky, and loaded with machismo. As a knowing look passed between Americo and Tim Richmond, he licked his lips and gallantly held the door for the women he had driven to court. Lauren had become part of the trap. Her feelings were hurt, and she started loading her pointed, sharp tongue with pretty, silver bullets.

Alexandra Kingston arrived looking like the fool. Unfortunately, dressed in jeans, a floppy brimmed hat and an expensive jade green, wool sweater; Alex had tried to copy Lauren's style. However, the critical, fatal mistake she made was wearing red cowgirl boots. The style, although not exclusive to Lauren, was a package that did not fit the woman.

Graciela clung to Americo's arm as if needing assistance. Her chic, beige suit accentuated the warm olive of her complexion and her richly black, shiny hair softly framed her face. The gold chain bracelet created by Lauren was on her wrist and in the charm that also served as a small container, was the remainder of Lauren's hair.

Lauren and Lydia put their heads together for a last minute conference. Lydia patted Lauren's hand reassuringly, wondering why Lauren had paled. "You don't have to do this."

Lauren had already loaded her tongue and was ready to roll. Looking defiant and determined, Lauren gave Lydia a warning. "All I want you to do is open the doors I told you about, and let me take it from there. Tim Richmond has portrayed me as having hot pants and I'll tell you, by the time I get through, the jury is going to think I'm the hottest stuff in town." Lauren feigned a chill, wrapped herself in the red silk shawl and took center stage.

Americo Rios watched Lauren walk across the room with her graceful dancers stride. He also noticed that she crossed her feet, knowing she was canceling out any commitment she made to the court, God, and the bible. Oh, the mistake the fathers make when they use a bible, not a cauldron, when swearing in a high-flying Witch. Although well disguised, his attraction to Lauren couldn't be ignored. "What is it about Lauren? There are many other women who are more beautiful. Her legs are a tad too long, her shoulders a little too broad, her eyes are a more deep set than I like, and her hair is always unruly. She chews her fingernails and sits with her toes together. I don't get it." Lauren turned to the side, looking at the judge with open contempt. Americo smiled at her audacity. "She's a dangerous beauty, so feline in her mystery, so deer-like in her demeanor."

Lauren caught the look on his face and knew she had accomplished her mission. At this time in her life, Lauren was learning the value of stalking and she was learning her lessons very well.

☪

The judge and jurors were stunned as Lydia opened the first door. They had been expecting to be led into the story less abruptly. Although Lauren had a full bag of tricks, she knew to remain flexible and had not yet decided on her responses. She had several disadvantages already; she was on center stage and could not watch from behind the scene.

Lydia opened the door. "Lauren, do you and Mr. Rios own joint real estate holdings?"

Lauren smirked at Americo. "We did, but he bought my share from me. He managed money like a big brother would, and he's very, very good at taking advantage of opportunities."

"Do you admit to having a twenty-five-year long love affair with Mr. Rios?"

Trey turned to Sunnie. "Did you know about that?" Sunnie stared at Lauren, totally shocked that she had over-looked the obvious. Trey mumbled, "Lauren's been crazy since she was a kid, I wonder what in the hell else she'll say to embarrass the family." Sunnie wondered if he should be passing judgment.

Lauren calmly removed her glasses and looked at the jurors as though explaining an abstract concept. "I wouldn't exactly call it an affair. A love affair generally means something. I'd call it a twenty-five-year long occasional tumble, a fling, an interlude."

Alexandra's hand flew to her mouth. Like everybody else, she had been unaware of the length of the affair.

Americo smirked back, provoking Lauren.

"I see. But, you do admit to having a sexual relationship with him even during your first marriage, am I correct?"

Lauren flipped her wrist as if to dismiss the importance of the issue. Arrogantly, she added more for emphasis. "I had sex with him during both of my marriages and all of my real affairs. However, our fling is over."

"Lauren, why did you continue the fling, as you call it, for so long?"

Lauren paused, squinted her eyes as if trying to come up with an answer. "It was the sex." Lauren paused. "It was also comic relief."

There was an extraordinary shifting of butts in the court-room, particularly Trey's.

"What kind of relationship do you have with Mr. Rios at this time?"

"We're engaged in a war."

Americo got it.

Lydia played the game by Lauren's rules. "I see, the parting was not amicable, I take it."

"It was necessary for survival."

Graciela gently patted Americo's arm, agreeing completely.

Alexandra felt assaulted from all directions, became confused and disoriented.

"Did you give him numerous gifts during your relationship, expensive rugs, crystal vases, and pieces of jewelry you created?"

Lauren looked directly at Americo and sent a silver bullet. "Yes, he earned them."

Americo laughed smugly, looking appropriately embarrassed afterwards.

"Why did you insist on keeping the relationship a secret?"

Lauren went for the heart, his laugh had infuriated her and

she had a sword of her own. Chuckling at her command of the moment, she thrust the sword. "I didn't think it was important enough to talk about, I mean, really. After all, whom would I tell? Most of the time it was only a few days a year, no big deal, considering my other deals. Like I said, it was a joke on life, a caper."

Lydia became nervous. "Let me get this clear, you didn't love Mr. Rios?"

Lauren knows how to dance; after all, she's had a lot of lessons and years of practice.

"I don't believe in love, unless you're talking about loving spirit, magic, the Earth, your Grandma, your other half, your dog, and your cats."

Alexandra and Graciela felt relief. Perhaps Lauren wasn't so dangerous after all.

"Why do you wear the charm bracelet Mr. Rios gave you thirty years ago when you design and create your own jewelry?"

Lauren grinned slyly, holding out her arm to the jury. For good measure she stood to show her bracelet to the judge. "Oh, this little trinket, I almost forgot, he did give me the bracelet and a few of the charms. I used to wear it to keep from getting lost, now I wear it because I'm not afraid of losing it."

There was not a single member of the jury that got that.

Judge Pyron called a short break to sign some documents the clerk handed him.

Lydia Fogel was no longer nervous; she was furious. She ushered Lauren into the conference room and shut the door, not wanting anybody to be privy to their conversation. "Lauren, you might as well tell the jury you did it. I can read a jury, and they didn't like you last week and they detest you today. You baffled me and everybody else in the gallery."

"It's my life and my stuff."

Lydia was not impressed. Although related by relationship, she had seen enough of Lauren trying to blow people away. "Tell me, Lauren, just where do you come up with your stuff?"

Lauren pursed her lips and blew a breath at the window. "Lydia, power moves, and I catch it. It's easy."

☪

Lauren took a break from Lydia to light one of the occasional cigarettes she allowed herself. Members of the jury were also standing on the front steps of the courthouse, trying to look occupied as they waited to return to session. Smiling at two women standing together uncomfortably, Lauren blew a smoke ring. It was not an ordinary smoke ring, the intent being to connect the women to Lauren. When Lauren saw them shift uncomfortably and look the other direction, she knew she had cast a spell, thus setting another perception.

Americo saw the magic and knew Lauren had done her work very well.

Confidently Lauren straightened her shoulders, saucily flipped her hair, and sashayed elegantly up the steps. Looking directly at Alexandra as she passed her on the stairs, Lauren smiled sweetly. Laughing to herself, Lauren looked at Alex's new red cowgirl boots. "There's more to come, cowgirl. You haven't heard anything yet."

Alex thought she heard Lauren talking to herself and wondered why Lauren called herself cowgirl.

Graciela went to work. During the break, while standing on the steps she became irritated at what she perceived to be Lauren's arrogance. Lauren's posture incensed Graciela, for it conveyed a natural elegance that cultivated charm is denied. The scarf Graciela wore to keep her hair in place seemed matronly compared to Lauren's wind blown, carefree appearance. The tasteful suit Graciela wore would have looked good if you were having tea at the palace, but seemed contrived and dowdy compared to Lauren's eclectic ensemble. Graciela, without knowing it, had allowed a few critical threads of her energy weaving to unravel. Yet, without considering that Lauren knew about her, she took a hair from the charm, ready to begin the war.

Thinking he was the manager of the frequency, Americo returned with his women to the courtroom, first kissing Alexandra and then offering Graciela a token peck on the cheek.

Barely speaking to Lauren, Lydia resumed the examination. Lydia decided to ask Lauren a few questions of her own before preceding with the list she had been given. The questions seemed unnecessary, but Lydia was determined to let the jury know there was more to Lauren than hot pants and sass. Lydia's attitude was cool and her voice unsympathetic. "Lauren, are you ready to begin your testimony again?"

Lauren could spin anything. "Lydia, it's a beautiful day in the high country of Arizona and although I'd rather be outside looking at the snow fall or composting my Grandmother's garden, I'll be happy to answer your questions."

"Are you a member of Mensa?"

Lauren thought that was a stupid question. "Yes."

"What is your I.Q.? It must be very high to be a member of Mensa."

"My I.Q., which by the way is the weakest of my intelligences, is 163. I'm what you would call a stupid genius. But not to worry, Counselor, my best thinking is done with the vortex in my womb and it's still intact, if not active."

Lydia resigned herself. "You spent the summer following your high school graduation in Monaco with your mother, right?"

Lauren had instructed Lydia how to pose the question, not knowing if she wanted to make full revelation. The bomb was dropped. Lauren paused wistfully.

Americo sat up straighter, looking tense.

"Yes I did and in January of the following year I had a baby in a private clinic in Paris."

"Who was the father of your baby?"

Lauren stood when she answered the question. "Americo Rios." Lauren continued standing, looking at Americo. "Our son died a few moments after he was born."

Lydia waited, giving the jurors time to absorb the impact of her honesty. "Did Americo know about the baby, before or after your loss?"

"No, I didn't tell him until last winter after I moved home to Sedona."

"Why did you keep it a secret all of those years, in spite of your intimate relationship with him?"

Lauren's voice became soft. "I didn't tell. He didn't ask. I made choices."

To the people listening Lauren seemed possessed. Words flew from her mouth with emotion and conviction. They didn't see Lauren deflecting a waving blanket of fragmented, disorganized energy. The waving menacing sound roared in Lauren's ears as she focused, concentrating, gathering her power. With her hands artfully manipulating the onslaught of heavy energy threads, trying to prevent the blanket from wrapping itself around her, it looked to others as though Lauren used her hands to emphasize her words.

"I was seventeen years old when I got pregnant; I was under-age. Americo is four and a half years older than I am and my mother said my father would have him arrested or maybe even kill him. Americo was not my boyfriend at the time I got pregnant. We got stoned and had sex the night I graduated from high school.

I didn't want to ruin his life with a forced marriage and after my son died, there wasn't any reason to tell him."

Without looking at her, Americo held out his hand to Alexandra and she knew that he did not want to feel her hand in his own.

Lydia was now blown away. "Didn't you write him a letter telling him you loved him?"

"Yes, he said he loved me after we had sex. I believed him, and I thought it sounded romantic, but it was silly, kid stuff. I corrected my mistake as soon as I realized it."

Tim Richmond sat down, bored, but pleased that Lauren was doing his job.

"Also, I didn't want to disappoint my father because he expected nothing but the best from me. I had always tried very hard to live up to his expectations and frankly; I didn't want to hear him yell. My mother told me it would break his heart and cause him to start drinking too much. I suppose she might have been right, but I shouldn't have listened to her. And, I didn't want my father to think I was like my mother."

Sunnie started to cry as Trey mumbled, damning Lauren for her deception. "Americo should have shot Lauren."

Waiting, Americo turned to face Alexandra. With her face burning, Alex slowly removed the ring from her finger.

"I've done a lot of thinking about my decision and this is my personal belief and one of the reasons I didn't tell many people who care about me about my son. My son came from my body, and he was mine. Women need to claim the power of giving birth. The father is the inseminator and ideally can play a very important role in parenting, but the child belongs to the mother. My tragedy was my business. I was alone in the world, and I dealt with it the best way I could, using a seventeen-year old mind."

Patting her knee, Americo put the ring back in Alexandra's hand, closing her fingers around it. With slow tears running down her face, Alexandra smiled and put the ring in her bag.

Out the corner of her eye, Lauren saw a fine thread of snaking energy rolling towards her. Skillfully, with her fingers moving deftly and inconspicuously, she blocked the energy, sending it flying back.

Graciela cleared her throat, becoming more absorbed in Americo and Alexandra. Americo played the game by almost inconspicuously moving closer to Graciela.

"I told Americo because we got caught up in the passion of spending more time together. In a weak moment, I confided in him. You must understand, my family has been enduring a great deal of tragedy, I was tired, and I was seeking solace. I might have been drunk when I told him; I don't remember." Lauren stopped, feeling the twisting of words in her brain. She reached in the air, grabbed one with her fingers, just not quite in time. "I suppose if I had been more mmmature I would have handled it differently. But if I had been older, it wouldn't have happened in the first place. I was yyyoung, naïve, under the influence and guidance of my mother, and mistakes were made. But, I don't apologize for them. I've lived with my gggrief, and it has shaped my life profoundly, in some ways good and in some ways tragically."

Lauren blushed furiously, hating it when she stammered. "For a long time, most of my life, I was frozen in grief because I never learned to process it. It was a journey through madness, self-injury, and agony you would never understand. But it was a foundational, pivotal experience. I think I've used the teachings sometimes wisely and sometimes not so wisely, because very often I act like a fool."

"Did you plan to keep your baby, Lauren?"

"Yes. I planned for us to live on a commune until I was ready to take the baby home."

"Do you regret any part of the experience? Would you change it if you could?"

Tears ran down Lauren's cheeks when she answered. "No."

A mature woman, with the appearance of a young girl with rosy cheeks and bright tear-filled eyes, looked at the members of the jury. Strain was gone from her facial muscles, making Lauren look vital and fully alive. The tears glistened, seeming to sparkle. The liquid crystal of her tears reflected light back to Americo. With a questioning look on her face, she saw him nod with a twinkle in his eye.

Americo mouthed the words, "Well done."

Lauren lowered her lashes, watching Graciela weave her filaments with Americo's.

Americo started to yawn.

With subtly wiggling fingers, Lauren activated the smoke ring. As she moved the ring up and down Graciela's body, the smoke ring severed the threads Graciela had so quickly connected between herself and Americo. Using the power of her eyes as a tool, Lauren gathered the threads and divided them. Working quickly she mended Americo's filaments with little knots, quickly coiling them into a small ball.

Lauren told Lydia to continue, after taking a sip of the water

Lydia offered to her.

"You ran away from your mother's home following the death of your son, didn't you?"

Rita felt the jolt. A jagged, silver-edged, black energy moved towards Lauren. The strike came like lightning, fast, thundering, and foreboding.

Lauren grabbed the bolt and without missing a word, she held it in her hand. Without making a move, Lauren transformed the energy into power, and holding her fist to her chest, let the power move into her body. "Yes, I stole a diamond ring from her, sold it in Paris, and traveled for awhile after I ran away."

"Why did you run away?"

"I was in deep shock, and I couldn't talk to anybody about what happened for a very long time. I didn't know what I was doing, and I didn't know what I was doing for many years."

☪

Strategically Americo created more intimacy with Graciela over an extraordinary lunch in a local historic hotel. The white linen was impeccably white; the silverware was silver and the plates, porcelain. Caressing her fingers, Americo looked romantically into her eyes, telling her how terribly relieved he was that Alexandra had rented a car and returned to Sedona, no longer a betrothed woman. With finesse Americo explained to her why he would be speaking with Lauren before the afternoon session commenced. He sounded innocent, betrayed, and hurt as he wove his words skillfully, portraying himself as a man of honor, whose reputation had been besmirched by a notorious liar and thief. "I can't believe that Lauren would tell a story like that about me. Personally, I've never believed her." Leaning towards her, Americo whispered so as to not be overheard. "Before she gets back on the stand, I'm going to warn her that if I ever find out she lied to me, I'm going to strangle her with a scarf."

Graciela smiled knowingly.

Wanting to establish that he considered himself to be her lover, Americo reached for Graciela's brown leather handbag resting on the table. She slapped his hand away too readily.

Americo laughed suggestively, lacing his fingers through hers. "Why, Graciela, my Darling, I never feel more intimate with a woman than when she let's me look in her purse. Do you keep secrets from the man who loves you?"

Graciela felt the pressure. Batting her eyes, she implied promise.

Americo sealed the promise, implying they had a future. "Graciela, someday, perhaps many times, you must show me what delights you carry inside of your bag because I'm fatally charmed by your mystery."

☪

Sparks flew as Lauren walked alone into the courtroom. Pretending, she yawned and stretched, capturing the sparks with her fingers. As she bent to release the hexed light to the underground, she felt a tap on her shoulder. The crowd, already gathered, was stunned when Americo led Lauren to the defense table and knelt down in front of her. Meeting Graciela's watchful eyes, he winked, confirming his threat.

Taking Lauren's hands in his, he put his cheek against hers and started to whisper. Clutching hands like two children, they spoke into each other's ears so nobody could hear their secret. Quickly he explained what he had discovered about Ignacio and Graciela.

Lauren laughed silently, but played the game. Appearing to tremble, she whispered.

"How in the hell did they get some of my hair?"

"They stole the hair you gave me at the airport. When I got pissed at you, I quit carrying it in my pocket and put it on the table in my house. They've been messing with your energy."

Lauren let a tear roll down her face, as if in fear. "Why?"

"To make you weak, to keep you from telling the truth so you'll go to jail."

"What should I do, Americo? I'm so frightened."

"Just follow my lead, Baby, I've got a plan."

Lauren sighed, knowing she had the Vortex. "Promise?"

"Promise." Americo stood and indicated for Graciela to follow him.

Lauren called him back, took his hand and wrapped his fingers around a soft, round ball. Whispering again, she teased him. "Did you feel yourself losing energy this morning?"

Americo felt the ball of his energy in his hand. "Yes, how did you know?"

Lauren giggled. "I told you I'd probably have to save your ass as well as my own."

It would ruin his disguise so Americo couldn't laugh with her, rather he whispered back.

"Lauren, you should be more careful when you bend over because when you do, I can see your panties."

Lauren couldn't resist. "Americo, be more careful where you put your... well, balls."

☪

Called to the stand, appearing properly chastised and apologetic, Lauren deliberately did not look at Judge Pyron. Stumbling as she walked to the stand, Lauren blushed when she saw Americo chuckling devilishly with his hand covering his mouth. Graciela thought he laughed maliciously, having not been party to their joke. Acting disoriented, Lauren didn't move. Rather, she carefully followed the delicate rope of twisting energy placed across the stair. Lauren wiggled her toes and coiled the rope unnoticeably. Pretending a charm had fallen from her bracelet, Lauren gathered the rope and carried it over her arm to the seat, then hurled the rope as if reaching for a glass of water.

At that moment, Americo, seemingly by accident, knocked Graciela's purse to the floor. Graciela screamed as the contents spilled, revealing the missing pink scarf.

Judge Pyron called the court to order, not noticing that Americo prevented Graciela from fleeing the room.

A thundering, hate filled, pulsing wall of energy moved towards Lauren. Suddenly she felt oppressed, smothered, and shy. White magic is more powerful if made with a dose of humor and levity. Lauren stopped the wall with a smile, a tarty smile. Tim Richmond postured himself, feeling manly, desirable, and wondered if Lauren had finally noticed his polished appeal. Holding her hand to her mouth as if to stifle a yawn, Lauren deftly spun the heavy dark filament into threads of light. The thunder subsided. Lauren blinked and when she opened her eyes, she saw Graciela's green scaly tentacles twisting into Americo's body. Graciela chewed subtly as if digesting the energy she sucked out of Americo. His eyes clouded, he wiped them furiously, knowing he was being depleted.

Lauren got it; yet another parasite had been sucking her

energy, leaving her weak and vulnerable, unable to fully express herself. Americo, too, had been a victim of jealousy and revenge and had been slowly losing his power, ability to see, and to love. Lauren looked at Americo, seeing the diminishment of his light. "Ignacio and Marquita may have wanted to hurt us, but their power is nothing compared to our own shadows."

Lauren stood outside of her body, and looked at herself. "Yet..." she quickly understood, "it isn't them, it's me. I've been stepping in traps, closing doors, making bad bargains, burning my own power, tripping over unseen ropes, falling in holes, and slamming myself into dark walls of my own design for thirty years. My power is mine and I'll claim my own shadows, my own dreams, and my own fears. I'll spin them around, turn them upside down and with my love for this man, I'll turn them into my strength."

A tunnel of pink light appeared. Lauren took a deep breath, sending the filaments of spun light to Americo. His eyes cleared and as they cleared, he saw a powerful woman on the stand, a woman who had reserved her right to have her own life, on her terms. He no longer saw a woman who needed him, but a woman who was made strong by her madness, foolishness, and magic. He grabbed the scarf, holding it for Lauren to see and smiled, feeling the infusion of wild, random, softened by age and experience, pure pink, female energy.

Graciela moved fast, this was her last chance. While helping Americo stay close to Lauren while in dreamtime she had discovered the gold thread that connected them. As if catching a small moth she grabbed it between her fingers. Lauren felt the tug near her navel, squinted and saw the delicate thread in Graciela's vicious hands. Almost moaning aloud, Americo bent with a stab in his gut. "Do something, Lauren. Marquita knows how to break our connection."

No problem, just a little distraction.

Judge Pyron jerked his head. He saw Lauren across the room, holding hands with Americo and kissing him on the cheek. He looked again. Lauren winked and waved discreetly from the witness stand. For once in her life believing in insurance, she also summoned the power of Grandmothers, chocolate, baby boys, deer, star baths, good men, champagne, and great sex. Lauren's war with herself was over. Her shadows were delivered and conquered and once again, Lauren was a girl with pigtails, spinning on a red rock mesa with her good buddy, Americo.

A light came on for Lauren when she addressed the jury in her own behalf. Judge Pyron closed his eyes in annoyance, preparing for more testimony in what he now considered to be a closed case. Planning the sentence he should give Lauren, Judge Pyron took a nap, only to be awakened when Lauren sweetly admonished him. "Please listen to me, Judge Pyron. I've just realized that although my Grandmother spins yarn, I'm learning how to spin yarns."

Judge Pyron shook his head, indicating for her to proceed.

Lauren spoke to the women of the jury. Meeting each of their gazes, she reached out to them with her story, knowing they had all taken the same journey many times on their own path. Lydia took a seat, waiting for Lauren to seal her fate with her madness.

Biting her lower lip, Lauren pondered where to begin. "I have a few things to say to you about shooting Americo. If I shot him, it was by accident. Although there's not any evidence that will prove it, I did not fire the first shot, because I don't know how to shoot a gun, even though I lied to Garry Baker because I was afraid and wanted him to stay away from me. My grandfather, the famous outlaw Jackson Auldney, laid down his gun and nobody in my family has shot a gun since then. But, if you find me guilty, I'll gladly pay the price for having the opportunity to unburden myself of my secrets. However, I still have to go home and tell my dying father what all of you now know about me. Can you imagine how nervous that makes a woman my age? He might yell and if he does, I'll understand. The only difference, is now I won't care, because I own my own life." Lauren took a sip of water.

Having felt the love and seen the light, Americo gave Lauren a salute as he settled back on the bench, stretching his legs, preparing himself to listen as she spun a yarn.

Many of the people present knew Americo. Many had known his parents and had watched Americo grow up in Sedona. They knew the hard working, dependable, good student, who matured into a reputable businessman and investor. Some knew of his efforts to set aside preserved wilderness land and his effort to maintain slow growth in his community. They admired his polish and his mild demeanor and they had forgiven him his one time propensity for barroom brawls. Americo had never married, yet his loneliness had never been displayed. Beautiful women were often seen on his arm, belying the empty space within. The style Americo carried was that of calm and reserve. Americo, wealthy, powerful, and respected, seemed to have it all. They didn't know Americo had always wanted something he could not have. The people watching saw only his apparent confidence and ease. Only Lauren knew of his anguish. Often, the outward appearance is a disguise for inward agony and only Lauren appreciated the torment of his long wait for the woman on the stand. They didn't know the now relaxed man felt a sense of joy, long forgotten. Americo leaned forward and rested his elbows on his knees. His gentle eyes were fixated on Lauren, willing her to unfold.

Embedded within Americo's awareness was the great cost Lauren's experience had been to her, for only he had witnessed her zest for life, her lack of inhibition, her joy, and her authenticity when safe within the boundaries of his home and living the life she had carved for herself far away from the restraints of expectation. With great sorrow he came to terms with the fact that he had tried, in his own way and without consideration for her reasons, to impose the same restrictions on a wild random soul. Only Americo had been aware of the shadows in her eyes, the fear of expectation, the reluctance to commit, and although she had kept a secret, her unrelenting honesty when she told him to seek a life without her. He interlocked his fingers, seeing the question in her eyes, recalling thirty years ago when she asked if he could see the real Lauren. The real Lauren on the stand knew that he finally saw her, and she smiled at the answer to her long ago question.

Lauren removed the pendulum from her neck, and surrendering once again to the twirling gold spindle; Lauren told her story. "On the day I was conceived, my star kicked a Fool in the butt and sent her spinning to Earth. She landed hard and broke her noggin. We know Fools are always female, chaotic and wild, but did you also know that it means they know how to do perfect somersaults and spin? As women, we take the Fools journey, each in our own way."

Judge Pyron sighed impatiently when Lauren took her day in court to the stars.

Still receiving her story from the spinning pendulum, Lauren continued. "This Fool is a lucky Fool because when I was born a Magician was waiting for me. I knew he was a Magician, because even though his eyes are gold, I could see the fire. The Magician took this little Fool under his magic and listened to all of her stories while he played spinning games with her. The Magician had a plan, and the Fool, like a little seed, needed a friend so she could burst open and grow."

Americo closed his eyes remembering the first time he saw Lauren when they brought her home from the hospital.

Crinkling her brow, Lauren continued to spin. The members of the jury seemed enchanted by the beginning of her story. For some reason the men seemed to be paying more attention than the women.

"The Fool was lucky a second time, because she had a power-ful wise Witch for a Grandma. The Fool's Grandma taught her the secrets of the moon, the power of being a woman, using your intu-ition, paying attention to your body, and the importance of being receptive. Maybe this Fool took that lesson a little too seriously."

Winking at Judge Pyron, Lauren thanked him for honoring her request to stay awake.

"The Fool got lucky again. The Fool was lucky a third time because she was raised in the country, close to the processes of nature. I've always been proud and grateful for being a country bumpkin because that means I was raised close to the Earth. I grew from the red Earth of Sedona just like a wild weed. I had open spaces to play in, the distance to view, and an abundance of time and freedom to roam on the body of the Goddess. The Earth opens your heart if you listen to her stories."

Lydia leaned forward, starting to appreciate the story.

"Then the Fool didn't get lucky. Somebody started to make too many rules, and the Fool cracked. Fools don't do very well if they have to obey somebody else's rules."

Americo looked at Lauren recalling a little girl cracking apart and not understanding why.

"The Fool was on a roll and kept running into more people and more rules. Everywhere the Fool went, somebody told her what she did was wrong, didn't fit, or didn't look good. Fools don't look good wearing other peoples boring rules. Rules make Fools crack, but when they crack, the light gets in."

Lauren smiled radiantly at Americo, reflecting the love in his eyes. "The Fool got lucky again and fell in love. She didn't know it at first, but once she realized it, the love never went away. When she fell in love with the Magician, he gave her a charm bracelet, and on it he hung a charm."

Lauren waited while strands of experience spun her story. "The Fool took a journey on her own for many years. On her jour-ney the Fool met wise Queens, a fun Page, a loving Knight, and a handsome Prince. Sometimes she made mistakes, and sometimes she had a wonderful time. Sometimes she cried, and sometimes she laughed, but most importantly, she did it on her own.

"While on her journey, the Fool didn't keep her equilibrium and had some problems. It was a very long journey and finally, the Fool saw the wisdom of what she learned. The Fool, realizing everything we do has a cause and effect, matured and gained con-fidence. The Fool accepted her destiny, but came to realize that in order to live free, she needed to further address her responsibilities. While the Fool journeyed, she spent a lot of time looking within for a wise old teacher she thought she might have lost. She spent a lot of time alone, finding meaning in her experiences. She made art, walked on the body of the Goddess, and learned about spirit. The Fool surrendered to her path. It was a time of all possibility, and she saw the round of all conceivable choices. The Fool was happy, even if a little afraid. We all fear the state of all possibility, when we have the opportunity to stand in front of the Wheel of Fortune. We also feel excitement knowing anything in the world can be ours."

Lauren stopped and looked perplexed by the spindle in her hand. Giggling softly, she confided. "I think this Fool spun the Wheel of Fortune a little fast and a few too many times for her own good."

The jurors wanted to laugh with her, but restrained themselves.

"The Fool returned to her home in the time of all possibility and found Strength she didn't know she had. She helped nurse her sick father and tended the garden of her soul. She worked in the garden, made art, and listened to her Grandmother remind her of stories she had already told the little girl Fool."

The spindle hummed, spinning in the next chapter. "The time came in the Fool's life to set things right with the Magician, so the Fool turned her world upside down. Fate had already been spun, and there was something the Magician should have wondered about. There was something she should have told him, but she was afraid of losing him. The Fool acted like a Fool again. She stood on her head and saw the world with a different perspective. She hoped the Magician would look the same direction as the upside down Fool. She told the Magician to spin it, and he did. The Fool surrendered in love and got bit in the butt."

Lauren looked at Americo and with tears in her eyes told him the truth. "Americo, I have always loved you and I always will. I'm deeply sorry."

Americo held his head in his hands, looking at the floor knowing if he looked up people would see the tears in his eyes.

The spindle started spinning faster and Lauren's voice started to shake.

Americo looked at Lauren and saw a flower bud, starting to unfold.

Mesmerized by her story the jurors listened to Lauren, gaining respect.

"The Fool had to let go of something very precious, and it broke her heart. Death hurts, but death heals, because then you can be transformed and reborn. The Fool had to let go, because she didn't have any choice. The Fool knew how to spin, but the Magician knew how to turn a world upside down, and a part of her died when the Magician picked up his cards and started a new game with somebody else."

The response to a stimulus can be deterioration, or further stimulus. One by one, Americo saw yellow petals of a wild sunflower unfold. The bud opened, presenting the flower, half open with promise. He whispered. "Lauren, Baby, I did fail you completely." Like a brat, Lauren stuck her tongue out at Americo.

"The Fool got lucky again when her Grandmother took her under her wing and gave her a task. The task was very difficult. The Fool had to look at herself in the mirror, face some truths, let things go, and find her balance. The Fool danced, worked, meditated, and cleaned a lot of cobwebs out of her mind. The Fool grew a lot of power fulfilling her task, and she needed it to vindicate her life."

Americo caressed the scarf in his hand. Holding it between his two palms, he felt the magic, the power, and the love Lauren invested in everything she did. With the scarf in his fist, he made a vow to right the wrong he had done to Lauren.

Lauren smiled at Judge Pyron. Foolishly and unsuccessfully, he tried to ignore her.

"The Devil came after the Fool and when that happens the Fool makes a fool of herself. There was an issue of power and old patterns, and the person who needs to understand this will. I will never surrender my power to another. My soul has been liberated."

The sunflower unfolded, fully and beautifully. A woman in her late forties, Lauren had blossomed, in spite of being a spinning Fool.

Americo understood the power struggle they had waged unknowingly against each other.

"I'm changing, my life is changing, and you will decide my immediate future. My entire structure is falling down around me and has been for some time. Sometimes we are immediately enlightened by the sudden collapse of our Tower, and usually one is thrown into a state of chaos or confusion. Most importantly it gives us a chance to rebuild our lives based on our truth. My circumstances at this time are these: I am no longer involved with the man I love, my father is dying, and soon my Grandmother will leave me as well. I might go to jail, I might go free, but however I go, I won't be carrying a heavy satchel on my back."

Lauren turned to Judge Pyron again. "If I go free or go to jail, I plan to do the same thing. I'm going to be open to the Goddess and bless myself for my journey. If I can't go home and have fresh flowers in my bedroom, I'll have them in my mind in a jail cell. The universe will heal me and I'm going to surrender. I have hope and like a Star, I'm free. I'm free because I am no longer hiding myself like the crescent moon. I'm going to be guided by my feelings, dreams, and visions, because I trust in the higher powers of the Moon to heal me. I'll stand before the Sun, try to grow my awareness, and pray that the sun shines his rays on me. The past is past and my heart is open, without Judgment. I can see what is real, and I am free. There is one certainty amidst all of this madness. You, Judge Pyron, can send me to jail. But I am now out of prison, and the World is mine."

Lauren beamed, light shined from her eyes and once again she turned to face the jury. Lauren spoke not from a place of self-pity, but from a place of self-acceptance. Tears fell softly down her cheeks, but Lauren's voice was strong when she stood before the court, with her hands clasped to her heart. "I'm speaking to each of the women in this room. I don't know if you have children or not. But, if you have had a baby in your womb and felt the heartbeat and flutter of the fetus, you know you will never forget the sensations. If you have ever felt your baby burst from your body, you will understand the pain of having empty arms and a shattered soul. A woman's soul shatters if her baby makes the choice to leave her. It shatters further if she doesn't tell anybody her secret. It takes a very long time," Lauren inhaled, "to gather the parts of a heart that was broken at a very young age."

☪

A thread of connection formed by destiny can uncoil to the farthest reaches of the cosmos, stretching, fraying, and thinning as time and circumstances unfold. As Lauren and Americo stood together in the hall of the courthouse, waiting for the jury to return with a verdict, the thread of connection between them very slowly and tenuously started to recoil.

The meeting was accidental. When Lauren stopped to make notes for the plan she started formulating the night before while being too nervous to sleep, Americo cautiously approached her. The exchange of energy between them during Lauren's testimony had created a delicate thread of hope that neither was yet ready to exploit. Initially, they stood together awkwardly, making small talk about Jake. When Lauren asked about Ignacio and Marquita, Americo answered abruptly. "It's been handled, Lauren, that's all you need to know for now."

Americo was amused to see the quickly written notes in Lauren's hand. Once again, Lauren had not written in straight lines or with an alphabet that could be translated by anybody but herself. Americo leaned against the wall with his hands in his pocket and opened a door. "What are you going to do when this is all over?"

Lauren lifted her head from her notes, tilted it slightly to the right and with a question in her eyes, was startled by her own answer. "I'm not certain yet, but I'm working on a plan. What about you?"

Americo laughed with gusto. "You'll never believe this, but for the first time in our lives, you're making a plan and I don't have any."

Unashamedly looking deeply into the other's being, their frequency aligned, and they recognized the gift the other had to offer. Americo saw Lauren's random, wild energy offering new vitality and sparkle to the whole. Lauren felt the calmness of an ordered structure, offering peace and stability. Each of them became aware of the harmony of balancing the two essential components of a relationship. No longer hungry for the missing ingredient, they turned to each other as a teacher. Lauren took his hand, smiling and thinking how changed they had been by the circumstances.

In that moment, the secret of their relationship was offered to each other as a gift.

Again, Judge Pyron shook his head as Lauren Auldney entered the courtroom on the arm of Americo Rios. The victim sat on the bench behind the accused, sending a message to those who judged Lauren.

Lauren stood with her shoulders straight, twisting the fragile gold band on her little finger when the judge asked the foreman to state the verdict. Lydia stood nervously beside her and as the foreman started to speak, Americo felt the vibration of his phone.

Having told Trey to beep him if Jake's condition deteriorated, Americo checked the digital message. "Bring them home now," was the message. Just as the verdict of guilty was announced, Americo handed a note to the clerk. Judge Pyron read the note, looked at Lauren and Lydia with not seen before compassion and called them into his chambers.

Judge Pyron returned to court, explained the circumstances and announced that a date for sentencing would be scheduled. Americo quickly ushered Lauren and Lydia to his car to drive them home to Jake, who was dying.

☪

With his mother, Trey, and Sunnie by his side, Jake waited for his daughter and woman he loved to arrive with Americo.

Lydia rushed into the bedroom where Jake had slept as a boy, kissing and holding him as her tears mingled with his in their private goodbye.

Struggling with his final breaths, Jake lifted his head and smiled when he saw Lauren and Americo waiting together under the threshold. Weakly, he motioned for them, recognizing the light he saw surrounding Lauren. The divine, sweet pleasure on her father's face was that of redemption, as he beheld his little girl in his vision. Reeling through Jake's mind were images of Lauren as a little girl with pigtails, a Princess descending a staircase, a wild bohemian artist, and the woman who came home to take care of her Daddy. But the happiest image for Jake was the gold thread of connection he saw between them. The realization came to Jake too late. "A single yes or no changes the path of many lives and for that I am sorry."

As Lydia held Jake's hand, Rita placed her hands on Jake's forehead, helping him to pass. Jake whispered goodbye to Trey and Sunnie and then asked Lauren what he needed to know. "Are you free, little girl?"

Holding Americo's hand, weeping freely as she bent to kiss her father goodbye, Lauren set Jake free. "Yes, Daddy, I'm finally free."

Jake looked last at his daughter. "Lauren, you're an outlaw," Jake whispered, smiling weakly, "just like your grandfather."

Lauren touched his cheek. "I know it, Daddy. It's in my blood, and I've tasted it."

☪

The dollhouse needed a good cleaning. The melancholy, moody winds from the north had blown cold and hard across El Rancho de Las Estrellas. Bringing warmth and harmony, the Vortex spun new filaments into the midst of new life and death. Lauren used a tiny broom to sweep the remaining debris across the threshold. When she paused, she heard the footsteps on the frosty ground. Four days following the sprinkling of Jake's ashes in the spiral garden, Lauren received a very pensive caller. Livvy Auldney had something on her mind. "Are you worried that you might go to jail, Aunty Lauren?"

Lauren stood, brushed the dust from her hands on her jeans and scrutinized Livvy's face. "Sure I am, Livvy. But, I should know in a week or two if they're going to lock me up or give me probation. Lydia thinks I might have a good chance of probation if I agree to go into therapy."

Livvy started to cry. "I don't want you to go to jail, but I've got a secret and it's driving me crazy."

Lauren knew the feeling. Carefully opening a door, Lauren asked Livvy if she felt like going for a short walk. As they walked Livvy confessed to Lauren something she remembered in a dream only a month ago. The cause unknown, Rita, Lauren, and Livvy experienced times periodically when they walked in their sleep, often waking up a long distance from their beds. Livvy confessed.

In the middle of the night of the shooting, Livvy had sleep-walked and heard Lauren and Americo screaming at each other in the Casino. Unused to the domestic quarrelling Livvy had been frightened by the threats she heard Americo making towards Lauren. Terrified that Americo was going to beat or kill Lauren; Livvy had picked up the gun under the scarf, planning to scare Americo. The gun, old and never used, misfired. Lauren, not knowing anything about guns, had been living with a loaded, cocked gun in her home.

The sound of the shot frightened Livvy, so she dropped the gun and ran away with the scarf still in her hand. Ignacio found the scarf caught on a shrub on his way to work the next morning and knew it belonged to Lauren. The bullet made a hole in the scarf, and the memory of the incident had been locked safely in Livvy's unconscious, waiting for a trigger.

Tearfully, Livvy told Lauren that she had kept it a secret hoping she would be found innocent. But, since Lauren had been found guilty, Livvy could no longer keep the secret.

Lauren was silent, pondering if Livvy should confess to the court, tell her parents and Lydia, but with wisdom born of experience, she knew Livvy could not keep the secret. While they were walking, the man and woman figures in Cathedral Rock sent a message to Lauren. The message being that of facing one another in honesty, rather than turn away from each other in times of fear. Nearing Americo's home, Lauren made a firm decision. "Livvy, the trial was the best thing that ever happened to me, but I wasn't the one who almost died that night. The second person you're going to tell is Americo."

Livvy panicked and started to cry again. "I'm so sorry, Aunt Lauren. Uncle Americo is going to hate me so much."

Lauren put her arm over Livvy's shoulder, and quietly they walked up the steps to Americo's front door. Lauren held Livvy's hand as they sat in Americo's living room, telling him the truth of the events the night of the shooting. Americo freshened Lauren's coffee and picked his cat off the kitchen counter. Acting busy, he listened to Livvy calmly confessing, pleading with her eyes for him to understand. Americo was stunned, having truly believed that in a state of rage, Lauren had tried to kill him. Feeling guilty that he had doubted her word, Americo's first concern was for Lauren. Giving Livvy a reassuring hug, Americo told her he wanted to talk to Lauren privately in the other room.

Lauren's heart stopped when she entered the bedroom. The collection of small carpets seemed as welcoming as the vase of fresh sunflowers on his dresser and a photograph of her on his nightstand. Resting below her photograph was the silver box that had once contained her hair. Sitting together on the edge of the bed, Americo took Lauren's hand, knowing the choice was hers. Lauren placed her feet on the small rug on what was once her side of his bed. "God, Americo, I don't want to put Livvy through a trial. This is such a great time in her life, but I don't exactly want to go to jail either. I don't know what to do."

Americo stood, put his hand under Lauren's chin, making her look at him. His face was freshly shaven, and he had a gleam in his eyes. He had an idea for Lauren to consider. "Lauren, I know neither one of you tried to kill me, so consider this."

Lauren walked to the mirror, seeing an old photo of them

taken at his hacienda on his dresser. While looking at his reflection, she saw him standing behind her looking at her fanny with admiration on his face. "Stop that, Americo, that's not fair. Tell me what you're thinking."

Americo laughed back at her in the mirror. "I don't think I need to tell you."

Lauren blushed. "Come on, tell me."

Americo became serious, sat back down on the bed and asked Lauren to sit by him. "What I'm thinking is this, we'll never know which one of the bullets hit me. One of them did, and one of them didn't. I think Livvy ought to talk it over with Dan and her parents, but in my opinion if you don't have to go to jail, what's the point? I'll go with her to talk to Trey and Sunnie and Livvy can tell Dan when she chooses, but I want to know that she did."

Lauren sighed, wondering about her sentence. "What if I have to go to jail."

Americo stood and walked towards the door. "We'll go back to court and save Livvy's butt, because I don't want either one of you in jail."

The wood in the potbelly stove sparked, startling Lauren, Sunnie, and Rita as they sat together after dinner, sipping chamomile tea, enjoying the quiet of an exceptionally warm December evening. Silhouettes of lacy junipers cast random shadows as if someone had draped an elegant black lace shawl over the yard. The outdoor lights flickered when Lauren asked if she could read something aloud. An old friend, a book by Susan Griffin, titled "Woman and Nature...The Roaring Inside Her" had returned to Lauren several months ago, offering her solace during the time of her task and trial. Pulling her chair closer to Rita and Sunnie, Lauren noticed an expression of Rita's face she had not seen before.

Lauren stopped reading and wondered. "Who do you think she's writing about, Grandma?"

Rita opened her eyes and clasped both their hands. "All women. All women who live and love, including The Beloved Woman and our beautiful Earth."

"I thought so, Grandma."

Rita closed her eyes again before speaking. "Lauren, I want

you to call Trey and Americo; I can feel death beckoning to me. My precious Zack is waiting, and I've been so lonely without him."

Lauren didn't answer, but quickly ran to the phone, wishing Lydia had not stayed in Tucson. With her voice calm and strong, the first call she made was to her brother's house, summoning Trey to his Grandmother's deathbed. The sound of Americo's voice startled Lauren from her calm. His strong voice provided an opening for Lauren to accept that her Grandmother, who had guided her through her life, would soon leave her alone in the world. Her voice shook breathlessly, and all she could say to him was, "Hurry, I need you."

Sunnie and Lauren quickly embraced, a long friendship offering comfort to both of them.

When Trey escorted his Grandmother to her bed, Rita stopped and for several moments looked at the nude portrait painted of her when a young woman. Quietly accepting his help onto her bed, Rita told Trey that she wanted to talk to him and Sunnie first. Lauren rested her spindle on the nightstand next to a small vase of flowers and placed a pair of Zack's boots by the bedside.

Americo and Lauren sat together silently on the floor, holding hands in front of the potbelly stove. Lauren stared at the skeins of yarn, stacked by color in the order of the rainbow. Mesmerized by the shadows on the yarn, Lauren recalled the hours she had spent on the same spot while Rita spun yarn in the cozy comfort of her living room studio.

Waiting for Trey and Sunnie, Lauren didn't know whom Rita would ask to speak to next. Americo broke the silence when he stood and pulled Lauren to her feet and walked to the bar. "What's this going to do to you?"

Lauren stood in the center of the room as the chill of approaching death forced her to ask herself the same question. With no doubt in her mind, Lauren looked at Americo and answered. "It's going to make me stronger, Americo, stronger than I've ever been before."

"Tell me more, Princess, tell me about the legacy Rita left you."

Lauren wondered how to sum up a lifetime of love, wisdom, support, and guidance. She took her time, the reel of her experience winding backwards into the Vortex. Spinning before her was her Grandmother, a woman who honored the woman within the woman, not the man within the woman, and was therefore loved and protected by the man in her husband. She saw a woman gen-

tly weaving her life into the background of her land, her past, and
the future of those she loved. She saw her Grandmother weaving
the fate of her loved ones within the central core context of the
home, the ever-changing spiral garden, and luscious time spent in
the wild. Lauren saw a woman with almost a century of accumulated charms, always refining the world in which she lived, while
never neglecting the Wild Woman within. Shimmering within a
swirling translucent body of energy was a woman with her hand
outstretched, her toes wiggling, with her eyes wide-open, ready to
dance. Standing before Lauren, was the Goddess.

Lauren spoke softly feeling the presence of something often
neglected. "Americo, the legacy Grandma left me was that of
appreciation for eroticism, sexuality, rhythmic and cataclysmic
Earth processes, the wild, the cauldrons of the home and the
womb, brooms, cookies, chimes, the garden, compost, mundane
repetitive work, the land, the body of the Goddess, eternal soulmates, destiny, red rocks, the continuum of experience, being a
femaleist; not a feminist, spinning yarns, and yes, Americo, loving
and taking care of the man who takes care of you."

Americo saw the presence hovering about Lauren and held
her hand, solemnly kissing the palm.

Lauren smiled when she spotted the turquoise earring she
lost over thirty years ago in his jeep on the way to the airport. "You
haven't worn that earring for years."

"I know, but it felt like the time to put it on again."

Lauren had wondered for months, "Americo, how did you feel
when I came to your house the night after my first appearance in
court?"

He cocked his head, arched his brow, and touched her cheek.
"Baby, I summoned you; you didn't have a choice. I needed to be
inside of you, even if it was the last time."

"I needed to feel you, I was so afraid and so confused."

"It'll be OK, Lauren, let's just get through Rita's passing, and
then I want to hear the whole story, the one I never let you finish.
We need to release TJ's ashes to the river, build a memorial, take
a long walk together and see if we can learn how to spin together
again. But there's something else I want to tell you, so listen
before you agree or disagree." Americo summed up their relationship. "Lauren, young love, first love, love with no reason, love with
every reason, comes once. We were two young people, conceived on
the same land, with our skin kissed by the same sunbeams and we
had no choice. We grew strong with minerals from the same soil in
our bones, the water from the creek in our blood and we saw the

same sights before our eyes every day. I feel sorry for those who have never known a love of promise, promise given from the eroticism of the landscape."

Lauren didn't know if she cried for them, TJ, or Rita's passing.

Americo recalled times when Rita had offered special comfort to him. Looking into the belly of the stove, Americo was reminded of the evening he told the family he was leaving the rancho for Mexico. He sounded far away, his voice was soft and when he turned to look at Lauren, he knew Rita had been right. "The night I told everybody I was leaving home, Rita made me a promise."

Lauren turned to Americo, intrigued by the tone of his voice. "When Rita hugged me goodbye, she told me she would spin us both home when the time was right. It wasn't the right time before now, was it?"

Lauren shook her head. "Sunnie and Trey are separating, did you know that?"

"Yeah, Trey told me. Maybe our problems are behind us, not ahead of us."

Trey and Sunnie returned to the living room, Trey looking remorseful and Sunnie glowing radiantly. "Grandma wants to see both of you."

Lauren and Americo looked at each other, each of them having expected to see Rita alone. Standing next to Rita's bed, Lauren fussed with the quilt and offered Rita a sip of water. Americo made certain the windows were tightly closed. There was a cool draft in the room, but it wasn't coming from the window, for Zack was beckoning to Rita, holding his hand towards her.

With her fingers moving rapidly, Rita reached towards Americo and Lauren. Unknown to them, she repaired the remaining tears in the weaving of their relationship. Also unknown to them, there was a little boy with energy sparkling like fireflies, coiling the thread of connection between them with his fingers. With her eyes already closed and with her hands reaching to those waiting for her, Rita spoke her last words to them. "I kept my promise when I spun both of you home at the right time. But, I didn't make a weaving for each of you." Rita paused; then spoke again faintly. "I wove a story for both of you and when the time is right, Lauren knows where it is in the attic."

Lauren turned to Americo as he leaned over to kiss Rita goodbye. "Thank you, Grandma, for doing everything when the time was right."

Gently Lauren held her right hand on her Grandmother's silver hair. Americo placed his left hand on Rita's heart and fully opened the energy centers, releasing Rita to her beloved eternal soul mate.

With one hand reaching towards Zack, Rita lifted her wrist and elegantly traced a spiral in the air. Lauren's eyes never wavered. She opened her left palm and fluttered her fingers, drawing the delicate translucent spiraling body into her hand. Receiving the transmission from Rita, Lauren held her palm first to her forehead and then her heart center. With Americo's hand in hers, she then gently placed her warm palm over the cauldron within her body.

☪

Lauren's dolls, her ladies-in-waiting, bowed at the sight of their Princess and her Prince reunited, once again, in the red rock castle of Sedona. "Welcome home from your odyssey, Princess, and have sweet, sweet dreams of your handsome Prince who now sees you for all that you were, all that you are, and all that you will become."

☪

From the other side of the two-sided saddle, Spinny and Weavy got a new perspective, because when you live on a two-sided saddle, there is always a different point of view. Their awareness was now keen and as they looked at the weaving, they considered the circumstances they had been dealt. Surrendering to the beauty of the imperfect weaving, they congratulated each other on a difficult job, well done.

The weaving was charming. The knots and unraveled yarn added texture, detail, and interest to what could have been a bland, uninteresting effort. The sudden stops and starts caused the viewer to pause and pay attention. The loops and returns, the delicate mends and the mismatched colors were the theme of the weaving. Although the lines were not straight and none of the surfaces flat, or the circles round, the negatively curved view from the two-sided saddle, was incredibly beautifully imperfect, under the perfect Sedona sky.

# Biography

The reason unknown to her, Sunday Kristine Marquita Larson moved to Sedona four years ago to write a story.

Living happily ever after on her star of origin, a wild and curious spirit tripped. A single stumble started her long tumble to the spinning orb called Earth. On a cold, late January morning, Sunday crash-landed on Earth with a scowl on her face, a crack in her noggin, her blue eyes open, and her dark curly hair unruly.

Raised on a Thoroughbred Horse ranch, Kristine grew up a worldly country bumpkin in the days of sex, drugs, and rock and roll.

Always stumbling ahead of herself, Sunday entered the university early and studied dance, art, anthropology, art history, and philosophy, reluctantly earning a degree that isn't worth mentioning.

Being closely related to an infamous attorney and a famous outlaw, Sunday Kristine Marquita believed that her dna bestowed the permission necessary for her to live life on her own terms, and she has happily done so.

Always living by serendipity, charm, cute red shoes, good fortune, and never a plan, Sunday enjoyed a successful career as a goldsmith and jewelry designer. Pieces of her erotic, one of a kind, gold jewelry grace fine collections worldwide. Dolls, collage, and installations are in her body of work and resume.

Presently, Kristine is writing the next volume of the "Sedona Witches Trilogy." In her spare time Sunday is also developing an oracle by the same name that will soon be available on CD and on her website (ASedonaStory.com). After she returns from meditating on the red rocks, she takes a wee nap before working on two series of dolls, "On Her Back" and "Witches Brains."

Contact Sunday Kristine Larson by e-mail at:
ASedonaStory@earthlink.net
or by mail at:
PO Box 1669
Sedona, Arizona 86339

# The Sedona Witches Trilogy

**Part Two:** *"Filament and Witches Knots...The Journey from Sedona" due 2003*

Although old enough to know better, Lauren Auldney and Americo Rios tied the knot and they now have to discover the karmic reason why. In the Andes, a land of Wizards and Witches, the search for the holy grail begins when a priceless weaving is unraveled and returned to strands of yarn by a precocious five-year old, Tia Masen, who is Lauren's grandmother reincarnated. The quest begins as time spirals backwards revealing a soul families secrets, reasons, and whys.

**Part Three:** *"Brooms, Wombs and Brains...A Witch's Handbag" due 2004*

The family saga of the Auldney-Rios clan continues as Tia Masen, home-schooled by her Aunt Lauren, discovers the most essential tool in her handbag. A child artist prodigy, Tia reunites with her soulmate, and fearlessly ventures into the future by reading the foretelling and foreshadowing map of art. Will the clan continue to be reunited in the red rock paradise of Sedona? If so, what will they find when they return? The Sea? Lemuria? Journey with them on the spiral path, and discover for yourself what Tia was born knowing.

Read more about the next two volumes of the trilogy on Sunday Larson's website, www.asedonastory.com.

**Coming Soon**

Watch for the Oracle *"The Spinning Game"* soon to be available on CD and the author's website ASedonaStory.com

A portion of the proceeds of this book will be donated to **"Best Friends Animal Sanctuary,"** in honor of Livvy Larson Lamont. There will also be donations made to **"The Club de Madres"** (*The Mother's Club*), in the village of Mollamarka, high in the Andes of Peru, in honor of my godsons, **Juan Palmino** and **Claudio**.

Printed in the United States
4945